Voluptas

Jonathan O'Brien

Dalcassian Publishing
http://www.dalcassian.org

Acknowledgements

To...

...Mrs. Brown, one of my high school English teachers. Your praise of my work in younger years motivated me to keep writing...

...Tim, your imagination, criticism, and creativity have always been a consolation. I couldn't have finished this without you...

...Seamus, your thoughts were of great value. You've always been an inspiration...

...All my family, you are my home, my love and my life...

...All the faces I've seen, stories I've heard, friendships I've made. They are the spark of my creativity.

Fr. Longchamps,
Thanks for being
there for me in some
of my times of
darkness.

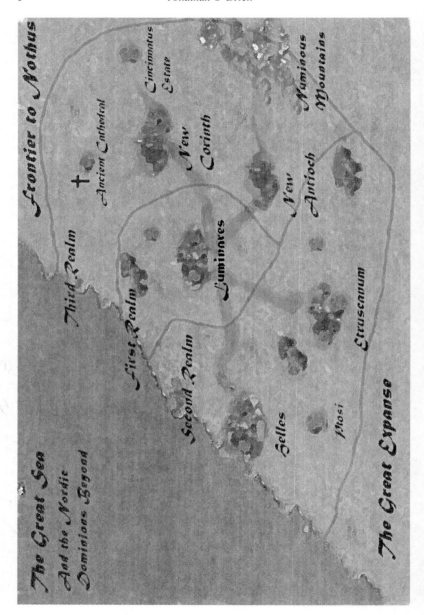

Prologue

A Forgotten People

AGES AGO IN A HORRENDOUS war, a crushing defeat was inflicted upon the peerless Roman people. The Parthian victor's cries of braggart echoed on a macabre battlefield. Yet his shouts masked fear, for a worse enemy threatened the Parthians from the East. This enemy outnumbered the stars and rode to battle in ceaseless waves. With enchained prisoners now begging at his feet, the farsighted Parthian King decided to settle three thousand of his Roman captives beyond the borders of Parthian lands. These hardened soldiers and their progeny would blunt the offensives of the hordes he truly feared...

Independent and free, the small colony became an isolated kingdom shrouded from the records of time. From this distant corner of the ancient world, a green land between the shadows of Parthian Empire and foe, between angry seas and the steppe of the Orient, a far off silhouette of the Roman Empire, comes the story of a people long since forgotten...

Chapter 1

Storm Clouds on the Horizon

THE HOOVES OF POWERFUL STEEDS trampled the meadows of Luminares. At the bidding of their masters, the beasts hurled themselves forward towards their riders' great city. The knights, sitting atop proud horses, seemed to recognize every blade of grass, though all had become shrouded in the thickening darkness. Waning crimson sunlight reflected fiercely from battle damaged armor. These knights would die for their honor and good name, for the heritage their forefathers called *dignitas*. They were the right hand of the king and the aid of the common folk. They were the Equites. Yet too few had returned from the perilous fight in the East.

Vincent Cincinnatus Kati was full of pride as he rode home in glory with his brothers in arms. Yet his heart did not burn with passion for the Order of Equites as theirs did. Their recent achievements seemed less to him and the armor that he wore only weighed him down with the coming of each restless night. What worth was *dignitas* to a man bitter against his past? Hard set he was to shake the relentless shadow of distant regrets from his back. The skill of this royal servant was great, yet of that which is not attained through mere bodily prowess, who can tell? Strains from a relationship with a woman of high bloodline complicated his predicament further. Always more glory there was to be attained to prove his worth.

It was to this person that Vincent directed his thoughts as he sped towards the city with the other Equites. For him there was no home and family to return to. With parents, brothers, and sisters dead, home was a place of terrible memories, of shame and anger. Home was a far off estate which gave him title and steady revenue. Home was three years dead in the grave, pushed beneath the sod of a forgotten life.

The Equites crashed through the opened gate and down the main city road. Horses reared and neighed as the body came to a halt in front of a tremendous crowd. Trumpets and flutes filled the air. The entrance was filled with splendor and a chorus of song and light. The men raised their spears up in a torrential fury and shook them with a war cry of victory and return. While their sharp, unstained ends glittered in the light of the many torches, the whole crowd chanted their beloved kingdom's name in unison. "Luminares!" they cried aloud. "City of Burning Light!" The people of the city joined the army of horsemen at the gate and encircled them in a wall of praise. Hearts, for so long caged in restless agony, were set loose to unbounded heights of joy when faces so dearly missed were seen again. Amidst the crowd of people, embraces and kisses sweetened by tears of joy initiated that time of celebration which demands tunes of dance. Their joyous songs seemed to echo into the ends of the earth, the people being certain that the ecstasy that filled their hearts would be without end.

However, it was not so with Vincent. All too quickly he rushed through the roaring crowd and pushed his way towards the palace. He did not see his fellow clansmen standing in a far corner of the crowd, three or so hundred foot lengths from the main gate. The slim, shrouded figure of a woman stood in the rear of this entourage. Beneath dark locks of hair dimly offset by the flicker of torches, a pair of golden brown eyes searched the faces of the many Equites flooding into the city. The figure of a man with his back to them riding out of the crowd caught her attention. His shape and the manner in which he rode seemed familiar. Her lips curled into a smile and she started off running to him.

As she ran, his head turned and she saw his eyes fall behind her, upon the other attendants of the house. Then for an instant his glance fell upon her. He quickly turned away, as if to pretend he had not seen her. He did not look back but pulled the hood of his glamorous red cape over himself and started off. A few more steps and she slowed to a walk, flooded with confusion, a tide of fear and dismay rising in her. Her eyes followed his movement as he now more speedily guided his mare through the masses and away from them. She watched and said nothing, her stomach beginning to quiver as her heart dropped. Three years he had been gone! Three long years of waiting. Had it been him? Had it been so long that she could no longer recognize him? Three years of being in the dark. She could not understand. Had he been somewhere else in the crowd? Would he still recognize her or Arlen?

Those eyes had seemed too familiar. Had he really seen them? Had he seen her? Was there room to doubt it? She heard the heavy footsteps of Arlen, a burly man of about fifty-five years, and she pulled her shawl tightly around herself and stood up a little taller to hide her concern. If it had been her Vincent Cincinnatus Kati, he was alive, that would have to be enough.

"Did you see him?" Arlen asked through deep breaths, his big belly moving in and out with each gasp of air. A capable administrator and leader, with both bulk and brains, Arlen was the headmaster of the servants. He was a hardy man, even as he came on in years. His life had been a happy one under the generosity and favor of the Cincinnatus house. Yet he had seen his share of hardship. Unlike many others, he had remained with the farms after the famines and burnings.

Iris Nuptiae looked up at the broad shouldered man. She took a deep breath. "No. I must have been mistaken," she replied.

Arlen scratched his half bald head and looked around. His hands were huge and gnarled from woodwork, his face wrinkled but firm. "Shall we wait a while longer?" he asked. Both paused, looking around at the people speeding off to spend the night merrymaking with friends and family.

"No. I think it best we return to our lodging for the night. It is getting late and we have a long march ahead of us."

"I agree; we have but one horse for our five. Night draws near and the city folk return to their homes. I see no more riders. Our master surely must be with another detachment."

Arlen held a torch before Iris as they walked back to the gathering of the Cincinnatus household. The irrepressible curls of her hair, escaping from her shawl and falling beside her cheeks and along her face, sprang lightly with her movement. The sun now completed its descent and disappeared beyond the horizon. Lonely moonlight shined brightly overhead.

***

It was ominous silver light, like the spying vision of tireless eyes, which gleamed on the massive veranda standing high above the front of the glorious palace. This was the only stone building in the city, a testament to the learned founders of the kingdom's mysterious past. Set atop massive pillars, the veranda projected a dark and menacing shadow upon Vincent as he walked beneath it to the palace entrance. The outline of two guards on watch could be seen atop as they went through their marching routines. Only the tips of their spears reflected any glint of light. The Royal Guard were not Equites. Being of the Guard, who called themselves Keleres, was a higher honor. They were given the privileged mission of protecting the King. They performed his most personal and important tasks. Vincent hated their sternness, their constantly rigid demeanor and how they saw their kind as more upright. It was all a big show that they put on! *Performances and décor matter little in the chaos of combat!* Vincent thought angrily.

He approached the gateway at a hastened pace. Apparitions of guilt seemed to spring towards him from every passing shadow. They were malignant phantoms from a time long ago. It seemed a hidden life was his to bear now, one numbered by days of regret and sorrow. He had to forget! His former life and all the people in it from years ago were gone forever! There was no use in stirring up the past by becoming entangled with the living clansmen! The memories would be too much to bear.

Yet what was there to cling to now? Behind the Lady's stimulating embrace was there not more fear and remorse? Metal plating in his leather boots tapped as he walked up the marble stairs. Vincent stopped at the palace entrance and saluted two

Keleres guards on watch. Up three flights of stairs and down a dimly lit hallway he would find the princess' private chambers. Finally up the stairs, Vincent was glowing with sudden anticipation. He had not seen her since her visit to the battlefield four months ago.

A torch from around the corner projected the moving shadow of a man onto the wall in front of him. He hurried and caught a glimpse of a body passing around the far corner of the hallway. It was not a Royal Guard. Whoever it was had been to see the Princess in her private chambers, something for which the penalty was death. Vincent was no exception to this rule; he simply knew he would not be caught. Perhaps what he saw was nothing at all, a production of his excited imagination and tired head. He pushed aside the drapes that hung at the entrance to her chamber.

She stood across the room looking out the open window into the deepening night. A few candles on a bedside table flickered and bounced soft light off of her body. There was just enough illumination to make out the color of her dark blue dress. Vincent approached Adeline slowly, as if not to awake her, and carefully placed his hands on her shoulders. He caressed her neck with his thumbs and she breathed in deep at his familiar touch. The fragrance of her long, fine hair filled his nostrils, and its texture felt soft against his sun baked face. A kiss he gave upon the softness of her neck and whispered gently, "Adela, did you not know that we had returned?"

A shadow seemed to have darkened her brow when she tilted her head to him. "I knew very well of your success. But how can you think me to be one who would mindlessly creep among the dirty crowds in a soiled form of celebration?" She walked closer to the window, withdrawing from his touch, and turned around. Her expression was even darker now, "I cannot even believe that you came straight here! This is the palace, not some tent out in the field!"

"You knew I would come," their voices seemed to invade the utter silence of the chamber and hall.

"Vincent! It is not the same now! I am the Princess and you but a knight of lowly stature! This cannot go on!" Adeline turned angrily to the window again.

Given fuel in but a moment, the silence burned up the perfumed air of the room for what seemed an eternity. Motionless stars, like countless witnesses of his humiliation, lit the night sky beyond the palace wall.

Finally she turned around and gently pressed her delicate fingers against his waist and pulled his hand to her side. Vincent was bewildered.

She continued slowly, "My husband must sit upon the throne of this kingdom. For this purpose you were not born, Vincent. You are the head of a House once enslaved. The Skilurus clan was among Luminares' ancient enemies. Your family is blessed to have been granted lands and title!"

"My lady, do you think that I am unaware of this?" he snapped back.

She calmed herself, looked upward to meet his eyes, "These things do not happen. My kind cannot be promised to yours. Vincent, if we are seen together your world will be destroyed, and—"

"My world is within your arms, there is nothing else for me."

"You mustn't speak such things!"

"Does your heart not race?" His palms moved firmly around her waist. "Or your blood boil when our eyes meet?" he questioned. She averted her gaze from his and looked down. He was acutely aware of her hand still pressed against his side.

"Hold me," she whispered. Vincent wrapped his arms firmly around her, taking in every curve of the Royal Princess that he touched, every strand of hair. Adela breathed in slowly. *I love you, against my will,* she thought.

***

Now the city of Luminares itself was situated upon a single large hill amidst an expanse of flat fields reaching as far as the eye could see. Beyond these teemed peoples of foreign tongue eager to gorge themselves on the Kingdom's fertile lands. They were fields long put under the plow and sickle until they submitted a fruitful harvest. Soil labored in pain to birth forth its nourishment while mankind poisoned itself with lies, lust, laziness and greed. The good with the bad were spewed forth, to serve their time upon this earth. As God's ruling hand, the Luminarian King sifted through this chaff and wheat and meted out justice. So the loyal still proclaimed. But rumor had long since spread that the insurrectionists grew in number and that the time of the Monarchy grew short.

The next day, many people gathered in the streets of Luminares to greet their victorious king in ceremonial welcome. Tradition demanded that the King be the first to leave for war and the last to return through the gates to safety. Celebration and merry making followed the wake of his parade through the city. Ornaments from the East were held aloft as trophies. The virtues of courage and fidelity, love for hearth and home, and the strength to protect these were commemorated by word of mouth in a multitude of festivities. The bliss of all that comes with Spring reached its apogee in this time. Yet few foresee ecstasy easily meeting its demise, or that elation itself can hide a jagged knife.

After the dust springing from the horses proudly prancing in formation, and from the stampede of citizens running madly to kiss the hand of their benevolent and protecting lord, settled down, most everything resumed its previous state. Yet in the air was felt something new. Luminares had not been strangled in the night by her enemies. By some grace she had survived. Yet it was not without great loss; too few of the land's proud Equites had returned. What did fate now have in store for the pained countryside?

The King of Luminares whipped his hands out from the center of his chest, releasing his hold on the giant cape he wore. The massive red fabric floated behind him, golden rays from the emblem of the sun going up and down the cloth to a purple edge. Stamping out of the room and down the hall, he waved his hand to dismiss the royal agent behind him waiting for orders. *How could he not be sure after all this time? Is it time to replace the agent?*

Is he incompetent? No. Wiser to let him remain. There are too few to trust in at this time. Turning a corner, two Royal Guard sentries put their hands on the hilt of their swords in salute. Thinking on whether they had held their salute long enough or if their armor was thoroughly polished, the young Keleres could not have guessed the depth of thought in their King.

But I told him to have spies in the tracks of everyone on his list. And no results! Impossible! The Plebs are planning rebellion. They are not content to let me be their caretaker any longer, they will have my blood! It will be somebody close. But who?

The great white doors opened and the King of Luminares stepped out onto the portico and greeted a small crowd of modestly dressed men below him.

"Sire, we representatives of the Concilium Plebis greet you. We regret to have appealed for an audience so soon after my Lord's return."

"Master Gaius you always look so tired," replied the king with a faint smile. "You're a worn out warhorse! These years have been harsh on all of us, but it is good to see your worrisome face again." His smile faded now as he peered at the other men and wondered if it was one of these who secretly planned his death. Traitors of the Pleb class in the Second Realm had long been at work strengthening their contacts in the Plebian council. Gaius was one of the few Plebs that the King wholly trusted.

A robed official spoke up, "My lord I come straight from the governor's villa in Helles and I must report that the conditions in the city are unbearable. A new and foul infestation has come from the sea and poisoned the people. The maritime traders have surely brought it with them from their stinking ships, yet the militia has done nothing! Moreover we are told the seafarers have been making *raids* upon the poor cordon of Helles! This has been confirmed by numerous accounts. Some say they even take slaves! This is an outrage to the honor of Luminares. The district must be purged of these outlaws!"

"The Praetor's militia will deal with them in time. Our Equites have just returned from war! Do you expect me to dispatch a contingent of them so quickly?"

"If duty demands it of them, yes lord. I don't trust the Praetor's army. It is more than capable of expelling the sea farers, yet it has done nothing."

"The royal commission will be the judge of that," the king responded tersely.

"*Royal commission!*" One of them whispered angrily.

"Few of these boatmen are even your subjects, my lord. They are foreigners from the north. Maleficus! The same which raped and murdered the people of the Third Realm three years ago!" added another.

"You speak of foreigners and brigands, yet what of these Numantine tribes from the poor cordon? Foreigners themselves but four years ago! Tell me, is it not the *same* people who so eagerly join the ranks of this rebel army which plagues the Second Realm? If the militia were not wholly concerned with this army, maybe they could deal with the seafarers!   I begin to regret my edict of amnesty to these Numantine tribes."

"I represent a Numantine tribe in the Plebian council my lord," spoke one who had before been silent. "Yes, some of my tribesmen have left the villages in anger to seek revenge with these lawless bandits. But they are nothing more than anarchists and thieves. The Praetor's army could crush them, should he will it. Mainstream Numantines remain loyal, my lord. But understand we grow more desperate each day in these conditions. My people have no hope at defending themselves against these northerners, these giants who come on sudden from the sea wielding axes of iron! Something must be done, or we will perish from the earth!"

"Men of Luminares, I understand your concern, but I have told you, I cannot afford to send a contingent of Equites at this time. And for what? To butcher the towns of the sea traders? We must allow the royal commission time to report on the success of the Praetor's militia."

"I believe the commissioner delays his report, my lord, while even here in Luminares we have learned that the situation worsens," responded Gaius with some trepidation.

"Some of us question the royal intentions," added another man tersely.

The King looked at him square in the eyes, "How dare you speak to me in this manner! When the commissioner has issued his report, I will take the proper action, and not a minute before. I refuse to bring in the sword blindly."

"Then my lord truly places the copper the Nordic seafarers place in the royal coffers above the welfare of his own people!" responded the man angrily.

Gaius turned aside to calm the man and then spoke to the king, "Sire, while you rule us we shall always abide by your will. Understand, however, that the council of the Plebs grows impatient."

'While you rule us.' Does Gaius betray his thoughts of murder? No. Impossible, his family has always been loyal. The king held his composure despite his distrust.

"I shall do all that is in my power to bring justice to Helles."

"Very well, my lord," responded Gaius. "But we all fear that these issues have revealed matters of grave consequence to this very city. The infestation runs deep, my lord, not only the borderlands have been infected, but the heart of your kingdom!"

"The disease is here?" the King gasped.

"No, the breath of horrible spasms has not reached Luminares, not yet. I speak of an infestation of heart. There are betrayers in your company!"

How ironic, thought the king. "Continue."

"Did my lord even receive word from the Praetor of the conscription of this militia which marches under the banner of Luminares?"

"Praetor Hydrus sent word from Luminares to my army many times, but the messengers were intercepted. I only recently discovered this."

"It is as we expected."

The king stared at them questioningly.

"Sire, we have reasons to believe that the Praetor may not have wished for you to know of the conscription of his militia."

"I find that the Praetor acted within his powers. His concern for the state in the absence of the Equestrian order was legitimate."

"Sire, he raises an army to quell rebellion while provoking it behind your back!" It was the loud angry man again.

"Councilor, do well to watch your words! The Praetor

possesses imperium. His judgments are final. I have entrusted him as a protector of the city, and I will not so easily withdraw my support."

Gaius spoke up this time, "Sire, my colleague speaks outright, yet it is the truth. We have the evidence. He is a traitor!"

"Traitors, they must grow everywhere like the green grass of our country!" the King exploded. "The Numantine Plebs of the Second Realm attacked the very citadel of Etruscanum! Were it not for the conscription the Praetor ordered, the capital of the Second Realm would now lie in ruins! You call him a traitor for doing this? How can I call him a traitor when he has brought a realm which denied my name back into the kingdom! When he has himself warned me of betrayal and so caught the hand of an assassin!" The king pulled a dagger from his cloak and flung it to the ground at their feet. Its sharp blade sunk into the wooden floor. "This blade was pulled from the hands of a traitor even as he struck for my body. Is there a knife such as this waiting to be plunged into the heart of my daughter also! I will not risk it! And you Plebs call the Praetor a traitor!"

"Sire, we *are* Plebs. My fathers were conquered by the steel of Luminares. We were a mountain people, wild and uncivilized, but free. Your fathers brought us under the yoke and no generation of my people has borne this thought lightly. But now we have seen the face of law and harmony. More than half of my people bear the title of Luminarian. Our destiny is with Luminares, and its King."

"Gaius, I do not doubt your sincerity so much as that of your fellow Plebs. The Plebian class has become filled with peoples who know nothing of our Roman heritage. With the hooves of Luminarian Equites I would mete out peace and justice, yet the times have been harsh: First the famines and now the wars. Many have died. Without the Praetor's actions, without the strength of this, this Legion, to use the tongue of my ancestors, I fear not only that more will seek to draw royal blood, but that the revolution will spread! And under its guise of empowerment will be spread anarchy so rotten and so terrible that Luminares shall slip into the night, never to see the dawn of peace and civilization again."

"Call the high council, my lord, and your eyes shall be

opened to the machinations of your enemies!"

The king paused to reflect. His face was worn and tired. "Very well, councilor, but do not disappoint me. I take great risks in doing this."

The king turned and passed through the white doors into the corridor beyond. His thoughts turned to his daughter, whose face he had not beheld for a year. *Will she be as strong as I hoped she'd be in these difficult times? She is so young, too young for so many burdens.*

Gaius watched the king disappear above him. He leaned over and pried out the upright blade, looked at the tension filled faces of the men about him.

***

Flickering torches illuminated the gait of her walk as she danced to the sound of the flutes ahead. Hand in hand they hurried under a night sky to the roar of the crowds. Excitement beat through Vincent at the rhythm of the drums. *Thump! Thump!* His heart pounded harder each time Adela smiled back at him. She moved along lightly, torches from the festival to their right revealing her countenance at intervals between the backs of tents they passed.

The music grew louder now, flutes singing a high and fast tune. Blazing firelight filled Vincent's eyes as they turned the corner and he had to cover his face. Princess Adeline, as if she lived to be the center of attention, danced right ahead to the beat of the music. The jewel of her tiara seemed to light a path as the crowd parted for her. She spun and waved her dress, clapped her hands and joined the circle of celebration. A great roar of excitement went up at her entrance.

Eyes adjusted, Vincent now joined the churning mob. His bright red cape matched that of many other Equites there. He was nothing special. He grasped the fingers of his female partner and the circle turned like a giant wheel, each person hand in hand. The excited young blonde peered up at Vincent as though he were all the world. Despite her efforts, Vincent's attention was wholly on the Princess. He stared jealously as she danced in the arms of others. She was high bloodline. Adopted by the King when the King's sister, Adela's mother, died of an infestation, she was now the immediate heir to the throne. She might one day be the very Queen of the kingdom and what was Vincent but the lord of a meager estate! A knight of worse than common blood, a descendant of slaves!

Finally his turn came to partner with the Princess. His heart beat faster at her knowing smile as she twirled and spun in his hands. The power he had to please her felt good. When the drums let off a final resounding beat and the circle broke up into a mob of talk, they slipped into the shadows behind a nearby tent.

The glimmer of her tiara was dimmed without the torchlight. It was just he and her. She was tall and proud and she was happy to be in his arms. He moved in slowly until the light warmth of her breath touched his face. Their lips touched delicately and then the wet of their mouths interlocked in passion. Oh what joy from a kiss! What endless delight from so simple a thing! Yet the bliss was stained with guilt, sorrow, regret and anger! Doomed to be cut short! She pulled away, looked to their left and right and then stared at the ground.

That day two years ago was still etched into his mind, when her highness graced the Third Equestrian Cohort with her appearance during a field exercise competition. Her gaze had locked onto him as soon as she made her entrance! He was young then, but had won all the competitions, many against his superiors. The coveted prize of kissing the Lady's hand had been his. He remembered the fire of her eyes for him as he approached. This became their beginning. It had seemed as if Vincent had forgotten what it was to live and breathe until that moment. As if he had at last found reprieve from long suffering and bondage. Yet now, after letters, meetings in the forests of far off lands and behind tent walls, after waiting, after victory, after passion, hidden chains tying her, keeping her from him, confounded Vincent.

Footsteps from close by broke the trance he was caught

in. Surprise flooded their faces when they saw the king himself emerge from the shadows. Almost seven feet tall yet still thick and powerful, he was arrayed in his red battle armor with the flaming insignia of the sun emblazoned upon the breastplate. Vincent went down on one knee and bowed his head as was the custom for men of the Equestrian Order.

"My daughter, my daughter! My weary eyes are lightened at the very sight of you." With a wave of his hand two High Keleres guards, forever with the king, stood silently beside the nearby tent, passively staring straight ahead at attention. Almost just as passively Adela gave her hand to the king. Her demeanor had always been reserved and independent, but she now appeared extremely cold. She had at some time hinted of some tension between herself and her father. Vincent knew her opinion of him was low. He had once known her deepest thoughts and passionate desires. He supposed that it would not be like that anymore. He wished he could tear her wall of stubbornness down just to show that he could see her and that he loved her through and through. Something had always attracted him to her mysterious, indomitable spirit, but lately he feared it.

The King kissed his daughter's hand saying, "The high council awaits the pleasure of your presence tomorrow." He was untouchable. Vincent knew the King took council but his will was his own and no man, no matter how big his purse, could harness him. While looking at Vincent he asked her, "And who is this?"

Adela spoke anxiously, "My lord, this is Sir Cincinnatus of the Third Equestrian Cohort."

"Aaah yes, I chose the Third to guard your person when you came to the front. But this is not Count Lothar, ruler of the Third Realm and commander of that cohort."

"No my lord, this is Vincent Cincinnatus, lord of the fifty-sixth estate of the Third Realm."

"I have heard the name, but do not know him. Who are his fathers?"

Vincent saw her face turn red with embarrassment, "He is of the Skilurus clan. His triumphs in the war were many!"

"Were they?" The King looked at Vincent, who was still on one knee. Vincent met the menacing stare. "Knight, do you know

the penalty for being caught alone with a woman of the royal line!"
        Without hesitation Vincent answered, "Yes sire, it is
death." Death. The word rang on his lips. For years he had
sought it in battle. Want of revenge was all that had kept him
alive, revenge and the cruel and unlikely fate that had brought him
to Adeline.

        There was a clanging noise as the High Keleres
unsheathed their long swords. They were poised ready to strike.
The king's words of doom issued forth, "Never again come into the
presence of my daughter. Never do this, and you shall live."

        The four began to walk toward the royal celebrants,
Patrician councilors and elders gathered in a far corner of the
marketplace. Vincent bowed his head again but looked up to see
Adela's swaying gown pass out of view.

                                    ***

        On either wall adjacent to the court were hung colorful oil
paintings of kings and other heroes of long past. This was the
legacy of the founders, the captives brought from western lands.
Wisdom had been their birthright. The palace, its pillars, paintings
and carefully guarded manuscripts were the living tale of a people
far away. A people all of Luminares was connected to by distant
heritage but with whom they were forever cut off. Purple drapes
hung from a stone ceiling held up by great, white marble pillars.
High up on the roof, burning red, deep purple and glimmering gold
radiated from an enormous painting of the Christ ruling as King of
all heaven and earth. Upon his throne, at the far end of the hall,
the king of Luminares sat beneath the painting. He alone claimed
full blood lineage with the founders. He alone bore the name of
the Roman family which had first led this people away from
paganism and despair. To his right was Adela and to his left the
Praetor Hydrus, speaker of the council. Vincent took his place as a
guest on the Plebian side of the council. Formal greetings began
and finished hurriedly and then an elderly man about twenty seats
in front of Vincent stood up.
        "Sire, knowledge that corruption has poisoned many of

your subjects, both lay and religious, has been proven. It is no longer a matter of speculation, but an issue concerning the life and death of the kingdom!" He paused for a moment letting his words sink in. Vincent saw Praetor Hydrus open his mouth to speak, but then shut it, obviously impatient and angered. He remembered the Praetor from years ago before the war, when he had sat nearer to the back of the hall. He had obviously moved up since then. The elderly speaker began again, "Efforts to raise not a mere militia, but an *army* free from the reins of the Order and the Guard have been put into effect. This is unacceptable! Without the restraints of the Code and any notion of fealty, this army will soon be marauding through our own towns and cities. Already they have set their steel against the Second Realm. I fear that Count Risar has come under their commander's sway. Mark my words, lawlessness follows in the wake of these men who call themselves soldiers. They stand by while Maleficus foreigners raid Plebian villages. Lands have been stolen from the Plebian peoples of the Second Realm. The entire kingdom will follow! This is all the work of men who wish to take new power for themselves. They wish to take power from you, my king. Before the end, these subjects, until now unnamed, will wrest the crown from your very head!"

The King took a deep breath and, as they always did when he gave orders or spoke in council, the Keleres guards in the hall, with one swift motion, put their fighting arm on the hilt of their swords. All were tall and strong, and not one moved his eyes or tilted his head, but remained straight and rigidly passive as always. They were a professional body, unlike the Equites, who were mustered when needed.

Wrinkles entrenched themselves along the ruler's forehead as he half frowned. His firm hold on the traditions had given the kingdom hope, though it be a disillusioned hope to many. Famine, plague and marauders had devastated many from the previous generation, and now invaders had nearly wiped Luminares off the map. It seemed only good luck that the Equites and their auxiliaries had even returned from the war, never mind being victorious. People were beginning to question the capability of the crown. New ideas were in the skulls of both the rich and the poor.

"Master Gaius, your words have long been respected, but this is a grave matter. I trust that you will hereafter present some evidence of your accusations." The king was firm, serious, and unemotional. "What does the Praetor have to say to these opening statements?"

The Praetor stood from his seat by the King. "When the great Praetor of Luminares, Lucius Aemilianus, met his end combating the Nothus hordes, I made a solemn vow to uphold what he began: To protect this kingdom from anarchy and division and bring it the prosperity and wealth that is its birthright. This high council will find that Gaius can no longer speak for the council of Plebs. He has been eclipsed by men whose only thirst is for the blood of their fellow Luminarians. These insidious rebels must be found out and punished! Master Gaius and his rabble stand in the way! These Plebian villages he speaks of are none other than the homes of the Numantine revolutionaries we have combated for so long. The militia cannot protect them from the Maleficus raids because they cannot go near without being attacked!"

The old Plebian councilor began again, "My King has returned at anxious times when evil plots are afoot. While our Equites shed their blood, members of the Patrician council took to scheming in the shadows behind locked doors." The old man's eyes became fixed on the Praetor Hydrus, who now stared back trying to look unmoved, and yet hate leaked out from under his eyelids. "This new army is fueled by the riches of the Praetor's men. It has become a tool of personal ambition and is a danger to your kingdom my lord! This I know, that the Praetor and his kind bring only darkness to this table. He has hid his workings from you so that they may come to their insidious fruition before your return. Flavius, the headmaster of Hydrus' own household has testified before Tribunal that the so called household messengers never left Hydrus' gates for more than a day the entire year!" The old man grasped a scroll and held it up before the council. "There were no messengers sent because the Praetor did not want our king to know of his army! His claim to have sent them is an outright lie! The Praetor has wrapped his crafty hand on the axe of fate, he has but to swing and our kingdom will break to pieces! We must stop him! With your approval my lord, I motion to vote for a new Praetor of the City before the end of his term. For too long our people, this very city, has fallen prey to corruption and to vile..."

Hydrus broke in. "Vileness! For the vileness of your outrageous accusation against myself and the other councilors, this court should be appalled! Your evidence is pathetically inadequate! And yet you sling insults against me in front of the King!"

Gaius shot back, "And you lie to his face! You snake!"

The Praetor stood fuming, glaring at the faces of the Plebian councilors surrounding Gaius. Regaining some of his composure, he refused to allow Gaius to finish his statement, "It would benefit the esteemed men of this council to know that my headmaster Flavius was released from service two weeks ago for stealing from the household coffers. He was replaced with one more capable. As such his testimony is moot."

"The Tribunal issued their ruling! It is final! What you say is of no consequence!" erupted a younger man at the side of Gaius.

Hydrus let out a controlled laugh. "If a Tribunal seeded with rebellious Plebs wishes to accept the ramblings of a young and greedy headmaster, then so be it. The minds of learned men of authority, however, should be on guard against such nonsense. What I speak of is simply the sad reality of affairs. Insurrection is brooding in the hearts of many. The order of Plebians has been polluted by the ungrateful. Numantines and others have no trust in our king. Their loyalty to him is but the whisper of a passing wind, their oaths of fealty mere parchment that is easily burned in the fire. Indeed, it is not men such as the old Gaius whom I fear. He is a relic of the past age. It is the rebels he unwittingly protects that I fear, and which you should fear as well! Only last week our king himself was attacked by a Numantine assassin! If the plot had not been uncovered by the Praetorian Guard, royal blood would have been spilt!"

Loud murmurs arose from the hall.

Hydrus continued, "Power must be given to restore order in the Kingdom. I have in my hands the sealed report of the royal commission to the Second Realm. I have faith that the King's trusted servant will be of like mind." He held the scroll aloft. All watched now as his fingers tore the blood red seal and opened the parchment. Anxious silence filled the room. "It says that the complaints have been found inadequate. The people of the Numantine tribe have been treated with nothing but patience on all accounts, yet still their men gather and rape the countryside in the name of independence. I humbly propose that our King bless the conscripts of this new militia and increase their number four-fold with recruits from the two other realms. Lead them to victory and so bring Luminares to a new age of peace!" Hydrus handed the scroll down to a Pleb who eagerly snatched it away. "The details of the report follow. Luminares is weak!" Hydrus walked confidently back to his chair. "Even Gaius can see this! Too many of our finest Equites have perished these past years. With the devastation wrought by the Nothus so evident, it is time we explore new methods of warfare. As for Gaius' disdain for the capabilities and loyalty of the new recruit army, I assure you their training and command is up to par. Legate Bassus, tell the councilor of the state of the army."

On the left of Vincent a broad shouldered, middle aged man clad in an unusual dress uniform with bronze breastplate and buckles stood up. He sucked in his big chest and spoke, "The Legion I shall call it, for in every sense does it compare with that most glorious army which our ancestors were members of before the transplantation to Luminares. The legion is composed of the finest young men of the Second Realm, trained in an astounding five weeks to be professionals. They are disciplined and skilled, and will serve Luminares well."

"Easy for you to speak thus here while this Legion rapes the second realm!" came a voice from the crowd.

The general hissed at the comment and continued, "Until now we have been unable to commit to pitched battle against the Numantines. Their forces are large and their tactics brutal. But with continued support, I have no doubt the Legion will drive the scum into hell."

Hydrus stood up again immediately. "Sire, under the guidance of your mighty hand, the great and powerful forces of Luminares stand ready for whatever the kingdom may require. This should stand sufficient. As Praetor I move to re-form this council in one week's time, when members may chance present more meaningful information and not waste your time. Until then the council merely presents these few motions which require your approval." Hydrus handed the king a stack of parchments and made ready to leave.

Gaius stood up in anger. "Sire, I protest! I beg of you! Matters cannot wait, not when royal officials leech money out of raised tariffs for their personal use, when Maleficus roam the countryside, when the Praetor has taken to defrocking and appointing whatever bishop he desires, and that legion pillages your kingdom! He has bribed the royal commissioner! And more evil lurks behind his designs!"

Hydrus spoke up, this time even more controlled than before. "What evidence do you bring councilor for these claims? His holiness, Bishop Archelaus, is in good standing and appointed in the traditional and rightful manner. First you accuse this council and now the Church! Perhaps you also have a quarrel with the King himself! As for corruption! Everyone knows that it is the land of your family that is being rightfully bought by the sea traders in the Sea District!" There were a few stifled laughs from Patrician councilors. "You are the one who is abusing the law, abusing the very sanctity of this high council! If the councilor has not one witness or even a drop of ink to support his claims, then I must recommend that the high council re-form at a later date, for the councilor's own good." Hydrus sat down with a bloodless smile wrapped on his face.

All eyes turned to Gaius. He hung his head low and covered his face with his frail wrinkled hands. The councilor did not speak.

As the mouth of the king opened, the Keleres once again went through their motions, their armor clinking in unison. "Gaius I have always respected your thoughts, you come from a good family, but we must have evidence. Bring it and I will listen to all your pleas. Praetor, you have been entrusted with great power, if I find that it has been abused the penalty will also be great. Years I have been gone in war, but I did not leave you guardians of Luminares empty handed! I expect as this kingdom always has, that you will live up to the ancient and just laws that we have always abided by. I will investigate these matters myself and will see some of you personally, including you Praetor. I expect a detailed explanation of events at the next meeting. My forefathers brought this people out of wandering and molded it into the most perfect forms that they had learned from their far-off empire. Unlike the pagan kings, I have always striven for the balance of freedom with responsibility. As our Lord's instrument of rule while I am on earth, I will see the conflicts of our time resolved! I hereby order a second high council in one week's time. In this, candidates will register and a vote for the office of the Luminarian Praetor will be held! I have spoken, so let it be done!" The King rose and all remained still and silent until he and his daughter had left. Vincent watched her familiar swaying gown disappear once again as she passed beyond sight.

Legate Bassus stood up just after Vincent and with his lumbering body brushed against him. The Legate blurted out, "A whimpering knight like you should have the courtesy to wait until his superiors have left before indulging his undisciplined manners!" The spit from his fat lips stuck on Vincent's face.

Vincent came to his full height, towering over the fat Legate. "And a well fed Legate such as yourself should know not to bother training his personal slaves for battle when the Equites are already off in war," he returned brusquely. This fool hadn't seen a day of real battle for the whole two years Vincent was away in war. What's more, he probably received his rank in return for some personal favor to some other monkey in the council. The king was a fool for having his nose buried in the codes of the law while all this went on. But then, Vincent had known for a long time that the councils were a foolish waste of time.

"I'll not have you slandering me in this court Knight! Guards!" Now he was in for it. Two Keleres marched over to the Legate. They were not under his command but were charged with upholding proper order in the palace. Vincent was promptly taken into the courtyard, stripped of his tunic and tied to a post.

"For slandering higher rank in this palace, you shall be punished according to the Martial Code," one of the Keleres proclaimed as another pulled a long strip of leather from a satchel.

These people are so unreasonable! To hell with the council and the Keleres! He kept his mouth shut, knowing he could dig his grave in a few minutes near that Legate. Then came the lash of the whip. One. Two. Three. Four. Five... Fifteen times the razor like rope slapped open his flesh.

The rusty blade of a barbarian grinding through one's skin felt worse. He knew. Vincent was untied and he stood up, half the high council was watching. He apologized to the Legatus Legionis, who then spat at Vincent's feet and walked away. Vincent suppressed a tide of anger.

Blood dripping onto the stone ground, he walked over to a bench, politely asking the councilor's to make a way for him to walk. Picking up a white cloth, he wiped the blood off his back as if he were drying himself from a bath. He then put on his tunic as the bystanders dispersed. Walking towards the hallway, the councilor Gaius barred his path. He put out his arm for Vincent to shake. *Is this man joking? This mongrel has the audacity to stand by and watch me whipped and then congratulate me for standing up against the Legate?*
"Am I to be the slave of the council or do I still walk by my own leave!?" Vincent pushed by, being sure that his blood came off on the councilor's pampered white robe.

***

"The Praetor has told me that this will not be a problem. He says that it is his hope you will continue to attend the high council." The princess was looking out a window again, only sparing a glance at him. Vincent walked away from her, letting his mind wander.
He decided to speak his thoughts. "Those councils have been nothing but a gathering of bickering fools! Let any of them come to the field of battle and I will show them who is master! I'm going to my novices. We will train."
"That's the problem with you Vincent! You're always comparing everything to battles and combat! The world is not a jousting tournament! Some things you just have to accept and deal with! Some things you can't change!" She began to desperately brush her long fine hair, looking at herself in a golden mirror. The finely designed object could pay for the service of twenty servants for thirty years. Horrible pain was beginning to shoot up Vincent's back again from the lashes.

"Why can't they change my lady? Why can't we ride to another realm? Where there are no more councils and meetings, where there are no more secrets? A place where we can forget everyone and everything and start anew?"

She looked at him, sorrowful frustration in her eyes. He was young like her but with a thousand more measures of determination. She knew that he was also a wandering soul, like herself. Deep down some part of her wanted to do just what he asked, but she knew it was impossible. It hurt her to think of it. "You know it is impossible, never ask me again," she commanded, unable to hide some sadness in her expression.

Vincent saw it in her and tried to draw it out. "What is there to hold us back? Who would stand in our way? We can go south! I know..."

Adela cut him off, "And forget everything? Leave the city behind? To go to some barren field in the south!?"

"Whatever you want you can do! Run with the winds of chance!"

"You are beside yourself! I have never dreamed of running away!" It felt like a slap in the face to Vincent. She continued, "I've already taken too many chances with you! You don't even know!"

"Is this all I have been to you, a risk? Or have you given yourself to someone else! I saw a man, not a Royal Guard, leaving my lady's chamber when I first arrived!"

"Well I see that your trust in me faded away long ago anyhow!"

"Only as much as your promises," he whispered angrily under his breath.

She brushed her hair angrily, ignoring Vincent. Finally she spoke again, "Tomorrow I go to Remessa. There are many preparations to be attended to. It would be best if you left."

"Who is the escort?" Vincent's face was red with emotion.

"Sir Lothar of the Third Realm with a detachment of a hundred Equites." He watched her eyes intently looking into the golden mirror as she finished perfuming herself. Silence again. He hated the silence and the mirror. He hated her fine brushes and escorts, he hated his Plebian class and his bloodline and Count Lothar. He hated how she refused to look at him, he hated her stubbornness, her wildness, and he loved her, by God he loved Adeline. It was all over.

He walked out, and he knew she didn't turn to watch him go.

The chill and damp evening air whipped against him and welcomed him. The slight sting in his face and the blood shooting out his veins to warm his skin was reasonable, a familiar feeling, and the wind an enemy he could deal with well. The stars shone gloriously above, and the saddle beneath him and sword at his side felt good. He guided his mare down one last alleyway and onto a dirt path which led into soft green hills with the moon overhead.

Chapter 2

Alone through the Dark

A SERVANT BOY INFORMED HIM dinner was served and
nervously ran out of his master's chamber before Vincent could tell
him to stop. The door slammed shut only to burst open again. A
shrouded figure entered.

"So it is the truth!" came a woman's voice.

"What may that be lady?" Vincent responded, searching
for her face.

She pulled her hood back, "That you have returned, but

not sent word!"

Vincent stared into Iris' fierce golden brown eyes, a whole vicious sea of the past arose within them.

"What are you doing here!" Vincent demanded.

"You never sent word once when off in the war, did you!"

Silence.

Finally Vincent answered, "You speak what is true."

"Has your heart run so cold!"

"For what purpose have you come here?"

"My lord, I've come to beg your return, if only for a while!"

"The days of that past are dead Iris! Nor shall the hooves of my horse ever tread upon that accursed ground again!"

"This is your clan, your people, have you become blind! They followed your father, who was a righteous man and died with honor! And now they look to you! Are you just going to leave us all behind?"

"Because of my father and his headmaster the Cincinnatus family lies under the earth with the worms! And stop saying 'us', us was a thing of childhood. There is no us! Love then was pretty flowers and games. Awaken you lax mind! Life is not the same anymore!"

"Oh that's why you think that I have come here! No, I guessed that you'd found a more stately woman! But there are other Skilurus families besides mine on the Cincinnatus land!"

"You can handle the farms just fine!"

"It's more than that! They've raised the levies unreasonably in support of the Praetor's Legion and who do we have to represent us before the lower tribunals?! Nobody listens to servants anymore. They ask where the head of the household is and we must submit because we cannot answer!"

Vincent looked away from her at his jeweled sword lying on his cot nearby. "Does Arlen still reside within the household?"

"Yes, he is eldest and still headmaster of the servants."

Vincent frowned, "So the old leech still lingers?"

Iris was appalled. *Doesn't he know Arlen is like a father to me!?* She brushed off her anger and approached him. "What darkness assails you Kati?"

Kati. He had not heard anyone call him that for years.

Silence.

"I remember too that dark day," she began quietly. "Do

its icy fingers even now claw at your heart?"

"Does the frost survive while winter endures?" he answered.

Iris searched his angry face, confused.

"So Arlen still resides in my family's household," Vincent whispered to himself under his breath.

"I do not understand what Arlen has to do with anything!" Iris watched him frowning at the floor, eyes lost far away.

"How could you? You've grown used to his foul stench," his voice trailed off. "Well I haven't."

Dead Silence.

He began again without looking up, "I tracked the Maleficus barbarians for months. My feeble efforts were of no avail however, for they departed across the sea. I hoped to die in battle afterwards, Iris. I certainly never intended to return home while I lived." He hung his head, and then lifted it to gaze on his sword glimmering in the dim light. "When I was chosen to be knighted, I was charged with recovering the sword and breastplate of my father. I did not tell you this was why I returned to the estate, but it was for this and nothing more."

"You spoke nothing of this before, Kati."

"I was pent up with rage against that day, as I am even now! I have nothing else, I am nothing else!"

"You are Vincent Cincinnatus Kati, son of Gilroy leader of the Skilurus clan!"

"Son of the stupid and prideful leader of an extinguished and obscure clan, a descendant of slaves! Son of a fool who abandoned his family to be slaughtered! God has cursed every step I take! He has taken away my brother and sisters and hid the Maleficus in order that I may not exact my vengeance!"

"Your father left to serve Luminares with honor! Don't forget that when you curse him you curse my father as well!"

"Curse the whole lot of them! They were blind fools!" he shot back.

"You shouldn't say such things," she protested. "You mock your very own blood and you mock God," she added quietly, though hurt was welling up.

"Do I mock God? Perhaps. He certainly mocks me!"

"This is not right, Kati. If you do not return now nothing will ever be the same for any of us."

"Nothing is the same now! Arlen certainly doesn't realize it, that coward! But I thought perhaps you would!"

"I cannot believe your foul words!"

"Well you should, lady!"

"I have no need for your mockery! You can rot in this city for all I care!" with that, the woman flew out the door.

The pain in Vincent's back flashed out as he smelled the aroma of roast duck in the hall. Food would have to wait. If only he could remember where they kept the wine! He wearily roamed out and grabbed a flask of black olive oil that was lying on a kitchen table strewn with dinner preparations. He kept walking. The chill evening air flew in his face as he crossed the palace's curtain wall. Far below, across the fields some two hundred fathoms away, red armor glimmered in the moonlight. Vincent leaned against the hard stone and peered out towards the gate. It was a contingent from the Third Equestrian Cohort. Rows upon rows of mounted steeds stood proudly in formation, their riders bearing torches. It was an impressive escort. Walking to a shining white carriage beyond the formation were the tiny outlines of two bodies. Vincent knew one of them was the princess Adeline. Anger burned deeper in his chest. *YOU thought to have her! YOU, a descendent of slaves!*

Finding his way into the damp and dark cellar, with some effort he uncovered the stowed away jugs of wine. The wooden stairs rattled as a young man and the previously seen servant boy came rushing down to the cellar. Apparently Vincent had made some noise as he rummaged about. They had thought he was some thief, or perhaps a very large rat! The two, at first prepared to defend to the death their precious vintage, eyed the large jug in Vincent's hand and then looked at him. Vincent had never seen workers dressed so raggedly before; the Palace must've brought in a lot of new hands after so many had left as auxiliaries for the Equites in the war. Since they remained staring at him, Vincent barked at the boys, asking what they were looking at. Both jumped, turned around and darted up the stairs. Vincent was perhaps only four years older than the taller one, but he had years of experience in making people fear him. He smiled to himself. Then, still hidden from the light seeping down the staircase, his thoughts wandered. Men had to fear him, for if they didn't it meant a line of pikes stabbing their faces. Legate Bassus wouldn't know about such things. The Legate no doubt stuffed his face while his Legion battled. *If* it ever battled. Vincent uncorked the jug and took a gulp of the wine. It was exquisite, best he'd tasted in years. Too bad it would all go to waste on rotting flesh!

Oil, wine and sage were proven wound healers. If not used on cuts, especially deep stab wounds, within days they could become infested with a detestable vapor and puff up with thick green or white spongy fluid which would eat away the flesh. Vincent knew this because he had seen many men die both in battle and on sickbed. However, he was willing to risk infection this time. He could not ask for help to clean wounds he received from being whipped in the public forum! And so soaking a cloth in a wooden bucket filled with these three ingredients, he began to clean his back. First he scrubbed the portions he could reach easily. His body shot out signals of pain as wounds broke open again and dry, hard scab gave way to fresh, warm blood. But his imagination was wholly absorbed elsewhere and he hardly recognized the sensations. He felt Adela's dark hair against his body, saw her eyes staring into his in anticipation, drawing him in. He had waited too long to clean the lacerations, any infestation would have likely burrowed itself by now. Her lips were close to his and dripping with the honey of excitement. His physical wounds not being extremely deep, he was able to simply wrap the cloth onto a rod in order to get to the places he could not reach with his hands. Her cold stare injured and bruised and then she turned her back on him. Clammy sweat dripped off his forehead. He suddenly felt totally alone and hurting, pain all over his body and mind. There was no consolation; no one could save him from the wreck he had become. He squeezed the rag. Red blood and wine fused together poured out into the bucket, a cruel chalice filled up with the catastrophe of his life. He stood up, hands clenched in fists of rage. Anger felt better than sorrow, and hate was easier than unrequited love. But in the end it didn't make it any better. A man cannot truly fool himself.

***

The novices were young, very young. Usually aspiring Equites had previous experience as auxiliaries in battle. Not anymore, the need was too great. Still, land and title were prerequisites and not guarantees to the Equestrian Order. This was unlike the appointment of officers in other nearby kingdoms less civilized. To be knighted one underwent the Seven Trials, an intense course of physical and mental tribulation, coupled with tests of devotion and piety. The ritual was finalized when the knight completed a vigil before the altar of God in the Great Cathedral, took his vows the next morning and was ceremoniously initiated by the King or one of his regents. Instruction was less intense than it had been for Vincent, who had spent an entire year as a squire following his Equestrian master to battle. Urgent need combined with a lack of respect for the old ways by the regents resulted in new Equites who knew little of combat. *At least the Trials remain the same*, thought Vincent. There was much work to be done, but a few of the novices were ambitious and willing to learn and so he thought there was some hope.

The students crashed through the attack course, lazily bumping into obstacles and missing most every dummy soldier with their sword strikes. Vincent threw up his hands in frustration. He charged out onto the field on foot, calling the new novices as well as his instructors to him.

"Sit!" He commanded. All eyes were on him, "You are nothing but tin toys on donkeys! The Equites rely on speed and agility! It should take mere seconds to attack this course! As a single rider you cannot destroy entire formations, you must keep moving. If those dummies were bloodthirsty barbarians, they would have put a spear right through your horses as they slowly chugged along. Every one of you would have been thrown to the ground where they would have cut you to pieces!" The young novices flinched at his ferocious yell. They were fully awake now. "Each of you is heir to a vast land away from here. I'll tell you right now, until you cross the threshold of the Great Cathedral with the Trials at you're back, you're nothing to me! I know your

unhardened minds at this very moment think only upon dining.
Well you can forget food! You will be riding for the duration of the
night or until every single one of you does this right! When you
think of food, picture your body all slashed up in the mud because
of your incompetence!"

Vincent jumped up onto his great black horse. "Spear!"
He commanded. His squire Evan, instantly tossed a spear to him.
Vincent pointed the tip at the novices and advised them, "The
spear and lance must be used at initial contact to break the
enemy's ranks! But in later close combat they are all but useless
and the long sword must be utilized." His tone was loud, clear and
commanding, demanding attention. "When in a sword attack,
have the weapon at the ready, anticipating which side the enemy
will be on next. One strike is the beginning of the next. All strikes
are lethal! In such dense enemy formations, pausing because you
missed the mark will only result in a pike thrust through your
steed."
One of the young Equites looked away from Vincent to the
road as an impressive looking carriage with a mounted guard
passed by.
"NOVICE! Who told you to look at the road!" Vincent's
fellow instructor was fuming. "He's instructing about life and
death and you want to look at a pretty carriage! Do you want to
revoke your vows and drive carriages for the rest of your life!"
"No Sir Proventus!"
"Your disrespect is as putrescent as your skill is inept!"
The instructor spat at the ground in front of them.
Vincent began again, "If you all have not realized it yet,
you will soon discover that the Trials lend you no rights! You
possess only your oaths and the duties they entail. Until these are
completed you will not have gained the respect due a lord and
knight. Now pay close attention to the way this is done!"

Vincent's glare seemed deadly; the novices fearfully
imagined what it would be like to meet him on the battlefield. His
great black horse turned and galloped away from them. At full
speed the knight's spear pierced the straw and cloth head of the
first dummy enemy. He then hurled the spear into the chest of one

from the next line of enemies. In the same motion he drew his sword and cut the next dummy over in two. Now to the left now to the right, he cleaved his way through the dummy ranks without missing a stroke, dodging the obstacles and remaining at near full speed the whole course. Each of the young Equites silently recalled how long it had taken them to get through the course, twenty, maybe thirty seconds. Their commanding instructor was on the road to the far side in no more than ten seconds. He did not halt but flew towards the fancy carriage passing by. The relatively untrained horses driving the carriage reeled at the sight of the black warhorse charging without any apparent intention of halting. They flew off the road and into the mud in panic, the carriage jolting around as it was recklessly pulled away. The novices smiled, enjoying the entertainment and their few minutes of rest. Three days of endless instruction had taxed their minds and bodies.

One sitting novice yelled out, "Hooray for the defeat of the purple draped carriage! Our war seasoned commander has won again." The others looked at his smirking face, surprised that he had spoken unasked for. *Was the angry instructor, Sir Proventus, nearby?* Laughter escaped from a few others. "HOORAY for Sir Cincinnatus the great veteran!" he continued. By now there was an uproar of laughter. Sir Cincinnatus still lingered on the opposite side of the field.

"Hooray for Sir Cincinnatus the Carriage Slayer!" yelled another a few seconds later. He turned to see if he had scored a laugh, but saw nothing but the tall Sir Proventus in red armor staring down at him. They were all in for it now.

***

Adela lifted her pearl necklace over her head and put it down on the bed. *A fine present from a fine nobleman and a fine suitor. Like so many others.* Cool evening air blew in from the window she liked to keep open. She felt alone. As she took off her blouse and stared at her image in the golden mirror, she wondered if ever she would even marry. Did she want to marry? The trip back from Remessa had been long and tiresome. She pulled off the purple silk dress she had worn all day, folded it, placed it in a great wooden chest and then lied down. The pearl necklace rattled as she carelessly threw it from the bed onto one of her bureaus.

Rest eluded her. The moon dimly lit the room, illuminating paintings on the walls. An angel clad in white knelt beside a child racked in pain and doomed with the Plague. To the right of the child, men and women crawled upon the face of the earth frantically fleeing death. Demons paraded over them while more angels above their heads attempted to break the demons' ranks. Adela knew it was all foolishness. Men always had to explain everything in terms of warfare and struggle; they couldn't accept things the way they were. In the painting dead bodies were strewn across the streets and in randomly heaped piles. Above all sat the Creator enthroned in majesty with the look of judgment upon his face. A poor Father would God be indeed if he abandoned his children to such suffering! She crumpled her body tightly into a ball and pulled the bed sheets over herself. She felt alone. Her mind traveled back to before she had been adopted, when she was still a young girl. The terrifying image of her real father leaving her and her mother invaded her head. It was as if it were yesterday, though she had only been ten years old at the time. His scruffy beard pressed against her skin as he embraced her, promising to return. His face was cold. Mother was crying, begging him to stay. He never came back, he had found another lover. He never even wrote. He had left her alone. Adela found herself squeezing the blankets in anger.

***

Kiathar Strongblade listened as Sir Cincinnatus gave them their orders. Kiathar was the descendant of a great warrior family from the Northeast and could not fathom the incredible shame of failing the Trials. At that very moment his family awaited his glorious return home. Kiathar took in every word that came from the great, although young, veteran speaking to them and let it sink deep into his blood, which boiled with restless anticipation. His hands ached to grasp his axe, to make use of his weapon and his training against a foe.

When the commanding instructor finished giving the platoon of novices orders, they immediately began preparing their weapons and gear. Kiathar stood up and looked to the caves where the Trials would begin. With his stare thus fixed, he placed his leather Nordic helm upon his head and slung his huge axe over his shoulder. The man was a giant among the other novices. His calf muscles alone were as big as an ordinary man's head. His biceps clenched taut with uncanny strength as he imagined facing the enemies he would soon meet.

Some of the younger novices who had never before seen people of Kiathar's race occasionally spared a glance at the monster of a man. Exander Quickfoot too looked at the great behemoth in awe, but then scorned himself for doing so. The shorter but more muscular Alexus left his sack by Exander and walked over to the towering Nordic novice.

"By what right do you seek knighthood outlander?"

Without looking down to the man, Kiathar replied, "By the same right as you," he turned his gaze to him, "Man shrimp."

Alexus laughed and carved off a piece of salted pork for the giant, which he accepted. "Perhaps my size disguises my skill," he was beaming as he spoke and devoured the rest of the dried pork.

Kiathar looked at him questioningly and wondered how a man could smile so much amongst strangers.

"In any case," Alexus continued, "My height will matter little to the enemy when he feels the tip of these." He produced a javelin from the satchel on his back. "I will never have need to get close to a foe."

"Combat *is* close and personal. It is inevitable."

The short, brawny man squinted at Kiathar questioningly then patted his forearm and trotted off happily.

Exander took a few steps toward Kiathar and mocked, "So the Maleficus turned knight can indeed speak our tongue!" He and a few others laughed.

The outlander picked up his satchel and slung it around his shoulders. "For two generations now the Strongblade's have lived within the territories of Luminares. Your language I have learned.

But I keep my Nordic blood." He started walking. "And it will serve me well in the hour sword meets flesh."

"You can't overcome the Trials alone outlander!"

Kiathar kept walking.

The first of the Trials was the Long Cold Dark. It extended from the westernmost edge of the Numinous Mountains to a tall peak in their center, where snow always blanketed the earth. It was a long maze of natural caverns filled with pitfalls and obstacles. The novices were to navigate these in pre-designated groups. Leadership, cooperation, and unique skill would get them through alive and ready for the next stage. At any point in this trial a novice could turn back, and while there was no punishment besides immediate dismissal, the lonely road behind was often more treacherous than that ahead.

After four days in those blackened caverns the will of the men began to falter. Torches had long ago burned away or been lost. Inwardly the warriors first struggled uncontrollably to pick out objects in the path ahead. Hoping their eyes would adjust, they searched endlessly for some sign of light or direction. With time the mind relinquished this futility, giving in to utter blindness. Constantly tormenting was the fear that each step would falter on some spike or boulder, or worse, give way to a giant chasm or a cliff stretching to some hellish abode in the center of the earth. This constant fear slowed the expedition tremendously.

The world became unbearably cold as the novices descended deeper and deeper into the frozen mountains. Laughter and jokes perished, even for Alexus. The reality of the solitary self closed in. More than a few lashed out with screams of frustration which leaked from the panicked mind. Without a word the novices unwittingly came closer together. Shoulder to shoulder and back to back, there was the unspoken comfort of knowing that one was not completely alone in the abyss. Still, the darkness trampled their hope and cut straight through their hearts.

Exander Quickfoot's stomach gnawed on itself, acid and

fluid churning within, begging for a piece of warm baked bread, a slice of salty ham or a juicy pomegranate. Soon his water skins would be dry too. He simply had not planned on bringing four days provisions. He had expected that there would be time and place to hunt and gather all along the Trials.

With a smack Exander's knees hit the rock ground. He clung to the waist of the man in front of him. The novices tight line formation allowed each to brace the other and conserve heat. Exander got up with a grunt.

"Curse Cincinnatus for sending us down here to our death! We have not even food and water enough to survive! How is this the lot of a knight? That insolent mongrel! What gave him the right! Mark my words, he is only a year or two older than any of us, and with a much lesser estate, and yet we are the ones sent to our death! Curse him and his squire!"

A few seconds passed and then a low voice responded from in front of them, "If you had but listened to the commander's words you would know that he warned us well of the perils of the dark." It was Kiathar, who refused to be part of the train of scared and cold men.

Exander didn't know how to respond. After a few seconds he cursed again. Kiathar tucked the fur end of his iron studded gauntlets under his coarse tunic of animal hide. Warm blood still flowed in his veins.

When they next lied down to rest in that endless night, Exander wrestled with hate, anger, fear and hunger. He espied Kiathar's body with his ears and closed in. The outlander was given away by his loud snoring. Exander Quickfoot pulled forth his dagger. Hidden by the thick darkness, the blade was sharp and ready. Lubber felt for the body with the slightest touch. Then, ever so carefully and quietly, he groped for the Nordic's satchel. Hard salted meat he pulled out! The Nordic had enough for many more days. Grinning unseen, Exander turned to head to his sleeping spot with his prize. But the Nordic took in a deep breath and the snoring ceased. Exander froze. The Nordic was moving! Beads of sweat accumulated on Exander's face. Finally came the exhale, he was still asleep.

"The Long Cold Dark breeds teamwork and mental

discipline," Sir Cincinnatus tried to assure the nobleman. The nobleman's son now traversed the rocky caverns far beneath their feet. "It fosters an inner solidness tested by the loneliness of the caves," Cincinnatus continued, "And a sense of honor and accomplishment common with all the Trials. Besides, the danger of getting lost and perishing is in fact minimal! Only a few have died in this manner in my lifetime. The caves are actually completely mapped out and not very complex. The darkness masks reality."

Uninterested in any fascination with the Trials, the nobleman continued to worry over whether his heir would live to inherit his family property. He argued more with Sir Cincinnatus, who soon lost all patience with the man. Cincinnatus motioned to his squire to take the man away. The squire tilted his head questioningly. *You want me to get rid of a nobleman?* Cincinnatus nodded knowingly and walked to the rock ledge. The boy walked in a tall manner over to the fussing nobleman and interrupted his mumblings.

"Sire, if you would follow me." He extended his hand to gesture the man to walk in that direction.

"Who is this boy you send against me!" He complained to the back of Sir Cincinnatus. "I will not be ignored, knight! This instant I want a detail of pages bearing provisions to be sent into those caverns. If I had any idea what kind of treatment..."

The squire watched his master walk away from them down the ledge. He needed no more excuse. Grasping the nobleman's arm and putting pressure against his lower back, he pushed him back towards his waiting entourage. The man made a fit about injustice and grumbled that a squire of no more than fifteen years had dared jostle him. In the end he actually did nothing but whine. Evan soon found himself back at the rock ledge alone.

Sir Cincinnatus was staring down to the green valley where the novices would emerge from the mountains. It was the first sign of life amidst the snow covered peaks, where memories of vibrant vegetation would be awakened after the long haul in the dark. On its fringes were bare evergreens stretching tall into the sky and colossal rocks guarding the valley like ancient sentries.

"Do you see that green valley, Evan?" Vincent asked his squire.

"Yes sire."

"That is where they will emerge from the mountain. That is where they will realize the darkness does not last forever. Soon their fear will evaporate like the morning mist which is now before our eyes."

"Yes sire, it is a wonderful thing."

"Is it?" Sir Cincinnatus breathed in deep and held it. Evan didn't know what to say. Vincent continued, "Or is this trial a lie? Is it an illusion which conceals a true fate of endless shadows? Do the menacing vapors of death and pain inevitably choke us, as the darkness chokes their hearts now, far below?"

Once again the awkward silence. Evan found himself searching for some words of encouragement for his master. He had carried his food and armor, prepared his meals, dressed his wounds and followed him into battle for two years now. Surely he could think of something to say at times like this! There had to be some way to express the pride he felt in watching the Red Armor charge three thousand Nothus horsemen, or the pain and glory of defending their beloved kingdom. *But who am I but a lowly servant and a boy of fifteen years?* he thought. *I cannot hope to wield words as weapons such as great men like him so easily do!*

"I can no longer tell," Sir Cincinnatus answered the deafening silence.

Vincent then picked up his burden of belongings, leaving the lesser pack for his squire to carry, and began the march down the mountain, towing his laden steed behind him. It took the rest of the day to reach the bottom, even after cutting a shorter path through hidden ravines, which the novices would be obligated to avoid. Evan set up camp under the cover of a patch of evergreen trees. The other knight instructors were nearby.

Fiery red sunlight descended behind the mountains and darkness fell. Evan could not sleep. Munching on stale bread, he dreamed of the battles that would transpire in the years to come.

How will I fare for my part in serving my master and the Kingdom?
His face became clammy at the thought of facing defeat, as he
knew the Equites one day would. He had seen Nothus horsemen
overrun cities as though they were mere insect nests. How they
had survived the campaign in the East he did not know. His
pondering was interrupted by a scream from the camp. Evan
lurched forward, threw off his cloak and unsheathed his long
curved knife.

　　Another low agonizing wale.

　　Evan sat back down and covered himself from the chill
evening air. The texture of his leather knife handle pressed safely
against his gut as he re-sheathed it. He watched Sir Cincinnatus'
face crumple up in pain as he moaned indiscernible words and
then raved in terror. Two years now and not a fortnight had gone
by without the nightmare. *While the other men of the Red Cloth
rest in peace, my lord does battle upon unseen enemies even in
sleep!* Evan was perturbed for his master's sake. Yet secretly it
won over even more of his admiration and respect for the hard
man. Putting his head back against the bark of the tree he closed
his eyes, hand resting on the knife.

***

　　The first stage of the Trials did not appear to be anywhere
close to being over to the men beneath the mountain. One long
hour of toil and disappointment followed another and a few were
beginning to give up hope. Had they lost their way? Perhaps they
were walking in one long and endless circle? Mouths were parched
and stomachs aching. The pace became hurried and the struggle
of the will over mind and body intensified.

　　Alexus jumped when his outstretched hands pushed into a
body. The train of discouraged novices collapsed upon itself and
curses flew in the air as man stepped into man. A few clumsy ones
fell.

　　"It's the Maleficus!" cried the train leader to those behind
him. Until then Kiathar had traveled just ahead of the group,
trusting to his own instincts and footing. In some cases he had

perhaps even led the group in their tired stupor, though they would never admit upon it.

"Wrap your hands tight around this," the Nordic tribesman commanded. He handed the leader one end of a long, tough twine his people used to fasten docked sea vessels. They heard him walk away but then turn around and yell, "And do not move!"

Soon he was beyond hearing. Without expending the energy to say a word, most figured he was making sure that they were not doing what they all feared they were doing: treading the same ground that they had walked on for days. Exander took up the opportunity offered by his absence.

"Though we have all rationed our food stores, soon they will expire. The Maleficus will hunger greater than us, being the fiend that he is! We must not allow ourselves to starve for him. Very soon he will ask for a share of your food. Do not give it to him!" His voice echoed so loudly that they feared the barbarian novice would hear. They waited. And waited. And waited. Finally footsteps could be heard again.

"All is well," came the deep low voice of the Nordic.

"You cannot know that all is well!" Interrupted Exander. "Your rope is no more than one hundred cubits in length! We still don't know if we've been traveling in a massive circle!" Most of the others assented and panic spread.

"He is right. I do not know. But the twine is in fact three hundred cubits in length and ahead lies a deep cleft which I feel we have not yet passed. It is wide and the edges steep, I suggest we hold onto this." Kiathar threw the end of the rope onto the men and raveled up the slack.

Slowly but surely they passed by the cleft. Only one man fell into the pit, but with some luck he managed to keep hold of the twine and was saved. When the group next stopped to rest, Kiathar sat closer and, just as Exander predicted, asked for a share of the other's food. All refused, except Alexus who traded a small bit of crusty bread for water. Exander begrudged Alexus for it. He hated the barbarian, as he called him. In the secret chasms of his mind he placed the blame of their situation upon him. This was against all reason of course. But darkness had masked the eyes of his wits. Enveloped in despair, hate became his food.

He pictured his fingers around the barbarian's mouth. The muscles in his hands were taut, smothering the giant's wakening howl of anger. He would hold him, yes hold the Nordic's massive flailing body down just long enough. Kiathar would be unprepared to defend himself weakened by the throes of deep sleep. Dreams would suddenly fade away into a dreadful reality as Exander pressed his knife into the soft skin under his chin. He would do it this time! Yes, he would do it when they rested.

He listened for the barbarian's footsteps ahead of them. Yes, there they were, heavier than the rest. *The stuck up mongrel! Pretending to lead us, pretending to know where we are! He knows no more than the rest of us!*
The Maleficus trudged along, loud against the rock ground.
The novices shuffled behind in tiny fearful movements.
Pebbles fell, bouncing off to caverns far below.
Still the sound of his trudging.
Exander pressed up hard against the man in front of him, they had come to a sudden halt.
The loud trudging began again and the journey continued.
"Maleficus barbarian!" exploded Exander. He could stand it no longer!
Kiathar came to a dead stop, halting the train of men behind him.
"Yes, you hear me," Exander exclaimed. "You know well what you are! That is why you halted at my command! Get back behind the line of novices now. There is no more need for you to walk in front. You know nothing more than the rest of us, and your foul stench belongs behind. You are a son of foreign invaders and carry a beating pagan heart! Your treachery and heresy are a curse upon this party and a danger to our God given rights to the Equestrian Order! Now get behind, I am sick of smelling your grimy barbarian scalp!"
Kiathar loosed the leather cord tying his axe to his back and pulled the weapon from its animal skin encasement.
Hands outstretched to feel their way, the novices

scrambled in all directions! Their heightened senses could taste the spilt blood in the air already.

Exander unsheathed his longsword. *So I won't have to wait until sleep, the sooner the better!*

Alexus fell to the ground hard, pushed by another novice running from Kiathar. Catching himself just before his face hit the surface, he let out a sigh of relief. His hand however, was gashed on a sharp rock. Blood oozed onto the cold ground. Alexus ran his fingers across the wound, feeling its depth. Unwittingly peering down at it, he saw the dark blood on his skin.

I saw!
Light!

Alexus looked up towards the faintest of faint glimmer of light and sprinted towards it. He tripped and fell again, his hand cut on another rock.

"LIGHT!" he screamed at the top of his lungs to the others! "LIGHT!"

There were boulders and rocks and pebbles and he could see them all! Alexus squeezed through a tight corner and the precious radiance became blinding, he closed his eyes in shock. The rest of the novices followed quickly behind, rushing towards the illuminating beauty, drunk with relief.

That was when Exander was knocked to the ground. His cry of terror pierced their ears with the sound of claw meeting flesh. Scrambling on all fours Exander crawled away from the roars of the beast towards his fellows. The bear hesitated to charge the men who now had their weapons drawn. If the animal had, it would have slaughtered them all because their human eyes were so stunned from the light which was now pouring upon them.

From hearing and what little vision they had, they discerned within seconds that Exander was trapped and that there was more than one bear assailing them. His cries became muffled under the fur and weight of one of the giant beasts, when with a flash Kiathar's axe smashed into one animal, breaking its spine. The others, their vision returning, surrounded the remaining bear as the cubs fled. They closed in, pointed metal facing inwards. Big paws wagged in the air, death and rage hidden behind the standing fury. No more than a second passed before a javelin hurled by Alexus was buried deep in the bear's stomach. Still the mighty beast roared, its rage heightened, when Kiathar's axe landed between its eyes and cracked its skull in two.

"Looks like it shall be meat tonight boys!" remarked Alexus between hard breaths. Kiathar was ritualistically smearing the fresh blood of the animal under his eyes. "In the name of all things sacred, Kiathar, what are you doing?" Alexus looked at the man in disgust.

Without paying him any heed Kiathar gathered up all the blood from his axe onto his fingertips and continued applying it to his face. Exander, lying on the rock and feeling as if his lungs had been broken, looked at Kiathar with loathing.

Finally Kiathar looked over at Alexus who was instead wiping his javelin and then his hands clean of the blood. Kiathar spoke, his grimy crimson face now looking very menacing. "My people teach that there comes a time when every man must prove himself. In my father's, father's country this was when he would become a warrior and one of his tribe. The blood of the beast he slays is sacred and a sign of his rite of passage from boy to man, from son to father, from child to warrior. The killing of the beast is an honor, not a mere meal," the Nordic tribesman scoffed at the smaller man. Alexus laughed and Kiathar looked confused. "Is this so hard to understand," he asked. Alexus laughed again and this time a broad smile came across Kiathar's face.

To Alexus it all seemed grotesquely hysterical; here was this giant outlander smearing blood all over his face while grinning and asking what was hard to understand. Not to mention that they had spent almost a week in the dark only to be nearly killed by bears. After starving for days they would soon be feasting, but Novice Kiathar preferred to smear blood on his face!

Alexus began skinning one of the animals with a short sword and remarked joyfully, "Well my barbarian friend, a good meal these bears will make indeed, and I for one am happy to keep it at that!"

***

Adela did not feel love for this man. Not truly, anyway. But what was true love? It was an apparition conjured up in the minds of a few privileged ignorant. What was real? The terror of being alone, that was real. And this reality wasn't so bad when he, or any man, was around.

Inflatus drained his mug and slapped it on the table. Adela saw him look over at her with a hungry look on his face. She gave him a little smirk, picked at a strawberry with her teeth and then pretended to ignore him. Inflatus laughed and moved over to a chair near her. His gold lined robe pressed up against her as he put his arm around her.

"My dear, dear Princess you provide the tastiest wine and the finest company!"

She giggled and put her hand on his shoulder. "And just how much do you love my company, Inflatus, prince of the Ptosiian colonies?"

"Tis sweeter than the most expensive wine!" He poked at her side and put his head against hers. "And I would know for I own the most expensive in the entire kingdom!"

Adela was surprised to look up and see Sir Lothar, Count of the Third Realm, walk in. He had escorted her to Remessa six days ago. He spoke, "My lady I came to call on you in hope that you would recline at my table tonight, but I see that you have found company."

"That she has!" bawked Inflatus, "But stay and have a drink with us!"

Lothar looked at Inflatus with what appeared to Adela to be anger held at bay. For a moment she feared that Lothar might challenge him to combat. But then his eyes fell on the table. "I think that I shall," he replied finally. Anger the Count felt for certain, but its root was a jealousy that not even the Princess with all her womanly awareness could comprehend. Content to at least be within her presence, Lothar sat and filled a cup with wine. The princess gave him a nervous smile. It was torture and ecstasy for him to be there. Through his blonde mustache and beard he forced a bright smile, looked at the cup fatefully and gulped it down.

Inflatus refilled the cup and began in a high distinguished tone, "The princess has given her consent to travel in my personal carriage in tour of my mansions on the morrow. I shall show her highness all my fine establishments."

"Alone with you Inflatus?" Lothar questioned.

"If you must know Count, yes, I shall have the honor of her complete and undivided attentions for so long as it shall pleasure her."

Lothar stood abruptly, "If my lady would excuse us, I must ask to speak with Inflatus alone!"

With a nod from Princess Adeline, Lothar bowed and Inflatus followed him out of the room and into the hall. The solid wood doors slammed shut.

"I know you Inflatus and in doing this you have forsaken all honor!" Lothar exclaimed in a low guttural tone. "As the son of my father's most beloved friend I have dealt with you patiently till this day. I shall reveal all your debauchery should you defile the honor of our future Queen by doing this on the morrow!"

"What is this Count Lothar? You look upon the soul of a simple merchant who enjoys a small number of diversions here and there in an otherwise dull life. Why should I not have the pleasure of entertaining such a fine and distinguished lady as our very own Princess?"

"Is this entertainment to be anything of the nature you performed with the Lady Easear?" the Count shot back.

Inflatus sulked.

"You have unscrupulously thrown your inheritance away in casting lots for the games, and still you seek more! Your lust for the flesh is only slightly less than that for the coin! Oh yes I know your secrets, Inflatus!"

Inflatus turned his back on the Count, walked back into the dining hall and picked up his goblet. In slurred words he spoke, "A toast to our most revered lordship the highest count of the highly unadorned Third Realm. Its walls rise high and its vintage runs low, while the condemned raise their cries from the dungeons of your mighty stronghold. May your reign be filled with more lonesome joy than your empty courts are with people!"

Lothar slammed his fist down on the table, "My lady do not leave yourself in the presence of this slanderous tongue!"

"But I meant no offense Count!" Inflatus came back. "I merely wished to express the sad reality that your halls are lacking in the lavish gifts and entertainments that our most adored lady expects."

"If this is so then I apologize to my lady."

Adela fiddled with a mango fruit uncomfortably.

"Adeline accepts your apology. Now with your permission, Adela, let us travel to my summer residence in the nearby town. There you may recline and munch on mangos and strawberries to your heart's delight. We must make the most of my time here in Luminares. Two days and I shall be gone. Behold my servants await our arrival."

Inflatus took Adela's shoulder, uneasily drawing her to himself. Two Keleres came to their sides to assist.

"Leave us be you nose prodding mongrels. She is only a woman and does not need assistance to merely move across town," Inflatus protested.

The two Keleres, younger than usual, looked at Adela questioningly. When she did not ask to the contrary, they slowly turned and marched back to their posts, unsure of what to do next. Inflatus continued towards the exit, his hand wrapped around her waist.

"I am so very glad that I was able to see you this day, Princess. I was endlessly disappointed when I was unable to procure a time to have with you when we met last month," exclaimed Inflatus.

"My lady I must protest!" Interjected Lothar. "This man makes a mockery of your honor. Writing off the Royal Guard and bringing you to his personal residence! Unheard of! Perhaps you have heard nothing of his endeavors. He spends away his family's inheritance at the games and thinks only to spend more. He is nothing but a hog that will use and then forget you, remembering only a dilapidated story to brag of to his peers or to use against you at a later time." He turned his eyes to the fuming merchant. "Have you forgotten, Inflatus, that this is the future Queen!"

"And have you forgotten that every woman of class has certain needs, or do you think in lands and titles only, you overgrown knight!" Barked back Inflatus, fumbling over the words.

"My Lady," came back Sir Lothar. "Say the word and I shall dispatch him!" Lothar was infuriated now.

"You forget, Sir Lothar," she began solemnly. "That I ask

for neither your company nor your aid."

With this the wind of Lothar was stolen from his angry sails and after a vengeful glance at Inflatus, he headed out of the room quietly. Inflatus smiled and wrapped his arm once again around the Princess Adela. She felt his lips on her neck and suddenly felt nauseated.
SLAP!
Inflatus was in shock as he reeled from her hand.
"Get out!" Adela screamed. "Leave me to my self!" *Leave me,* she thought. *Alone.*

As Inflatus reached for the door, he was slammed into the wall behind it as it swung open. Disoriented, he had trouble recognizing who the man entering was when the door wheeled shut once more. Astonished to see the king, he attempted a courteous bow, but was grabbed by High Keleres and hauled out of the room.

The King's bodily prowess dwarfed Inflatus and the Keleres guards, even at his age. Adela looked annoyed. When the hall was empty he began, "You reclined with that mongrel of a man?" he asked his daughter.
"What is that supposed to mean?"
"I mean only to indicate that the High Council is a few hours from now and you are here carousing with that foul likeness of a man! How will you govern the people if I have to be constantly looking over your shoulder?"
"You know nothing of how I will rule for you are never in the city! If you had but been around you would see the wisdom with which I have chosen my political paths! So do not judge me! You know nothing of me at all!"
The King was stern and unmoved, "I've always been very clear with what I've expected of you and I've always watched you very carefully."
"You've always treated me like a child! Never have you shown any trust in me! It doesn't matter. When the time comes I will capably rule from your throne until I find a husband of proper rank and character."

"Will you, I wonder?" The gnarly old man replied.

Adela scoffed at his harshness. His inquisitive stare cut through her as if he was searching for an infestation which he had overlooked. She looked away and down at the half eaten food on the table. "Since when do you even care what I busy myself with anyhow?"

"Ever since I took you as my daughter I have treated you as such! I have always been a good father to you." But Adela saw no care in his eyes.

"Oh yes, you are a good father," she sarcastically remarked under her breath. "Where were you when I traveled halfway around the world just to hear your voice last year?"

"We were at WAR! I had no time for pleasantries!"

"Indeed," she paced around the room. "Your servants, however, informed me that at the time you were celebrating with your legates and refused to be disturbed. I might add that my presence was also concerning matters of the state. Matters regarding the Second Realm, which now spirals out of control!"

"I corresponded with Count Risar of the Second Realm when I could when on campaign. There was nothing you could have told me of value," the King answered with disregard.

"Oh really! Did he tell you that shamans from the Far East have taken root in his largest port city? That these foul pagans with painted faces command the sea trade of the entire realm!? That they may even kill their own as sacrifice?"

The King crumpled his face in a look of consternation.

"No, I suspect he didn't. Yet your will precluded me from doing anything!"

"There are more important things in the Second Realm! I am more worried about this spreading infestation and the Numantine rebellion than a few pagans!"

"Go ahead, write me off again. But let us go back further in my life for the sake of the truth. Five years ago when my dearest friend and companion Lydia was handed over to the plague, I had no one left in this world and there was not a soul to offer me comfort. I locked myself in my quarters for days without eating. If the headmaster had not taken an axe to the door I should have perished! Where were you father!"

The King's eyes wandered toward the ceiling as he tried to remember. "I was away, away in some far off land. But I sent a message by courier! I recall offering my condolences and prayers for Lydia's poor soul. For I knew how much she meant to you!"

"Liar! You were in the city Father!" she snapped back. "You were in Luminares on business. Did you have any idea how heartbroken I was! I was only sixteen years of age!" Red in the face from yelling, Adela now sighed. The King was shocked into silence. "Truth is you probably did know how forlorn I had become, yet still you did not come, nor did you send anyone to my aid. In reality, I, an adopted daughter, fruit of another man's loins, have never meant anything to you. Long ago I'm sure you were very careful that the kingdom should observe you as you took me from my dying mother in a sign of loving adoption. You've always been careful to let your courtesies to me be shone in *public* affairs. Yes, you're a *very* good father. Yes, Indeed."

"You will not speak to me in this mocking tone!" the King was livid now.

"And what if it is my will that I do? You're not my father, you never will be!" Though she stood firm and motionless, her heart was fluttering, secretly hoping he'd show contrition and care.

"I don't have to listen to this!" Barked the angry old man, towering over his daughter. He barged out of the hall and walked to the courtyard. Pacing back and forth he let his rage spill over in more yelling. He pulled out a skin of rum from his cloak and consumed it. Able to relax a little now, the King finally left for the palace in his carriage. Cushioned seats softened the bumps of the dirt road as realization set in slowly. The shock of her words had released old pains, pains he had no means to deal with.

The sundial was two marks past. The High Council was scheduled for less than one hour from that time and he could not concentrate or think. *I cannot govern in this state!* Years ago he had ordered the creation of a small chapel for himself next to his bedroom. It was adorned with magnificent paintings. The King's scheme to re-imbue beauty and devotion in the form of art to Luminares' buildings and halls had begun here in this tiny room. He walked past the red curtains. *I have always tried to do my best, where have I gone wrong?* He had always wanted but never had time for a wife. His reign had been assaulted with too many crisis for a slow life! After he had aged the adoption of Adeline became something of an answer to prayer. *Did I make time for her?* He did love her, his little Adela. *Does she not know it?* He never failed to give her fine gifts on the day of her birth or the anniversary of her adoption. But had he *lived* his fatherly love for her? *What a sack of hog skin to think in this manner,* he thought angrily. Still, the question provoked him, *have I shone my care?* He pulled out another wineskin and tasted the sweet and calming elixir. Close to the entrance of the chapel there was a painting of Marcus Solis Invictus, the powerful ruler of his ancestors who had crossed the great expanse. The warrior was standing tall upon the hills of Luminares with the remnants of the Twelfth Legion behind. The ragged exiles, countless leagues from their homes and abandoned by their pagan gods, stared at their new king in awe. The King of Luminares touched the massive sword at his side. Many wars he had fought to defend his people. His victories now seemed empty. *What is a man without family?* There was another painting of the Christ blessing a few loaves and fish in order to feed thousands. *I have tried to help the poor, to curb the effects of the devastating famines.* The faces of dying children, their bones protruding from the skin of their tiny famished bodies, still echoed in his memory. *But I have no Dignitas to my name if my own daughter rejects me!* Another mosaic of Jesus was at the center of the chapel. This one had been passed down from the first days of Luminares, when the King first claimed primacy over the Roman exiles. The Savior had a gold crown upon his head and a red garment around his shoulders. His eyes were soft and quiet and his pierced hand extended out in a sign of peace. The King of Luminares felt the weight of the crown upon his old head. Perspiration was accumulating around his long gray hair underneath the heavy gold. *I have failed my daughter all these years!* Bracing himself with his hands, he kneeled below the mosaic. The pressure brought pain into his knees despite the barrier a rug provided against the stone. He took off his crown and laid it on the floor. After all this time, now that his body had faded, now that his kingdom had descended into near ruin, despite all his efforts, the crown above his head was worth nothing to him. He only had his daughter and now she was out of his reach. A simple prayer came to his lips, he doubted it even as he spoke, but he spoke it nonetheless.

    The curtains rustled. Someone had entered the chapel! The King raised himself from his knees, secretly hoping that this intruder by some miracle would be his beloved daughter. He turned. A man in the armored uniform of the High Keleres stood before him.

    "Who shall rule this kingdom when death knocks upon the door, my lord?" asked a mouth full of rotten teeth. His countenance was hidden from the King's searching eyes by the battle helmet which he wore.

    "You break your manner of dignity in addressing your king out of order! I shall have you removed from service for this intrusion!" Two pale eyes stared back from the sinister concealment the helmet offered the Keleres.

    Might my assassin arise from within the ranks of my most loyal Guard? Impossible!

    The King reached for his sword, that massive blade which had seen the face of war and victory for countless generations. The metal rang sweetly in his ears as he unsheathed it, but it was too late.

Chapter 3

Masks in Shadow

THE NOVICES MADE THEIR DESCENT down the mountain with bellies stuffed full of bear meat. Their joyous faces populated the ancient forest, awakening it anew once more. The illumination and warmth of daylight was ecstasy to all of them but one. Exander alone still reeked of the dour pestilence of the shadows. Rather than solidify that which is the palladium of the soul, the crucible of darkness had unclothed the wickedness within the novice.

Alexus' hands were sweating. He could see the spikes beyond the distorting fumes of the hot coals. Rising beyond this in the distance was an intimidating wall which had to be nearly twice his height! Instructors at that very moment were dumping fresh coals into the infernal mote that lay before them.

"Novices, you have traversed through the caverns of darkness and come back to the light." It was another Knight of the Third Realm speaking to them from the ledge where the trainers poured the coals. "Your determination and firmness of mind have been demonstrated. But the Trials are not over. Nay, they have only begun! Here in Luminares we value the soul of mankind, for God has placed him above all beasts. Yet to become a Knight of the Crimson Cloth, one must readily lay their own life down. Cowardice must be as far from the sanctum of your hearts as the East is from the West! The Trials are the most timeworn tradition of Luminares, do not fail now, for failure may mean death! These flames before you are but a symbol of what lies within. Do not tarry long, for in the halls of this ancient and defiled pagan temple your fidelity shall be tested. Drink nothing you are given!" The

Knight pointed to a furry animal beside the novices. "Bring this goat, a sign of your wayward past, through unscathed. On reaching the other side, may you wander heedlessly through life no more, but instead lead others in the footsteps of the Good Shepherd. Bring this rusted armor also to the far side. It is a token of your previously un-harnessed furies and lusts for bright gold and sensual flesh. When you have carried it this distance may your passions be forever harnessed and honed, as is the bright red steel of Luminares. Now for the sake of your family's honor and your own, go forth!"

The first team stepped forward.

There were five men who looked in fear upon the obstacles which lay before them. Exander took the lead, "You two balance the armor between yourselves," he pointed to two fellow novices. "Alexus you harness that goat, do not let it fall to its death, for our success will slip away with its life. Maleficus," his tone was harsh. "Grab a hold of-"

Kiathar was already in the process of hurling the huge log onto the coals. Alexus watched as he fearlessly charged across this makeshift bridge and jumped into the field of spikes beyond. They could not have missed his flesh by more than a finger's length. Weaving through the spikes he came to the wall, which he scaled in a single bound.

"Hurry yourselves," Exander demanded as he began to cross the log. "We shall have to work without that traitor!"

On the other side of the wall, Kiathar found himself in a darkened room. Candles were placed beside a door on the far side. With the softly placed footsteps of a hunter, he snuck across the ancient stone floor. Clothing rustled from somewhere in the room. Kiathar looked behind himself to see FACES! Silent. Women's faces painted in white, staring directly at him. Kiathar jumped from the startle only to stumble into something else. He turned to face the direction of the door.

A Man!

A cruel smile was on his lips and like the women, his face was eerily illuminated by the white paint. Kiathar came back to his full height, recovering his composure. With a kick of his left leg he

knocked the man to the ground whilst he drew his axe from its fur
sheath on his back. The giant blade in hand, he stepped towards
where the man fell.

And walked into a wall.

Bewildered, he watched the candles flickering. Kiathar
found himself walking to them, a sick feeling growing in his
stomach. He would bust open the door with a roar and frighten
away whatever pale skinned men lay within! Yet as he grasped
the latch, the sick feeling grew and he could hardly push on the
frame. Stumbling into a room filled with light, somebody touched
him.

It was a soft and secret touch, as of a lover gesturing to
her beloved in a crowded room. It was a woman, a beautiful
woman! Her face was not painted with the eerie white, but was
soft and golden. Bright and eager eyes blinked at him.

"Follow me!" she commanded.

Off she ran, as lightly as a gazelle, the simple silk robe she
wore bouncing lightly around her small waste. Kiathar followed,
putting his axe away as he passed around a great bonfire. The
heat felt good. *Why had the outer rim been so dark! This place is
warm and vibrant, as if a festival will soon begin!*

Kiathar watched her stop in a doorway and turn. He
approached and soon found himself directly in front of her. He
could see the moisture on her lips and feel the warmth of her
breath. The atmosphere of the whole place was sweetly
intoxicating. Hands on her shoulders now, the Barbarian wanted
to tear the robe from her soft shoulders and devour every inch of
her body. The silk robe began to slip off.

"Stay with me." She pleaded with a smile, drawing each
word out. A mask of golden yellow she procured from behind her.
Then, placing the mask lightly onto her face, she squeezed his
arms more tightly around her body.

Then he smelt it: the honey sweet and spicy odor from
long ago, the smell of the grotesque snake cults from the Island.
When his father had taken him to visit their ancient home across
the seas, they had seen them. The sweet smelling worship huts
had come to dominate the temples of the traditional gods, Thor
and his kin. Father detested them!

Kiathar tore his eyes from the golden beauty and looked
inside the darkened room. She continued to beg him to enter it

with her. A bed could be seen. But two merciless eyes stared back at him from beside the bed. They were eyes of a man and his face was covered with the paint.

Kiathar angrily pushed the woman into the room and turned to go. She aimed a piercing shriek of fury at him as he began to walk away.

"How dare you!" the golden skinned woman demanded!

The Nordic didn't turn back. A sick feeling was devouring his stomach again. He could hear the weeping of a man echoing now from somewhere in the halls. He was running now and fumbling for his axe once again. A large metal bowl by the bonfire spilled as Kiathar clumsily ran into it while looking behind. Mutilated flesh, the hand of a once live man, flew on the ground from the detestable red soup. The spicy smell issued forth from the spilled liquids. Jugs and flasks were piled nearby as if ready for a celebration at the novices' coming! Kiathar ran harder now.

Back out the door lighted by the candles, the giant gulped down air in relief. He didn't know what he was afraid of and he mocked himself for having fled like a child, yet never had he been so happy to flee! Feeling his way around the room, Kiathar easily found a narrow passage leading outward. A torch seemed to be at the end.

Suddenly he fell three or four feet and found himself in a pool.

The waters were green and murky, full of foul spirits. He looked up to the torch; it hung from a rusted roof of iron which caged the pool, hiding what lay beyond in the darkness. There was only one way forward. Kiathar began swimming. It was a prided talent of the Nordic tribes, being an island people. Nothing was visible now, only the splashing water and smells of rust and rotting wood remained. Kiathar's head hit hard against the wall. *Where is the exit!* He felt around, above the water at first, then below. *Nothing!* He searched again. This time when he came up for air he was startled to feel his head hit the wood and iron roof. *The water is rising!* Frantically now he dove beneath, searching for the gateway to safety. His fingers felt a plank holding doors shut. Planting his body on the ground he tossed it aside and felt for the doors, which he tore open. *Light!* He swam towards the blur of brightness and soon found himself walking up stone stairs. None other than Master Cincinnatus stood at their top.

"Forgot something have you?" The Knight asked him. Kiathar looked down at his dripping body and then back up, puzzled. "Novice, you shall not pass this threshold until all the tokens of completion accompany you!"

The stairwell was suddenly shut off and Kiathar was left alone in the rising water. *I tire of being trapped in the dark!* He thought as he impatiently returned to the chamber with the painted faces.

Flesh was thrown on their bodies. The soft skin of long legs and luscious faces, wrapped tightly, begging tired and confused men. It was a mesh of human sickness, of frailty and loneliness and power and addiction. The bodies writhed in sumptuous agony as they were pulled further into the torpid waters of enslavement. One by one they followed the witches through the doorway lit by candlelight.

Exander entered first, hands wrapped tightly around his captor, feeling her breasts against his body.

Kiathar watched in trance for a moment, enraptured by the beauties until the sick feeling in his stomach warned him to move, but it was too late.

Sharp pain in his right side!

Kiathar reached out and grasped the arm which held the knife stabbed into his flesh. A cold painted face stared back at him. Slowly a smile crept upon the deathly pale face.

Kiathar roused himself!

With one twist he broke the man's arm and in the same moment kicked him to the ground. As the monster hit the stone a low and terrified cry echoed through the defiled walls, awakening the novices. Kiathar had his axe in hand within a breath.

He paused to pull the knife from his side.

"You call that a weapon! HA!" So the giant mocked as he threw the knife to his cowering enemy. With one blow he put a finish to him.

Alexus tore the affectionate fingers from his face, backed away from the embrace of her legs and enchanting hips. The body of the woman with the white painted face was unblemished and clean.

"Pardon me, my lady, but I must press on."

"Drink with me. I don't want to be alone." She tossed a wineskin to him and began to drink from a pewter jug in her hand.

Alexus looked at the wineskin in his hands for a moment. He was a devoted enthusiast of fine drink and meals. He stuffed it into his belt and turned to go. One last look he allowed himself at her and then suddenly found her atop him once more! He was slipping away. Intoxicated.

Her saliva filled his mouth with a strange and exhilarating hotness, as of brilliant spices. It was from the jug she carried! He swallowed hopelessly as her tongue reached inside him, caressing every cavity of his mouth with its sweetness. Thoughts faded as he was absorbed between her legs...

She moved atop him in a slow rhythm now and gently poured the jug into his mouth as she caressed his forehead.

The tension of her thighs...The Second Trial...Knighthood...

How great her desire!...

Fidelity to King! To wife! to... her fingers like warm waters on my skin...

Knighthood! ... The thrusting of her hips... I am disarmed...In a daze...

The Second Trial! Knighthood! ...

The other novices!

"NO!"

Alexus stood up in a daze and tripped as he sprinted by a dozen tables to the doorway. On hands and knees, panic stabbed him as he realized his strength had left him. Whatever he had drunk had robbed him of his energy! Crawling inches at a time, his stomach went into agony from his sudden efforts. Churning and exploding, uncontrollably he spewed vomit onto the floor. Undigested food, rank liquids and blood smeared onto his face as he continued to crawl through his own mess. Screams he heard now which were not his own. Terror clouded his mind! *A few more feet*, he thought.

It was too much, the darkness surrounded him.

Kiathar picked up the shorter man and pulled him to the entrance. Throwing him on his shoulder he grabbed the goat token with his other hand and they walked out of the nightmarish hall. The other novices, shocked and bewildered, left the witches and followed Kiathar's commands.

"Wait," whispered Alexus.

"What now novice?" exclaimed Kiathar with exasperation.

"The lights," he whispered weakly. "Blow them out."

The flickering candles were silenced, to save those less careful of novices who would come after, and darkness filled the wretched hall.

Through this shroud walked Exander silently as the echo of the others pattered far ahead. He tied his trousers as naked bodies with golden carved faces laughed hatefully at their victim from the shadows. Unperturbed or unnoticing, he walked tall, the poison drink burning happily in his veins.

Strength returning, Alexus found himself comically applauding the half drowned goat, one of the tokens of completion, for its efforts. He scaled the stone steps towards the re-opened exit with the other novices. Soaking wet they approached a Knight with a red hot iron poker. Kiathar was the first to exit and the first to receive the emblem of Luminares upon his flesh. Thus emblazoned with the sign of the sun rising over a field, the novices took a step from which they could never turn back. If in failure they were sent back to their estates, the emblem would be erased with fire: A permanent sign of incompetence. If of their own volition they turned their backs on the Trials to flee, the penalty was now death!

"Sire, we have left one behind! Should we not return for him?" asked Alexus as he approached the Knight.

"What is his name novice?"

"Exander Quickfoot, Sire."

"Does he carry one of the tokens?"

"No, but I fear those who dwell in that foul place may have him enchained within!"

"Yes indeed, but not with iron or steel! Many who come through this evil place never again see the light of day! Yet of their own will they are slaves to this dungeon." The knight looked down the wet stairs to the cold, black waters from where the novices had come. "Any one of them may at any time leave. But no one ever has."

"Then the Equites should bring freedom to them and destroy this pagan temple!" exclaimed Alexus with unusual ferocity.

"Silence novice! For you do not know the paths of history or destiny! Many times did the Equites in decades past purge this defiled place. But always did the cultists return! Their source is of no town or village, but the heart of evil itself! Of all the Trials, the Second alone touches true darkness!" The knight's eyes were wide and aware and Alexus remembered that this man too had been through the *same* Trials. "I dare not speak more," continued the knight in a whisper. "A Knight of the Red Cloth must resist the trickery, and so does even the wrong work for our good. Now step forward and receive the seal, for *you* have passed the test!"

The sweet, spicy taste suddenly came back to Alexus and inwardly he desired more. He remembered the wineskin stuffed under his belt. *It is venom,* he cursed. Guilt panged his innards.

As he moved forward, Exander emerged from the misty shadows and silently took his place behind. No words were said.

Alexus winced from the pain of the fiery brand. Strangely, his spirits returned and the shameful thirst immediately left him. "Not that I don't appreciate being stabbed with a hot iron after hauling a goat through eerie waters," he remarked afterwards with a laugh to Kiathar. "Which reminds me, I had forgotten to bid the instructor give me permission to slay that delicious animal. I noticed, while nearly drowning, that it possesses a pair of very tender chops. I have no doubt they would compose a most delectable meal! If concocted with the right brew of onion and leaf, it just might trounce that fine meal of bear we cooked in the mountains!" Alexus laughed and then paused to reflect on the pleasures of sitting down to a three course meal at his estate.

"Wolf," answered Kiathar. Alexus stared at him puzzled. Kiathar pointed to a pack of some twenty wolves in the pen ahead of them. "I came of age in the wild. Wolf meat makes you hardy. It is better than goat."

***

From beyond the Numinous Mountains deep in the Third Realm, Vincent rode back to the city. The second convening of the High Council would commence in two days and he was determined to be there. Little authority was his as a mere member of the council of Plebs, which consisted of exclusively non-royal families. The council's chief power came from its six Tribunes, who retained the right to veto any law passed by Patrician or Pleb. The power of the Tribune, Potestas Tribunicia in the old tongue of the kingdom's founders, was the key to Vincent's political rising. One day it would be his. This was how he would answer the cheating Princess, this was how he would take vengeance against Lothar and all his enemies! Naturally then, he wouldn't dream of missing the High Council.

Vincent made his way to the front of the court, ambivalent to the ruckus of yelling and argument which presided around him. The meeting was overdue by an hour, but a large number of attendants were still absent, including the King himself. A minister in a white tunic barged into the front of the hall and called the crowd's attention. Praetor Hydrus voiced this man's demand even louder and soon all eyes were to the front of the hall, where the three chairs of the throne lay, all empty except for one.

The tremor in the minister's voice was pretentious, "Oh what horrible fate! I was searching for our King, knowing that the council was ready. He was not in his chamber so I went to his private chapel. I was too late! The King is dead!" Silence held the air as all waited in disbelief, wondering if their ears had deceived them. "The King is dead I tell you!" He repeated. "He has been murdered! Stabbed three times whilst he prayed!" At first outbursts of stifled panic filled the air as men attempted to grasp the situation. Then there was a roar in the council such as has never been heard! Heated argument accelerated into violence. Vincent moved to a corner and watched in disgust as the pitiful men bickered, then pushed and then struck each other. So much for the greatness of Luminarian law! No Keleres were to be found to enforce their precious order now. Ironically enough, they had disappeared when they were finally needed.

Only the Praetor Hydrus held the power to restrain the mob. Up he rose from his white Curule Chair. His voice climbed above the crowd and demanded attention, "Silence!" he commanded. "Silence you bickering fools!" The henchmen of Hydrus, his Praetorian Guard, rushed into the crowd and restrained the more violent minded of the councilors. Hydrus began again, "The perpetrator of this horrendous crime must be hunted down!" There were many shouts at this and some of the fighting broke out again. The Praetorian Guard pulled out their threatening clubs and silence returned. "I will see to it that justice is done! Our Lady must be protected from this insidious plot! Let all here and now swear loyalty to the Queen of Luminares! Only in unifying under her sovereign authority can we hope to find out these traitors and defeat them! Swear now to the only heir of our departed King, hail Queen Adeline Solis Theodora!"

"Hail Queen Adeline Solis!" the body repeated. "Hail Queen Adeline Solis!"

"Let the Equites of all three realms be mustered," Hydrus commanded over the resounding din. "Blood will be spilt for this atrocity!"

Vincent followed Count Lothar out of the hall behind a sea of red armored Equites as more orders were given in the clamor of the court. He could hardly believe what his ears had heard.

***

Word of the murder spread like wildfire through the whole countryside. Men gathered together with arms in the markets and the wails of women mourning filled the evening air. Vincent couldn't help but feel a guilty satisfaction at the turn of events. His relationship with Adela had for a long time made him bitter, but he knew it was wrong and he rebuked himself inwardly now.

Vincent hurried his black mare towards the southern tower where the Third Equestrian Cohort was tasked with protecting the Queen's compound. It was a familiar task for Vincent and the rest of Count Lothar's Equites. Ironically, the

King's choosing Lothar to court the Princess had given Vincent ample opportunity to see her in the past. *Not so now. Now I bow to her in silence only. The Queen.* Vincent was still in disbelief. The winds of momentous change were in the air, of this alone was he sure.

A small contingent of Keleres foot soldiers crossed in front of the dirt path Vincent's horse trotted on. Snorting, the shining black beast pulled to an abrupt stop.

"Clear the way!" The Keleres commander yelled. "There is much work awaiting us." They were cutting across the hills to hurry towards the front of the palace, but Vincent was in no mood to be trifled with.

"Yes there is much work because your kind were not there when the life of our King was snuffed out!"

The Keleres commander stopped short while his contingent continued marching. He barked, "It was not the fault of the Royal Guard! We could not have possibly known that his own daughter would attack him you ignorant fool!"

Vincent spurred his horse towards the man, "What did you say!"

"I said the Guard couldn't be found at fault!" He responded annoyed.

"No! Who did you say killed the King!"

"His very own daughter, God help us."

Vincent wondered if he had gone insane. "You say that the Queen, Adeline Solis Theodora, killed her father?"

"Listen *knight*, I don't have time to talk, I have *my* orders!"

"You will answer me or I will have your life!"

"Yes, yes I told you it is being said that his daughter killed him, yes Adeline Solis!"

"You lie!"

"Do not heap disdain upon my honor knight!"

"It is a lie!" Vincent repeated to himself as he flew ahead of them towards the southern tower.

"Let me come with you master!" yelled his squire as he rode off. "I too will fight for our lady!" Evan ran after with the sack of belongings on his back, but it would be an hour before he could catch up.

Vincent barged through the tower's boarded up northern entrance, disobeying Count Lothar's orders to assemble. He threw aside the rotting timbers his horse had knocked loose and ran up the stone stairs. It seemed an eternity before Vincent finally reached the hall of the Princess' private chamber. A Keleres attempted to halt him at the top of the stairs. Without hesitation Vincent hurled the man down the stairs. The crashing fall silenced him. As he charged to her bedroom two more men, both Keleres, fled the hall. Vincent pushed the purple curtains aside and entered the room.

"Adela!" He beckoned. Wind blew in from the windows, and light illuminated the Queen as she lay on the silken covers. Vincent knelt by the bedside. "Is it a lie?" he asked softly, his voice trembling.

"Vincent darling," she smiled and slowly reached out with her closer hand to touch his face. Her fingertips were empty and chilled.

"Tell me it is all a lie!" Vincent demanded desperately, taking her hand roughly.

"I don't understand what you are saying, Vincent." She didn't move as she spoke.

"Your father!" he responded angrily.

"My father is at the high council."

Vincent looked at her confused.

"He is always away when most needed," she added.

Her face seemed strained with a strange exhaustion. Vincent's heart began to race. Each thump exploded out of his chest and he was afraid to move. He didn't want to know any more! He wanted to forget. He wanted to go back to the way things were. But he reached out and he held her, kneeling on the bed. He pulled her up close to himself, but her body was nearly limp. The fingers of his course hands braced against the small of her back and felt the familiar contours of her body. Her blouse slid up with his supporting arm. He felt her familiar soft skin, and then time became like an actor's drama which is watched from afar as his hand slid into a gory gash in her back. He immediately pulled his hand from beneath her, bracing her body with his other arm. The warm wetness dripping from his fingers flooded his sensations. Gasping in horror he watched the thick dark blood spilling all over the bed and himself. Crimson death stained the white blankets. Like an army laying siege to a fortress, tears began to collect in his eyes. His mind clouded over in confusion and distress as he pulled her close to himself. Fumbling behind her, he tried to plug the wound with his trembling hands to stop the bleeding.

"I never thought it would end like this," she whispered weakly.

"Adela, Adela, Adela!" He could say nothing else. The tears flooded out from his eyes.

There on the wall opposite the two was the painting. In its corner, the little girl infested with Plague. A magnificently white angel knelt beside the ravaged girl. Adela again looked at the picture, this time from over the shoulder of Vincent as he held her failing body. She was amazed to notice this time that the dying girl was full of joy. Adeline mustered her strength and reached to Vincent kneeling before her and stroked his long brown hair with her wavering hand. "I am glad that I am not alone." She kissed his ear and whispered softly, "All will be well. Don't be afraid." He firmly grasped her hand with his right and enclosed her with his left. Repose from the icy fatigue of death she found staring into his blue eyes, blue like the sea raging in a storm. "I wish I could've made things better with my father." Suddenly panic came into her expression; she squeezed him with all the strength that remained in her empty veins. "You will tell him, Vincent, tell him that I am sorry for being so harsh with my words. Be sure that he knows it! Vincent!"

Vincent nodded, holding her closer.

"Don't store anger against this day, as you have done with your past. You gave me joy," a smile spread wide across her tired face. "Kiss me," she asked in a most faint voice, her eyes already falling into emptiness.

And into that kiss a thousand moments and feelings were brought forth, unchained from jealousies, freed from forced forgetfulness, dragged forth in bitter ecstasy, to die in Vincent's arms. And he would die to hold them a moment longer, to let her live but a second more. He felt all the warmth and love that the world could offer absorbed up in his arms, and then it was snatched away. As her lifeless body slid down to the bed, frozen forever he knew his heart would be from that day forth. Closing his eyes, he shut the doors to his mind in denial. But he was forced to open them, to accept the reality that invaded his world.

Inwardly trembling with hurt and shock, he stood. Her lifeless body was sprawled on the bed, eyes staring into emptiness, dark black hair bathed in red. He covered his face with his hands. Fingernails pressed into his forehead, into his flesh with the hurt, the hopelessness, the anger. The horror remained when he pulled his sweaty, blood soaked fingers away.

***

Vincent barged into the council chamber. Underneath the battle armor, fury pumped through his veins, waiting to explode from his muscles which flinched in tense exasperation against the metal.

Is there no one on this wretched earth that my arm may protect! Must my hand always be late to strike down the offender! Never again! My God! How could this happen? Did this happen? Is this not a nightmare? Twice have I failed now! Never again! Her innocent blood has been spilled and Justinian will pay for it! I will not stray from the path! Never again! He will find his lies against her rewarded by a grave sooner than a crown! Never again will I fail!

Justinian, master of the Keleres and the King's second cousin, would pay for his lies, of this Vincent was sure. He felt rage flow through his body, overcoming the pain. Somebody was going to die for this scheme, blood for blood.

Evan followed behind him now, still out of breath from the run to the palace.

"What happened master?" he asked between breaths.

Vincent turned to him in surprise and took hold of the boy's shoulders. As if in a dream Vincent searched Evan's face, looking for a clue which might spring him back to reality. Terrified, Evan backed up against the wall, not understanding why his master seemed to not even recognize him. The Knight let the boy loose after a moment.

Vincent covered his eyes to hide his grief, "Much has happened Evan," wiping his face the Knight stepped toward the hall. "Now stay quiet. Much now must be done."

Hydrus stood at the front of the hall, quieting the chamber once again. "It is beyond the realm of credibility to think that the King's daughter would ever dream of harming her father! Justinian has spread this lie only to justify an arrest and execution. So that he alone might be heir to the throne!"

"We must not jump to conclusions!" came back Gaius.

"Yes, we stand with the Keleres!" came another voice.

"Ever has the word of Justinian been trustworthy, should we so easily doubt it now?" Gaius added.

"Arrest her!" yelled yet another.

"Silence!" Hydrus demanded. "You will refrain from the use of profanities in this house of justice! Our Queen is-"

"She did it for fear that the throne would fall to another!" Interrupted the wealthy Inflatus. "I heard it in the district of Edessa myself. The lady had graced me with her presence when our King unexpectedly arrived. I could not help but overhear their arguments as I was dismissed."

"You scoundrel!" Count Lothar came forth to challenge Inflatus.

"When our Queen expressed how she would rule capably, our departed King's exact words were: 'Will you! I wonder?' Every person here knows how strained the relations between the two were!"

"Who paid you off this time, Inflatus?" Lothar returned.

"I fear that Justinian's hand has been most swift," added Hydrus. "Already he draws supporters in the council to himself. With the Keleres utterly loyal to him, how can he be stopped? Our Queen must challenge him herself, demand that he lay down the sword! Let us call upon her, for with-"

"The Queen is dead!" Vincent broke in. Blood stained his hands still and murmurs arose from the crowd at his entrance. With his red cape swaying behind him and his helmet under his arm he walked by Hydrus and stood in front of the Praetor's Curule Chair. "I myself held her body as life fled from it! The Keleres have murdered her. She did not even know-" he choked on the words.

He swallowed hard and began again, "She did not know of the King's death. Her life was snuffed out in retribution for a crime she did not commit!"

Another uproar exploded in the hall as the hundreds of councilors bickered and crowded to the front.

"Can this be true?"

"It's not possible!"

"Arrest him so that he may be questioned!" yelled still others.

Hydrus stepped up beside him. "Silence!" Vincent saw the Praetorian Guard waiting in the wings. "Guard Commander!" Hydrus spoke to a Praetorian Guard with a purple crest above his helmet. "Investigate this matter and send twenty men to bar off the Princess' chamber! Nothing is to enter or leave!" The Praetorian Commander bowed and ran off the platform. Hydrus looked at Vincent now, "Knight, how did you come by the princess's chamber?"

"When approaching my appointed position as prescribed by my lord, Sir Lothar, I fell upon a contingent of Keleres. These men marched to the palace under supposed knowledge that Our Queen had herself murdered our beloved King. I knew this could not be so! If the council would but forgive my imposing upon the sacred royal chamber, they would see that I have uncovered a most vile plot! What I did I did out of devotion to our lady, who had not even any knowledge of her father's death as life seeped from her veins!"

"Did you see the assassins Knight?"

"They were Keleres. One I killed, two more fled."

"How can we trust this man who comes before us with hands sullied in blood!" came the exasperated voice of Gaius.

"Justinian has poisoned the Keleres with his foul tongue! And as far as I am concerned, he may have poisoned you too!"

"Look at how the Keleres have fled their posts," Hydrus remarked. The people looked around them to realize that absolutely no Royal Guard were present. "Something is going on of which we are not aware. I suggest an immediate investigation of the Guard's Quarters!" The council motioned its overwhelming approval by a raising of hands and more praetorian guards hurried away.

"One thing is for certain," Count Lothar continued. "Councilor Inflatus cannot be trusted. This very day I gathered witnesses before the Tribunal. Their testimony is certain, the Tribunal's ruling complete. Inflatus has dishonored his name. He is a philanderer, a fool and has accepted bribes in court! As a member of the Patrician Council, this is an offense against the state! Inflatus belongs in the dungeon!"

Even before Lothar had finished Inflatus fled from the hall in terror, but was stopped short by Praetorian guards and arrested.

"And if Inflatus is to represent Gaius' followers," Lothar continued. "Then no longer shall my support lie with him. I stand with the Praetor and with my Knight Errant, Sir Cincinnatus."

"Years I have attended the Concilium Plebis, few times did I give address, for it was not my place as a lowly knight. Yet I say to you now at this High Council," Vincent's voice became louder, "To both Pleb and Patrician, subjects of Luminares, if you do not redress this wrong with all the vigor now burning in your veins, then you are both cowards and fools! Justinian must be confronted and arrested! Only then will we know why the Keleres have done this evil!"

"Let the vote be cast!" commanded the Praetor. "All those in favor of putting the master of the Keleres into chains so that he may be brought before the Tribunal and justice done upon him, step to the left!"

The hundreds of councilors began moving. All those in favor walked to one end of the hall, those against to the other. It looked as if the measure would pass, when Gaius came to the front.

"As Tribune of the Plebs I cannot allow this! Master Justinian has always stood for our rights. In the Second Realm his Keleres restrained the marauding seafarers when your militia would do nothing to protect the Numantines. He has always abided by his word. Consider my veto in effect!"

The councilors froze.

"I expected as much," returned Hydrus. "Alas, Potestas Tribunicia cannot be overruled. Yet it seems Sir Cincinnatus may have provided a way around this dilemma. We have standing before us a most distinguished Servant of the Red Cloth. I am informed that Sir Cincinnatus, though only a Knight Errant within the Third Equestrian Cohort, won great fame in the battles against the Nothus. He is strong willed, as we saw from his actions at the last session of this council, though it only won him blood stripes then. Yet this should not be counted as a fault, for times may soon be upon us when the strong are needed. I propose Sir Cincinnatus take the seat of Gaius as first Tribune of the Concilium Plebis. Do you judge this as fair?"

"No Praetor! You cheat the council!" roared the old Gaius. "You think to throw me out before my time is complete when only the Royal Person may confirm such action! You forget that you yourself were judged to be voted upon at this same council!"

At that moment the Praetorian Guard Commander returned to report. "Our Lady's chamber is secured, Praetor. All is as the Knight said. Our beloved Queen has perished. One man in the armor of the Keleres lies dead in the stairwell. As for the Quarters of the Royal Guard, they are empty!"

Gasps of horror escaped from the crowd.

"Will you now consent, Gaius, to bring Justinian to questioning?" Hydrus challenged.

"I will do no such thing!"

"Then indeed folly floods your mind! Let the vote be cast!"

"I shall not allow it!"

A man stepped forward from the Plebian circle of councilors and pushed Gaius aside, "We have but two questions, Praetor, before this vote is cast."

"Ask and make haste!"

"Afterwards, will you consent to having the vote cast for the position of Praetor as was decreed beforehand?"

"I shall abide by the law as I have always done. Yes, the vote shall be executed."

"Then our only requirement will be that the command of this recruit army, this Legion in the Second Realm, be given over completely to our new Tribune."

"Impossible!" exploded Hydrus.

"Impossible? Then also shall Gaius remain Tribune and Justinian, commander of the Keleres be left to his devices."

Hydrus covered his face with his hands in contemplation.

"You broker a tough deal, councilor! Yet there is no time to waste, it shall be done!"

"Then let the votes be cast."

Chapter 4

Blood of Sacrifice

ALEXUS WATCHED SIR CINCINNATUS LEAVE the platform which was raised above the ring. The master would not be seen again until the novices gorged upon the sweet fruits of success at the completion of the Trials in Luminares. *That day seems too far beyond the horizon, beyond hope*, thought Alexus behind the palisade. He heard the novice ahead of him enter the arena and shivered at the howling pack of wolves. *I'm not going to make it out of there. I'm going to die.* He wanted to run, but there was no choice left. To run meant death, as was agreed in the last Trial.

On sudden Alexus reached under his tunic and felt the leather wineskin he had saved. He pulled it out but hesitated to drink as he remembered the red hot coals and painted faces in the dark. Now the leather pressed against his lips and he tasted it. The sweet, spicy fluid flowed into his stomach, into his veins, warming and relaxing him. He saw the masked women and felt their bodies pressed against his own. He felt their soft skin. His muscles relaxed and he slumped against the wooden wall. Much time passed.

The escape was over now.
He clutched the bronze shaft. Use of ranged weapons was banned from this trial, and so his sack of remaining needles lay outside the arena. He would have to use the javelin as a spear. The giant wooden gate stared at him. He was next. A horrendous scream came to his ears from just beyond! Now there was a rustling and angered yelling! Alexus rushed to the gate and peered through the crack between the doors. The novice was

walking toward him in a hurry, tears and dirt on his face. Then
Alexus saw it; his right hand gnawed down to the bone! Nothing
was left but strings of torn flesh hanging from the elbow! His
wrist, even the bones of his fingers were exposed to broad
daylight!
The gate opened!
Alexus shuffled out of the way in fright, but the man came running
through moaning and crying and knocked into him. Alexus saw his
eyes!
Terrified!
Blood was everywhere now, all over himself!
The gate closed behind him.
Alexus stood motionless.

He could see the trainers now. They towed between them
a fur filled net of ferocious teeth and claws, a pair of starved and
beaten wolves thrashing and howling.
The beasts scrambled out of the opened net as it was
dropped into the ring. *Watch for the moment when the animals
spring towards you,* Kiathar had said. *Do not let them encircle
you!* Alexus gripped the single shaft tighter, his palms were
sweating profusely. Heart beating furiously, he was frozen in his
tracks. *Why does my very body shake with fear?* he screamed at
himself. He had thought bringing javelins to the Trials would allow
him to remain safely away from any enemies. *Impossible now!*
Putting his shield ahead of his body, he walked towards the beasts.
I WILL myself to fight! He brought the single javelin to the
overhand position. *Still my forearm shakes with trepidation!* He
could see their desperate eyes and grinning teeth as he
approached.

Alexus felt the jaws clamp into his left shoulder. In a
panic, he had thrown his javelin into one of the beasts. The other
creature at the same moment leapt upon him. He felt it clawing
and biting for his neck. Teeth scraped against metal as Alexus
pinched his helmet to his shoulder to protect the soft, exposed
skin.
BAM!
The wolf whimpered from the strike of the shield. Getting up from
the dirt, Alexus ran headlong at it and struck again. Then,

grasping the beast in his hands, he squeezed hard and bashed its skull onto the ground. Blood exploded from his wrist as the wolf bit everything in reach with insane fear.

When both furry carcasses lay motionless on the ground, the trainers rushed into the ring to cover the novice's wounds. As he was carried through the gate, Kiathar walked in.

"Strangled it with your hands? HA!"

"You couldn't have done it better yourself!" Alexus answered still quivering, he forced a bold smile and was taken away. The servants poured wine and warm aloes onto his arms and then bandaged them up.

As the gate closed a fiend of most horrendous proportions was let loose within. With teeth the size of a man's fist and a grossly muscular structure, the Extraho Prodigus feared no other creature on earth. Fur of orange with stripes of black covered its giant body. As long as two men standing, it extended the razors of its paws, ready to pounce. Kiathar broke the adversary like stale bread. It's guts were smashed in the dirt before Alexus could even take his seat in the audience once more. When finished with the beast, the outlander straddled the animal and ripped its jaw apart. One by one he cut its giant teeth from the animal's mouth and stowed them away, blood soaked, in a sack.

Next morning Alexus would note with humor that the warrior had donned a twine necklace laced with both bear claws and the gigantic teeth. Kiathar proudly displayed to him more teeth from the monstrous beast mounted onto a sturdy handle; A most fierce slashing blade.

The novices individually put all the beastly adversaries to death in a timely manner. The whole pack of captured wolves lay dead in the ring next morning. Alone in the battle chamber with but a shield and a weapon of his choosing, man had tested himself against beast. Only Andreis of the Golbini family, Alaric of the Vistacini and Radamasis of the Volga had been dismembered or killed. The seeds of courage were planted; it was up to the novices now to ensure they continued to grow.

Given back their horses for a race along the great expanses of frontier, the fourth trial brought them back towards Luminares. One poor fool rode his horse straight into a ditch and the steed's front left leg was shattered. Despite protests from the nobleman's father, Viscount Narcissus of the First Realm, the novice was immediately dropped from the Trials. When a messenger reached him in Luminares asking for commands, Vincent's only remark had been 'Never was there known a Luminarian knight who could not ride.'

A mounted test of arms against dummies, much as had been practiced, comprised the Fifth Trial. All went well. To ensure mental capacity, the Sixth Trial tested knowledge of battle tactics and Luminares' history as well as the obligations of each novice to their liege lord. Now, in sight of the walls of the ancient city, on the doorstep of success, would each novice make everlasting vows to God and kingdom. The last trial awaited.

***

Evan watched the ranks of Keleres fill in fifty fathoms across the field. They too had breastplates of red but their helmets afforded less visibility with only two vertical slits for the eyes. Their legs and groin were also more heavily armored than the Luminarian Equites. They looked terrifying.

"Spear!" Vincent commanded his squire.

Evan tossed a spear to him. He had two spares left on his back.

The Keleres suddenly unsheathed their swords in absolute unison. The echo of the metal against metal was terrifying.

"Let me fight master, I will hold true," Evan asked, eyes still glued on the formation across the field.

"This battle is not for you, squire," answered Vincent as he tightened the leather and iron studded gauntlets on his forearms.

"Justinian will not parley with us!" bellowed the voice of Sir Lothar before them to his Equites. "So let us show him the wrath of true Luminarians!" Lothar, leading the Third Cohort, turned to face the Keleres and drew his sword. Vincent wondered why he had hated such a man for so long. The whole world had fallen into shades of unfamiliar gray now that Adeline was gone.

The Equites began to ride forward toward their liege. To their left were the Equites of the First Realm who had been mustered and to the right those of the Second.

"Tribune!" came the voice of the man on horse beside Vincent. "I would have you know that I honor your words this day! I am a Numantine of the thirty-second estate of the Third Realm, also of the Plebian order. There is not a man of truth in the Concilium Plebis who would not prefer your youth to the cowardice of our late Tribune Gaius. I have the greatest faith that you shall lead well Sir Cincinnatus! Godspeed! And may the hand of St. Michael himself guide you!" With that the knight lowered the visor of his helmet.

The Equites picked up pace, first trotting then galloping towards that red wall of steel. Evan watched their backs with anticipation. The neighing of the horses filled the air and spears were lowered. The squire's heart was racing, flooding with desire, with anger, with pride, with a need to be amidst that coming chaos. For in that chaos would the brothers of the Order lay down their lives. Then came the crash! Evan darted off toward the melee the moment he heard it. As fast as his legs would carry him he ran, while screams, yells, and the clashing of metal against metal filled the air.

***

The letter could not bear good news. Iris Nuptiae, daughter of a servant and descendant of slaves, broke the wax seal. The symbol of sword and star peeled in two as her fingers pulled apart the leaves of the folded correspondence. It was the mark of the Third Realm, used only by the Count himself. The royal messenger who had brought it waited impatiently to see if she would send a reply. He made himself perfectly at home, pouring a little water into a mug on the table and downing it. Without second thought he then took a bowl of grapes from the table and devoured them. Iris glanced up at him with anger, *who does he think he is!* Almost rebuking him, she held her tongue, *he is the representative of the Count while he is here! I must maintain composure! Sir Lothar has always been a chivalrous lord, and yet what does it matter if he sends mongrels such as this to do his bidding!*

She read the writing too quickly the first time, went through it again. Her attention gathered nervously around the two names. A summoning for Arlen signed by the Count Vincent Cincinnatus! She looked up from the letter, confused and sorrowful. *Arlen will learn nothing of this!* She could see Kati as if he were speaking the words to her in person. Tall, strong, his sharp facial features regal in element, and anger in his eyes. *So has the impossible been done! Yet now is your soul worth even less, Kati!* "Tell my lord that his orders will never be obeyed! Not if he sends a thousand messengers! Not if he sends an entire army! Now begone!"

The shocked messenger stood in confusion. Iris picked up the bowl that he had been picking at and threw it straight for his head. After lifting his hands to block the blow, he made a short bow and hurried off, the grapes still in his hand.

***

Having returned full circle to the outskirts of Luminares, the Trials were nearly over. But not yet. Each novice was sent, without food or rest, to individual chapels within the Great Cathedral. There in the Cathedral, without falling into the welcoming arms of sleep, the novices knelt until daybreak next morn. Their orders were to contemplate the solemnity of their office, to realize their obligations not only to liege and Luminares but to the very King of Kings, God himself. They were to solidify a vision of their knighthood as bound by *dignitas*. No hardship would cause them to forsake their family's honor now. Over a hundred years, the Trials of the Equestrian Order had changed dramatically, but this last test had always been the same. It was with this trial that the Nordic tribesman was destined to have the most trouble.

Kiathar looked at the wooden box on the table. Inside it he knew was the bread that the priests constantly held aloft. Such absurdity! While Christian by baptism, Kiathar could not understand this Christ or his Father and Spirit. Assuredly Kiathar did not disgrace himself by falling asleep or losing his posture before the altar! But that was just it! Why was he kneeling before a simple wooden table with an even simpler wooden box atop it? The Nordic gods of his fathers were strong in their mountain! No pestilence or suffering touched them! What was to be gained from worshiping this god who was nailed to a tree and gave himself to be eaten? Odin, Thor, Iresiturne and Brodir would brook no such abuse! They would burn the world if any man dared touch their mountain! Always this talk of the ancients the Luminarian crown spread! The ancient empire which encompassed half the entire earth! They whose knowledge was without bounds! They who founded Luminares amidst a sea of unruly tribes! Sojourners far from home who carried civilization itself on their backs! They who demanded salvation through the holy Christ. Then the tales told of how the ancient's ancestors themselves put to death this god of theirs! What absurdities! Thor would have left scorched earth of this ancient empire should any of its warriors have laid hands upon him! What good is a god who cannot even defend himself! The Nordic gods understood protecting that which is of value. This iron principle was clear in Kiathar's will. He had a woman and heirs on his estate. He had land and servants. He had cattle and dogs and endless fields of wheat and they would all be safeguarded! No Luminarian would ever again lay claim to his land because of his foreign blood! After his knighting Kiathar would have satisfied both his fathers and the realm. The sacred blood of the warrior would run through him and the title of an Equites and sole lord of the twelfth estate would be his and his alone. Without fail Kiathar knelt before the altar, awake and awaiting dawn.

***

Vincent ran his finger along the parchment and went through the numerals again. *There has to be some mistake!* The thought came to him with outrage, *The Maleficus has won the platoon pilum!* He ran his fingers through his brown hair, felt a piece of dried leaf. He had yet to bathe before the ceremonies. *This honor cannot go to a barbarian!* He looked over at the pilum he had placed on the table. A steel spear ornamented with gold, it was given as a sign of the most honored position within a platoon of Equites. While officially given by the legate instructing to a champion of his choosing, it was traditionally put under the care of the novice with the best scores from the Trials. This was a time honored tradition passed on in some form since the rule of the ancients. Vincent closed his tired eyes. He couldn't have slept for more than an hour earlier that night. The Keleres Guards had been more ferocious as enemies than any could have imagined. Nearly surrounded by the charging Equites, they still held for hours. When at last defeat was upon them, their retreat was as flawless as their stand. Vincent could still see Equites falling to their death onto the sea of red armor. *So much death because of one traitor!* Vincent clenched the pilum and walked out of the chamber onto the stone porch. The nightmare of his past had assailed him again that night. Brought to life in the vision of his sleeping dreams, the memory of the Maleficus barbarians who had destroyed his family so long ago was reinvigorated in his waking mind. Life itself was drenched with the blood of mortality. As the crimson sun rose up above endless green fields before him, Vincent became resolved. *No Maleficus will receive any such honor while I live!*

Hydrus stood leaning against the porch wall. He turned when Vincent came, "Well done Legatus Legionis, they shall be the most superior of Equites. Although you must remember that your greater responsibility now lies with the army in the Second Realm." He put a hand on Vincent's shoulder. "The lot of a most glorious fortune has fallen upon you, first the tribuneship and appointment to rule the Legion. Then Count Lothar dies heirless! I am glad that you went through with my proposal. For the Tribuneship passes away with the coming of elections, but blood lasts forever!"

"Call it fortune that our King and Queen were murdered, Praetor? That the Lord of the Third Realm gave his life fighting fellow Luminarians in order to avenge their Majesties? For these were the deeds that gave me this authority! I do not know if it be fortune, my only hope is to wield this power well against such a monstrous host of wrongs. For indeed *their* blood calls out with that of so many others, and I shall not rest until it is avenged!"

"And you shall have this opportunity," Hydrus answered

Vincent. "You shall go to the Second Realm with the Equites of the Third at your side and take command of the Legion. Face down the fleeing Captain of the Royal Guard and crush his entire army! Only then will you be able to search out the Numantine Plebs who have conspired to rebellion. The Keleres will be racing against you to unite with the Numantines. Act with speed so that nothing may come of this! Do you understand what it is you must do Count Cincinnatus?"

"Yes Praetor, I will depart in three days time."

"Why the wait!" Hydrus snapped.

"There is a matter of some personal significance to attend to on my father's estate. I shall soon be making use of New Corinth's dungeon."

"You try my patience, Count!"

"My Equites hail from many leagues over mountain and range. It will take at least three days time to muster the rest of them in the Third Realm's capital. But have no fear Praetor, for the Guard is on foot, we shall make up time."

"Lock up whomever you must and then make haste!" Hydrus began to walk toward the stairs but then turned. "I almost forgot, Count. I too have a matter of personal significance. You see, there is a port in the town of Helles, on the eastern coastline of the Second Realm. I own this port, and you see, the shipments that go through Helles happen to be of particular value. They are collected in a great mountain in the center of the city. Knowing this, conspirators and friends of the Numantine rebels have constantly raided the area. They gain some sick pleasure in hurting the interests of a man of position such as myself."

"I will send a detachment to guard the mountain, Praetor."

"There is already a century of legionnaires there. They were emplaced when Bassus was in command. I only ask that they remain."

Vincent nodded.

"If you do all that I have bidden you, all will be well." The Praetor smiled. Vincent couldn't help but notice how sickly pale his expressions seemed. "Remember that it is I who have given you this power," continued the Praetor. "It is I who wrote down your family's name in the ancient scrolls of dominion. Without this imposition the council would never have recognized your claims to Lothar's title. Without this, you have no lineage! For this, Count, you owe me a debt of servitude."

"As you have said, it will be done," answered Vincent. He walked by the Praetor and led the way to the Great Cathedral. At that moment a strong wind blew and the rising sun was partially covered with dark mists. Vincent did not turn, but led onward, the golden laced red cape on his back flapping rapidly. Golden insignia of sword within white star flared in Hydrus' eyes. The markings of the cape were a Great House emblem and indicated the person of a Count. In that moment the Praetor wondered with inner trembling if the young knight's hands would prove too haughty. *One foul move by this upstart of so-called royalty and all my plans could go awry!*

The novices wore red. Red tinted steel armor was the great secret of Luminares. No other metal smiths in the known world could imprint such a color upon metal. Nor did many know the secret to steel, that unbreakable solid from which was wrought the most deadly weapons and armors. Pride was in the posture of the novices. Though they had been up all night and likely the night before, there were none who slouched or dozed. The sunlight of dawn tore in through the open doors of the Cathedral, lighting up the rows of armored bodies. Latched onto the elaborate breastplates at either shoulder of each man was a beet red cape which fell down his back, knee high above the floor. In the left hand of each were grand helmets, fashioned specifically to fit the heads of their wearer's. On top of their thick red dyed tunic they wore straps of iron studded leather about the waste to protect the groin. Full metallic greaves, also in red, with a softer leather backing protected the shins. The novices had been given their armor the night before, to wear during the vigil. A symbol of their promises to fidelity, justice, and courage, they would wear it after the ceremony as a most sacred sign of the Equestrian Order. If ever a knight were to fail any of these three virtues, it was said that the mere sight of his armor or sword could cause an inner spurning so great as to make drinking, sleeping and even eating unbearable while on this earth.

Chapter 5

Blossoms of Malice

IRIS KNEW HE WAS COMING. SHE slammed the door of the house and hurried into the field. Pulling off a head of grain she began plucking at it and unwittingly scanned the horizon. The anticipation was killing her! Arlen had asked her to inspect the work of the day while he helped repair Ruben's cart. *If only he knew what danger he is in!* She could not tell him, or no good could ever come of the situation. How could she even think when she had disobeyed their liege and lord! *But Vincent Kati is no Count! He has not a drop of royal blood! Even if by some intervention of heaven that power were his, how could he dare throw a friend of his father's into the dungeon! I am a lady, not just some groveling servant, I will stand up to him!*

Her heart jumped a beat when four horses trotted over the hill and interrupted her thoughts. They were a stone's throw away. Not knowing how to act she quickly fumbled through some of the grain at her feet and then began to walk back home pretending not to notice him until he was closer.

She heard his horse getting near.

"Has Arlen relegated you to the most astute position of retracing grain fields?" he asked her.

"The more I see you of late, the more I realize how little you do know!" the exasperation in her brown eyes was suddenly like lightning. "Arlen holds this very estate together! He is a father to us all! And your father counted him as a brother! And you dare condemn him!"

"This is the Count of the Third Realm, Lady. You may refer to him as Sire or my lord," spoke a knight from behind Vincent.

Iris looked from this knight to the peasant boy on horse beside him, Kati's squire no doubt. He could not have been more than fifteen years old but he tried to give her such a deathly stare that Iris would have laughed had she not been so angry already.

"Sir Exander," Vincent spoke to the knight. "Go with my squire and the two others and find the stables. See that the horses are provided water."

"Yes m'lord."

"You will find Iris," Vincent dismounted as the others rode off. "That it is you who are so poorly informed about our Headmaster."

"And what precisely should I know, Kati?" She stood a little taller as he walked to her.

"That Arlen is a liar, a cheat and a coward! He let them die Iris! He watched them die! And it is time he paid for the crimes he has hidden from you all!"

"This cannot be the truth. He has always been faithful and wise as long as I have known him!"

"You were so young then, you could not have seen the falsehood in his character! Let this letter open your eyes!"

Vincent handed an old parchment to Iris. She read it over, disbelief covering her face.

"I don't believe it!" She exclaimed.

"Of course you don't!" returned Vincent. "You were young and foolish then as was I! It took me years being away before I accepted reality, and that reality is that Arlen had an affair with my own mother! He took advantage of her when my father abandoned us to serve the Count. And when she told him it must end he would not accept it. This letter came from his hand two days before that day of hell! When the Maleficus came, he stood by and watched! He did nothing! He looked on while they destroyed my mother and sisters! His sins must be punished! The time has come, I have returned, and now as Count I will bring justice!"

Tears were running down Iris' cheeks as she listened to Vincent in absolute horror. She wiped them away and looked at the parchment. "I must hear it from his lips." Iris sprinted away with the parchment between shaking fingers.

The headmaster Arlen threw some of the seed onto the freshly tilled ground. A dark brown horse stood by him, its body shimmering with sweat. Latched onto the work animal was a plow, its metallic snout smeared and covered with rich earth. He heard someone calling for him. It was Iris. He looked back at the horse, "Ruben!" He waited until the young man was looking at him. "Ruben, see to it that she gets some water soon!" Arlen gestured toward the muscular animal beside him.

Iris ran up to him, he could see the tear stains on her face. "Is it true?" she showed him the letter. He took it, wiped sweat from his brow, and began to read. Dirt was all over him, covering his clothes, under his fingernails and on his face from where he wiped away the salty sweat that would sting the eyes.

He looked at the horizon fatefully, "Sir Cincinnatus has returned?"

"Is it true?" she pleaded.

"My love was but a passing comfort to her, she would never have had me." He paused. "Yes, I wrote this many years ago."

"And on that day did you stand by while his mother," she couldn't bring herself to say the words. "Did you stand by while the Maleficus-"

Arlen looked back at the farmhouse, at all the Cincinnatus land, and then back at Iris. "To my everlasting shame."

Iris broke into a sob. Arlen was going to hold her, but held back. He saw Sir Cincinnatus standing at the great house, he dropped the letter and walked to him.

"You come here, you come after years to shake things up. Who are you to do this? You have been off pursuing royal mistresses and now you come here to tear apart the estate? You wear highly garments, but it is of no consequence, you're nothing next to the elder Cincinnatus! You're still a boy running away from life! Here we face life, in the dirt we grind away our past until all that remains is the new harvest! You've never worked the ground in your life, if the elder Cincinnatus-"

"Do NOT mention that name! For you are unworthy to pronounce it, betrayer! You cheated my father! You lied to Iris! And you are a coward! For it was you who ran away, after letting her die who would show you no affection, you ran to me!"

Arlen bowed his head in shame.

Vincent could feel the anger beating in his heart. He grabbed hold of Arlen's neck and held him against the wall. "You shall spend the remainder of your days in the dark! For as Count of this realm I pronounce final judgment! BIND HIM!" Vincent let loose his neck and turned his back on the man.

Exander snickered under his breath and then clapped irons onto Arlen's feet. The man kneeled, a tear falling from his eyes to the ground. "Master," he pleaded, "Master I know what you think. But it was not out of hate. It was plain and poor cowardice."

There came no answer but the flap of the red and gold cape in front of his face.

"I'm sorry that," Arlen looked from Vincent to the dirt, "That I wasn't the one who died in place of your mother and sisters."
Silence.

"I'm sorry too," Vincent replied coldly. "Take him away!" the Count stepped by him without looking down.

***

Iris watched the boards above creek as the young squire walked to and fro, keeping watch. A few rays of light leaked through the hatch in the roof down onto Arlen's face. He stared blankly at the cellar floor in despair.

"Why did you do nothing?" Iris asked.

"Cowardice," the broken man said without moving his gaze. "My life too might have been snatched away."

"You did not stand by on account of vengeance against her?"

"I loved her Iris. How ashamed I was of it, a servant loving his master's wife! When she recanted her feelings, I could have torn the house down in anger." Arlen looked up at Iris, "But I never wished her harm. You must believe me!"

"I believe you."

"There has not been a day that has gone by that I have not wished I did something other than stand on that cold grass in fear!" He paused, listening to the boy above tirelessly marching the hall on guard. "You will be headmaster when I am gone-"

"You're the headmaster, Arlen, I can't do without you!" she protested.

"Iris listen to me--"

"No! How many years have you been here! How many years have you served his family!"

"Sitting alone, one's thoughts become clear. I deserve what is coming to me. Sir Cincinnatus is our master and liege lord. And you, you must obey him!"

Iris looked down with a frown. "I cannot run the farms without you Arlen!" she begged in a lower tone. "The men, they all look up to you, respect you. They listen to what you say!"

"As they will you. Iris, look at me."

She lifted her eyes to the old man's, tried to hold back tears.

"Young lady," he continued. "You pull yourself together, for them! You're kindness and compassion must be tempered by firmness. They will learn to follow you. You know what must be done to make it through winter. The belongings in my chamber, they are yours."

He reached out to her, the chain holding him back some, and hugged her with his big old arms. Gnarly hands wiped the tears from her face. "My dear Iris. I remember when you were born. You were the joy of your father's heart, don't ever think otherwise! Fate has a way with things we cannot always understand. You were the light in his heart despite all the pain of your mother's death that day. They would both be proud to see you now, and by the grace of heaven perhaps they do!"

***

Icy laughs poured out of the mouths of loud hairy faced men and chilled the cold morning air. They were disfigured with huge masses of muscle and had blood tipped bull horns mounted to their helms and human bones strapped to their shields. Sobs and cries from every direction polluted the vapors of the atmosphere. Blood oozed out of his mother's stomach, dripping down her naked body.

Violently Vincent sat up, his muscles flexing and tense, sweat dripping off his brow. Throwing his blankets aside he groped around for his tunic and put it on. He rushed outside to the reprieve of fresh air and open space. Those images never faded, sometimes they became more lifelike, and sometimes worse than it had been.

Clouds had covered up most of the morning light. A storm was coming. Vincent leaned against the doorway, staring out onto the road. Laborers were beginning to pour onto the fields like bees. The bodies of his sisters were under that earth, food for the very plants that these ignorant farmers toiled over endlessly. Dark mists overcast the horizon. Their waters collected, waiting to burst forth in violent downpour. The same restless agony of the brewing thunderstorm clouded his heart and the lightning of hate still flashed in his mind; Hate for the Maleficus who had destroyed his family, still alive somewhere in this world; Hate for Arlen for having done nothing. And he had hate for God, who did nothing to save those who pleaded to him. Adeline was the one shining star in his heart, but a black haze covered all now.

From the early hours of the morning till well after the evening meal Iris slaved daily over the most meticulous details of sales in the city. Today, however, she walked the fields to inspect the state of the six or seven crops they grew on the farms. She bent over to examine the leaves of a potato plant. Soft light from the sunrise and droplets of due adorned their buds. The little pink flowers gave off the crisp smell of vibrant vegetation. Potatoes sold cheap. They also were reliable and easy to grow. After the Maleficus ravaged the farms, the families of the Cincinnatus land had survived off potatoes for some time until new grain fields were planted and livestock bought.

She recalled when her father first brought her into the fields to learn to weed and garden. It was long before then. She had wanted to go swimming in the cool river that sweaty day. His words still resounded in her head. As real as the pregnant soil she now touched with her hand. He had said, "God's creatures are like the life which springs from the earth; Each with their adornment of beauty, but concealing a greater treasure of nourishment deep within. One cannot utilize this prize without first digging deep and working hard." He popped a potato up as he said this, a gratifying grin reaching all across his face. That was one of her few memories. These precious few moments were forever gone. Iris wished he had spoken more to her.

She had never known the caresses of motherly affection. Mariana had given her own life in giving her life. Father always said that Mariana had died happy, holding her tiny Iris in her arms. But her death had broken him. He was often darkened by spells of despair. These were evident not in idleness, fits of rage or pithy crying, but a quiet sadness. She felt the quietness sting her now; her old guilt reaching down deep, like the grasping roots of a tree, silent and powerful. Guilt for being alive.

Iris stared at the potato in her hand, her thoughts lost in a maze.

Thunder rumbled in the distance.

In every prayer Father had asked that Mariana look down

upon them. Maybe he had finally gone home to her side. She
pictured his grin as he looked at her, mapped out his dimple, bushy
eyebrows, big nose. She locked it in memory.

There was a rustling behind, she stood and turned.
Vincent looked at her, "Iris," his eyes were full of pain and
questions. He looked as if he would say something more but did
not. Vincent helplessly stood there, trying to find the right words
as he held Iris' gaze.

She wore a simple light brown working skirt and an old
short-sleeve white blouse. A dark curly lock stuck to her sweaty
forehead and the rest of her hair was tangled in a bun behind or
frizzled around her ears.

The cool winds blew against them, pushing out the warm
air.

Iris looked away from him and across the horizon, "I wish
that I could behold the countenance of my mother." She pulled
the hair from her eyes. "It somehow seems wrong to imagine.
Whatever image I conjure up will never be the real her."

"I remember my mother. All too clearly I can hear her
voice. It pierces my ears, the screams. My sisters too. I am
plagued with memories! But I cannot see their faces, Iris. Try as
I may I can no longer picture them. It has frustrated me for
years."

A drop of water was on Kati's forehead. He stared into the
distant sky at the storm. Another drop fell. Iris came closer to
him, took hold of his hand with both of hers. It was scarred across
the palm and along the knuckles.

"What of your lady in the city? Is there not memories
waiting to be made in her arms?"

"No. She was lost. In the tide of this coming war. Murder.
Dying when I found her," he spoke it matter of factly.

"You cannot blame yourself."

"If I had been earlier. If I had not gone to the blasted
council! I could've come to her. There were only three I could
have-" his voice trailed off.

Iris felt his hand squeezing hers. A drop of water hit her.
And another. A downpour of rain fell now all over the fields.
Vincent did not flinch. She put her arm around him. It was like
nights years ago. He would come to comfort her from the clashes

of thunder, screams of lightning. She came to feel his arms wrap around her, their hearts beat in rhythm.

"It will tear you apart, Kati, if you hold on. You must forget all these terrible things."

"You think that I have not tried?" came his voice, empty. Water dripped down his face.

"They have departed. Be at peace. None of this was your doing, it is no fault of yours! All that you can ask of yourself is to do what you can do, no more."

Vincent's eye's flared up at her words.

"There is nothing more you could have done!" she added.

A grimace came on his face, "It was Arlen who stopped me! I came as soon as I heard them, but when he saw me he ran to me. He held me back, though he would not go himself! I could have stopped the Maleficus! Arlen! It was he who killed my mother, my sisters!"

"Arlen was a coward, yes, but he did not kill your family, Kati!"

"Don't tell me that!" He took his arms away from her, pushed her back. "I had a spear with me, a shield! I should have killed Arlen then and pushed forward!"

"What then! So you might have slain one of the Maleficus! And then what? I'll tell you, they'd have killed you along with the rest, Kati!"

"Better that than standing by, like the cowards and weaklings!"

"Arlen saved you from your own childish carelessness! Perhaps it was the one thing he did right!"

They stood apart looking at each other, drenched by the continuing rain. "All we can do is that of which we are capable, you said it yourself! This was all I wanted. To not stand by, to fight!"

"To die?!"

"Yes, if need be!"

"Well you might as well be dead now! The way you act! Gone for years without a word! Not a shred of care left in you for us!"

At first it bit, but then Vincent saw her wavering. He

grabbed hold of her and she hit him pitifully, eyes red with fitful tears.

"Iris," he wanted to say more. He touched her face with his hand. Trickles of water dripped down her hair onto his skin. "I cannot let it go. I am a Count now, and the Legate of a vast army. Arlen must pay for what he has done! He is only the beginning. I have power now, and a name. The betrayers of our King and Queen will be judged. Justinian, that usurper, will die! And one day, one day, I will find the Maleficus who brought hell to this farm!"

"One day, Kati, you will see that these things. Titles. Wealth. Revenge. They are nothing. Until then, you are nothing!"

Vincent scowled and released her from his grasp. He walked to the stables without looking back. Thunder shook the air. Iris was left in the storm.

Of the objects of combat, Vincent carried only his steel sword and its scabbard with him. Sharp enough to cut through bronze and copper as if they were bindings of straw, this blade's deadliness far exceeded any common weapon of war as did its beauty any handcrafted ornament of metals. He looked at the gem adorned blade in his hands. He felt the weight of it in his arms, but the heaviness was in his chest. The fearless steel and bright gold radiated into him, shining light deep down into his stomach. There resided a burden unable to be carried. A Luminarian Knight never turned away from danger! Always he did what was right no matter the cost! *Why did I run away!* He asked himself. Vincent remembered that day. *I lied to Iris. I did not come when I heard them.* He had seen it a thousand times in his dreams. He stood quiet, still as a statue. He did not want the Maleficus to find him. But his sister they found! Still he did not move. They were harming her! No movement, he could not be discovered. She screamed! He ran. Ran and ran. Ran away with hands sweating and heart racing. Ran until he could run no more. Only after many hours did it sink in. Oh what had he done! Only then did he work up pitiful determination. He found a spear and returned, trembling with fear. Then he saw Arlen, crying in fear. Arlen wouldn't let him. *It was his fault and not mine!*

On Vincent Cincinnatus Kati rode, pushing the world away before him, as one with a shield attempts to dispel the oncoming tide. A dark chasm had been chiseled into his heart, one that was too close to be seen and this disease grew.

***

"Fifty Equites died battling the Keleres! Fifty, Kiathar!" Alexus took a bite from the peppered sausage, spoke while chewing. "All were fully armored, all upon the finest warhorses. It is unfathomable that so many lords should perish in one battle!" he swallowed.

Servants came and placed ten silver dishes of fruit on the long table. There were glowing red apples, imported nectarines and bright green grapes.

"I must say, I find New Corinth most pleasant!" Alexus bit into a crisp apple. "If only knighted earlier, I would've paid the Count of the Third Realm many more visits."

Kiathar looked up from his plate of cleaned chicken bones, grinned and tore into a loaf of bread. "You'd likely be dead now with those others!" He laughed. The white teeth, his personal trophies from the Trials, dangled from his neck.

"Have you ever been in battle?" Alexus questioned.

"A real battle? Against men? No," came the outlander's deep voice.

"Just think of being amidst those Equites before they charged the Keleres! Knowing one third of them would soon die! Those are the men whose ranks we will soon fill!" Alexus fiddled with his fork. "How can you be sure, having never seen battle, that you will not falter when that time comes?"

"How to be sure? There is no surety! There is but to do!" Kiathar poured dark red wine into a stone goblet, tilted his head back and emptied it. "Cursed wine! Have you no real drink in this fortress!"

"Real drink? What do you call real drink, outlander?" Alexus sipped his wine.

"Ale!" Kiathar answered.

"Ha! What may be this barbarian concoction?" Alexus

laughed.

"You ignorant fool! Thick, strong. Made from grain, a froth on the surface," Kiathar closed his eyes and smiled, his blond, wine stained mustache twitching.

"Grain? What manner of a man would drink liquid muddled with the heads of grain?"

"HA!" Kiathar slapped the table. "You will see! Tonight! Two jugs I brought with me! You will see that ale conquers petty Luminarian wine!" The Nordic finished the loaf of bread. "You want to test yourself in battle, challenge our lord Cincinnatus to a joust!"

"A joust? Count Cincinnatus?" returned Alexus pensively. "Very well! I shall." His hands secretly shook at the daunting thought.

"HA!" spittle and bread bits flew from his mouth, he slammed the table again. Silver plates rattled, table torches shook. "You're serious!" he shouted. The other Equites looked down the table, in shock that he had violated the codes of dining respects.

"Of course I'm serious! Do I lie? I win and you provide this, this ale. I lose and you still provide the ale!"

"Deal!"

***

"I demand that my appointment be restored!" Bassus bellowed. "I had no intention of abdicating command of the Legion so easily! You must rectify this situation immediately!"

"I will do nothing of the sort!" exploded the Praetor Hydrus. "I gave you that position and now I have taken it away!"

The two stood glaring at each other in a musty ship hold. The smell of rusted iron and rotting wood mixed with the salty sea water. Bassus sucked in the dank air angrily. Hydrus braced himself as the room rocked back and forth.

"Sir Cincinnatus was the only way out!" burst the exasperated Praetor. "His appointment as Tribune was necessary to replace Gaius and his placement as Legatus Legionis was necessary for him to be accepted as Tribune. Without putting him in command of the Legion all would have been foiled: my position replaced, my guard gone, the Legion retired!"

Of vastly greater importance, the Keleres might have escaped uncontested! thought Hydrus. *If the edict of arrest had not been procured as a fruit of the new appointment, Justinian might have been allowed to spread words of conciliation! Because of Sir Cincinnatus, even the Plebian side of the council had worked themselves into a fury! But Bassus is too obtuse to be given more knowledge. No, and there are very few to be trusted now.*

"In presuming to demote me without so much as an arrangement, you have forced me into an unfortunate situation. Those legionnaires owe me allegiance; I will go to the Legion, stir things up. Whatever I have to! I will destroy your ports. Your precious cargoes will sink to the bottom of the Great Sea!"

"You wouldn't dare!"

"I would!"

Hydrus bit his fingernails.

"Alright!" the Praetor relented. "Your pay shall continue."

"Don't peddle with me! You know as well as I that the pay means nothing. I want my men, I want victories, and I want a part of the earnings from your ships! And I know all! I can reveal it before your time!"

He thinks he knows all! thought Hydrus. *But perhaps it is time to extinguish Bassus. He demands as though he was the designer! My Praetorian guard waits on the upper deck, I could call them now. No. Perhaps he is still of some use.*

"Very well, Bassus. Beat Sir Cincinnatus to the Second Realm and scrape up your most loyal officers. The Sixth Century of the Legion safeguards my mountain and I told the Knight to leave them untouched. They will be an ideal unit to base your headquarters out of. I want you to see to it that the shipments to the ports and from my mountain are kept secret from him! If he attempts to interfere in any way or tries to remove the Sixth from my mountain, stop him! I worry that our new Legate may prove disloyal in the end. He is unaccustomed to such a degree of power and may come to folly in wielding it. Men of steadfast devotion are so hard to come by these days, are they not?"

"Indeed," answered the fat Bassus.

"I will contact you when the time is right to rid ourselves of

Count Cincinnatus. Until then, you know what to do."

"A royal pity his line will be so abruptly ended!" scoffed Bassus, body heaving with his chuckles.

"Most pitiable, indeed," answered Hydrus, as he opened the hatch.

Chapter 6

Into the Fallen Realm

VINCENT LOWERED HIS LANCE SLOWLY, timing it to hit the chest of the enemy just as he would come within range of the weapon. He tucked it in tight against his body as the great black horse jolted beneath him in great exertions. The enemy was closer now, Vincent could make out the emblem of the sun and meadow on his shield. Mud flew from the hooves of the two beasts leaping, flying, and charging across the wet field. Two seconds more passed. He was closer now, not close enough. Vincent squeezed the massive horse's body with his legs, bracing himself for impact. *NOW!* Vincent's mind screamed. He instantly spurred the horse to the right. The enemy's lance missed Vincent's torso by a sword's length, but Vincent's smashed into the enemy's stomach! The man flew from the horse to the muddy ground, his horse whinnying from the shock of the impact transferred to it. Vincent pulled his steed to a sudden halt. It wildly pulled its head up and stood on its hind legs. Vincent leaned forward and grasped the horse with his left hand to stay mounted. When the animal settled, he dismounted in one swift motion while taking hold of the reins and drawing his sword. He walked over to the fallen enemy who was smeared with mud and lying motionless.

"Do you yield?" Vincent yelled with all the fury of war.

"By God I think I shall!" remarked a comical young voice from behind the closed helmet. The man lifted his visor, revealing a broad smile.

"Next time perhaps you will think twice about challenging your master, knight," Vincent pulled the young man up with one hand.

"Next time I won't fall for your sudden flanking movement, my lord!" Alexus unlatched his breastplate, a giant dent in its center. He rubbed the bruise on his stomach. "Did you really have to be riding so fast when you hit me?" He complained as he let out an exaggerated groan.

Vincent gave a loud laugh and then took a deep breath of the fresh air.

Alexus began again, "Sire, I want to thank you in person for most graciously opening up your most glorious fortress in New Corinth to such humble Equites as myself. We all have been most wonderfully entertained! Although I would recommend that as the new Count of this realm you supply your stores with a drink which is named *ale!*" Alexus' facial expression lit up, waiting for a response.

"Ale?"

"Yes, Sire. It is an interesting drink. Different from wine. It grows upon you. Excellent stuff! Lord Strongblade and I shared some yesterday. When we heard the Equites would be leaving so soon, we decided not to delay our celebrations until after this joust!"

"Do you always talk this much, knight?"

"No, my lord - I mean yes, my lord - My apologies, sire."

"No apologies necessary, knight. But there is much toil ahead of us. The Second Realm is already in shambles and Justinian and his Keleres race against us to its borders. We leave New Corinth today."

Now Alexus really did feel defeated.

The two mounted and trotted back to the road. Evan stood there, beaming a mocking smile at Alexus. Alexus stared back questioningly.

"You laugh at me squire?"

"That I do, sire," answered Evan.

"My squire has bested many Equites in tournament, Alexus," interposed Vincent.

"Is that so? And no more than fifteen years old! Most astounding."

Evan frowned, "Were I the lord of an estate I too would have finished the Trials. But my place is to serve my master."

He hardly knows who his parents are, never mind his lineage. He would make a fine knight were things different! thought Vincent.

***

The Keleres peered out at their commander, Justinian Marcus Solis, descendant of the Great Kings, of both Roman and native blood, heir to countless chiefdoms in various districts, hero of the Second Malefican war, savior of Luminares and rightful King! His voice boomed over the troop formation of the Royal Guard,

"Let your fidelity be firm as the iron in your right hand! Your courage as endless as the rays of the sun! Now affirm your oaths to lord and land! To the true King of Luminares! How answer you?"

In chorus they responded with the oath, "We pledge our faith and our bodies to the King and his domain!"

"Against sword and axe?" roared Justinian back at them.

"Let them grind against our shields!" They recited.

"Against darkness?"

"Let it come, for we have the Monarchy of the Sun above Meadow to rule us!"

"Against death?"

"Only grant us fall at your side!"

The thousand voices were suddenly silent. The Oath of the Guard was finished. A tiny flicker of gold glimmered above the mass of red armor. Not the old crown, rusted and worn with time. This ruby speckled ornament was a new diadem for a new and glorious line of Solis Kings.

"Then let it begin!" roared their King.

The Keleres smelt the black oil. Sounds of burning permeated the pure earth. Distorted on the horizon lay Etruscanum, capital of the Second Realm. Hundreds of Luminarian Equites would cross that expanse in a day. But the rebels wouldn't make it any further. Rusty spikes, ropes and oil, walls of sharpened cedar, ditches, grunting mules towing boulders; all was in preparation for them. Over the din of yelled orders and back breaking work, some say they heard the King call to the Lord of the Third Realm. "Come then," he commanded with dusty winds giving ear, "Come O Tribune, Knight, Count and Legate, come usurper of titles and feast on the throes of death!"

***

The Second Realm imposed an air of sacredness and ancient greatness. Colossal feats were its heritage and glory, yet everywhere one breathed the dust of a graveyard. Massive pillars, each toppled and smashed, lined wide stone roads. Buildings of such height as to scrape the sky were filled with gaping holes like empty eyes from a past life. Breaking apart they knelt to the ground in submission to the chaos which had worn them through to the concrete bones of their foundation. Such damage only war machines produced. Catapults and ballistae had bombarded this city ages ago in the War of Ancients. The ancestors who could build as though they were giants had extinguished their own city with their vast powers! Since then anarchy had been a lasting disease for the Second Realm's capital, Etruscanum. It seemed to be waiting to burst forth from the very street corners! Still, the Counts of the realm had insisted on setting up their government in the city's old and illustrious palace. For Count Risar, it had not turned out well.

Sweat dripped from Vincent, Kiathar and the other Equites of the Third Realm riding down the road. The salty liquid burned in their eyes and soaked sore backs enclosed in steel and iron. Vincent wiped the dripping sweat from his brow. It reminded the new Count of the blood which had been spilt there. The blood of anarchy and rebellion was oozing forth from some hidden and festering wound, waiting to explode in a torrent of brutality. *Count Risar doesn't deserve to rule this dying realm any longer!* thought Vincent angrily.

"The buildings," began Alexus, "No wood. No clay. Each is built like the lone palace of the First Realm! What this city must have looked like in its glory! This is amazing! It is as though we have ridden to another kingdom!" Alexus was stunned.
"It's the handiwork of the ancient ones!" added another.
"Besides the stonework, perhaps you've noticed that the knocked over walls, fires and dead bodies also are unlike anything found in the Third Realm!" mocked Kiathar in humor.
Vincent watched the Nordic foreigner closely, he was

right. "Do not overlook what we have ridden into," he added tersely from the front of the formation. "Here death has raged for twenty years. And here we will be dealt death and deal it until the insurrection which runs rampant and the betrayal which flees to it are destroyed."

As if to affirm the young Count's words, the whitewashed, sun baked bones of a man came into view alongside the road. Most of his decaying skin and organs had been eaten by the birds, but some of his hair remained. The Equites peered at the body with a new sense of foreboding. The Equites carried on.

"Etruscanum is a waiting trap," Sir Cincinnatus broke the overgrown silence. A great palace was now looming before them. "The Keleres have beaten us to the city, God alone knows how. And the Legion is nowhere to be found. Be on guard! Count Risar has much explaining to do!"

Vincent unsheathed his sword and pointed it to the right, directing the right line of Equites to make a sweep of the palace grounds. Picking up pace, he then led on past a mud spewing fountain to the broken gates. His powerful black horse galloped through the courtyard, a train of his Equites in trail behind. Past more dead fountains and baths, they came to another gate. Vincent dismounted and budged it open with a push. Swords in hand, the other Equites followed on foot, towing their steeds behind. Vincent rushed down the hall, his eyes searching for life, for anyone in the empty palace!

A scream came from ahead!

Vincent charged after the fleeing man and brought him to the ground.

"Don't harm me! Don't harm me!" cried the frightened clerk.

"Silence!" Vincent commanded, the force of his breath alone taking the wind out of the scared man. "Where is Count Risar!?"

"He is in the royal chamber just ahead to the right, now let me go please!"

Vincent loosed the man, tied his horse to a pillar and stepped off toward the chamber, gripping his sword tightly. A line of Equites followed fearlessly behind their impetuous lord.

***

Kiathar watched the Equites spread out across the field. His brown mare sped across the ground and locks of his matted hair escaped from the sweat soaked, steel helmet. The wind felt refreshing. A series of pillared structures were coming up. With a pull of his hand he guided the horse to the left of one of the structures, saw Alexus do the same further to the left around another building. His axe clanked against the back of his oversize breastplate as he slowed the mare. Saving his weapon of choice for a time of real trouble, he drew his shorter sword.

The veranda was empty. Kiathar spurred his mare upstairs onto the tiled cement porch. Large basins filled with dirtied waters lined the platform.

Another bathhouse! It's no wonder these lazy fools have been conquered! Kiathar thought mockingly.

Pillars were knocked down and roofs falling in as with everywhere else in the city. He looked through an open doorway, empty. Nobody. Not even any bodies. Kiathar suspiciously moved closer to the opening for a better look, but found nothing. He turned the horse around and the great beast crushed a pot which was in the way. Kiathar had chosen a horse of much greater strength and breadth than the other Equites. Its giant hooves pounded the earth with unchecked ferocity, but its speed lacking. Kiathar thought this exchange suited his style of warfare. Going back down the stairs the beast grunted on the awkward footing. Brushing the animal's mane comfortingly Kiathar muttered, "Stupid beast."

He looked up to the hills from whence the Equites of the Third Realm had come and saw the outline of a man on the horizon. Suddenly Kiathar saw five more, all armed, move up beside him! Without a second thought the knight spurred his horse forward as fast as he could force it to move. The creature panted and raved and the grass flew by beneath them. Over and up the hill now, Kiathar pulled the horse to a stop. It's mouth frothed from the work. Before the Nordic's eyes was arrayed an entire army marching toward the horizon. Even at that distance the noises of the mass of men at arms could be heard like the echo of a distant earthquake. They were a disorderly rabble without uniform or banner, but numbered at least a thousand strong.

***

Alexus was momentarily separated from his brothers and his heart quivered with fear. *Where are the Numantines who have ransacked this great city?* He cautiously entered into a broken down building, leaving his mare outside. He opened a rickety wooden door. Leg muscles twitched, ready to dart to friends and safety at the sight of drawn swords. Two men stared at him from inside, their conversation frozen in fear. One was of common attire but the other wore a great black cloak. Alexus failed to move or say a word, but the men saw his sword in hand and shifted to the door.

"I beg you to let us go, Knight. You can have it! I swear I respect all the King's edicts of old!" the commoner promised Alexus.

Alexus stared at a wineskin in his hand. The man dropped it to the floor.

"I am leaving!" the same man said to the one clothed in black as he pushed by Alexus.

"You owe still more for this! Your debt grows beyond your measure," said the one who remained. He stared then upon the wineskin as if it were an object of great value. Deciding at last not to take it, he strode by Alexus without another word.

Alexus knew what was in the skin already. The same cursed elixir as in the Second Trial! *What dark power gives me this knowledge?* he wondered with trepidation. The uncanny certainty troubled him. *Leave!* his conscience screamed. *Walk away!* He uncorked the skin and breathed in its contents. Memories of a place black and hidden rushed back to him and he was ashamed. He corked the skin quickly for fear that he would gulp down its contents there and then! Yet he could not bring himself to cast it away. Before Alexus strode out again to the sunlight it found its way deep into his satchel.

***

"What do you mean the Count has left? Is this not his city? Is this not his palace?" Vincent demanded of the older man in royal garb. He stared Vincent down and then took a seat in the royal chair.

"You are the most ignorant and insolent person of royal blood I've ever encountered! Count Risar is in Helles with the Legion and has been for weeks!"

"Weeks? On what business?"

"His own business, I surmise. He is a Count!"

"As am I." Vincent stepped closer to intimidate the Viscount. "Where are the Numantine rebels? Does he oversee their destruction?"

"The Numantines? In Helles? HA!" the Viscount scoffed. "The Numantines join the rebel army to escape Helles!"

"Why? What is in Helles?" Vincent questioned.

"You obtuse juvenile! Go back to your newfound throne and gorge yourself on royal pleasures. There are too many secrets in this old realm that you will never understand."

"Let us have him beaten from this court, m'lord! He should not speak thus of your royal person!" exploded a knight from behind.

"No, we will not beat the Viscount from his empty courts this day," Vincent declared to the man in the royal chair. "But after I take up my place in Helles, that day may come; if he is not murdered in his sleep by Numantines beforehand. Watch your back Viscount, for you will find no friend in me to guard it after today!"

"You waste time in going to Helles! Count Risar and the Legion's Legate will not greet you kindly!"

"I do not go to greet the Legion, but to command it!"

"Impossible," he was dumbfounded.

"The council believes that those who are now in command have not dealt with the situation fittingly."

The Viscount smiled and stood. "Very well Count. Do what you will. You must excuse me for I have to finalize plans for my departure."

"Is the whole city to be emptied?"

"I'll say it again, you've come to an older realm. We have

our ways in place. You will not understand them."

At that instant the door to the chamber burst open and Kiathar stormed in. "An army!" he declared as he caught his breath. "An army is here. They have no banners or uniform but number at least a thousand strong."

"Numantines?" questioned one of the Equites.

"Perhaps. They were already at a great distance. We must move now if we are to catch them before dark!"

Vincent scowled at the Nordic knight. "You would waste our time with your intuitions! Exander, take five from your platoon and investigate. We will finish scouring the premises."

"But Sire, by the time he has returned they may have escaped our sight!"

Vincent pointed his finger at Kiathar, "My words are final!"

Peeking eyes disappeared and the door to the antechamber behind the throne slid shut ever so slightly. The Viscount continued with his preparations as planned.

***

He was home. Not that desolate place which he had seen so short a time before. Instead it was the home of a lifetime ago. His mother was in the room across. The smell of freshly baked bread wafted into his room. She was guiding the servants in creating her favorite meal. Fresh strawberries would be cut and mixed with the sugarcane. And then it began. Screams! Pewter plates crashing! Low voices commanding in a foreign tongue! A table crashing against the wall! It was all too familiar. Vincent began to run. His mind wanted so badly to stay with his sister, to hold firm, but his heart and hands quaked with the fear. He could not control himself, no matter how much he demanded courage. Always the same. He ran.

No, but this time something *was* different. Vincent turned! Not his sister, but a radiant woman with flowing black hair stood calling to him! He moved to her, slowly at first, and then running. Adela! He held onto her, staring into her, filling himself up with her! Then came a hard bang against the wooden door. Vincent throbbed with anger and hate! He knew who was on the other side! Vincent would crush him and spill his guts on the floor! He released Adela, the rising hate was intoxicating! Finally he would fight and kill! She squeezed his hand as he pulled away! Blood! Too late! Vincent turned to hold her in his arms. There was a wound in the small of her back! Dark red poured over the clean sheets. The blood covered him!

***

"I will tell you a secret, Kiathar."

Kiathar jumped to his feet when Exander awoke him from sleep. A distant flame flickered against the two in the darkness. Only shadows of their faces marked the night sky, but each could feel the mistrust of the other.

"Wake, foreigner, and hear my words of doom. I will tell you why our master chose me to be the First Spear, why the Trials were harder for you than any other and why you must leave this expedition."

"I refuse to have words with you, Exander."

He continued anyway, "The Third Trial. The Extraho Prodigus was not put into the ring at random. You were meant," Exander paused and leaned against a nearby tree. "Well, you were meant to die."

"I'll show you who's going to die if you don't remove yourself from here at once," responded Kiathar tersely.

"Sir Cincinnatus' family was massacred by a band of Nordics, outlander! This is why he has treated you unfairly. Of all the novices, you earned the Platoon Pilum, not I. He gave it to me because he could not stand to see it in the hands of a *Maleficus!*" the word hissed as it came off Exander's lips.

"You are a deceiver! How am I to believe that you came by this knowledge!"

"I am not the lord of many lands for nothing! Ask your friend, Sir Alexus, he will tell you it is the truth. The master hates you because you are a barbarian! You know it to be true. Five days ago he would not even believe your report of the Numantine army until another knight had also seen it! Of course by then it was too late. He has set himself against you. You must know it?"

Kiathar knew he was right, but would not accept it.

"I've put our past grievances aside. I'm trying to help you! If you do not leave now," Exander continued. "You will end up dead; in sleep or in battle, it does not matter. *He* will see to it one way or the other!"

Kiathar put his hands on Exander and lifted him clean off the ground, "Get out of here *knight!*"

Even with Exander's considerable height, the barbarian held him a whole foot's length from the dirt. When his toes touched the solid earth again, Exander strutted off in a hurry, but he was really quite content.

Kiathar sat in the shadows and pulled a coarse bear skin around himself. He could faintly see the other Equites sleeping at a distance from him.

He didn't look, dress or speak like them. He slept and ate apart.

I am not one of them...

Unable to harness his suspicion, Kiathar went to find Alexus.

"I am sorry friend, Exander is right."

***

Vincent had Evan's throat in his hand as he awoke.

"Master," the boy pleaded through gasping breaths. Shocked at what he was doing, Vincent released the boy. "Master, we have spotted fires to the west. The Equites believe it could be Justinian and his Keleres!"

Vincent sat up. He could not have lain down for more than an hour. "Very well squire, get my armor."

"Yes sire. Sir Exander wishes to speak with you sire."

Vincent pulled a cloak around himself, covering his face under its shadow. Sir Exander stood under a willow. Its boughs bent around him sorrowfully and sparks from the embers of a fire lit his face with a fearful gold. Vincent perceived the excitement on his brow.

"Sire," Exander bowed low at the approach of Vincent. A dark patch of trees shaded their meeting. "The Keleres have been spotted! They are at unawares and we should strike true while we still can!"

Kiathar peered out from the morning darkness at his lord, Count Cincinnatus, as he spoke with Exander. He growled at the two under his breath. *Damn the Count and Exander!* Kiathar roughly grabbed the young girl sobbing in the shadows and pulled her toward the Count.

"Exander is a fool! He would not even tell you of the raid going on in the nearby village because he cares nothing for humanity!" He pushed the girl in front of the two, into the light.

Vincent already had his hand on his sword at the sight of his handling her. He eyed the Nordic cautiously and finally observed the young peasant before him. Tears stained her mud smeared face, her bare feet and knees bled from bruising.

"Who is this?" Vincent demanded.

"I told those Equites to keep her under watch! How dare you bring her here Nordic!" interrupted Exander.

Kiathar gave him a cold stare. "She comes from Ptosii Sire," he answered. "It is a small village two leagues from here. She found our camp but an hour ago. Speak girl!" he commanded.

"My lords," the thirteen year old looked to the ground in shame. "I was sent to beg your aid! Forgive me, for no man could be spared." She looked up at Vincent now. Two starry and fearful eyes glared at him. "The Numantine rebels are attacking us! There cannot be much time, my father left to fight, you must come, you must, you must!" she broke into tears.

Vincent looked away, "Of what significance is this girl now, Nordic?" he questioned Kiathar.

"But-"

"Take her away!" Vincent commanded.

"Sire! Send me with a detachment. We will do great damage to the rebels in the confines of the village when their army is spread thin!"

"You cannot trust this outlander alone, lord!" Exander demanded.

"That is out of the question, Kiathar!"

That double crossing imposter! Kiathar was fuming now. "The Numantine revolutionaries have already begun the siege of this town! As we speak their homes burn! With the reinforcements of the army we lost pursuit of, the town will be entirely annihilated! We must catch these murderers before they can escape!"

"This news is no longer of any relevance!"

"M'lord, how can you say this! If they escape it will mean continued violence throughout the realm! We have all gained word of their outrageous acts. They kill children without compunction, rape the women, and kill the elderly for greed! There is no honor in this! Every one of them must be destroyed! Let us finish the job now!"

"Only the Queen matters! Her betrayers must be brought to justice!"

"The Queen is dead!"

"Silence! Have you learned no respect for the deceased! Justinian must be killed for what he has done! His ills outweigh all else!"

"By the Code of our Order! We cannot allow this massacre whilst we wield the power to stop it!"

"Don't speak to me of the Code! BARBARIAN!"

Kiathar met the Count's fiery stare with one of equal fury. Finally he took a step back and without a word walked into the shadows. The girl ran in fear.

"We attack at dawn! With the rising of the sun we shall crush the Keleres rebels!" The Count commanded Sir Exander in a raspy voice.

                              ***

Iris pulled her shawl tightly around herself. The servants of the house had spent hours preparing her for this trip. Her hair and body were cleaned. Fine oils wafted a temptingly distinguished aroma from her skin. A gown of purple with embroidered red flowed around her as she walked up the giant steps of the palace. Around her eyes was a hint of dark paints, in the way of the highest ladies of the First Realm. Her gaze was steady and concentrated, entrapping attention. She was prepared, she was ready, yet still she pulled the shawl more tightly around her face.

Two menacing Praetorian Guards stopped her at the entrance. Hearing her explain her business, they chuckled and then let the visitors pass. Quivering inside, Iris glanced back to her escort of servants for reassurance; they were just as disturbed at the snickering. There were many halls and it was all a trifle disorienting, but these emissaries of the fifty-third estate of the Third Realm soon found their way to the adjudicator's quarters.

"My lord we humble subjects of the Third Realm come before you to beg your mercy concerning the fate of our homes," Iris bowed her head very low. She was unused to the formalities but she would do everything she could to make her respect apparent. If she failed here, she would fail as headmaster, fail the Cincinnatus house, and all the families of the estate.

"In whose name do you bring case to this house of justice?" croaked a man from behind a giant stone table at the forefront of the room. It was set upon a high platform that looked down upon the court below.

"In the name of House Cincinnatus, m'lord."

The adjudicator leaned forward from the table and Iris caught a glimpse of his clammy skin and cold stare. She wondered if she had forgotten some part of the procedure. Were there some words she was supposed to use?

"Are you Cincinnatus blood, lady?" he interrupted her thought.

"No Sire, I am the appointed headmaster of the fifty-third estate of my lord, Count Cincinnatus."

"Hmm." The adjudicator examined Iris. "Could the Count not afford to send an emissary to do his bidding? Or even a male of the bloodline?"

"No sire that is not why I have come. My lord Sir Cincinnatus is away at war, as you must well know. I thought it best that we take care of matters by our own devices if possible."

"By your own devices? You should have sent someone else! Now tell me your complaints and be quick about it!"

"M'lord, Prince Nicephorus Puter of the district of Edessa attempts to force my hand in selling our estate. He would swallow up our living to gorge his thirst for endless vineyards. Vineyards run by slaves! For long now he has violated the Royal Command in taking men into bondage, yet the kingdom did nothing while our departed King was away at war! Now he presumes to force me into selling and at such a price that we too will be forced into slavery in order to survive!"

"Why have you not brought this before the courts of the Third Realm, this is a matter for your Count, not the Luminarian Court!"

"But m'lord, our Count is away at war and cannot be called upon. Moreover, the Count's regent can do nothing because Prince Nicephorus threatens him with suffocation in the marketplace. Prince Nicephorus controls the caravans and ships of the Third Realm which transport our goods to cities here in the First Realm. Only you can intervene with the force necessary. It is injustice that our royal lord, Count Cincinnatus, should have the lands of his birth stolen from him in his absence!"

"Aww yes, Count Cincinnatus is both Count and lord of the estate in question. Well then it is settled, bring it before your tribune, perhaps the Plebs can do something about it." There were snickers from the corners of the gigantic court. It was clear none of these men were Plebs and that they doubted the sanctimony of the Plebian council.

Iris froze up for a moment, hearing replayed the jabs of childhood at her Plebian class. She was angry, "Is it out of ineptitude or mere stupidity that m'lord the adjudicator does not realize that Count Cincinnatus is also Tribune of our people!"

"How dare YOU mock ME!" erupted the adjudicator as he stood and slammed the table. "Take her away!"

Praetorian Guards in purple came running and Iris saw her folly. She got on her knees.

"Lord, I beg of you! Help my people! Save them from shackles, save their children from starvation! Give us your protection!"

The adjudicator put his right hand up and the guards halted only feet away from Iris.

"You do well to kneel, lady. Now that I behold your countenance fully," the adjudicator rubbed his chin and lips as he took her fully in. "You are very beautiful," he remarked quietly, perversely.

Iris was disgusted, but at least here, even if in his lusting eyes, there was some hope. She held herself erect, allowing all of herself to be seen.

"Hmmm," the adjudicator chuckled dirtily as he sat back down. "This will serve you well, for I am afraid the only protection you will find will be behind the walls of a brothel. Take her away!"

"Yes my lord Hydrus!" responded the guard commander.

"But wait!" she screamed. It was no use, the guards picked her up by the arms and dragged her out.

She stood staring at the closed iron studded gates. The heads of her retinue of servants were sunken, defeat was at hand. Worse, slavery, starvation and death knocked upon the doors, and not one of them could stop their barging in.

Iris pulled the top her dress back above her shoulders. There was one way. She had not considered it before. She could marry. Yes, she could marry *him.* *Return before I do it!* She prayed angrily, desperately.

***

Vincent Cincinnatus stood upon the bodies, the blood red morning sun burning in his fiery eyes of hate. He was consumed, his soul obliterated, his conscience stamped far beneath the ground. For no higher purpose did he strike men down, nor for his brothers did he fight. A pack of red tinted survivors fled down the treacherous ravine. It was not over yet. Justinian was there with them. Standing on a mountain of death Vincent watched him run for all he was worth. Through a maze of rocks they ran into shadow and the forest beyond.

It had been a trap. The Equites had charged their way through ambush and encirclement, spikes and flame, arrow and boulder, hill and rock...and crushed the Keleres. So sudden was their fury that the maneuvers of the Keleres had been late, their closing box of death shallow, their formations thin. Yet still would the Equites have utterly perished had not Cincinnatus seen the gap.

Alexus pictured it now as he shivered with the horror still filling his veins. They were in the midst of the enemy's camp, or so they had thought when the horns suddenly sounded. Keleres

formed ranks on their left and right, front and behind. Alexus
could still vividly see the Count turning back to wave his men to
follow him deeper into the camp. *Deeper!* Towards the advancing
line of pikes they rode at full speed! *What is he doing!* they had
thought. That was when the fear came for Alexus! Not a mere
heightened anxiety, but an entire paralyzing of the mind. The
danger gripped and choked him as the wave of death came closer
and closer! Alexus' horse carried him without guidance. Arrows
were at their back, flying by the men's ears, stabbing into their
necks and into the muscles of the horses. The pained whinnying of
the beasts and piercing human screams punctuated the thunder of
the stomping hooves. Alexus knew an arrowhead would strike
him! The inevitability of it laid siege to the sanity of his mind. He
had no choice but to turn and look behind.

Alexus wiped the sweat off his face as his heart pounded
with the memory. Grasping the reins of his horse, he had turned
his face back to the front only to then find the formation far ahead
of him. They had pinched through a fast closing gap between the
charging phalanxes. The spurs of his boots dug into horse flesh!
He had to make it through the gap! Glistening points were aimed
at him now. From two directions they closed in, like the late hit of
a blacksmith's hammer. He was just behind the other Equites
now, and it was too late! Suddenly lurched forward, he soon felt
the hard dirt hit his face. He scrambled to get up, but the torn up
earth slipped under his feet! Heart exploding, Alexus was frozen
watching his horse stabbed and overrun by the two waves of
Keleres. The Guard broke formation in a panic to turn to their now
vulnerable rear. They faced him. *Get up! Just get up!* His mind
had screamed. The Equites were far away now and cutting the
Keleres archers to pieces, so Alexus learned after the battle.
Finally his legs had obeyed him and in that moment he could only
think of one thing: to run as fast as he could. Like a cold blooded
coward, that is exactly what he did!

Alexus held the hand of a Luminarian Knight in his. The
man shivered as if immersed in snow. Blood spewed from his
coughing mouth. His eyes fluttered about in panic, looking at
everything and nothing. Twice he looked at Alexus and held the

stare, only to return to his panicked searching. Once he attempted an utterance, but there were no words. Only the sound of his choking on blood and spittle emerged. And then he died.

Alexus cried. Not for that brave soul did he shed tears, for he had died well. For the great evil that he himself had done Alexus wept, for the men he had betrayed. When Alexus opened his eyes, he knew what he must do.

Equites were bleeding to death, years of life spraying out of them in seconds. Others gasped for air, slowly suffocating from the darts shot through their backs. Many who lived could hardly be recognized, so bad were their burns from the oil. Vincent walked away from his dying brothers. He drew his sword and walked to the bound prisoners. Only moments ago they had, with smiles on their faces, hurled iron spears into the flesh of his Equites.

One by one Vincent demanded of them where Justinian would retreat to and one by one he cut off their heads. Darkness had consumed him. Far was he from the path of God! His royal garments were stained by the spray of the blood. It is written in the Code that after a battle was finished a knight was to love even his enemies and treat those who injured him with compassion. He was to kill without hate. Only for love of justice and duty was he to raise the sword! All Equites knew this. Alexus knew it as he watched, his heart pounding in utter confusion. He was to confess to this man? Who was this Count that executed helpless prisoners by his own hand? Alexus' thoughts were suddenly disturbed by the glance of Sir Cincinnatus at his approach.

"Master, I have failed you! My courage was lost in the fight! To my endless shame, I fled from the enemy in fear! Tell me what I must do!"

Silence.

"I will lay down my life gladly! Give me a hopeless quest that I may right my wrong! Have mercy!"

Vincent picked the man up from his knees and with a fierce stroke of his right arm knocked him back down. "Neither barbarians nor cowards belong in my company!"

Alexus knelt there for an hour, maybe more. The others set up camp for themselves. Despair collapsed the caverns of his heart. He had joined the Equestrian Order for his family's honor and to make a true man of himself. To sanctify his worldly position of royalty with heavenly royalty! With chivalric purity! What was he now?

The taste of the woman in the caves of the Second Trial suddenly came back to him! He remembered her body and the sweet and intoxicating sensation in her mouth! He pulled the sensation into himself; wrapped his body in its caresses. He was empty for its absence; he had to have that taste back! He knew it was this Drink that he craved. His mind was calling for it! He needed it to move! He needed it to keep on living! Fumbling through his satchel he found the skin he had taken from Etruscanum. He uncorked it and emptied the contents into his mouth! The soothing numbness covered him.

"I have more of this, drink, if you are willing to listen to my counsels," came a voice from behind him. It was Exander.

Alexus turned in surprise. He stared at the knight momentarily and then snatched the full wineskin from Exander's hand.

Chapter 7

Symptoms of Disaster

THERE WAS NO TURNING BACK NOW. The Luminarian Equites were far behind.

Let them die fighting the Keleres, thought Kiathar.

The Nordic jumped off the powerful warhorse, bringing the forlorn girl from the town down in his giant arm. She flinched from his tight grasp. Kiathar, who had forgot his strength for a moment, quickly set her down. Urging the young Ptosiian on as encouragingly as he could, the Nordic followed her into the town towing his horse behind.

Angry fires roared against the soft rays of morning light. Black smog wafted low in the sky, thickening as the two crossed a broken down wall into the village. The smoke hung in the air as a macabre memory of the night before. It was above them and around them and in them. Distant noises it carried to their bodies.

They were the sounds of death, which need not be spoken of aloud. Deeper and deeper they weaved themselves into the maze of hatred and killing. Agony around every corner, horror on every path, never had this son of a Strongblade witnessed such atrocity. Bodies lined the streets, blood drenched the dirt. People hewn in pieces still squirmed in agony. Kiathar felt the hardness in his stomach, the iron indifference he had put there, completely erode.

The young girl frantically pointed ahead and then darted off. Yelling for her to stop, the Nordic Knight was unable to follow as his steed lost control of itself in fear of the fires. Pounding the ground and rearing over and over, it took all of Kiathar's strength to hold her steady. Sweat poured down the shivering beast as the Nordic knight stroked it calmingly. From the corner of his eye something appeared between a wisp of smoke. Kiathar looked but saw nothing.

No, there was something. A man!

The giant mare, like a panicked dog, fled as the Nordic let it loose. Kiathar drew his axe.

Five other men closed in slowly.

"He is a knight," the youngest said to his fellows in his native tongue. His face showed doubt.

"But he is one of *them!*" yelled back another.

The ring closed in tighter around Kiathar.

"His blood is barbarian. Just like those who plundered our villages."

"The Equites are an Order!" responded the first. "They are sworn to a Code! They're not like the Legion which looks the other way at a gold coin."

"I told you to leave him at home! This is no job for him!" remarked one angrily.

"We have no allies in our war," spoke their leader. "All this was done to us first!" the voice rose, as if trying to justify their actions. "We only return the favor. Attacked we attack. Stolen from, we steal. Plundered, we plunder."

Then the Nordic let out a roar that shook the very bones of the oncoming enemies! When they heard that sound and saw his muscles flexing around the massive axe in abject fury, each one secretly thought to turn and run. But looking at each other reassuringly, they closed in, like a pack of timber-wolves on a horned bull.

One went down immediately as Kiathar rushed him, then another in the next axe stroke. Two were behind him now and Kiathar felt a sharp pain as a sword pierced the flesh of his side between the plates of armor. His axe clanged on rock as it fell from his hands. Aware now, Kiathar turned without hesitation and picked up the very man who had stabbed him. In a flood of wrath, he hurled him headlong into one of his fellows. Then, drawing the blade from his side without wincing in pain, he swung at the other charging warrior. Missing once, the next stroke hit the mark and he fell dead. The two others were on their feet now, but Kiathar let out another roar as before, and they fled faster than he could take another step!

There was noise vibrating the moist and decaying wood walls of the shack. Sounds as of fists falling on flesh and bodies crashing! Kiathar ducked under the doorway. Now there was a scream! He hurried for he recognized the young girl's voice! One man laid on the floor in blood, the father. He knew the girl was in the corner of the darkened room, he could hear her crying. Before him was the back of a man in leather armor with studded gauntlets. A lady stood before him in defiance. From the torch the man held, he could see that her face was stained with tears and blood. The man, of similar raiment to the warriors Kiathar had just vanquished, hit her again. Her body smacked the hard wood floor, smashing a pewter pot beneath the force of her fall. Now he was on top of her and tearing at her clothes as she scratched him in a last ditch effort. Without one more moment of hesitation, Kiathar stepped forward, picked him up by his head with one hand, braced his body with the other and snapped his neck. Throwing the corpse out the front door, Kiathar called the woman and girl to himself, but only whimpering came from the mother. With two gnarly hands he picked her up and held her close to his breast while the child crawled onto his back. Out into the night they went, while cries of battle polluted the morning air.

***

The monk looked at his face. It was sickly white, with ruffled and matted hair along his forehead. Abnormal beads of sweat accumulated around the wrinkles of his frown. Fatigue had painted black circles beneath eyes. The pupils focused on the rustic boards of the floor, shame freezing them in utter relinquishment of purpose. But it was more than shame, the despair ran deep. His stare was empty. The sickness was hauntingly familiar to the monk. He had seen it a thousand times when the monks had journeyed to Helles. But now their monastery was empty. Only the recently come refugees from Ptosii gave it any feel of life. Alone, he had returned from the ghoulish streets of Helles. No longer song, but the tortured memories of his brothers echoed in the monastery's hall.

The monk unfolded his hands from prayer and spoke, "I can do nothing to remove this addiction except to pray, brother. Would that my prayers would heal you, but that gift has not been given me. A foul pestilence this is! And it strikes the Second Realm at dire times! You must face it! But you are not alone."

"If I do not get more of this drink, if I cannot taste it, I will lose my sanity! All day it passes through my head, shadowing every thought! It is with me when I lie down to rest and when I rise. As I eat I taste nothing, only the longing. It wrenches my mind! A great rage so often fills in me that I must scream! Yet still it does nothing, I am trapped inside myself!"

"A tough cross this is to bear."

"I am lost," Alexus answered. "And I have no will to fight it if I could. There is nothing for me left in this world to fight for."

"There is always hope, Knight."

"Do not call me that! I am a coward, and the Order is not what I thought it was! I am alone and drowning! As well as I probably deserve..."

"Do not dare mock the forgiveness of our Lord!" Alexus' somber voice trailing off in self derision was cut in two by the monk's explosion of anger. Alexus was taken by surprise. "You have received his covenant but moments ago with the sign of the cross and now you push back his gifts in dark tones? How dare you spit upon the promise of the King of Kings! When he has forgiven, who can accuse? What's done is done." The voice of the monk now lost any sense of anger, but urgency remained in every utterance, "A knight you are. All sometimes must be reminded of their duty, but there is no being on this earth that can change what you are! What you do with your knighthood, however, is up to you. Will you be the royal, anointed slave of elixirs and passions? One who runs forever from his past, who puts his failures out of his mind rather than confronting them head on? One who associates with the traders of this foul drink? One who sits by idly while his frame wastes away in the pits of despair, when all the while the world groans in pain? Or will you take up your sword and conquer!" With those words the monk on sudden reached forward and unsheathed Alexus' sword. Brandishing the shining blade before him, the monk stared into the Knight's startled eyes. "It is not men alone that a Knight must conquer! You learned this from the Trials."

The flimsy wooden door busted from its hinges as Kiathar barged in, axe in hand. "I heard a sword drawn!" he mumbled to Alexus, looking a little embarrassed now.

"Kiathar, my good man," beamed the monk. "Stay a moment."

Outside, the mother and child Kiathar had rescued from the village gnawed on freshly baked bread. Other refugee families slept beside them on the stone floor. Kiathar shut the door behind himself as he walked in.

Alexus reclaimed the blade and sheathed it as he stood. "Just what would you have us do, monk. We have abandoned our master, to whom we swore fealty and undying faithfulness! Our Equestrian vows are broken!"

"You speak of Cincinnatus?! He would not take us back now if we brought a carriage laden with gold behind us!" added Kiathar.

The man hunched over in his dark and brooding robes. His eyes closed pensively and scraggly black eyebrows twitched along his pale face. Then he looked directly at Kiathar and then Alexus, "You will serve him!" Fire was in his eyes and his voice. "You know well enough that you have entered the oath of fealty! You spoke it, and so it will be. You will return to him, for you are brothers of the Red Cloth unto death." He covered his bald head with the menacing hood. "The Count needs his brothers in this time of darkness. Be warned! This business of war with the

Keleres bodes ill of Luminares! Christian fights Christian, Knight fights Guard! Unheard of! But there is much worse in store and your counsel will be needed."

"Our counsel?" Alexus questioned mockingly. "It will be a grace if our lives are spared, but he certainly will never listen to anything we have to say again!"

"Very well," the old man responded tersely. "At least then you will have done your duty. The fault will be his."

"Easy for you to speak, *old man!*" Alexus came back. "When it is *our* heads which will be severed as if we were no more than the Keleres prisoners!" Panic was in Alexus' eyes already.

"Of what counsel do you speak, monk!" broke in Kiathar.

The monk took in a deep breath, "The wounds of this land run deeper than the Count can imagine. If he thinks to right the Kingdom by vanquishing a few disloyal, but valiant Keleres guards, then he has been fooled!"

"You speak of the Numantine army! The Count knows well of them and they will be destroyed when he has taken command of the Legion. With that army none will dare oppose him!"

"The Numantines are NOTHING!" boomed the small man. "Legate Bassus had but to wave his hand and the band of marauders would've been destroyed years ago!"

Alexus gave the monk a look of disbelief, "What of the reports of battles lost, of need for recruitment in the Legion? What of the sacking of Ptosii?"

"Of the need for more gold from royal coffers?" added the monk. "Count Risar and Legate Bassus did well in perverting word of all that transpires here. The First and Third realms have been blind and the Legion has grown without bounds."

"To what end?" Alexus was dumbfounded.

"If only we knew," the monk gave a faint smile.

"Vincent will soon take command. Whatever the Legion is up to will be under his wary eye! I know my lord, he may be vengeful but he is loyal to the end! If there is sedition or corruption, he will root it out!"

"Is that so? A knight of the old order taking command of the Legion?"

Kiathar saw where the man was going but chose to keep

silent. It all seemed beyond him. In five more months his obligation of service to his lord would be up. It was his right as lord of an estate to then return home. Home, where the hard ground alone stood against him, where he paid lip service to no man, where he carved out his own life.

The monk continued, "I am not here to command you, my lords. I only offer counsel. Many days I have seen the Legion march past these lands and I tell you that their might is unmatched! The stamp of their boots is as the rumble of thunder, the might of their arms unequaled. Countless shining spears and bronze helmets! The throw of their javelins is like a thousand lightning bolts! No thing on this earth can withstand them I tell you! Your lord will attempt to harness them. But they have no land, no lord to whom they owe fealty, no code of honor, and now they have no King. They show no mercy. Perhaps they are adorned as were the ancients, our Roman ancestors. But do not be fooled, there is no *dignitas* in them. However, they have one weakness, there is one thing which they fear."

"What can they fear?" came the big voice of the suddenly inquisitive Nordic.

"The truth, knight; That the Legion will be deemed too powerful and disbanded before she reaches her prime; That the First and Third realms will discover that innocents of the Numantine tribe are enslaved daily under the Legion's watch. But most of all that a deep secret will be revealed, for in the bustling streets of Helles crawls some darkness so foul as to poison all Luminares to her roots! And Legionnaires already protect it!"

"Slavery?" wondered Alexus.

"What is this secret you speak of, monk?" questioned the Nordic.

"Perhaps you have also wondered why I live alone in this great monastery? My brothers were killed for trying to discover the Secret. We are ministers of God, we go where He calls us. In desire to minister to the *sick*," the monk eyed Alexus eerily as he spoke the word, "We came to Helles; a city teeming with disease of body and mind. There is a great mountain in the city's center." The monk's words were suddenly chilled with horror. The white of his eyes became smaller beneath the hood as he focused in on the memory. "Ever since the coming of the Legion has its peak been a pinnacle of darkness and fear. I believe the sickness emanates from the mountain. You have not seen the sickness yet," he glanced at Alexus again. "Not much of it," he corrected himself. "When you have stayed in this realm longer, you will see. Day and night, dark smoke rises from the mountain's top. Townsfolk are loathe to venture up its slopes, yet constantly are carts wheeled down its single roadway. On some nights, when the moon is bright, one can see Numantine slaves being force marched up to its peak. They never come down. The brothers, we demanded knowledge about this mountain from the city prefect. When he refused, we defiantly marched up its roadway." The monk shuddered. "I have no desire to recount what horrors then transpired, but needless to say, only I returned."

"You would have us demand our lord heed warning of a mountain in Helles?" Kiathar scoffed. "Perhaps we also should tell him of some other scenery in neighboring towns! I've had enough of the madness of this realm! I have done my duty, I have done what I could to protect the people here. You tell me that the Numantine rebels are no real threat? That the Legion can crush them? Then I can do no more here. If I return to the Count, I will take up my place and do what is required for a short while. My family and estate await me, it is my noble right to return to them after a time!"

The man seemed hurt, but they couldn't tell since he had retreated beneath his cloak and left to walk the main chamber lighting candles. "As I said," he spoke from a distance beside the flicker of fire on wax. "I only offer my counsel; The Count may be in need of friends soon enough. But you are lords and not I, do what you will. I have already said too much, you best leave now, darkness comes." There was an unearthly fear in his eyes.

***

Kiathar put on a stoic face as he came to a stop near a wooden post of the sparring ring. Alexus stood in his shadow. Count Cincinnatus heard them but did not turn. Wood rapped against wood as their master fought an armor clad opponent in mock battle. Cincinnatus maneuvered quickly, parrying a blow here and striking there. His bare back dripped with sweat. Smells of rotting wood and damp hay filled their nostrils. Vincent took a step back and blocked a high blow, following it up with a strike to the opponent's torso. The armor clanged under the force of the oak weapon. Under the helmet, the man snorted and returned with another more powerful high blow. Cincinnatus parried with both hands and then came down hard on the man's neck. The cuirass and helmet caught most of the force, but the opponent still felt a biting sting. Without hesitation, Master Cincinnatus took advantage of the moment and kicked the opponent onto the hay matted floor. He threw his fighting stick down beside him.

"Good fight! Now go find some meat and bread for yourself."

"Yes, master." The man bowed low and left, one hand massaging the wound on his neck. Vincent turned toward the two Equites.

"Sire, we come bearing a message and requesting your orders."

"Am I to excuse your absences as if they did not occur?" the Count wiped sweat from his face with an old hide blanket and began to unbuckle the armor he wore.

"Sire," Alexus took a step forward.

The Count interrupted him, "That I even allowed you to enter these grounds astonishes me. You will both be punished for your insolence!" he stared hard at Kiathar. It seemed to the Nordic knight that he was daring him to say a word or make a move.

"You," he spat, "Nordic, will oversee the care of our steeds with the servants. Alexus, every day you will spar as you have seen me do, until fear is beaten out of you. If you fail in either of these duties, your estates will be penalized in the following harvest season."

"We have a message, *Sire*," Kiathar had a trace of sharpness in his address.

Cincinnatus glared at the Nordic Knight for half a second, "Report."

"We have heard reports from the outskirts of Ptosii that the slave trade has been renewed within Helles, against the kingdom's edicts."

"When I take command of the Legion in a week, I will deal with lawbreakers appropriately. Thank you." Vincent spoke matter of fact and without any gratitude.

Alexus began, "Sire we also heard tales of," Kiathar gave him a look of disgust. He ignored the Knight and continued, "Of a mountain in Helles where some dark conspiracy is kept. People have been murdered for merely walking up its lone road. The Legionnaires protect the mountain and there is reason to suspect their complicity."

"And they shall continue to protect the mountain under my orders. Do you wish to waste any more of my time, knight?" Cincinnatus retorted.

"No master."

"You two are dismissed."

Kiathar stormed out of the wooden building and away, leaving Alexus behind.

"I told you not to go after that outlander." Exander was around the corner waiting.

Alexus kept walking, head hung low.

Exander put his hand around the man's shoulder, "I have many friends in Helles and in the Legion. All will be well for us, you will see."

In those days Alexus did as he was bidden by Vincent and grew strong of body. However, his resolve against the mysterious drink weakened daily. Many acquaintances he made within the Legion under the shadow of Exander Quickfoot. Exander grew in the eyes of the legionnaires and knew of their many rumors and secret meetings. Strangers who delivered the wineskins of the Drink became as friends to Alexus and Kiathar judged him gravely for this and his companionship with Exander. The two spoke never again.

Chapter 8

Oaths, Masks and Pain

SEVEN MONTHS PASSED IN THE LAND. As the monk foretold, the Numantine army was crushed to a man in a single battle. Still Justinian defiantly claimed the throne and still he eluded the wrath of Knight and Legionnaire. The old crown of the King was locked away in Luminares, unworn. Bogged down in a foreign realm which now depended on him alone for rule, Vincent found himself unable to confront his arch enemy, the master of the Keleres, because of civil concerns. His memory of things dear was dimmed and his hate burned as embers beneath a blanket, hidden but bursting into flame without warning.

Slavery spread throughout the kingdom unchecked and as summer came to a close a decree went throughout the realms protecting the bondage of exotic peoples. The vetoes of the Tribunes were totally ignored. "Your praetorian guards should fear the day I return," Vincent wrote to Hydrus in answer to this outrage. The Council of Plebs contented themselves with the hope that their Legate would soon arrive with the Legion at his back. Meanwhile, Hydrus grew fat off the revenue generated by the sale of his cargoes and even some Plebs were pleased with the influx of copper coin from the kingdom's growing trade. Uncertainty filled minds, but the wealth of a kingdom ever quiets a disease of heart.

Iris dried her tears. It was Christmas day! She must be cheerful! Her delicate hands pushed open the hard wood door and she walked proudly down the corridor. Torch in hand she brought light to those dreary passages. Brightness and dancing flame filled the wide hall of the Cincinnatus house. Should it still bear that name? The letters were carved above the mantle of the fire pit. It was but a memory of an age past now. The Cincinnatus masters had not ruled this house in over thirty years! Now counted as royal blood, the Cincinnatus line had better beds upon which to sleep. No matter, this night a feast would be served! Salted pork with roasted apple, fine oatmeal, oiled wheat bread, and plenty of wine to flow while the moon yet shone! The fifty-third estate of the Third Realm had a new master! One rich and gracious, one who was strong yet tender, a lord and gentleman! Iris wiped away another tear. So she dreamed it would be. But it was not so.

How had she come to love this man who would've seized her plantation and thrown its people into the night had she not intervened? Had she seen the good in him and tried to draw it out? He had been proud and handsome no doubt, but she remembered the dark weight of those times. Her people depended on her to survive! She had done what she had to do to carry on! Yet it had been more; a gnawing emptiness, a relentless shadow always a footstep behind and in hard pursuit. It was as if Kati had infected her with his curse before he had left forever! The shadow of her father's silence had been replaced with Kati's absence; Kati's harsh words froze over all memories. It was her frantic surges chipping away futilely at this iron ice that brought collision with Nicephorus Puter. She couldn't remember her thoughts of Nicephorus when they began a life together. *Why not?* she wondered. The *hurt*, however, was recalled all too easily. A pain which hides black beneath cool skin it was; a neediness that consumed all of her life. She had needed Arlen's strength then as she needed it now! She was weak and insufficient! The gait of her walk, the pride of her voice all crumbled away when she saw herself here reflected.

They had met in the Great Feast Hall according to her devices. All the fairest ladies of the realm and the stateliest men had come together for the annual celebration of most extravagant proportions. She had spun the web which was to catch him, though herself she entangled also. All the rumors and messages which had hardened her heart against him faded too quickly. His body and eyes would blot out a cold present, cut away a hurting past.

The lord for his part had no idea whom his eyes had fallen on as the ladies and men paraded about each other and momentarily caught hands in the courtly dance. Just as she planned, his heart fell for her. The most elegant lady in the hall paired with the finest lord. Iris kept this *visage* up as best she could, still fighting back her harsh, uncouth upbringing. Amazement overcame Nicephorus when he realized who his acquaintance was: a servant from a lowly estate. Still, an oath he swore to protect her and the plantation and for months did he abide at her side! His love was real, she felt it! It had to have been! How his desperate appetite raved! At last she was a woman. But not so now. It was all short-lived.

Iris sat in dismay. Silver platters covered the long cedar table. Each shining plate awaited the coming of the servers who would bring the succulent morsels of pork. Beside the dishes were shining goblets thirsting to be filled with the dark luscious wine. The people would drink and be merry and smiling faces would fill the hall. Rubies and sapphire glittered from the goblets at the head of the table where the lord and lady of the estate sat. Lord and Lady always drank first. The fine cups were empty, awaiting celebration. Iris knew her husband's would remain so for the duration of that Christmas celebration. No matter, there would be celebration anyway! Iris stood from her chair and went to find the headmaster. If her husband Nicephorus and his guests would not come, then she would invite the whole estate!

That night the hall was filled and overflowing with guests. The voices of families great and small echoed against the stone. Old men were brought to tears as slow and mellow songs of kin and heritage were sung. Then laughter bubbled up from the hearts of the young as a joyous dance was stamped out by quick moving feet to the accompaniment of flute and drum. The hall was bright with heart pounding life!

Iris kept her mask on tight. This façade of joy was strapped snugly around her smile and about her movements as she jumped into a dance here or spoke to friends there. It formed the words which came from her mouth. *I have them all fooled,* she thought in the corner with a frown creeping back upon her face. Iris covered these thoughts with more wine and looked back out on the tide of happiness before her. *Arlen would see right through me if he were here! Not for one moment would I escape his attention!*

So the feast continued for many hours until at last, he came. Not as a delayed and wearied sojourner did he make his entrance, nor did he bring gifts to amend his delay as an apologetic husband and tactful lord might do. Instead the step of his legs was of a pompous king, and his demeanor said that the guests had intruded upon *him*. All fell silent when his retinue crossed the threshold; a path was made to the head of the table. Iris waited there for him anxiously.

"What is this," Nicephorus looked away from Iris to the crowd, "*rabble* doing here!" he whispered angrily. She could still remember when he would whisper sweet things to her, now no more.

"This *rabble* is your people!" She whispered back, the wine in her blood making her all the more daring.

"HA!" he mocked aloud as he took his seat. A woman dressed in silk and furs pulled the chair out for him and stood by his side. Nicephorus Puter touched the long fingers of the woman's outstretched hand dotingly. Iris watched his motions and wished that it was her that he touched.

"Gerard!" Iris called out after drinking another glass of wine. A handsome man made his way over to the sound of her voice. He had a rough beard around his square chin and along his face. *His features are sharp and hard from the labor of a true man's work*, thought Iris deceitfully. He was a year younger than her, and he was single. "Gerard!" She exclaimed again as he drew near with a broad smile on his face. Iris pulled him closer, beside her and Nicephorus. She walked her fingers up his dark sinewy arm tantalizingly and then hugged him tight with a laugh. It was inappropriate for a lady to be so close to a man, but Iris was sure to hold him there long.

"M'lady?" Gerard questioned, there was confusion in his eyes.

"Oh Gerard, this is my husband Nicephorus!" As she

spoke she looked into Nicephorus' eyes to see if there was any envy. She saw only anger.

"Delighted," Answered Nicephorus dispassionately from his chair, hand still on the woman's.

Iris lost resolve and Gerard, suddenly feeling lost, made his way back into the dancing circle on the floor. Iris did not even notice his going as she stared into the emptiness.

"So where did business take you this month?" she asked Nicephorus blankly.

"To New Antioch, of course! More vineyards have been bought in my name on the city's outlying territories. My tenants, however, were having some trouble with the dispossessed population. The usual. You would have found the trip quite tedious!" he kept his hand on the woman even as he talked to Iris.

"Would I have!" she snapped back. "To the contrary I have taken up a great interest in the vineyards! The amount of wealth brought in by each, how one taxes the..."

"HA!" he mocked. "You have never had any understanding of these things! You sit around here busying yourself with trifles, with stupid silly things! You're a farmhand Iris, and you'll always be one!"

"You underestimate me." She spoke quietly but with a well of anger behind the words. "Gerard!" she called again.

"You forget I saved you from disaster!" He snapped back quite loudly. "Without me you would be nothing! Without me you'd be a scamp crawling in the streets!"

"Gerard! Take me to dance!" She put her hand in his and tried to imagine that Nicephorus had not just insulted her in front of the guests.

"Yes, m'lady." Gerard responded, looking a little more uncomfortable than last time.

"I should have let you rot in the streets!" mocked Nicephorus so that all around could hear. "I could've taken all I wanted by visiting you in the local brothel!"

Iris walked away, hopping to the beat of the music. She could find delight in appearing happy while he writhed in anger.

Perched like a merciless hawk, his eyes spied her from the chair. Even as his wiry fingers stroked the lady wrapped in fur he watched intently, irritably. It was not love or regret he felt. It was not even jealousy, which Iris had hoped to imbue on his stony heart. But hate he felt, and the need to reclaim his power, the upper hand which was his. *How dare she walk away from me!* He could not endure it.

"There has been a mistake!" Nicephorus stood up and declared with a loud voice. "You must all leave at once!"

Iris walked back to Nicephorus with rage in her fists. "How dare you come here and..."

"I am the master of this estate! I will do as I please!"

She slapped him hard on the face and he reeled in shock. Wild murmurs rose up from the exiting crowd.

Nicephorus waited until the rest of the guests had departed.

Then his fist rammed into her jaw, knocking her body to the ground.

She lifted her frame slowly, first with her arms, then her legs. Blood dripped but she held back tears. She wiped the crimson drops from her mouth.

Nicephorus grunted approvingly.

"You are master," she continued. "But one day, Count Cincinnatus will return to this people. And he may wish to reclaim what was once his. Perhaps you should be careful not to bring his wrath upon us on that day."

"You dream, Iris." He sat down and neatly cut out a slice of ham. "I doubt the Count remembers you or this little tract of land. When he gets back, *if* he gets back from that God forsaken realm, he will have far too much to concern him in New Corinth to worry over such a small estate." He began chewing the ham.

A small flame then burned in her chest, which she had not known for countless seasons. She cut into him in a low guttural tone. "You squabble over shining coins and force families off their land. You fill their earth with choking vines. You manage vast dominions and attend fine gatherings but ignore your own people. And you bring back women you can use because you can no longer comprehend love! You take and take! One day it's all going to come back to you!"

"Your wisdom astounds me!" he mocked. "Why did I come back to this rat's hole anyhow?"

"Leave!" Iris screamed. "Your comings and goings mean nothing to me! I only married you for them!" she pointed to the archway where the gathering had left. "So that you wouldn't steal this land and throw them into the night!" How she wished her words were the whole truth! Perhaps then the knife cutting her open from inside would lessen its tortures.

"To think that I saw something more in you. To think that I took *you* as my wife! Now I know why you begged like a hoar to aid in managing my affairs. To keep that rabble!" Nicephorus laughed. "To think that if you had refused my seeds, and the grapes had not been grown, the lot of you would be begging in the streets now!" He smiled vilely. "No one buys grain from the realms any longer. It is all produced in the north by, dare I say it? Numantine slaves. Dirt cheap! Soon this will all be revealed to the likes of you, when the last high council is convened." Nicephorus' eyes faded off into the distance. After a few seconds he looked back at her in disdain, "Without me, you have no vineyard, without a vineyard, you are all lost! Face it, you are quite dependent! *I* have saved your people!"

As though her lungs were ripped out of her body, she could say nothing.

"Which brings me to my business here," he continued. "You've kept on too many hands my dear! And paid hands too! It has cost me a little more than a trifle and my debts will soon be called. No worries however. Those who are relieved will be replaced with slaves from the Second Realm."

Slavery was a nightmare of the past, something she knew of only through the memory of her grandfather's stories.

"But there is no king!" Iris snapped back in disbelief. "Who has authority to revoke our laws?"

"The way of the world is changing, my dear."

"But the people, the farmhands. They have homes here! They will be forced onto the streets! You cannot do this to any of them!"

"I can do what I please! It is the affairs of my estate, dear."

"Don't you call me that!" she snapped back.

"I will call you what I please!" he grabbed hold of her. "You deceived me! You tricked me into marriage with perfumes and fine clothes! You descendant of slaves!" A minute passed, perhaps more, and the touch of his hands became less harsh. "But you are mine and mine you will remain."

That night they shared a bed. His brief love making was rough and distant. Afterwards, she lay awake for hours as he slept. Beneath blankets whose rough edges of worn flax pressed uncomfortably against her, echoes of a silent God convinced her that she didn't deserve better.

***

Evan watched him. It was sickening, the way he looked at her; eyes full of gluttonous desire, dripping with putrid thoughts of abuse, like the green soupy foam at the man's mouth. The man dipped his spoon into the bowl again, this time pulling it out and splashing the muck onto the girl. A grisly laugh protruded from his gut, and the rest of the legionnaires were amused too. Evan wanted to strike the man! He harnessed his anger and leaned back against the portico wall. *This fortress is seething with insolence and depravity! The master should banish these men, purify the legion! If only he could see! All day he mutters of the spreading plague and Justinian's plans! Can he not see what is happening at his very feet! The Order of Knighthood is perishing, being surpassed by fools with swords!*

Her serving done, the woman got up to leave. She hurriedly walked toward Evan and the exit, but a Legionnaire stepped into her way.

"Not so fast Missy." The soldier put his hand along her stomach and pulled her towards himself. She pulled away but another Legionnaire jumped up and took hold of her by the arms. The tray she held fell crashing to the floor as she let out a cry.

"We'll miss you if you leave," the second soldier mocked in a gentle tone. He rubbed his face against the back of her neck, boring into her skin. The other soldier began to grope more of the lady's body and laughs erupted from the table where the soldiers had been seated.

"Let her go!" Evan commanded as he walked out from the shadows to the soldiers.

"Well if it isn't the Legate's little helot! Why don't you go find some metal to polish!" This second soldier, still clutching the woman's hands from behind, let out a loud drunken laugh and continued, "I said get out squire! This is *our* barracks!"

The first Legionnaire, who was in front of the girl, reached out with his right hand to push Evan, but the boy caught his arm with his left hand. In the same motion Evan unsheathed his long knife with his right hand and held it a finger's width from the soldier's neck. He squeezed the soldier's bare arm tightly with his left hand and said aloud, "I say again, let the lady go."

"You're a relic of an age past, squire." Remarked the second soldier as he angrily threw the woman's arms back down. She sped out of the room, whispering a thank you to Evan as she passed by. "I don't know why the Legate keeps you around," he continued to mock. Evan still kept the curved blade up close to the other man's skin. "The whole lot of you, squires and Equites, will be a dead letter of history in another few years! Riding horses on high in that shoddy red armor!" The soldier spat. "Proclaiming yourselves noble and high born! Nobility! HA! The King is dead forever! The crown has crumbled! We are the tomorrow! The Legion, the force of the land!"

"You speak treason, soldier!" Evan gasped. "Another will soon wear the crown. Now revoke your cries and this one will yet be spared!"

"Who will wear the crown? His murderer, Justinian? No, the monarchy is dead, as is the fealty that was borne with it. We are the future, boy, Legionnaires! We come from all over the earth, rich and poor, but no ragtag formation of hastily assembled Equites can stand up to our professional army. When those hundreds of bright spear tips are arrayed in kind, nothing on this earth can stand in our way!"

"Kill him," remarked the first soldier behind the blade.

Evan twisted the man by the hand around backwards and put one arm around his neck so that the whole knife was pressed close to his neck. "You speak awful freely for one so bound!"

"Kill him," the soldier repeated, this time gurgling beneath the weight of Evan's left hand. "He has no friends left to protect him. There will be no one to lament his gorged body. The Equites are gone!" Evan squeezed tighter but he continued. "They have returned to their hearths, as is their *royal* right after a time."

"Sir Strongblade will stand for me!" The name rolled off Evan's tongue like a bugle call and for a split second the hall was silent in fear. Soldiers looked around and over their shoulders. Eyes became set down the long hall of the barracks to the distant dark corners where the Nordic sometimes sat alone. Many a man had Kiathar Strongblade laid low with his fist. He had earned the respect and fear of the Legion, though none understood his mind.

"Kiathar? Kiathar!" The soldier called out in a mocking tone, a little louder as the boy's grip loosened. A few of the other soldiers gave him an angry stare in fear of the wrath he might incur from the Nordic. "He is not here either, boy! Packed his things and left last night."

It was like a stab in the heart for Evan. The soldier saw his chance and wrenched himself free of the boy's grip. He picked up a short sword from the table where he had sat and started for Evan.

His slash was stopped only by his fellow Legionnaires.

"Let me go!" he cried. "His blood is mine!"

"We dare not let you, Macius," spoke one who had jumped up to hold him. "We fear the Legate's anger!"

"Yes, the Master will see, he will know, his spies are everywhere!" remarked another.

"He will whip us all and have us caged for your crime," came a frightened voice.

"Another day, Macius, not when Legate Cincinnatus is here."

The soldier relinquished his fight and merely watched the squire with eyes of hate. Evan backed away slowly, keeping his long knife drawn and eyeing the Legionnaires.

Abandoned.

Fury built up in his eyes now and he was anxious to run back and fight. Half of him wanted to show that Legionnaire what he was made of!

Evan walked up the stone stairs toward the fortresses' court to report to Sir Cincinnatus. The Legion had built the fortress in the midst of the city in defiance of Count Risar. Vincent now denied his incompetent rule outright. But it was a claim to Ptosii's neighborhoods which was never followed up upon. The *plague* had brought delay to Cincinnatus' objectives by crippling the Legion's offensives with ailing soldiers. Only in the impregnable fortress was a Legionnaire truly safe. Keleres assassins waited in every corner of the realm, or so it had seemed over the past few months.

In the upper corridor there was a small and rustic hall before the entrance to the high tower, where the Master resided. Evan walked across the hall's first wide tiles and thirty or more eyes followed his every move. *City dwellers in the citadel of the fortress?!* It was a rare occasion that allowed for such laxness. Evan looked around at the crowd. Invasive smells intoxicated him! The rank vapors were sweet, spicy and putrid all at once! It burned his nostrils and it came from the people! Each one of them sick to the bone!

And then he saw it! Two bloodshot eyes stared angrily at him from near the tower door. The form shook in uncontrollable agony, but the eyes were steady. Suddenly he knew there was some dark secret in those eyes. They blamed the Legion for the pain! Evan reached for his longknife in fear, so ferocious was the gaze. But his hand returned awkwardly to his side as his senses were awakened to a bulky Legionnaire walking toward him.

The muscle-bound soldier pointed a finger to his face, "And what is *your* business here?" he demanded.

Evan looked back at the Legionnaire and fumbled for words. He could still feel the shrouded stranger's searing stare from the line of people next to the door beyond. The pupils were radiating unworldly anger and pain. He sat without moving, but Evan could feel his clenched fists and taste the infested sweat dripping from his brow. Evan knew it was *his own* fault. Knew that somehow, *he* through his part in the Second Realm, was responsible for their disease, guilty! It was like a bedroom doorway which one can only feel in the dark yet is immediately recognizable to touch. The doorway of this man's eyes was to an agony unheard of.

Evan swallowed hard and answered, "I am the Legate's squire. I have come to report."

The soldier lowered his outstretched hand, "Humph, you again eh. Move along then, and be quick about it. There's enough folk waiting around as things stand already!" The Legionnaire invitingly stretched out his hand to the door in mockery.

Evan shuddered as he passed the stranger and crossed the threshold. Four more guards stood post at the top of the winding steps. These were not regulars, but elites hand chosen for this purpose. They bore the Count's crest of sword pierced star on their gauntlets and stood nearly seven feet tall. Yet they were not natives of the Third Realm, but rather had been the personal guards of Count Risar of the Second Realm before Vincent had seized the title. Throwing Risar out into the cold of night, Vincent increased the wages of Risar's household retinue and kept them on duty. So easily did such men change allegiance! It made Evan uncomfortable. The four guards recognized him, but eyed him suspiciously as he was allowed to pass into the chamber.

White robed men stood silently before a great stone throne, leaning towards the darkly cloaked figure which sat upon its heights. Crimson red fabric flowed across broad shoulders and veiled the cold stone around the figure. Clenched fingers crumpled a parchment and a stern face stared off into the unknown. The thin white figures stood perched, waiting for an answer. Like birds waiting for a massive dog to be finished with his meat, they were dwarfed by the Master's presence. Evan had walked in on something important. The master had noticed his entrance, but paid the squire no heed. Evan felt insignificant in this gathering of what must've been very powerful men. He took heart; *I still have my part to play at my master's side. I am responsible!*

Sir Cincinnatus, Count by blood to the Third Realm and by force to the Second, Commander of the most powerful army to walk the land, Tribune of five tribes and Knight of the Red Cloth, the most supreme man in the kingdom, lifted his head slowly. All in the chamber watched him, transfixed. He put the document he held to the orange flame of a nearby candle. The parchment lit up in his hand and crumpled in on itself. Seconds of intense silence passed. All stared at the flickers of light. Fire licked the flesh of his fingertips, but Cincinnatus didn't flinch. He was cold as death. The Master slackened his fist and blackened embers slipped from between his fingers and floated slowly to the rock floor.

"The High Council would tie our hands behind our backs," came his brooding voice from the throne. "And send us thus hindered, to fight!" There was a deep guttural fury in the Master's voice, something unknown to the squire before these dark times. "The powers that rule this kingdom," the Legate continued, "Are plainly in disarray. The High Council no longer speaks of its free will. But the Praetor will regret his demands when my troops finally seize his trading ports. The whole of the Legion will continue its preparations to march on Helles. That letter," the Legate pointed to the ashes at his feet, "Councilors, advisors and my fellow Tribunes, never arrived at this fortress!"

Evan suddenly felt the Master's smoldering gaze sear into his eyes and he knew that he was party to something more momentous than he could imagine.

"It is our duty to vanquish the betrayers," he continued. "The pretenders who called themselves Keleres. Yet we cannot do this while the seafarers make raids on the peoples across the realm. Or while plague spreads from their foreign ships. I do not need the words of my fellow Tribune to know the effects of this plague. It has injured my Legion dearly already." There was an anxious pause as the Master eyed one of the robed men darkly.

The Legate continued, "As the new sovereign of the Second Realm, I cannot leave this land in chaos. Count Risar could not, or would not stop the insurrectionists. In doing so he abdicated his rights to rule. This realm's problems have now become my problems. The Maleficus have fled entirely from their outposts throughout the realm. Their residence is now solely in Helles, where they have killed or captured my entire Sixth Century of Legionnaires." Cincinnatus stood now.

As the gold laced folds of his cape fell away from his shoulders to his back, Evan saw the glint of his black and silver breastplate. *He no longer wears the armor of a knight.*

Vincent's voice became louder, "I will take my Legion into the heart of Helles and there stamp out house by house, block by block, these criminals and thieves. Furthermore every household infected with plague will be burned to the ground, regardless of inhabitant! Only then, when the land is rid of this foreign infestation, will I be freed from these crowds of pleading peasants!" The Master threw his hand towards the door and staircase down to the waiting chamber. "No more will I hear of this plague!" Evan could feel the tension in the air at the mentioning of the disease. "This foul curse of the mind and body, which putrefies the flesh, burns the eyes and possesses the spirit, will be no more! For I am sure that it is these foreign Nordics that have brought the putrescent infestation upon us! When they have been crushed and Helles is purified, you will see it disappear. You will see the greatness of my ruling hand."

The clean, white robed men with their oiled hair, swallowed hard at the mere mention of the plague. It was a nightmare still on the fringe of their consciousness. They would rather ignore its ravages and hope it forsake them.

"When this is done," the Legate's voice rose. "Then will I have a free hand to cut down Justinian, the King of Lies!"

"And what of bringing order and the rule of law to my people?" the Tribune he had eyed earlier broke in. "Will you abandon them when you have this traitor in sight? Or leave them behind after you have severed his head and are free to return to your own realm and lands? If you attempt to rule the two realms at once, the Second will surely get the worse end of the deal. How can we trust you?" the Tribune scoffed, and the others wondered at his daring. "You who are a foreigner yourself to this realm! You who, had we not fallen into such desperate times, would be called Usurper!"

Vincent smiled darkly, "Plans are already set in motion, Tribune, for over one hundred fortresses such as this one in which you stand, to be constructed throughout the realm."

The robed men gasped in disbelief. Not even a Luminarian King had undertaken a project so vast in a century! The Tribune would have nothing of it however, "Impossible!" he retorted. "Where are the workers and the silver to pay them! It would take more supplies than the Second Realm has been able to come upon in--"

"What you fail to see, fellow Tribune," the Master interrupted, "Is due to the snobbish manure poisoning your eyes. Ample supplies were sent for from stores in the Third Realm before I even stepped into the Second Realm. And the Legion, my distinguished guests, will accomplish the feat. The Legion, *is* the arm of the kingdom here. Is *my* arm, and it will act swiftly."

The Tribune tried to mask his surprise. "I misjudged you m'lord, forgive me. But I do not trust these Legionnaires," he came back in a cowed tone. "They are not like your kind. Not like the Equites, Count. They have no families of their own, nor the marks of hands that have worked the land." The Tribune waited for an answer from the shrouded face before him and shuddered when he received none.

The silence was finally broken, "They will do what they are told," came a final and cold response. "We march in two days time. Battle orders have been sent out to each centurion already. Consider this council now dismissed!"

One by one the robed figures walked out the door and down the hard stone steps until the master and his squire were alone. Evan eyed the ashes at his master's feet nervously and couldn't hold back a surge of curiosity. "Did the High Council order my lord to retire the Legion?"

"So have they been led to believe." The Count motioned to the door where the men had only just left.

"But in truth there is more?" questioned the boy.

"They ordered your master to relinquish control over all but two centuries of the Legion and then return to Luminares for a meeting of the High Council. Furthermore, the Plebs' addendum ordered me to turn over Count Risar's powers to the Tribune you just saw in here."

"Perhaps we have done what is right, master. For it as you say, we cannot abandon these people to anarchy and division."

"I know what I have done! The Praetor fears the Legion now that it is wholly mine and he dares to withdraw his support! He and the Plebian councilors presume to remove my rule from the Second Realm forever! I would rather have my hand on a sword and have ten enemies than hold scrolls in council with five enemies at my back!"

"Yes m'lord, but it is better to face defeat with an upright walk than to gain victory hunched over in shame." He knew the words were bold, but well spoken. Evan braced himself for a harsh response.

"You converse as one aged in years, squire." The Legate's

response was cool but unsympathetic. "But you are young and have not seen much of the world. The Nordic tribes here will be annihilated and Justinian the betrayer killed. Only then will I return to the First Realm."

"Only be careful you do not become what you set out to destroy, master."

The Legatus Legionis stared down Evan darkly at this. Then, without a word, he returned to the throne and set to work. Evan exited quietly.

***

It was an exultant hour in the lighted regions of Luminares at twilight; a time of food, love and song. Revelry occupied the minds of the people and drunken laughter paraded the streets. Yet in dark corners, the Beast lurked. A few tribal leaders still called it by this name, for its lore had been passed through the generations. Ages ago the same Beast had fed upon the royal ancestors across the sea. It was told that its fangs were the red blood of young thieves, its mouth the watering saliva of addiction, its muscles the sweat of slaves, its stomach the skin of a thousand starving poor, its talons the charm of a hundred prostitutes. The Beast's name was Depravity and day after day it tore its own flesh apart. Each part bled and oozed as the other's tore into it endlessly. Each day the Beast grew to full form again and more. Tribal leaders whispered that its dominion had spread from the Second to the First realm.

Nicephorus Puter tossed the coins between his hands. They gave a jingle that felt sweet in his ears. "It's not enough," he said, pressing the silver back in the trader's palm. "I offer you twelve able bodied males and sixteen females and that's all you can come up with? PAH!" Nicephorus threw one hand in the air in disgust, with the other he reached for a wineskin from under his cloak.

"What you offer me are twelve males who can hardly be sold in the market!" shot back the exasperated trader. "No lord in this kingdom will buy a Skilurus male. There's already a surplus of Numantines for heavy labor! Now the females, they can be sold.

Many places will buy them. I take the males off your hands as a favor, you should be happy with what I have given you!"

Nicephorus took a swig of the wine and swallowed hard. He watched as the last rays of daylight disappeared beyond the horizon. "Perhaps I would be happy with, say, four more silver pieces."

The trader reached angrily into his sack and pulled out more shiny round coins and stuffed them, along with the rest, back into Nicephorus' hand.

"You have robbed me in this I tell you!" Nicephorus pointed his laden hand at him. "I may never deal with you again!"

The trader grunted in response and stormed off. Nicephorus turned, took another drink and smiled to himself as he turned the silver over in his hand. A lady's gown swished in his ears. He turned to spy a wealthy maiden pass him on her way down the dark street. Night was coming. Nicephorus knew he was in luck. Pulling his mare behind him, he patted his own hair down and hurried up to the lady.

"Such a fine lady shouldn't be roaming down these streets alone."

"Oh I fear that I am lost Sir!"

"Then I must help you find your way!"

With a hand on her chest she leaned her head back in relief. "Oh thank you kind sir!" she exclaimed. "I was in the market searching for my sister. She had been out to buy a ring. I *told her* to send a servant," the lady made a look of disgust. "But she would not listen to me! A stubborn girl! Why should she act this way?" the lady questioned as if her new friend could answer. "Our family is full of stubborn people, my father not the least. He shall be very angry if I am not back on the manor soon!"

"And where do you hail from my dear?" Nicephorus moved a little closer to her.

"I live on the west side of the city. We came to the east side only because she, my sister that is, had heard of a golden ring of great value in these parts. Rumor had it that it belonged to one of the lords who were recently executed! Oh it was so exciting I just had to come!" the lady squeaked with enthusiasm and smiled at Nicephorus.

"Well my lady, all will be of good accord in no time. Trust in my care! I am Nicephorus Puter, ruler of the village of New

Antioch and lord of many vineyards, I know a good person when I meet them and I will not see you come to harm!"

"Oh thank you Master Puter!" the lady wrapped her arms around him and Nicephorus smiled at her directness. She giggled, "Forgive my openness! Daddy always corrects me for that!"

"It's quite alright my lady. But what is your name?"

"Oh! I haven't told you! I'm so sorry, I am the lady Sara of the House of Selker."

"Well, dear Sara, I am afraid that we will not be able to make it to your abode this night. There are thieves and bandits about in these parts. Yet have no fear for we will find an innkeeper and come morning we will ride nonstop to your manor!"

"Oh my poor father will be so worried!"

"There, there now," he patted her back. "He will understand when you have returned. Now up you go," Nicephorus lifted her up onto the horse. Another broad smile reached across his face as he pondered the night's adventures. The smile melted from his face when he saw a multitude of torches and the Praetor himself staring down at him. The Praetor's henchmen blocked the road. The guards carried wooden clubs at their sides, ready to beat down anyone who insulted the Praetor or crossed his path. Nicephorus hid his mortified expression and feigned delight.

"Why, the great and noble Praetor! He who has brought light and law to this tired land!"

"Spare me, Nicephorus Puter." He looked at the girl.

"Lady Selker, get down," Nicephorus commanded.

"But I thought we were going to find a place to sleep!" she demanded in confusion.

"Indeed you did, but that is not possible now." He pulled her off the horse.

"But the night is dark and I fear bandits, Master Nicephorus."

"LEAVE NOW!" he screamed and she stumbled off crying.

"I see that you have not lost your touch with fair maidens." Remarked the Praetor dryly.

Nicephorus was not amused, but he forced on an air of flattery. "What does the Praetor desire of his humble servant?"

"You know you are about to become a wanted man?" Hydrus circled the wine seller.

"The Praetor, jokes, I am a law abiding subject in this Kingdom."

"Citizen, wine seller, you are a citizen, our King is fallen."

"Yes, Praetor. It had slipped my mind. I —"

"It seems a great many things slip from your mind. For starters, paying your dues. You are the most wealthy plantation owner in the Kingdom and you set this example?"

"Dues Praetor?" Nicephorus pretended to be confused. "Oh you mean the new taxes! Yes I just sent a shipment to the capital! It will be here most any day."

"Nicephorus, how is it that you reached the city before the shipment?" the Praetor questioned from behind the taller wine seller. He enjoyed seeing such men tremble before him.

"Uh, Praetor, it was, that is, I sent the command by courier."

"Must've slipped your mind, just like the instructions that you received regarding those lords." One of the Praetorian guards uncovered his club and stepped closer to Nicephorus.

"Praetor! I ordered the plantations to cease giving tribute to those lords! I told them, Praetor!"

"Then they have disobeyed your commands and you must find new headmasters!"

"Praetor, these lords are Equites, with steed and arms. One cannot expect mere peasants to disobey their lords, they have nothing to defend themselves with."

"Then arm them!"

"Many of them are loyal, Praetor, much blood will be spilt."

"That cannot be helped."

"Yes, Praetor." Nicephorus put his hands together and squeezed them nervously. "It will be done." Nicephorus took a deep breath then, trying to regain some semblance of calm. "Praetor, this has been a great honor and surprise and I thank you for reminding me on these matters. They will be remedied immediately I assure you." He tried to back out of the circle that the Praetorian guard had formed around him.

"Nicephorus, it seems you have forgot something."

"Aha! That memory of mine! Always forgetting! What have I forgot now?"

"Did you not just complete a trading of slaves?"

"Oh, yes Praetor, but they were not foreigners. They were

my own property, they are not included in the slave tax."

"They were your own hands eh? Ruthless. Yet still taxable, scribe what does the law read?" Hydrus motioned to a short man carrying a sack of scrolls and books.

The man ruffled through some papers and hastened to find the right page in a handsomely inscribed book. "The law according to the Council's five hundred and sixty second declaration reads, he who shall sell or buy slaves of any race is entitled to do so, except when pertaining to those restrictions listed hereunder or by further declaration of the Council. The seller is subject to a one in ten deduction to be paid in silver to the authorities in Luminares."

"Thank you scribe." Remarked Hydrus triumphantly. "Those slaves were worth at least twenty pieces of silver, therefore you owe two."

"But Praetor, I only received fifteen pieces!"

"I have had just about enough with you! Your forgetfulness and insolence trouble me!"

Nicephorus handed over the silver regretfully.

"Farewell Master Nicephorus!" the Praetor and his cronies continued their walk down the road.

Nicephorus frowned and took a turn down a brightly lit alley to find a nearby inn. This was the part of town full of energy and life! So Nicephorus thought to himself. People were everywhere even though the night had come. Traders blanketed the street with their yells, demanding attention to their merchandise of exotic pleasures: sweet delicacies of sugar, herbs which made the mind waddle in a fit of giddiness, the pleasures of women for a single silver piece. Some also said the Drink from the Second Realm was bartered in these parts. *Is it possible its essences are mixed with wines from my very own vineyards?* The thought excited him.

A great black marble building with one pointed tower stood in the midst of shacks and its lonely spire reached into the night and blotted out the stars. A chill breath reached out from the black silhouette. Nicephorus had never seen it before and hurried as he passed by. White eyes stared at him from the darkness of the building's surrounding hovels. The eyes had the look of worms and lesser creatures. Nicephorus turned his head forward and walked away from the menacing black house, but warm hands stopped him. Slender feminine fingers reaching and tickling, felt his body, reached down his cloak. "Come, the night is cold," inviting voices pleaded. "You deserve all the pleasures of this world," they said. "You will not have known them until you come inside," the other added. "It is warm and well lit within our halls, friend."

He was pulled back to the dark edifice slowly, neither trusting the voices nor willing to pull himself away from their touch. These were not poor and dirty prostitutes; these were vibrant, beautiful girls with warm skin, silk cloaks and shining jewels! Light shot out from inside as the door opened. Nicephorus knew where he would spend the night now! A strange man with a white painted face greeted him kindly.

***

Hydrus' remaining visits were scheduled. Many a man groveled and crawled to him that night, as landowners, officials and lords did regularly in those times. When the day's work was nearly done, the Praetor and his guards came to the loudest section of streets. Hydrus entered the predetermined brothel alone. There was yelling and off color singing from forty men or more. Beautiful women clad in low fitting, loose blouses and flowing dresses paraded between seats or on top of tables carrying rum, wine, bread and other spirits. A great racket it was! Smiles were all about and laughter too, except for here and there where things had long since spun out of control. Hydrus looked about in dismay. *How am I to find him in such a place?*

"Why it's an honor, Praetor!" came slurred speech from a stranger. "You who stood up against the King's betrayers are saluted!" he nearly fell on the Praetor as he walked by.

"Yes and we have grieved his death long enough. Luminares must not fall prey to inaction in the throes of mourning," Hydrus responded curtly.

Rum dripping off his shoulder, he searched the place for the wretched individual. *This is humiliating! Invited alone to a strange place! Why do I ever listen to that man!* But Hydrus knew why, and just as he thought this he saw him sitting in a corner. Hydrus marched over, unafraid to show outwardly his anger.

"I've had quite enough of meeting in such places, from now on our meetings will be on my terms," Hydrus grumbled.

"Very well, Praetor. In one month's time report a place to my acolytes in the black palaces and I will come there," spoke a low voice from behind a black hood.

"Good! Now to business, where are your promised shipments? My servants in the northern ports say that they have had little business of late."

"Patience, Master. If things hadn't gone ill in the Second realm of late, my acolytes would have served up plenty. The Keleres remain a nuisance and there are other matters."

"I know, that damned Cincinnatus was too slow! But this will be resolved. I had the Legate recalled to the First Realm. If he is unable to find and defeat Justinian Soli, then the Council will find someone else who can! Besides, I tire of his insolence."

"He has not left as you promised," remarked the hooded man with anger held at bay.

"How do you know this? I received no such news!"

"There are many in my following."

"You speak of the acolytes from your inns?"

"Some are closer to the Legate than even your spies."

Hydrus was dumbfounded. "How close?" he demanded.

"Very," he answered with finality.

"He left the Sixth Century of Legionnaires to your protection. Surely a whole century is sufficient protection! Who could be troubling you?"

"The Legionnaires performed admirably before, they allowed the Maleficus to gather the bodies we needed and kept the villagers off our backs. But things are changing of late with Legate Cincinnatus. He will not leave. Nay, he draws all the Legion to himself. The Sixth Century no longer guards my mountain. Your pawn Bassus has them manning the city's defenses."

Hydrus remembered his instructions to Bassus. *If he attempts to interfere with my trade in any way or tries to remove the Sixth from my mountain, stop him!* "If that upstart Cincinnatus wants civil war, then that's what he'll get!" he boomed at the hooded man.

"The Sixth Century will not be enough," he answered dryly.

"Bassus commanded the Legion for years. It will not fight against him!"

"Bassus is a pig! His men never respected him! But he is more *clever* than I imagined," the hooded man laughed pitifully. "He has invited the fleeing Nordic warriors into Helles' city walls! The whole city is in chaos and fear now! So you see," began the hooded man again. "Without the collectors available for work, we are left without provisions, leaving you without shipments. I have been forced to take certain precautions."

"That are wholly unnecessary, no doubt!" Hydrus fumed. "The situation is well under control, Octar. With or without this Malefican rabble, I have but to spring the trap and this whelp, Sir Cincinnatus will be crawling at my feet."

The hooded servant made no comment.

"Will the shipments be there for my men to pick up from the base of the mountain?"

"I can promise nothing."

After a long pause, Hydrus questioned, "What will it take?"

"I have many," Octar paused, "*Inns* throughout Helles and the Second Realm. They can gather the necessary provisions from the lower tiers of the populace and bring them to the Mountain."

"It must go unnoticed. I don't want to hear of a Patrician councilor's relative being abducted!"

"No!" The hooded man waved his hand in dismissal. "Of course not! Only the broken and forgotten!"

"So the shipments will be on time?"

"They will be there, this time, master."

Hydrus slipped a sack of silver coins to the man, "They better be! I am finished here." Hydrus stood to go.

"Master!" there was anger beneath the black cloak. "You have not heard the complaint I said I would mention."

"Oh what now?" Hydrus refused to sit again.

"My shamans and acolytes have been bearing themselves against unwarranted persecution here in the First Realm. I ask where is your promise of freedom for my followers? Or is this yet a land in thralldom to the condemning aspects of the past?"

With a look of frustration Hydrus responded, "I have had

quite enough with these incidents as well. Your inns have brought commerce and excitement to the realm! There is nothing wrong with either of these! The people of this kingdom will not be held under the grip of any tyrant. They will be free to go and do what they please and to worship who they see fit. This shall end now, you have my word."

"Aww, your word, and what is that worth?" the man chuckled darkly.

"What is your meaning by this Octar?" Hydrus demanded.

"It is nothing Master, I believe that it will be done."

"Do not try my patience with all these things again! I have some affinity for your kind, I respect the power of your crafts. But my forgiveness only goes so far."

"Many pardons, Praetor."

That same month, Hydrus, the most powerful of all Praetors in Luminares' history, completed his weeding out of the powers in a final High Council. It had begun with Gaius, after the fleeing of the Keleres. Now his rage had grown. There was no man who would stand up against him. But in his heart he shared a secret fear of Vincent. Would this boy whom he had used for his own devices overturn his plan after all? He had usurped governorship of the Second Realm more readily than Hydrus would've guessed. Now he ruled two of the Land's realms with an iron fist! Hydrus had had much difficulty in wresting troublesome nobles out of the Third Realm already. Spies and warriors had constantly beset his Praetorian Guard as they went about their business. Cincinnatus' voice was noisy and reckless in the councils, even from afar. Virtually the whole Plebian side of the council was won to his side by his vehement letters. Hydrus had not even been able to pass an edict terminating Cincinnatus' command of the Legion without granting continued control of at least two centuries! The dirty tillers of the land and the tribes of many foreign breeds preferred this bastard's hand to the Praetor's.

When a courier arrived from the usurper Count Cincinnatus with a message full of fiery threats and a refusal to relinquish command, Hydrus had had enough. The Praetor prepared for the High Council. It would thereafter be called the

Great Betrayal by the Plebs. Idealistic to the bitter end, the Plebian tribunes and councilors assembled at the call of need and one by one the Praetorian Guard beat them to death in the streets of Luminares. The Council was purified of all Tribunes but one, and his time would come soon.

Hydrus reveled over the ease with which his edicts then became law. Copies in parchment were issued to all the great city centers and to the governor's mansions of each realm. Hydrus' fellow Patrician councilors listened well to his spell binding speeches of liberty, trade and wealth. Henceforth men and women would be unhindered in doing as they willed in all things but theft and murder. Even with their bodies they could make earnings in silver if possible! The worship of foreign gods would be protected. It was repelling to be afraid of what was new or merely different! People who practiced the arts of magic could now do so publicly. Most importantly, the inns with black spires, the cultist's miniature palaces, would be allowed unlimited access across Luminares. For anyone who knew anything knew that these were the most fashionable places to spend the night in all three realms!

Those who believed against these edicts were breakers of the law. All citizens of Luminares were free to do as they willed, but those who taught close minded and backward traditions against these things were treasonous. All were now citizens, and nevermore subjects. The King was beyond return and there was no suitable heir to wear the crown, Hydrus told them. It was time to move on, to build to greater heights and to grasp the people's full potential!

Chapter 9

Dungeons of Three Souls

ALEXUS HUNG HIS HEAD LOW and stared at his feet. The
Legionnaire behind him pulled the rope round his neck taut as he
leaned. He felt himself despicable. He was not worthy to stand in
his master's presence.

"You have failed me for the last time, lord Alexus, knight
of the Red Cloth."

"Send me to the front, Lord, let me die in battle!" Alexus
managed to beg in a raspy voice.

"Savor those words which I have pronounced, for no
longer shall you bear either title. No, a death in battle is too
honorable for you now. You shall be stricken from this court as a
beggar. Homeless and without a single possession you will be cast
out to rot away the remainder of your years in agony. Nor may
you set foot in the Third Realm again or death will surely answer
your call."

Alexus stumbled to the stone floor, the fall bruising his
knees badly. The Legionnaire behind him tried to pull him up, but
Alexus stubbornly refused, laying his body on the floor. He did not
look up to meet his master's eyes, but spoke to the cold stone
floor, "Master, all that you pronounce against me is just. Only
spare the people of my land, my lady and family. When their lord
is cast down, surely all their livelihood will be confiscated. Don't let
the wine sellers and Patrician councilors take any more land from
the Third Realm!"

Now Alexus' words, as lowly and untrustworthy as they
had become of late, troubled Vincent. For he had heard other

rumors from councilors and spies of these spreading powers in the Third Realm. Despite the warnings, his mind had been occupied with pressing the advantage against the Maleficus and Keleres until this point. Yet Vincent's wrath was already hot and hate for Alexus had taken deep root so that any thought of mercy he might have had, he quickly pushed aside. "Take him away!" was Vincent's command, and so it was done. Two Legionnaires dragged and kicked him out of the hall. Two others enthusiastically rushed off to plunder the former Knight's belongings. Three couriers were sent out: one to notify Vincent's regent in the Third Realm, another to record the change with the authorities in the capital and the last to tell Alexus' household of their sorry fate.

Alexus cursed himself even as the Legionnaires tore his red cloak off and beat him. He knew he deserved every bit and more for what he had done. He did not try to block the blows nor did he scream and yell, though he could not help but groan from their ferocity. Left in nothing but a loincloth, the Legionnaires kicked him out of the tower and onto a precipice above the main gate. Alexus pulled himself up and leaned his back against the wall. Out from the tower came another man, this one in armor that shone red like dark blood in the twilight. He was a Knight and with a red hot iron he abolished the mark of brotherhood from Alexus' shoulder. The timeworn tradition was kept sacred even here, even in the Second Realm, in the midst of war, in a fortress of the Legion. Alexus could not wear the mark a moment longer since he had betrayed his brothers and stole from them. All the work of the Trials was for naught! In his desperation, in his hour of need, he had given in and failed! Not a tear did Alexus shed, he knew his fate. Yet when he stood, wavering from the pain, he saw the jagged rocks below. Looking down he was entrapped.

He could jump and end it now.

I am alone. He thought, and even the thinking bore pain.

The spires and deadly spikes of earth's stone swam up to meet him. He saw himself meeting his doom and then he leaned forward and lifted his knee.

But a fire arose within Alexus' bone, maybe it had been born of old in the Trials, maybe it was conjured up on that spot. Either way its flames licked clean the putrescence leaking from his beating heart. *I will make it right somehow! I will repay the wrongs I have committed! The Count will see my deeds and be content!* A new light sprung up in him then, weak and feeble, even pathetic, but it would not die out until its will was accomplished.

Alexus rushed down the fortress stairs, clutching his side the whole way. Many of his ribs were broken, but he refused to groan from the pain. He knew exactly where he had seen it last. Alexus hobbled down an alley hoping not to be seen and embarrassed. Past the third tower he stopped at the spot of a few moldy barrels. Reaching deep down into one, he pulled it out. It was a long brown cloak some Legionnaire had disposed of. A rat came squealing out with the clothes and he had to shake the thing off. Alexus wrapped the cloak around his all but naked body and made for the ledger's office at the front gate.

A fire was burning inside, bringing warmth to the room. Alexus waited. His eyes turned to the dark gray smoke traveling up the tower to a hole in its roof. *So much of my life; wasted now.*

"That will do for now, Recruit! Just make your mark here and you're but a step away from being a Legionnaire!"

"How long will initial training last before I am given a real post?" asked the teenager in front of the desk.

"You just make your mark and the training station will take care of you lad." There was a hint of exasperation in the Legionnaire's voice.

"Alright, I'll do it!" responded an excited voice.

"Good! Now, Duplicarian!" the Centurion called one of his junior Legionnaires.

"Yes, Centurion?"

"See this young recruit out and then get my things."

"But Centurion, there is one more!" the young Legionnaire pointed to Alexus.

"Curses be on you, Duplicarian, I thought you had closed the gate!"

"No, Centurion."

"Well." the Centurion gave a nod for him to get on it.

"Well what, Centurion?"

"Well, see the recruit out and close the gate, boy!"

"Yes, Centurion!" the Legionnaire moved frantically.

"With any luck you'll outrank the Duplicarian in three months, recruit!" he yelled after them as the door closed. "Now come here, man." He motioned to Alexus hurriedly. "What is your business here?"

"I wish to fight in the upcoming battles in Helles!"

"Why you! Who told you such a thing! Where did you hear word that the Legion was marching?"

"With such a vast and powerful force, it is only a matter of time before the whole world knows, Centurion." Alexus hoped the man didn't recognize who he really was.

"Umm, yes. I suppose." He was still dumbfounded. "Well you might catch the tail end after training. That is if we don't make short work of the Numantine hideouts! HA!" The Centurion was amused at himself but Alexus was still too serious.

"Give me the papers, I wish to make my mark."

"Very well, my good man. I'm in a hurry as well."

Alexus walked into the night hanging onto a strand of purpose. *Can God even use unworthy wretches such as me for any good?!* The fire in his heart was burning low and he longed for a soft bed and the chance to forget. *To forget about everything in this world, oh how sweet a thing!* The thirst overtook him then, and it could not now be sated except with the blood red elixirs of the poison. Even in his subconscious he had planned for an event such as this. He tasted the sweet nectar in his mind as he hurried down the steps to the cellar. It was a dungeon of forgotten things. Crates and sacks there were aplenty, but nothing of use. Broken swords and rotten wheat littered a wet floor. Alexus crawled into a far corner, the only human to lurk in that dark place. Here he was safe, he would not be discovered. Neither would his treasure of Drink and the silver he stole to buy it. Oh yes! The coveted substance! How his body ached for it! Sweat poured down his arms and chest and his eyes burned with a hurtful flame. Every limb, every nerve called out for the juice, the foreign wine! He drank!

It set in slowly, first relieving his pain and then evoking pleasures of insanity. He breathed it in, he gulped it down, felt it in his fingertips and in his toes. After some time he lied down, the strange fluids taking control of his muscles. Relinquishing his

control of self, he felt wonderful. A climax came and then faded slowly. And before it was gone he saw his family thrown from his home into the streets in a vision pure and clear, a mocking gift from the Drink with which he had poisoned himself! He was chained somewhere above them, unable to move, unable to help as they too were thrown into darkness. Powerless.
I cannot come. I'm sorry.
I'm no good, he thought, and then it turned to a whisper out loud. "I'm no good!" and tears finally came.
And he was forgotten, in his dungeon.

***

Iris grappled the silver brush and pulled it through her hair. Dark locks and curls straightened under the force of her pulls. She knew he liked her hair straight. That brush was the finest ornament she had owned at the time Nicephorus had given it to her, and she loved it. Horses neighed on the other side of the velvet carriage wall. Rocky ground threw the carriage to and fro, but she was almost to the vineyard and Nicephorus would be waiting. She hurriedly began to apply to her face and arms the powders and oils that she had just bought. The fragrance filled the carriage until the coachman himself could smell her from outside. Scents of luscious pomegranates and spiced herbs permeated her fine tanned skin and sunk into the purple seats and drapery. Iris removed an old rusted mirror from her breast. It was one of the few items from the old farm that she had held onto. It was the most prized heirloom of her pauper parents. Looking in the glass, she put little drops of the oil on her face, she frowned. Dark purple still remained from a bruise.
Did he really hit me there? No, that was a different man. A side of him that occasionally creeps out, but has now been put away for good. He is enduring much stress in these times. Affairs of his estates require him to travel across all three realms! He will be tired when I find him and I will have to put away my own selfish needs and be caring!
She put the mirror back and sat contently as they passed by green vineyards that stretched out beyond the horizon.

Three servants aided Iris as she entered the fine home. An enclosed garden shaded by a roof of clay and wood pillars protruded from the front of a flat house. She was still not used to all the attention that the servants happily gave her.

"Bring me to the room where your master is," she requested politely.

"We beg your pardon my lady, but he has not yet arrived," they answered.

She immediately dismissed the servants and began exploring the building alone. When Iris tired of being confined under roofs, she found herself roaming the fields as she had once done as a headmaster of servants. She marveled at the vineyard, which was more lush and expansive than any she had seen in the Third Realm.

It was as she walked between the vines that Iris came upon Golro, a poor brute descended from peoples of the outer lands. A mix of the Numantine and Nothus was his blood and by great misfortune he had lost his small shop in the City of Burning Light, Luminares. He now spent his days begging on roads and in churches, and stealing what fruit the earth offered up. With great trembling Golro dropped a handful of grapes and bowed at her approach. He feared that she was some Lady of great nobility come to rebuke his thievery, for her raiment was fair and her manner of walk majestic. But Iris was moved with great pity for the man. Knowing instantly that his livelihood was a pitiful one of begging, she procured a sack of silver from her belt. Without a thought of deliberation she gave him the whole treasure. A great amount it was in fact for any man poor or rich, but she gave freely without any expectation of return.

By some ill chance Nicephorus at that very moment came speeding down the road on horseback. Seeing her handing out such a large sum of silver, his heart was overcome with greed and anger. With a fell swoop of his riding stick he knocked the beggar to the dirt.

"Who is this scamp who takes my earnings?"

The raggedly dressed stranger got up from the ground and held out the sack. "I meant no guile, Sire, and will give back all," he answered fretfully.

"No," broke in Iris. "What I gave was mine to give freely!" She pushed the sack of silver back to the man. "Take and leave."

Nicephorus stared at her angrily.

As soon as Golro thought he could escape the mounted lord, he sprinted back into the vineyard, clutching the silver tight to his breast. "YIP-YA-AY! I'm free again!" His screams of joy loosed a flock of frightened crows and the black birds flew low over Nicephorus.

Nicephorus shook his head with cold wrath and galloped away.

Iris found him alone later that night with a strange paleness over his face. His hands shook and there was a hungry look in his eyes as though he were staring across a thousand leagues.

"I need the drink!" he demanded in a whisper.

Iris looked at him questioningly and walked closer. "This is a vineyard, dear. We have wine aplenty." Her hand jumped at the feel of his sweat soaked blouse.

"No. There is none here. You don't understand."

His quivering intensified and Iris cradled him against her bosom. *He is mine again*, she thought. So tight he squeezed her that for a moment she feared he was dying and ordered the headmaster to fetch a physician.

"No! Nothing can be done for it!" Nicephorus rebuked her between gasps.

In time, the attack stopped and he sobbed upon her breasts until his strength was renewed.

"Forgive me-" the words were hard in coming out. "For striking you."

Yes, he is changing, thought Iris. But her soul was already too sewn up with his to see wisdom.

***

The siege of Helles had come at last. The engines of the Legion: tall towers, hardwood battering rams and ladders, were scattered around the city in an enormous ring. Thousands of unarmed city dwellers fled but none passed except through the bulwarks of the Legionnaires. As the desperate moved across the ditches and fortifications along makeshift bridges, many were harassed and stolen from, for the Legionnaires had no code except the very force of their arms. Legate Cincinnatus would not have approved, but such oversights seemed trivial to him in comparison to the battle with the Maleficus lying ahead. If he had known the true extent of practices gone unseen, things might have been different, but Vincent was blind to it all.

On the dank floor of a wooden siege tower a mere bowshot from the city walls, candles were lit. Doors were shut. The rite of appointment was prepared. Lord Exander, once himself a knight, was to take the name of Grand Cyclops within the Cult. It was a coveted title. The whole century knew of the appointment and understood the prestige of the title. Few had heard the actual words of a Grand Cyclop's oath! A centurion stood at the dike beyond and watched the walls of Helles, dismayed with the new obsessions of his century.

The Equites had their Trials. The Black Legionnaires had their holy commencement.

Humming like a deep earthquake came from the tower. The hymnists sang in low tones while the darkly hooded Grandmaster brought out the Scepter of Power. Exander kneeled with pride in his heart while the screams of a victim echoed behind the curtain.

"How will you mark your oath to us?"

"With a promise of blood," Exander responded following the ritual.

The Grandmaster unsheathed a jagged blade and stabbed into Exander's outstretched hands. The blood he let drip into a vessel of gold upon the dark altar. The scepter he then placed in Exander's hands.

"Rise, Exander Cyclops, guardian of the Third Century of the First Legion, and make claim."

Exander rose and looked out upon his fellow Legionnaires in the darkness. Even then anger burned in his heart. The screams of the victim became chillingly loud and then were cut off.

Goblets were brought forth to all in the tower by hooded

servants and frightening white masks peaked out from the folded cloth covering their brows. Exander raised his vessel of gold. Its spicy contents churned as he turned them round. Scepter in one hand, glass in the other, he drank, and the Legionnaires followed suit.

***

Far off and away from the sorely set city of Helles, Praetorian Guards thundered through the streets of New Corinth. Like a hundred bees they delved into the halls of Count Cincinnatus' fortress, beating and clubbing their way to the inner sanctum. There the Praetorians greeted the Count's trusted regent, an esteemed knight, with a sword thrust to the neck. Even to the dungeons did the Praetorian Guard make there way, a spectacle of extravagant purple in those damp works of iron and rock. Officials and prisoners alike were herded out the gates, a common bondage their new destiny. Far off in the Second Realm, word reached Vincent's ears of this abomination and his anger burned as a great lake of fire against Hydrus.

So it was that Arlen, once headmaster of a fair estate but condemned prisoner for life, found himself walking on frail legs in the open air. With eyes aching for having not seen light in years, he peered at the train of captured slaves stretched out before and behind him. The overthrow of Count Cincinnatus meant a new life! Yet still he mourned his lord's downfall, thinking that surely he had met his death at the hands of the Praetorians.

A teenage boy shackled beside him asked, "Do you cry for yourself or for your family?"

"I weep for our Master. Surely he has now met a tragic end!"

"Of what master do you speak, for you bear the look of a prisoner of the dungeon? Whom do you love that has been wronged? Surely not he who condemned you to the darkness and chain!?"

"My sentence was just, but our Master deserved no such wrong! If only the Equites would muster and drive these foul Praetorians into the earth!"

"My father once told me tales of the Trials and what it took to become a knight. But there are few that remain, he says. Most were killed fighting the treacherous Keleres. I have never seen one, save for our late regent, may he rest in peace. Our life will be very hard now I suspect, don't you think?"

Arlen's heart was too troubled at these words to answer.

"Shut your gabber and walk boy!" the teenager's father commanded.

A line of mounted Praetorian Guards flew past the train of captives and off into the sunset. Their steeds were smaller than any knight would dare claim, for the breeding of a knight's horse was an art perfected over a hundred years. These praetorians cared for nothing but expediency. Gold and lust were their gods! Arlen cursed them under his breath.

"Where do they go?" he finally gained the energy to ask the teenager's father to the front of him.

"To the Forty-Ninth Estate, likely. Rumor has long spread that the lord of that land is in rebellion against his new master, the owner of the vineyards, and against the Council's decrees. He harbors all who are of like mind. A troublesome force he has been, but smoke rises far up from those fields lately and we all suspect trouble has come back to him."

The forty-ninth estate is only a day's ride from the fifty-sixth! Arlen thought of Iris and home and was troubled.

An old man spoke from behind them, "Our Regent was too much like that fool! If only he had kept quiet, none of this would have happened! Instead he had to babble on about ideals in the High Council. Take care to your own affairs and let your neighbor do as he pleases, I say! Do I care if a fellow stays at the inns of black stone? No! It is none of my business if he wants to have a night of exotic pleasures! As for slavery, it would have only been those foreign rats! But now we are all slaves ourselves! How is this better? If only he had believed that men have a right to do as they please, as was decreed in council! But that was too hard for the Regent! Now we too must pay for his sedition!"

"Tell me stranger, for it is long since I have heard news of the world, is it now sedition for us to believe one thing or another?" asked Arlen. "And since when did the three realms relinquish their power to enforce their own laws of tranquility?"

"A man should be free to do what he pleases!" the old man responded brusquely. "Or were our lords meant to be tyrants of our daily lives? If so then we are better off without them!"

"There are many things which mankind would do in private, were he allowed, which should never be permitted." His words suddenly became solemn. "I have witnessed such horrid acts myself. Besides, the private lives of the many become the public life of the state."

"Well aren't you the Philosopher himself, right from the stinking prison!" the man spat on the back of Arlen's feet.

Arlen's confusion and pain was too deep to respond.

Chapter 10

Helles Falls

Now had come the time when the fate of Luminares would be determined, sang the troubadours of the Second Realm. Surely the Legion would crush the Nordic raiders who remained! With the pestilence of the foreign plague they had brought from across the sea eliminated, who then could stand against the Legion's might?

The Twice-Scepter, as the people had come to call Count Cincinnatus, manifested unfathomable power. The banner of sword pierced star flew over every fortress and town from the sea in the north to the far reaches of the kingdom in the south and east. In the First Realm there was trembling at the thought of his forthcoming return. What repayment would the Count give for the deeds of those in power? Their hands were sullied in Plebian and Equestrian blood.

Still, many flocked to the Praetor's banner as he heralded an age of freedom. It was a time of things new and exciting in the First Realm. Marketplaces of all sorts grew, guilds were strengthened, and the exotic black palace inns brought animation to an agitated city.

In the Third Realm too, rumor spread that the Praetor and his lackeys were in for it when Cincinnatus returned. Folk fond of older days told this in whispers as purple draped Praetorian Guards ransacked the country-side. Lady and lord were driven out wherever the Praetorians went. New masters were put in their place and they brought in slaves from afar or forced former tenants into bondage. The land was faced with a cruel fate.

Rumor of these foul deeds had reached Vincent's ears and he saw opportunity in the people's suffering. He set forth great plans to overthrow the entire Council, for he had become great in his own eyes. Even the thought of becoming King by his own hand was set upon him in the recesses of his mind. *They will all bow before me, Praetor, Patrician, Pleb and slave!* he thought. One battle lay before him and his goals. Afterward, enemies would surrender at the very word of his coming.

Bassus shuddered from atop a battlement as he looked upon the vast siege works moving toward his city. It was only a matter of time now. The angry words of Hydrus echoed in his head. How could he not have won over more centuries to his command! He had after all been Legate for well nigh four years and the Knight upstart only two! *A moot point now! Battle is upon me!* His servants thrust his hefty breastplate onto his oversized body and he hurried to the field, breathing hard all the way.

Vincent saw a great cloud of dust arising from beyond the city gates and the glean of metal was mixed therein. He was troubled and asked, "What foul secret have the Maleficus unveiled now?" For the numbers of the enemy gathering there were far greater than any his spies or advisors foresaw.

To this Evan replied, "Foul indeed, Master, but they have the whips of their warlords behind their backs, whereas we fight in the right." His words were beyond his years, but Vincent was no longer used to listening to such expressions.

A horn blast was heard and the shining of red metal off of foot soldier's armor was seen on a hill far to the west. *Justinian!* Thought Vincent in rage. Bassus laughed then, for the Legion stretched itself out to check its now uncovered flank, and he knew his opportunity had come.

The siege engines began their work that night. Each section of wall was fought for inch by inch. Luminarian spilled Luminarian blood and Bassus used up the city's militias on the battlements, thinking it better to save his finest soldiers for the clash on flat ground. Lies were told that the Twice-Scepter would burn the entire city to the ground and that he would suffer no survivors to escape. This was believed at face value, for many had heard rumor that the Twice-Scepter himself had once cut off the heads of an entire cohort of Keleres prisoners. With this in mind the militias held onto the walls savagely. Knowledge of Vincent's ruthlessness had grown much out of proportion. Still, the power of the Legion was relentless and it was a night of doom for the militias.

A full moon shown down on the silent camp of Keleres while screams and clashing metal echoed from the city walls. Vincent observed the Keleres guards vigilantly and pondered how best to use his troops against the skilled enemies. Suddenly the watchman called out the alarm. Without another order a mass of Legionnaires formed a line of pikes before Vincent. A small party of Keleres advanced speedily against the formation. Javelin throwers flanked the party and swordsmen ran around to encircle the intruders. *I have taught this Legion well,* thought Vincent. His commanders passed on his strategies like sacred doctrine. When the party came closer, it was clear that it was only a parley. Vincent came to the forefront of his line of pikes, as did his field commanders and a number of centurions.

"What do you seek here, betrayers?" Vincent questioned coldly.

A tall Keleres stepped to the front, "We seek out Sir Cincinnatus, your lord and commander, so that we may parley with him."

Vincent saw that the whole party had put their hands on the hilt of their swords. A heated melee could erupt at any moment! "He stands before you, now say what you will and be gone."

"Well met, Lord Cincinnatus. I speak on behalf of my master, the commander of the Keleres and my message is for you alone."

"Behind closed doors and in secret did you plot the death of my King and my Lady. Now you will speak plainly in the open or will not speak at all!"

"Very well." The demand was unexpected and the tall man paused to collect his thoughts. "For years now have our men fought and evaded each other. My master has been pinioned by your sentinels and fortresses in this Realm so that he has been unable to receive or send word. Now at last does my master see that you are not in league with the servants of Bassus, who surely betrayed our King. He asks for a peace between us."

"Liars!" shouted a centurion from behind Vincent.

"They sue for peace so that they may escape," whispered a field commander to Vincent, as if he had not thought of it himself.

"Late has my master discovered what truly divides us," continued the Keleres. "It is not you that betrayed our King, nor was it us, but another."

"Impossible!" Barked Vincent. "The Keleres were in the royal chamber! With my own eyes did I see them! The Keleres would've had the Kingdom believe you exacted quick justice against our Lady. If it had not been my fate to be there, your foul hand might have succeeded. Late I arrived at such a horrid scene, yet still did I smite your servants and will do so again!"

"Stay your anger, lord. I tell you no Keleres did this evil!"

"Did a passerby then steal the armor of the Royal Guard? Such negligence is rewarded with death, thus was the rule of our King. No Keleres would dare be so foolish!"

"If Keleres committed this murder, then it was done without support from the brothers or the sanction of the Master! But such a thing is impossible! The Guard knows its own. None would've done it!"

"And what is your word worth?"

At that the tall Keleres unsheathed his sword and the Legionnaires behind the party followed suit.

By some providence no blows were yet struck. The Legionnaires put their weapons away when they saw that none of the Keleres had imitated the messenger.

"I am Justinian Marcus Solis, commander of the Royal Guard." The tall man held the sword aloft, point down. It was a glorious weapon, jeweled and shining palely in the moonlight. The blade's size dwarfed not only the short swords of the Legionnaires and other Keleres, but also Vincent's Equestrian long sword. It was the prized heirloom of the Keleres. "I tell you that no man of mine harmed our beloved king, nor laid a finger upon our Lady!"

The crowd was shocked at the commander's appearance. Even the Keleres appeared awestruck. A few of the Centurions left and readied their men, hopeful of claiming Justinian's head. Hatred for the Keleres had run deep.

"These are not the only tidings that I bring," continued Justinian. "Within those city walls lies more than an army of Nordic seafarers. Nay, they have not commanded the peoples of the city. Rather has the city consumed the Nordics. You fight also true betrayers."

Then it came together in Vincent's mind and he knew why he had received reports of desertion amidst the fighting on the city walls. *Bassus!*

Justinian resumed, "The Legate who was in office prior has raised revolt against you. He has joined with the Nordics in order to smite you to your ruin. As a token of our peace, I offer you this promise, that we Keleres will fight at your side through the heat of this battle. For Bassus has proven his duplicity in siding with the Maleficus raiders, whose actions the old council hoped would be stopped without delay. You have taken up arms against him and your actions I have marked well. I know now that you are no traitor; only an unwitting pawn in Hydrus the Deceiver's scheme. That forked tongued fool has the world begging at his feet. When I return to my throne, as is my duty as the King's cousin, I will cast that snake down!"

At these last words, Vincent's pride was awakened in him, and it was a hot coal because of anger and hurt. He saw the truth in Justinian's eyes and knew then that he had been duped. Hydrus' betrayal he had thought rather to be something grown late of avarice and jealousy, not a plot to overthrow the King and his daughter! How could he have been so blind! Yet too hard it was to admit weakness in front of his Legionnaires, a fate of his own doing. Moreover, there was still a lust for the Crown in his own heart. Knowing that Justinian was the only surviving heir, he found himself callous to fighting subserviently beside him, or even as an equal. Vincent had become great by his own hand, it was too much to now be asked to lay his ambitions down!

"You come gallivanting up here in the dead of night and speak fiery words, Justinian," Vincent walked toward the Keleres. "Yet how are we to trust you after these years. Nay, not so quickly will we turn our backs to your sword points. Your allegiance has yet to be proved, but not with our blood will this be done!" Vincent's gaze challenged that of Justinian and neither relented. "We ask for no aid in our endeavors and none will we receive! The Maleficus mercenaries and this rabble of Bassus will be crushed by my own hand! Now begone with you and when you return show more respect to the army of Luminares!"

So the Legion took the field of battle alone and the Keleres returned to their camp. The walls of Helles had all but fallen by dawn. When Vincent arrived at the front, the demise of the defenders was quickly engineered. Over the vast stonework climbed countless Legionnaires using their ladders and siege towers. Within an hour the court guards had been slain and the gate of oak and iron was opened from within. The sun rose just as the Legion poured through the gateway like so many ants. They made crisp battle formation, while just beyond Bassus and his men advanced down a green hilltop. Momentum was on the betrayer's side. *They will smash us against the walls!* thought Vincent. Yet too quick was his mind for Bassus, who had spent more days in the baths and brothels than in the practice of his profession. The Legion turned the wall mounted ballistae against their enemies and added their bolts to the darts and javelins which already pelted the oncoming enemy. Too quickly had Bassus given up the walls. Besides this, two centuries were ordered to rush to the far left flank of the Legion. There, hidden behind huts and shops, these centuries rushed the flank of the enemy as it came down against their fellows. Unnoticed, they threw the Maleficus mercenaries into a panic and Bassus knew then that he was beaten.

Like a single wave which crashes and breaks against a stone breaker would these enemies have been against Vincent's Legion, had not the acolytes betrayed their brethren. The Third Century was among those that flanked the enemy. Exander, Grand Cyclops of that Century slayed its Centurion proper as they knelt silently in waiting. A horrific purging then began and afterwards Exander claimed sole leadership. The fourth Century likewise had many acolytes in its ranks. Also with them had a secret purpose long been spread so that, when the century sprang forth, many backs were cut down as they ran. Thus when these flanking detachments should have met the sides of their enemies, they charged into the already collapsing flank of the Legion. Still more joined their rampage of betrayal from that main body. Everywhere, acolytes threw down their helms and donned hoods black as tar. Confusion paralyzed the entire Legion.

Vincent saw what transpired from atop the wall and a great fury raged inside him as he leaped from the bulwarks to the battlefield below. Seizing an axe from a fallen Nordic, he rushed to the front and a great number of faithful Legionnaires rallied behind him. The waving gold and red of the Count's cape was ever in the forefront of the battle now! For the third time Bassus' heart quaked with fear, for the Legion punched a hole through the center of his forces. For a moment it seemed they might sprint up the hill and overtake the false Legate himself! But it was not so, for they were overtaken from the sides and their energy was spent running up the hill. Vincent alone pushed on, crushing all who crossed his path. Yet even he at last was surrounded by an insurmountable sea of enemies. First a wound to the arm, then an arrow in the back and the Twice-Scepter, whom the world had feared, was cast face down and bound for some dark purpose. Dark, pulsing life rushed from his back in gushes of red. Vincent passed into darkness.

***

He awoke to white robed retainers leaning over his face, and hands bound with thick twine. Days must have passed.

"He is awake!" a man hollered above him. Vincent's eyes tried to focus on the figure but saw only a blur of skin and hair. "Fetch the master!" the man commanded. The noise pounded painfully in Vincent's brain.

Moments passed.

"Cut him loose," spoke a voice.

Hard hands picked him up by the shoulders and placed his feet on cold stone. The blood rushed back through his veins. He felt his strength returning now and thought he recognized the face before him.

"Accursed, will be your name from this day forth!" It was a voice familiar from years ago.

Hydrus!

"Hail the Legate who would take my place!" Wet saliva splattered on Vincent's neck from the voice close behind him. His knees suddenly buckled at a blow from the rear and he hit the floor hard.

"I wanted you to have your wits with you for this, Count." Hydrus walked closer to his front. Vincent could see his face now. A cruel smile stretched across his face. "I have been told that your family and kin were gutted like cattle before your eyes many years ago?"

Vincent felt his heart throbbing at these words, his energy was coming back! Anger was burning in him and the twine restraining his hands cut into his flesh as his muscles tensed!

"You watched them die, my agents tell me. You could not protect them." Hydrus continued. "You failed, just as you have here. You're going away to a dark place, Count Cincinnatus. You will have time to ponder your faults. But you need not worry about your remaining kin any longer, for they are all lost. My servants collected taxes on their enslavement a month ago. Every one of them will work behind the lash! Just as your forefathers were doomed to slavery generations ago, so shall they be. You are no more than they! A false Count! A farce! Instituted by my power and removed by my hand in the same stroke!"

"You are the cheat, Hydrus!" Vincent spat back. "The Council will have its revenge soon now. Every lying tongue receives the smiting blade in due time!"

"Look at you! Speaking of the powers of a Council you abandoned for the might of the Legion! Who controls the Legion now, accursed one?"

Vincent shook his head in disgust, flexed his muscles against the rough twine.

"But you are right Count Cincinnatus," Hydrus added. "I am a cheat. Far more than you ever imagined! You failed our Lady, Queen Adeline Theodora, the same as you did your family. You could not protect them. You could not protect her. My mind was too quick for you! All men have weaknesses to be exploited, Accursed. Yours is hate and lust for power. Inflatus, who discredited Gaius by simply siding with him, fell for only a few silver pieces. Sure, the Keleres would not fall for this ploy, but it was easy enough to find a smithy which produced their armor! So in battling Justinian Solis, you cut off your only true ally."

"How great your wrath was, fool!" mocked Bassus from behind. He broke into a fit of fell laughter.

"Not great enough," remarked Hydrus coldly. "But that will soon be remedied. You have been outwitted, Count. Yet before you meet your fate, know that I alone engineered the fate of our King and Queen! I am the killer! I designed their death and you wasted your wrath on friends!"

Vincent gritted his teeth in anger. Shock was in his eyes. He had distrusted these two, but never had he thought them capable of such long grown duplicity. He stood to his feet in defiance only to fall from a blow to the back.

The fat Legate leaned over close to Vincent's hair after the kick. He too was surprised, though Vincent could not see it, but he cared more for gloating over battle than politics. "The entire Third Realm, stubborn as a mule refusing the slaughterhouse, will be sliced to pieces when my Legion returns!" Bassus boasted. "Hail Accursed! Your people are doomed and death or slavery will soon come upon you now!"

"Worse," Hydrus corrected. He looked over his shoulder and four black hooded men immediately emerged from behind him and ran towards Vincent. They grasped him by the neck, arms and legs and began to carry him away. "You should have obeyed the decree and returned to the High Council. Even a murderous death would have been fortunate to the fate that awaits you now!"

Stifled cries passed into silence as Vincent was carried away.

Hydrus stared hard at Bassus. His fist swung forward and hit the Legate sharp on the chin!

Bassus winced from the pain. He snorted angrily at the smiling Praetorian guards behind Hydrus. "I bring you victory and you repay me with this?"

"You bring me to near ruin!" Hydrus cut back. "I gave you this Legion for years and you could not muster more than one Century to your side! It was not you who won the battle for Helles!"

Bassus was silent. He remembered clearly the hooded men coming from within the enemy's ranks, cutting apart their fellows just when the Sixth Century and Maleficus would've been overcome.

"I am left with no choice," Hydrus turned to go.

"Retain my appointment for the invasion of the Third Realm! I will retire after! I will not send the Legion's loot to your ports if you cut me off again!"

"You have little real control of the Legion, Bassus." Hydrus shut the door behind.

"Do with Bassus as you will. They are all yours now," Hydrus whispered to a shadow in the hallway.

"I will need more than a single Legion," the faceless man

responded.

"Whatever means are necessary. Only march on the Third Realm as soon as possible!"

"Yes, master."

"You see that I give and I take away. Do not forget it!"

"I serve."

Hydrus mounted a white horse outside and immediately began the long journey back to Luminares. A colorful train of guards and courtesans followed closely behind. But the retainers in the house of medicine later told the tale that in that very moment a low rumbling of laughter and words had shook the ground beneath the building; a foreign tongue with the voice of a monstrous human. As Praetor Hydrus passed by in brilliance, they crouched behind doors in unreasonable fear.

Chapter 11

The Secret

VINCENT BREATHED DEEP. His lungs were on fire with pain. The stench of rotting flesh filled his nostrils and moans and cries filled the air. All of them stared out the rattling cart's back, wounded Legionnaires, Numantine men, even women and children. Each stared down the path to a wooden gate at the base of the mountain, a gate which no one ever returned through. Legionnaires with black capes and hoods stood guard, ready to kill anyone who might venture up, or sneak down.

Muscles in Vincent's arms flexed to no avail as he tried to break loose from his bindings. Others were in the same predicament. But where were they headed in this cattle cart of bleeding flesh? *Why the women and children? They surely did not take part in the battle!* With one eye he peered over the side as best he could. Bristle and thorns of enormous proportion covered the jagged slopes the cart slowly climbed. The road to the top was long. Idle time anxiously bled them white with horror.

Through iron gates they were pulled and the cart's writhing captives were consumed beneath the slopes. Down they traveled now, down into the bowels of the earth where neither men nor beast live freely. Dark caves they entered where candles speckled jagged rock and hateful faces stared back from beyond. Shrouded in the darkness, only their cruel eyes could be seen peering at them. These caves were made by man, but there was a sickening feel to them, as though infernal forces held them together.

Suddenly all went black! Ritualistic candles cluttered the

rock no more. The cart continued, for the horses leading it were bred in the pit. Repulsive horrors now emerged as if the captives were trapped in a nightmare!

A baby crying somewhere in the blackness. Somewhere alone in the maze of rock.

A man covered in blood nailed to the wall beside them.

Several of the captives puked and Vincent gagged as he saw a woman cut to pieces on spiked rocks, a mocking candle beside her dead face. Her lifelike eyes begged him.

Then, as if there had been no darkness, the cart rolled into a great hall filled with light and the shine of gold. There worked hundreds, each man heartily set to a task. The ground turned to elaborate tiles of purple and gray. Torches flamed brightly from mortared walls and hung from silver chandeliers attached to a lofty ceiling. Ornate wooden pillars carved with images of monstrous gargoyles reached high overhead. The workers ignored the cart entirely. Still the captives cried out, but it was as if they were not even there! They called to deaf ears in a hopeless anticipation of help. All screamed and yelled. Many cried now. Vincent alone remained deathly silent. A fell mood was upon him. He cursed the doom which had pursued him for so long and burned away all he held dear. Damned he was to hurt those who meant most to him! Now had it brought utter ruin to all!

The Mountain's workers did not mine the cavities of rock. No metal or treasure of the earth did they seek. The cover of darkness was their friend, for human flesh they cut and whittled, sifting finely into pots and brews of grape, leaf and powder. The putrid mix of sweetness with flesh, of green life with death filled the captives' nostrils and covered their skin like a dank blanket. Hooded men worked happily in this mist.

The captives became delirious from fear after the workers came among them. Half were taken away; Tied down and destroyed on the spot in the foulest manner imaginable. The others, Vincent not the least, swooned from disgust and from the smells of the unclean drink being concocted before their very eyes. The very friends and Legionnaires who had just been sawed to pieces were poured into bowls of wine. A tall cloaked man with a gem adorned scepter approached now. While incanting the words of a ritual, he dunked one hand into a bowl and held his scepter aloft with the other.

Vincent recognized the word "Benedictus," come from the man's mouth. *They bless it!* he thought with disgust.

The recitation ended and he walked towards the cart. "Who desires to live? Two of you will receive this grace," spoke the tall one again.

"Take me! Please! Take me!" screamed a skinny man from the back of the cart. The hooded servants immediately came to the side and cut him loose. Hands and feet still tied together, he crawled over the Legionnaires and atop a mother and her child until he reached the back. He tumbled out clumsily. Two hooded servants clasped one of the bowls into his hands roughly.

"Drink!" they commanded.

The skinny man hesitated at first, but then gulped down the contents. Those in the cart grumbled furiously. Rank vomit spewed onto Vincent's feet from the sickened Legionnaire to his left. One of the workers pulled out a clay mask from his cloak and pressed it onto the skinny man's face.

"Who else?" the one with the scepter asked. "You!" a long boney finger pointed at Vincent's nose.

Vincent spat on his face.

"Bring him here!" the tall acolyte called out in a commanding voice as he wiped away the spittle.

On his knees they placed the bowl to his mouth. Vincent bit hard but they forced open his lips and plugged his nose. *I can do nothing to stop them now. Providence has abandoned me again!*

"Wait," spoke the tall man. The gems of his scepter glowed in the firelight like the eyes of a dragon. He fetched a sack from the nearby tables and emptied its powder and leafy contents into the frothing bowl. He thrust his hands toward Vincent's stomach while speaking curses in a foul tongue and then dipped his long fingers into the bowl. He motioned with his hand and the servants bowed very low and continued. Vincent growled, bit and spat to no avail. They forced the entire bowl and more down his throat until he lost sensation in his muscles and the world faded to black.

When Vincent awoke he felt a cutting pain in his stomach. He stuck two fingers into his throat and gagged, but nothing came up. It was as though a knife were lodged in his gut and slicing his insides apart! His hands clutched his stomach while he coughed up flem, but there was no relief.

His captors had released him near a high ledge. Chained prisoners cried and moaned all around Vincent. Far below was the golden hall where the black hooded acolytes worked. Their tiny forms moved about doing their horrid deeds with speed and efficiency. One by one the prisoners' limbs were being drained into large aqueducts which traversed the roof of the golden hall and descended to the drink preparation tables below. Vincent walked towards the edge. *I will end this nightmare now. I am abandoned by God and man.*

It was then that a brilliant light blinded him. Vincent fell to his knees and covered his eyes.

"Release him!" Boomed a commanding voice, a noble voice, of one respected and powerful.

Who is this? Thought Vincent, but just then he recognized its tones. *Justinian will take his men back out of this Mountain! I will rot before being rescued by his hand!*

***

Iris closed her eyes and remembered the green glades with pink flowers where she had spent her younger years. *So far away now! It is lost in the tide of time along with my kin*, and also *myself!* She slapped her hand on the wood door in anger and lifted her head up. *It is long time this ended!* She felt the bruise on her arm and then tightened her fist as she remembered.

The door slammed open and Iris stormed into the study. There Nicephorus Puter sat by the fire, the fur of a lion wrapped around his neck.

"It has come to this!" Iris demanded his attention with her fist in the air. "You are my husband by God and man, but no longer will I abide your fell moods and rapacious greed! Not a moment longer will I linger! Never should I have abided to join with you, who are a disgrace to my kin. This is beyond my power now, but some freedoms I still have. I will go back to the land of my kin and dwell there. A simple and hard life it may be. Yet a fairer one also! Some day you may return to me, but I will not think this should come to pass. Wrong I was to believe I could change your faults, for they are the fruit of a black heart. Each day that passes you sicken more."

Nicephorus spared a disgusted look at her and then gazed back into the fire.

"This I pronounce to you," Iris continued. "One day will you be so weakened that no longer will you call yourself a man. A wretch of the underworld rather you will be; an imp burning inside and begging for death to end the plague in your heart."

The words of the simple wife were more profound than she knew. For even now a sickness joined of mind, body and soul wracked Nicephorus. A sickness nurtured by the Drink of the Religion of the Dark, but brought on by his own naked ambitions. He looked on Iris and remembered the staggering beauty of her will, but of late his mind was only driven by lust, and too much to bear was this splendor. He turned away in pride and cast aside all hope of renewal.

"Go then lady Iris Nuptiae. And keep the name that was once yours."

But Iris would have none of his gloom, "No Nicephorus, a covenant is binding. Not you nor I have the power to break it, except in death. Someday may you have the grace to see this!"

Then was his anger kindled. "Return home, Iris. But you will find no friends or kin to welcome you! Look instead in the Southern Mines, in the dens of thieves, the slime of brothels, and before the whips of slave drivers! For all your people are sold and scattered!"

"You lie!"

"Ha! Other times yes! But not today!"

Iris slapped him hard across the face and in his lion skin he reeled from the sting. "How could you?" she asked. "Who are you? No one that I know!"

Before the words had finished coming from her lips,

Nicephorus rose and grasped her in wrath. Yet terrible was her stare to behold and he could not abide it. Gone forever was her complacency, and the deception he had had her trapped within.

He pushed her away, "Leave now and join them. Look not for my aid any longer!" And without looking back, Iris took her leave.

At that hour there was still some hope in her long journey. The rebellion of the Lord of the Forty-ninth estate had been greater than any could've foreseen. Even now his small army, which he named The Few Faithful, waged war against the invading Praetorian Guard. Wherever the Few Faithful came, slaves were freed and the Old Law restored. Some of Iris' kin, dwellers of the Cincinnatus estate of old, fought beside him. Their hopes were high, their hearts proud and they anticipated one day returning to their homes.

***

Vincent's thoughts of Justinian were harsh as he shielded himself from the blinding light. Hardly could he believe the thoughts were his, but he still harbored hate for the Keleres and he certainly wanted no pity or help from his former enemy. By his own hand he had failed, by his own hand he would now perish. He asked for no rescue!

Nonetheless, strong fingers grasped him at the back of the neck and lifted him up. Vincent pulled his own forearm away from his eyes and squinted at the figure above him in awe and anger. To his great amazement it was not Justinian that he saw, but the expelled Knight Alexus.

I myself banished this man!

"How is this possible?" Vincent whispered, and he realized his own bodily weakness as Alexus pulled him away from the ledge.

"My lord, forgive our delay. A dreadful maze lies behind us. But fear not, we will reach the peak alive!" With these words the banished knight led Vincent. His lord was the last remaining from the cart that had woven its way to that dreadful place. All others, besides the traitor who had drank from the cup, had perished in the pit or at the hands of the infernal workers. Legionnaires bore blazing torches before them. Around their faces were wrapped cloths to protect from the stench of the Mountain's concoctions. In their right hands were swords with which they cut a way through enemy after enemy. Vincent saw then that Alexus too wore the garb of a Legionnaire and the insignia of a lowly recruit. Then he was amazed. Evan too was there. When his eyes had adjusted, Vincent spied his squire's guarding glances back at him. The young warrior was with the few Legionnaires rushing through the black maze.

It was not long before the whole Mountain of Darkness was alerted to their presence. A swarm of black hooded men followed behind them, drawing ever closer and increasing in number. Axes, spears, maces, whips and all kinds of dreadful weapons they carried. Vincent's awareness was almost fully returned and he perceived that the party of enemies was lingering behind them with purpose. *Perhaps they wait for us to make a wrong turn.* Trapped before a rock wall or an invisible cliff they would be pushed and battered to oblivion! Another party of enemies could also be waiting around each corner they turned. Yet Alexus and the Legionnaires did not hesitate to find out. Every foe that crossed their path they cut down. Onward they pressed without slowing and Vincent wondered at Alexus' superb navigation of the vast underworld. Moreover, he directed the men as though he were ten years a Centurion!

Now they were come to the entrance of the foul Mountain at last. One of two things could lie beyond: another party of enemies waiting to meet them with ready blades, or an open path down. Strength all but fully returned, Vincent stepped ahead of Alexus. With anticipation he peered down the slope. At first his eyes were unable to tell, for the rays of the sun were a shock. Again his eyes had to adjust. In time he saw, however, that there was indeed a party of Legionnaires marching up the Mountain just over a stone's throw away. These ones had no intention of helping them escape. Again Vincent fell into despair. He leaned against the Mountain entrance hopelessly. Alexus too looked down the Mountain and saw his fate, but was not deterred.

Alexus tucked away the weighty fear that would have him paralyzed and put on an air of confidence. "Fear not lord!" Alexus proclaimed. "These betrayers shall yet taste the steel of a Legion that still follows its master!" Alexus pointed to their left off a cleft. "Jump down that ledge and look to the east, there lies the narrow and jagged path to the base. I learned of it in my days of folly and addiction before banishment. Now make haste!" Alexus eyed Evan. The squire nodded, sheathed his sword and came to his master's side.

Vincent peered at Alexus in awe and regretted his bouts of wrath against him. His thoughts asked, *why?*

"You were right, lord. I had become a pitiful wretch. Long have I run from all my fears. Not again. Here I make my stand."

"Come with us!" Vincent asked.

"Impossible," Alexus responded. "The cultists will be at our back in another moment and an entire Century of turncoats lies before us."

Beside Alexus was an older Legionnaire with wiry gray hair beneath his helm. He looked at Vincent and then out on the Legionnaires. In a loud voice he called out. "Here holds the last of the Legion that brought the Second Realm to its knees! The foe of Numantine rebels, Maleficus mercenaries, flesh-drinkers and traitors!"

Alexus turned his head back to Vincent and Evan, and no shadow of doubt returned to him. "Look for us now only in the land which never fades, where the warmth of light will ever be about us, where there is but one King whose reign cannot end."

The exiled knight did his best to conceal his shivering limbs and then made ready to charge the approaching enemy. Evan had to pull Vincent away, for he was in a stupor of wonder and pain. The squire knew his master would have preferred to die there with them.

They formed a line of the sixteen faithful Legionnaires, eight long and two deep. It was just enough to cover the path up the mountain. They marched down the road to meet what were once their fellows. Blade pierced flesh and bodies were split. Black robed cultists also attacked at their backs. Those seventeen

each breathed a last bloodied breath, but not until every ounce of
their strength was utterly spent, and the pass was held long
enough for their master to escape.

A mile away now, Vincent and Evan leaped over rock and
ledge following a narrow path down the mountain. The sun rose
up before them. Had they beheld the scenes which followed
within the mountain, they would have seen a man who gave no
quarter to weakness. Again and again they tortured Alexus'
wounded frame and again and again he rose to take more
beatings. Stretched and lashed, cut and burnt, it made no
difference. Finally, death came to him. He met it with a spirit
unbroken.

***

Once down the Mountain, Evan and Vincent rushed into
Helles and blended into the throngs of people. So many surveyed
the battlefields in wonder but so few understood their implications.
At a local inn they spent the day and night healing wounds,
resting, and replenishing their famished bodies. Vincent was
greatly taxed from his defeat and capture. Evan too had not come
out from those dark places unscathed. A watchful eye they kept,
however, and concealed their true names and aching battle
wounds except when alone. When they had slept and ate their fill,
the two sojourners joined a small gathering in the main hall. They
sat at a long and high table, behind which the innkeeper and
workers cooked a sundry of meats and breads.

"What news is there of the great battle within these walls?
For we two are travelers from afar and came upon the scene too
late to tell. Tell me, for you must know from the make of your
visitors." Vincent asked the Innkeeper that morning. And indeed
many Legionnaires were now resting in the inn, if only for a night,
so news was close by. The two kept their cloaks tight and hoods
low about their faces.
    The innkeeper smiled graciously, he loved being the
bearer of news and wisdom. "A horrendous battle it was! We all
dreaded the coming of the Twice-Scepter, but knew that at last he

would arrive. Immense was his army! The ranks of his troops stretched beyond sight." He put his hands far apart in a sweeping motion, as if to demonstrate how big. "I was afraid for my inn! Pack up all my most precious belongings and ready myself to leave I did! We were all quite terrified!"

"But why?" broke in Evan. Vincent gave him an angry look, for he feared that he might blow their cover. Evan still finished, "Have you not heard that this Twice-Scepter is gracious and just to his subjects?"

The innkeeper's mustache twitched as he looked at Evan with confusion. "I never heard such a thing. The Twice-scepter beheads all his prisoners and cares nothing for his poor and lowly subjects! People like myself are dust in the wind to him," he added.

Vincent held in his anger at these outrageous complaints.

The innkeeper came close and stared each of the two in the eyes before continuing, "It is said that in the Third Realm he sent away the servants of his own household to slavery and the dungeon, for naught but his own cruelty!" His attempts to inspire fear in the sojourners failed however, and he poured himself a goblet of wine to rest his efforts.

Yet his words had struck truer than he could've known. Vincent's anger was overcome with unlooked for guilt and he cringed inside as he remembered Arlen. How far and wide did ill tidings travel! He hoped Evan didn't perceive his discomfort. In truth rumor of more than this had spread, thanks to the Praetor's devices. Even Nicephorus' sale of Iris' kin and the other hands had been attributed to the Twice-Scepter, though he had nothing to do with it. So had Vincent's faults multiplied beyond reckoning and been promulgated throughout the realms. Yet mostly in the First Realm and here in Helles did Hydrus' darts strike true. Even without this knowledge, Vincent suspected the machinations of the Praetor. He knew too well the guile of Hydrus now and his hate of that man continually burned brighter. These thoughts took precedence over any remorse he may have momentarily felt for the coward Arlen.

"But hope has returned now," continued the innkeeper as he served a plate of smoked beef to a customer. "The older commander of the Legion, the true Legate, laid the Twice-Scepter low in battle yesterday morning."

"How did this come to pass, since the army of the Twice-Scepter was so great?" Vincent now anxiously awaited an answer, for he wondered how the people had come to accept the patronage of the barbarous Nordic mercenaries.

"An alliance was made with the vagabond seafarers, a foul people of the Plebian class, may they leave at once. You must've heard how they tie the very skulls of their vanquished enemies to their armor?"

Vincent started at the mention of his own Plebian class in association with the Nordics, but he suppressed his anger a while longer. "That I have," he replied. "So why hire the outlaws?"

"Foreign fool! We could not have held the city alone against the tyrant Lord Cincinnatus!"

"And what reward does the ever so generous Legate offer these barbarians? Vast lands and a title?" Vincent joked.

"No titles are to be given in the kingdom again, by decree of the Council. Do they have no ears and mouths where you hail from!?" he mocked.

"Forgive me, the rule of the Twice-Scepter hid us from much news." Vincent responded, but he had not forgotten. Though the decree had reached him in that same month that he was ordered to abandon the Legion, he had laughed at the audacity of it and paid no heed. Then it had been meaningless parchment. Now things were different.

"The Praetor removes us from under the boot of royalty," the innkeeper proclaimed with pride. "Never again will we suffer the rule of such a Count as the Twice-scepter! But word has it Bassus did promise them land and gold."

"Do they not doubt that his word will be kept? Whose land will be given them?" asked Vincent.

"What does it matter?" the innkeeper answered.

"What kind of a ruler does a liar make?" Evan retorted, hardly able to stand the innkeeper longer.

"A capable one, in these times."

"A man who changes his character upon the whims of circumstance is like driftwood cast about by the surf in a storm. He is worth nothing!" Evan's fury was growing and Vincent had to check him.

"Where exactly do you come from strangers?" questioned the innkeeper, looking somewhat worried.

"Cast out by troubles with the lords of the Third Realm." Vincent answered before Evan could. "We wish to forget that now and start anew."

"Indeed, I have heard the Council has had the most trouble in keeping order in that realm. To this day there are skirmishes with the authorities." At this Vincent's heart was gladdened. The innkeeper continued, "Rebellious and haughty lords likely. But from what parts do you hail?"

Vincent dressed himself with a sad face, "It is painful to recall those places, many friends and family were lost to our lord, for much the reasons that you say. But too close a time it is to bear the telling." Vincent intended to put the man at ease, but Evan wondered at his weaving and desired to come straight out and declare who they were. He tired of this gossiper's insolence.

The Innkeeper took the bait. "You want to hear real news?" he whispered closely. "Only last night did I hear it from a wearied Legionnaire. The Legion itself provoked the rebellion of the Numantines!" he soaked in the surprise of his guests happily. "For years a blind eye our garrison of Legionnaires turned to the raids of the Nordics and their masters upon the Numantine lands! Always after a battle many slaves were taken through our ports. And this even before the New Law allowed the trade! For the past year they have been taken up the Great Mountain in the city's center, never to be seen again."

"And the Legionnaires posted here allowed this lawlessness?" Evan asked with disgust, for he now knew full well the horrors of the Mountain this man talked of casually.

"The Sixth Century." Vincent muttered to himself. *Always late to follow orders, cryptic in response and pawns of Bassus in the end.* He cursed himself for having not seen it earlier. He had left them in the city alone, in accordance with Hydrus' wishes. When they failed to return for the mustering, he had assumed it the violence of the Maleficus, but he had been wrong. Horribly wrong. It was the Sixth which stood upon the bones of Alexus atop the Mountain.

"Yes they went along with it quite fine," the innkeeper answered Evan with some delight. "They were under orders to guard the ports, the pass to the Mountain, and the Nordic slave trade. Nobody asked questions as prisoners were hauled by in chains, but we all suspected them Numantines! Serves them right! Living on lands that belonged to our forefathers long ago! The King was wrong to grant them this land, for they are a foul breed and worthless in all things." The innkeeper leaned on a shelf behind the long table. "So you see, the Legion has really been working *with* the Nordic mercenaries for a long time!" The innkeeper smiled with crafty delight.

Vincent was then struck with horror at the working of his own deeds. Again he saw the terrible doom which he deemed caused him to destroy his loved ones, allies and all that he valued. He cursed God. For his eyes were opened and he saw that these provocations against the Numantines which encouraged their rebellion were the same deeds that led to the sanction of the Legion in council, a sanction that he was the key proponent of. Moreover, it was under his own orders that the nightmarish secret within the cultists' mountain lair was protected! Behind his back his own soldiers had wrought evil leading to rebellion and worse. Who knew what darkness the Legion would spread now and in other realms too! Their power was unstoppable. *What ill fate! What evil!* This was all the design of the conniving Hydrus! Vincent would have his blood before he was beaten!

Yet as Vincent brooded further, the blood of Evan boiled into outrage. He was obedient to death, but could only pretend to accept the talk of a deceitfully hearted bigot for so long. Evan too was of the Pleb class and his blood was a mix of many foreign peoples. Yet not least among them was his grandfather, a full-blooded Numantine! Though he knew neither father nor mother, his grandfather had sired him for five years before death. A stouthearted man who brooked no aggression or slander, he certainly wouldn't have stood for insults to his ancestry. Strong his grandfather's blood ran in his veins!

"Pray that you have not breathed your last, for Numantine blood runs in my veins! Your complacency in these deeds is as foul as though you had committed them yourself!"

Evan grasped hold of the innkeeper by the neck and

heaved him across the table before them. Vincent was amazed at Evan's words no less than his deeds, for he had no idea of such ancestry in his squire. Wood was splintered and drink spilled, but the innkeeper survived the fall.

"Forgive me for the outburst, m'lord," Evan asked as the two exited in a hurry. "It was not good of me to lose command of my temper."

But Vincent made no response for he no longer knew what was good.

"We must go to the Third Realm, lord, before the war is ended! There may be some hope in a final muster of the Equites to rout the Praetor! Surely even now he maneuvers against you in your homeland!"

"Nay, squire. My wrath, like yours, cannot wait. I will go straight to the First Realm to destroy the Praetor himself."

Then Evan feared the fell mood of Vincent and wondered if it was still pride that gained the better of his master.

***

Three weeks later Vincent once again scaled the giant steps of Luminares' palace under pale moonlight. Evan obediently waited below, keeping watch from the shadows. Yet the squire was filled with angst. All his warnings and pleas to his master had been ignored. Vincent was surprised to see Legionnaires on guard. *How could the Legion have been stationed so quickly!* He wondered. Little did he know that the Second Legion, one far superior to his First, was already being fashioned. Vincent stormed past the guards without a word. Seeing his Legionnaire's armor and officer's helmet in the darkness, the two saluted and made no attempt to resist. Now weaving in and out of the halls within, Vincent avoided the patrolling guards and found the Praetor's chamber, for he knew the building as well as his own body. He unsheathed his sword with stealth and crept within.

Now at last would he have vengeance! Now would Hydrus rue the day he had dared plot against him! Now would the betrayer reap his just reward! Oh sweet retribution, the finest of wines! Vincent could almost taste the blood already. He approached the bed where the body lay in sleep. Carefully, slowly, anxiously he tiptoed. He pushed away the bed's curtains which shrouded the man from the light. Then he saw the white of his eyes! Wide open they were and staring at him in terror! Yet life was not in them, and he saw in the moonlight that blood already pooled in his clothes. *What? Already dead!* Vincent cursed the heavens for being robbed yet again of his designs. Hate burned deeper in him than justice.

The body he would have thrown to the dogs if he had not been interrupted by the rustling of curtains in a corner. A dark shape stood before him then and a great shadow of fear leapt upon Vincent. He desired to dash from that place, but the shadow held him in thrall.

A deep voice spoke from the shadows, "At last have you come, Vincent Cincinnatus, acclaimed Twice-Scepter, feared in all three Realms."

Sweat dripped down Vincent's face as he heard his name mentioned, "Who are you and how is it that you know me?" he asked in perplexity.

"I am Octar, and I know many things. I know that you entered into my Mountain in Helles. I see your malice and know now that Hydrus was a fool to have discarded you so quickly. But I suppose he only did it out of fear for himself." The figure chuckled darkly at this comment.

"Hydrus was ever a fool in politics and war. Now tell me if I judge rightly that it was you who ended the Praetor's life." It was a sinking feeling in his stomach that told him he was right.

"You judge rightly, Count. Of course, the Praetor did his part. A finely engineered recruitment of soldiers and assassination of your king he designed. But the arrogant fool never suspected treachery could touch his own cloak." The shadow of a man laughed curtly again, "He was but a chisel in the end, a tool with which the kingdom was split and the new life implanted within!"

Vincent wondered at the man. *Octar? A name unheard of! His claims are absurd!* "Perhaps you will not find the Praetor's designs so useful should they turn upon you, Octar." He somehow felt dirtied by using the name.

"I know you too well, Count. You who would reclaim the

Legion and take the Kingdom for yourself! The Legion, however, is well beyond your reach. Even now it crushes the last of your loyal servants in the Third Realm! Moreover, a Second Legion twice the size of the first is being recruited in this realm. Even if you should reclaim your troops from the First Legion you would face annihilation! However, they are *all* safe from insurrection. Not by trials and oaths are they confirmed, but by blood, ritual and indebtedness to me! They are all now acolytes of my following. The warriors have been purified, Vincent. They are my Equites now."

Equites? Vincent thought in bewilderment. Without willing it images of himself in the Trials flashed back to him. He thought of the Numinous Mountains and the lands to their east, where they had ridden back from war only a year ago with the late King.

"Your accent is not of our realms. Please, tell me again your name and from where you hail," Vincent asked.

"I am a Luminarian, Count. There are many different peoples in these lands. And I told you before, my name is Khan Octar."

"Khan? You are Nothus!" Vincent exclaimed.

"I am many things to many people."

"You are a descendant of the horde kings!"

"Again you prove your worth! Yes, my fathers were from the tribes you speak of, but Luminarian blood also runs in my veins! This kingdom was destined to be joined to me."

Vincent was repulsed by this figure, this pretender. "You speak of dark secrets and plans. Ill indeed it is that things have taken this turn."

"Do not be naïve, Count. Would it have been ill had you done the *same* after defeating Bassus and that Nordic rabble? We are not so different, Count Cincinnatus. No, not at all."

Vincent caught a dim reflection of himself in a mirror to their side and his thoughts became lost in confusion.

"The powers will it," Octar added.

"And what powers do you and your frail shamans worship?"

"The princes of this world, Count, the princes of this world! Tell me, does your god reward you, or when you think you have gained an upper hand, does he strip power from your side?"

Vincent was silent.

"Does he give you what you desire, or does he cut you down like grass?"

Again Vincent didn't answer.

"My promise to this kingdom is one of freedom! To go where we could not go before!" He pointed to Vincent's stomach, "Your pain, I can heal."

Vincent felt the sharp sting in his stomach returning. The cutting edge growing within him ever since his captivity shot pain out into his whole body like lightning! Ever since the mountain he had hidden its recurring pangs from Evan.

What does he want from me? Vincent wondered.

"You have a choice," the voice spoke out as if reading his thoughts. "Retain your titles of Count in both realms, and serve me. Or, become a commoner, a lowly vagabond, landless and forgotten! It is not a hard choice I deem, Count."

Vincent held his stomach and coughed hard. He took a step toward the shrouded figure. "That I should rule and walk here and there only by your leave?" Vincent questioned.

The voice hissed as teeth came together like ice, "The greatest man in this kingdom, second only to me! Must I show you reason! All things would be yours, the women you desire, guards to command, endless lands, and retribution upon your enemies. Now, there is an offer I judge you will look twice upon! The blood of Legate Bassus: he who reviled and embarrassed you so many times."

"You would trade him for me?"

"That fool! Without hesitation! I know that he has long been a hindrance to you. There are still scars on your back from when he had you whipped in court, yes I know even of this. Would you also have it go down in our histories that his genius defeated you in battle? But he will not have the last word! No, he will grovel at your feet."

Vincent stared at the floor in contemplation.

"And think not that my power only extends to him!" Octar added. "It reaches far into the North! Up river and into the Great Sea from whence come the Nordic peoples! For my dominion is great, but also is my mercy. Do not think that the innards of your heart are hidden from me, Count. I know well of your childhood.

And also of a tale of foul ones who murdered your family."

It was a hidden organ that this stranger had touched. Vincent tensed from shock and adrenaline rushed to his veins. "How do you come to know such things?" he demanded.

"My dominion is vast, as are my subjects. I command great knowledge of both friend and foe. All these long years have the perpetrators of this horrendous crime along with their kin roamed free. And this at your expense and while you crawl without rest through this life! Because of their actions! End it Count! Take vengeance, Vincent, and gain victory and peace at last!"

It was too much to take in at once. "Silence!" Vincent demanded. "How do you come to know these things!" The blood was rushing to Vincent's head.

"It is out of my goodwill that I tell you. If you should spurn this opportunity to wreak destruction upon the murderers, then so be it. But if you do so then you have truly lost the path of reason, and justice."

"You speak of the impossible!" cried Vincent.

"Impossible? The names of the raiders have been in my keeping for many long years! For I was there in the North accepting the patronage of their King when they set out and remember the day that they returned! It was a great and fell expedition that sailed six summers ago."

Vincent was bewildered, for that was indeed the season of the attacks.

The shrouded figure continued, "But now all those lands belong to me and the power is mine to send the perpetrators where I will. Or, to direct you to them, if you so desire."

Vincent stood thinking, but his pounding heart blotted out thought. He didn't know whether to attack the dark figure for his audacity, or clasp hands in thanks.

A long moment passed.

Vincent stepped forward. His arms he outstretched.

He spoke.

"Take me into your service then, should all these things be mine." The pride surged in him as he saw himself standing over his enemies and subjects at last.

"Very well, Twice-Scepter. Your name will be acclaimed for ages to come because of your wisdom!" Octar pushed down his hands, "My servants drink Voluptas in promise."

Then the shrouded figure snapped his fingers and two other men appeared out of the darkness. Vincent was amazed, for all this time they had been beyond his notice. They brought forth a cup and it seemed as if its contents were smoldering in the dark. Octar lifted the cup to the level of Vincent's eyes, "Drink, and be healed of your thirst and relieved from your struggles!" He waited for Vincent to accept.

Vincent reached forward and saw the face of the shrouded figure for the first time. In the dim light, he noticed a broad and confident grin of red lips and shapely jaw. The eyes though, were still hidden in darkness. Vincent took the cup and brought it to his lips. He realized then how greatly he in fact already desired its contents! With an uncanny sense, he knew it would relieve the pain in his stomach and satisfy the thirst he had secretly suffered since his captivity. His fingers clasped tight around the goblet. His lips pressed against the metal.

Then did he smell that foul Mountain and in a sudden wash of memory revulsion grew in him. He remembered the dark caverns, the puking Legionnaires, the bloodied tables and cutting saws, the stench of death. The nightmare returned. Though he feared the consequences, he threw the cup down in sudden disgust!

He exploded in frustration, "No, no, you seek to bite more venomously than the Praetor! But I will not also be your pawn!"

"Oh but you already are, Vincent. You already are."

Sudden fear consumed Vincent in that enclosed room. He desired to run above all else but could see no escape.

"What then, will you fight me, to your death?" Octar laughed piercingly. "No, I will let you go freely. I have no reason to fear you, you serve my will already!"

Vincent started at the accusation, but found himself sinking back against the wall.

"You who would have stolen Princess Adeline Theodora away for yourself long ago! All so that you might enjoy a private escapade of love whilst the Kingdom fought rebellion! But your selfishness proved a useful tool. Your witness of her death was better than that of Lothar, who was intended. A blameless Legatus Legionis he would have been if the council had forced him into the position as they did you. However you, Vincent Cincinnatus, served the Khan's designs well. And your selfishness and hate will continue to serve me. Go now, vagabond! For even Nothus such as I have honor. Your flight shall be unhindered. Yet look not for solace in your fortress, for you will find New Corinth under my banners! Run to your old home along the plains, for its ruin no doubt is at hand! I fear you are no better than your father, who abandoned all his kin to death! Indeed, you are alike, crusaders and fools! Now run, and perhaps you will save some of what was once yours, though I doubt it."

With these words Vincent felt the footsteps of his doom following behind him again. Silently, he cursed God and the relentless shadow which pursued him. Then without another word, Vincent pushed past Octar and dashed out the Palace. In his haste he did not search out Evan but instead stole a stabled horse and sped away in terror, for Octar's words burned in him like a firebrand.

Within the palace, Octar called many guards to himself and only then breathed easy. For even the greatest of lords and magicians remain mortals.

Chapter 12

Nobility Reborn

SOMEWHERE IN THE THIRD REALM, a knight strapped on his armor. He tied leather straps tight and placed gauntlets on his hands. From the mantelpiece he took down his double edged sword, once wielded also by his father and his father's father. On a proud warhorse he came out of his sanctum's gates and rode forth to do good deeds. Little did he know that he was the last of his kind. He was the last of those stately men who daily laid their most precious possession, their lives, in the jaws of danger; the last of those who exerted against the throes of chaos by the courts and by their own sweat and blood; the last of those whose lives would end before the promise of their oaths be broken; the last of those whose common word was of as much worth as an oath; the last of those who valued dignity over naked flesh, yet rescued princess and harlot just the same; the last of those sworn to protect the weak and feed the hungry; the last of those who respected both friend and enemy; the last of those who challenged thieves and wrongdoers and meted out justice with a fair hand. Galloping down a winding dusty road, he disappeared into the grassy plains. No knowledge possessed he that the maelstrom of revolution and lawlessness was already within his lands. Yet had he known he would have rode out alone to meet it just the same.

Within his fair estates there was a village that of late bustled with travelers and excitement. It happened that Golro passed through this place clutching happily at his sack of silver, for it was not long ago that he had run upon the Lady Iris. Her generosity had given him life. A great journey east he had already made and he was eager now to spend his newfound fortune. The lusts of the world weighed heavily upon him, for he had known naught but poverty for many years now. In this village there were many shops and the sparkle of jewels shined tantalizingly in his eyes. Many adornments he bought and fine purple garb to match it. In these days after the Monarchy, anyone who was worth anything wore the royal colors. No longer would he be left out! All fine things would soon be his. Voluptas also he bartered for. Loading the drink into a great sack with many other things, he looked for a place to spend the night. Only the best would do.

He found himself walking up black marble steps, a smooth tower climbing far above him. Warm, smiling faces greeted him, some of them ornately painted. It was a place of spice, of action, of goings on. Even the shining walls draped in finery voiced a world both foreign and exciting. Many bodies roaming about filled the room with heat and perfumes and a slow rhythm beat out the sound of some melody from a portico above.

There also were servants who poured down Voluptas from these heights. An exquisite work of masonry funneled the tiny red waterfalls down to the bottom floor where hooded moneychangers stood ready to sell off the Drink to eager bodies. Many people wore masks, and Golro wondered at it. The masks were colorful and magnificent, but made it difficult to discern the wearer's expressions. Golro found himself uncomfortable with them. Yet the wearers assured him all was well and that the masks were a privilege attained through many nights stay in the Black Palaces. For so had these inn's come to be called. Golro noticed that while the masked dwellers gathered tightly in packs, they often stared into the warmth of the fire pit as if alone.

Those with the painted faces had slept there even longer and seemed to possess some intimate knowledge of the Palace that was beyond the average caller. It was all very mysterious and stimulating! Golro talked to many as dusk drew near and tales of wars in the Second Realm and of rebellion in the Third he heard aplenty. Yet he deemed these things far above and beyond him. There was one long un-tasted pleasure that he now yearned for above talk and mirth.

A room was set aside for him, but he was surprised when they brought her to him in front of the others. *Do the others also have to see?* A sudden pang of guilt crushed his gut and he had to push it down with the thought that, *By the Council's decrees, I am still a law abiding citizen!* The porter with painted face also reassured him saying, "Be not ashamed, for we all share the same pleasures and fates, Sir." Then he added, "Yet here is a key to lock your room if you wish it so." Golro took this iron ornament of secrecy and stuffed it hurriedly into flaps under the folds of his purple garments. The wooden door creaked open. A great closed chest stood across from him against the room's wall and atop was propped a mask of gold. The two slits for eyes stared back at him. He felt shameful. *I asked for no mask!* The girl entered now and he angrily shut the door behind her. She walked slowly, as if in a stupor. The key turned. The lock clicked.

His bed linens were soft and so was her skin. Yet terror hid behind the painted eyelids and he could not look away. She kept them closed as she lay there. It was as though her arms would fight him if they could. Then they opened! Terrible eyes! And they fought him with great fury! There was recognition in them, as though he were already a monster of her past. Then realization swept over him and he greatly desired to vomit, for he knew very well who she was! He rolled off the bed in horror as she ran to the door. The key he slid across the floor to her without moving from his spot or daring to look upon her. With some trouble she opened the door, for her hands were unsteady from the spirits they had prepared her with.

A great ruckus was heard in the hall and Golro ran out to discover its meaning. Terrified screams pierced his ears. Looking down the stairs at the gasping women in masks, he knew that theirs was needless panic. But black robed attendants streamed out the inn's wide gate and in their hands were scythes of fearsome design. Moreover, the lady from his chamber followed behind. At that instant Golro sprinted down the stairs. Had some protective instinct returned to him? He didn't know. He wasn't even sure who he was at that point.

Out the door he sped only to meet the raised hooves of a warhorse. The neighing animal came down from its hind legs with a crash, nearly crushing his body. Turning with a kick, robed bodies flew to the ground and it dashed off to a hill fifty paces away. Golro saw the lady knocked against the black marble walls when the men fell against her. He rushed to help the unconscious woman, his heart still ringing with guilt. A loud voice stopped him in his tracks. It was the knight sitting atop the warhorse. Golro peered up the hill with sudden awe.

"For the last time have I asked thou to depart." The knight said to the porter of the Black Palace, who stood before the others, torch in hand.

"The days of your pompous prancing about are over, Knight," replied the porter with malice. The sun had disappeared now and the robed men appeared as shades in the twilight. Golro was filled with a sudden dread.

"Maybe so," spoke the Knight matter of factly. "Either you

and your acolytes will perish, or I shall. Yet if my life should end, as anyhow it one day must, let it be in just such a fashion! My hand alone may not rein in this tide of darkness. Yet may God smite me down himself if my soul be bribed or sword grip loosened before that day comes!"

"Look at him! Idealistic martyr! Ready to die and be erased from the memory of the world! Foolhardy he goes out to meet emptiness!"

"Not emptiness, but fullness, nor darkness but light."

"Your hopes are in vain, for your god is dead!"

Golro saw the shades of men surrounding the knight in the darkness. He picked the woman up, his liberator whom he had repaid with wrongs. Yet his feet were stayed by the glimmer of the knight's red armor against the torch, and he listened once more.

The knight spoke in a voice of command, "Slave masters, deceivers, jail keepers of addiction's prisons, murderers and usurpers you are. But day will come again! Taste now my father's steel!"

There was a flash from the brandished sword and then a mob of battle. Men fell, stabbed and trampled, metal clanged and blood spilled. Golro ran to the site, the woman still in his arms. *Hopeless!* He thought. The robed men were soon finished with their work, though a different acolyte directed them now. Golro stared without blinking at the Knight's body, the neck and face cut to pieces. The Shades took the woman away from his frozen hands, giving him looks of disgust and questioning. Dragging her to the gate, cries of anger now came from her wakened body.

"STOP!" he suddenly cried to them, tears in his eyes. "She will stay with you no longer!"

"What say you traveler? She belongs to us, as do all the others so painted!"

"She does not! She is Iris Puter! A lady pure as flowers! Gracious as a Queen! She will stay with you no longer!" Golro cried again, his hands shaking with nervous fury.

The Shades ignored his cries and laughed at his pity. Yet when they were nearly at the gate, they saw from the corners of their eyes the gleam of the Knight's steel once again and were afraid. *Has he returned from death!* came a phantom of their thought.

"You people, you are tricksters!" Golro spoke between sobs. He grasped the sword tightly with his two hands. "I gave in, but not again. Foul things you have done and I tell you that this woman will go with you no longer!"

"Ungrateful wretch!" barked the leader as he swung with his scythe. Golro was outnumbered, yet his rage grew without bounds. Throwing and thrashing, he overcame his opponents. The new leader perished and also one other. The others fled in terror but Golro let them be. Now before Iris alone, he knelt.

"I am sorry, my lady." He declared with a sob.

She said not a word, for all was still a blur of shock, pain and elixir induced confusion. But she touched his head in mercy and then ran with great speed away. For from the battles of rebellion in the Third Realm she had come, and her mind was even now for her people and land.

Golro for his part came to the side of that great Knight, the last of his kind. Burying his body apart from the others he prayed and cried with great fervor the duration of that night. Then, selling his entire possessions next morn and giving the silver to the poor, he took up the sword and red armor of the fallen hero and bought a great horse. From there he set out on the first of many great journeys. So it was that even as the last faithful man of the Order disappeared, a new seed was planted. It is said that that day, above all others, the sun brought a great heat upon all the lands.

***

Kiathar cringed at the site of the poor soul being whipped. One could already see the ribs bulging from his emaciated body. Now the tight skin burst to reveal the white of the bones below. The more he bled, the more the man clung onto something hidden within his palms. Whatever it was, he clasped onto it as though it were life itself! *What can mere men do against such wrath?* Had he his sword and shield, Kiathar would have cut down ten, perhaps twenty of the onlooker Legionnaires and mercenaries before they could have taken him down. But his shield was bent and broken and his sword the booty of a drunk Centurion. It had been no real fight when they took him at unawares. His lands were confiscated, his wife raped and children crushed beneath the timbers of the burning house. The same timbers he had put up with his own two hands! He had been able to do nothing tangled in their nets and traps. Nothing! He had prayed to Odin for aid, to Thor to incinerate the wretches. Never had he prayed so hard in his life! Never had he been so helpless in his life. He could only hope that his family waited for him now in the halls of Valhalla.

His vows he had renounced unto himself as he left the frontier of the Second Realm. Since that day the duties of the Order had been far from his mind. There had been only the toil of the harvest and many strong children to raise up. But oh what he would give to hold his Equestrian weapons again! To peer at the frightened faces of his enemies from behind an iron helmet! It could not be. He was bereaved. Chained. Helpless.

The blood dripping prisoner sunk to the dirt in exhaustion and those who flogged him finally ceased their work. Crowds dispersed and the prisoner was left tied to the post in the midday sun. Coarse rope pulled Kiathar's hands as the troop began to march again. They moved over the body of the prisoner as though he were a rock in the road. The slave masters cared not and his fellow captives were too exhausted to struggle against it. So did each one trample upon him relentlessly, except Kiathar. With a hard shove he knocked down the man to his right and pulled the others back so that they were forced to follow his lead. At the sight of the ghostly frame of a man before him, he wondered of the fate of Alexus. He regretted abandoning the poor, addicted wretch.

Kiathar reached down with all his strength to open the hands of the dead man, the prisoners ahead of him fell from the tug. Inside was a blood stained crucifix. *I am with you!* A voice seemed to say as he picked it up. It was the god-man nailed to wood. He remembered his vigil on the last night of the Trials when he had knelt before such an icon and the bread that was supposed to have been the god's body. Kiathar would have laughed at the irony had he the strength of heart. *Does this god not know that I would rather him rescue me than suffer with me!* Still, Kiathar accepted the tiny object as a sign and clutched tightly to it as they entered into the mines. Deeper and darker they went, sliding through crevice and crawling through tight holes until the light of day was far behind and they were buried beneath the earth. There they would cut away iron ore for the remainder of their lives. Before they had even halted Kiathar's hand was bloodied from holding to the icon so tightly; for many long runs and hard battles can a Nordic endure, especially one of the Strongblade kin, but endless slavery in the tombs of the earth is a hard thing. Every man has his breaking point, Kiathar knew his would now come.

***

It was three days ride from the capital to the old Cincinnatus estates. When he finally reached the lands, the steed he rode was crippled with exhaustion. He left it in the fields to die as he sprinted to the house. He had seen the smoke rising from afar and now realized all his worst dreams had come true. The dwelling was nothing but a ruin and its dead inhabitants were strewn across the tall grass. In the distance smoke rose from fifteen more sister homes of the Cincinnatus clan. Vincent dragged his feet through the ashes and turned over the dead. *Someone must have survived!* He came before a pile of smoldering bones and fell to his knees in complete mortification.

Not Iris too! he thought in pain. *This evil should not have reached her doorstep!*

"Forgive me master!" came a voice from behind Vincent.

Vincent turned in a startle and stared at the bloodied mess of a man. *Arlen!*

"I have failed you again! I tried! I tried!" the old man broke into tears. "I could not stop them! I tried!"

Vincent crawled to the old man, a man he had known since childhood, a man he had hated, a man he had blamed. Suddenly the horror of his own deeds flashed into his mind and he reached out, cradling the dying man's head in his hands. "Rest now, friend," Vincent spoke into his ear so that he was sure to hear. "For you have served the Cincinnatus House well, though I have been late to see it."

"I tried, Master. I tried," he repeated until his breath was no more.

Thus passed away one of those tormented souls ever striving against the faults of their younger years. So greatly did he strive that in this, his dying moment, he only wished he had been able to give away more. But he had tried, and though in his last hour he knew no gratification except to please his master, there was victory even in the attempt. For at last had he overcome his weaknesses of heart in the bone shaking drama of deadly confrontation, in action.

Vincent, however, was left alive and alone in torment. His will sank, for all his deeds had turned to evil and the fruit of his works was too rotten to behold. He remembered Iris' words the day he had thrown Arlen into the dungeon. *One day, Kati,* she had said. *You will see that these things. Titles. Wealth. Revenge. They are nothing.* But he had not listened to her. He had walked away without looking back. He had deemed himself one utterly bereaved that day, but he was wrong. He wished he could go back now, he wished he could tell her she was right! His quest for revenge and glory had been a prideful parade put on in the dark. Now everything was truly lost!

Vincent Cincinnatus Kati sank into the earth on that spot and wished never to move again.

There would he have died had not a slave train come by. This foul trade was bountiful in those days of war and depravity. One of the long caravans had seen smoke from afar and turned toward the estate. So did the Twice-Scepter, the most powerful man in all the tales of Luminares, sink into morbid obscurity. Two more Springs came and passed. In those days when written records were kept only by the Council, his name soon became but a short verse of the troubadour's many songs of distant wars and feuds of the old order.

Meanwhile, another sat upon the throne in that same year. Past ages were spitefully forgotten and the people cursed their forefathers. Old laws were thrown down and the black palaces spread through every realm.

Chapter 13

Whispers in the Dark

WATER DRIPPED ON ROCK. Slowly. Steadily. Repeatedly. The same splashing sound echoed in his rotting ears every few seconds. It crashed down hard on the stone over and over again. Hopelessly, the drop shattered into a thousand pieces on the rock each time. Hopeless. In the absolute darkness, he made no noise as a body crawled across him to sleep on an open spot on the rock face nearby. There was no effort in life anymore. There was but to wait for death; to wait for the time when the guard would strike true; when the lash would be followed by a sword thrust through the heart. Miners picks clanked and clattered meaninglessly against the earth day in and day out, removing metals for the Legionnaires. Like a lifeless rock to be crushed by a miner's hammer, he waited.

Yet there was one man there, who had lived well beyond his allotted time, who still had eyes sharp enough to glimpse gold beneath pale stone. His shaky old voice pierced the darkness, "Vincent Kati, of the house of Cincinnatus, last of the Skilurus clan, Tribune of the third realm, Knight of the Red Cloth, GET UP!"

His name suddenly came back to him as from a dream. For years, there had been nothing but the lash to answer to. *Vincent Kati, yes, that is my name.* Shocked, Vincent felt with his hands for the man's face, "Who, who," it had been months since he had spoken a word, "Who are you?"

"I am the one who has been sent for you," responded the figure with a spark of enthusiasm which Vincent no longer had the capability to detect. Vincent took his fingers away from the long scruffy beard and pulled back in alarm.

"Sent? Sent? From? Do you come from..." Vincent hesitated in search of words.

"Sent from outside? Well, you could say so I suppose. But I've been in this hole for years, same as you. Probably longer. Too long in any case! My time is almost up," he said matter of factly as he sat down beside Vincent. "If you will not get up then I will sit. Ha!" He jabbed Vincent energetically as though he were not the enervated and aged stack of bones that he really was.

The two sat there in the darkness while a thousand thoughts came back to Vincent, like a pile of collected dust which springs into the air when disturbed.

"I have waited for *my* time to be up!" he snapped as his memories returned. "But it does not come." he added despondently. "If in any case you must sit with me, then call me not by such names and titles! They have long been dead. Call me instead The Accursed."

"Nonsense!" came back the feeble old voice.

"No! There is nothing for me in this world! All that I held dear outside I brought to ruin! The accursed of God, I am! All that I strove to protect was destroyed! First my family, then our Queen, next my kin." He paused and breathed deep the rough air of the pit. "Late was I to miss an old friend's company. The name of my fathers is damned! We are doomed to fail forever in protecting those we love. And so it is good that my name will die with me."

"It is a dark thing to wish for one's seed to be wiped out."

"Do look where we are, old man!" Vincent let out a weak

laugh in mockery. "*Darkness* consumes us!" He began to wheeze and cough now from the rock dust in his lungs.

"But the darkness cannot last forever, Knight."

"Do not call me that, old man! Long ago I forsook my vows, long ago did the light of God fail to shine upon our order. Now tell me how then light shall come to us while we pass year after year in these dungeons awaiting death?"

"Even death cannot withhold the light of God! But you speak the truth if you suggest that the Equites are no more, for I doubt that any faithful survive. But our God did not abandon the Equites; his light always shines upon them!"

"Are you a priest old man? For you speak in mindless riddles of hope and mystery! What does God mean for *me?* What does God do *here* and *now?* God is nothing but a jumble of nonsense I tell you!"

"The resurrection is no less real than you; though I see but a shade of your form, and hear only whispers in the dark."

"Fool! What sign is there that my body will not remain forever with the worms when I soon die," demanded Vincent, his pale eyes staring at the priest through the darkness. They were as torches on the brink of expiration, hope and vitality all but vanished. Yet not without a glimmer.

"The sign of the resurrection is our Lord, Jesus Christ, whose own body after mutilation and destruction had corrupted it, came back to walk this-"

"Don't tell me that!" Interrupted Vincent. "All in our kingdom have heard the story of that man from the empire across the Great Sea! He rose after three days in the tomb Luminares' ancient founders said. But I ask you for evidence here and now! Why is my perishing body of any more significance than a corpse?!"

The Priest let the silence absorb the feeble cries of the former knight and then spoke, "Very well, but then you also must give me one reason why your body should not be raised back up, should you die a Christian death."

"I am no stranger to death priest! Wars and feuds I have seen beyond count! I have walked upon bodies and seen thousands lain beneath the mud! The worms devour them and they are no more! We are nothing but dust Priest! We are no different than this rock which I shall soon lay upon in last anguish!"

"Awww yes, we are like the rock," he noted assuredly. "You have spoken a truth. You *have* had a beginning in the womb and you *will* have an end, when lifeblood no longer flows. The rock also will collapse and crumble under the weights of time; become the dirt beneath our feet. Is this not true?"

Vincent made no response.

"It is true," he answered for Vincent. "But did the rock also have a beginning? That is the question!" added the Priest.

"I see no significance in this." Vincent responded drearily.

"But you will. If a rock crumbles with time, it could not have always been there, else it would have crumbled long ago!" he exclaimed with satisfaction. "Therefore there was a time that the rock came into being. You will find it so with all things of this earth, even flesh, which is birthed through bread; bread through grain; grain through soil; soil from many rocks and small things. If the rocks of the world have not existed for all eternity, how can they exist of themselves? Anything birthed by another outside itself is in fact no master of itself. Who then is Master? Who birthed the tiniest of dust? Who made it so that all things must fall when placed at a height? Who designed the turning of the seasons and the rays of light? Who set Time rolling down its course in the first place? It is God who breathed all these into being. God is the Father of all. God, who alone is High King of all creation. Therefore the dust to which you would degrade should you die, shall indeed be raised up to life again, for he who made the four elements, he who is master over rock and sand, and all that is, loves mankind and desires to raise him up."

"Love?" Vincent came back sarcastically. "And what is that?"

The Priest paused in thought and then answered, "To lay down one's life for a friend."

"Ha! An overused maxim!" but the words had, in fact, struck home. He remembered Alexus. He thought of Arlen's last moments too and wished that he also had died in that battle.

"A simple saying no doubt," answered the old man. "But one which rings of a deeper truth."

"I wanted to have died for my kin when I saw their bodies burning like wood, their bones baking in the sun. But if there be a Father in control of all, it was *he* who bended my fate away from them! If God watches us from above, it was *he* who prevented me from laying down my life, from defending loved ones!"

"Was it, friend?" the Priest questioned in a quiet voice.

"Don't question me, old man!" Vincent exploded in sudden anger. "What can you possibly know of the cruel turns of my life? I may be a meager shadow 'neath these rocks, but I was to be feared years ago! A Knight, a Tribune and a Count, my wisdom was prized as gold! Above all do I know my own life I think!"

Taken aback, the Priest ruffled despondently through his thick beard. It was tangled and twisted with dry mud. "I have truly been a vagabond and a wretch nearly all my long life, and duly so, for my sins were grave in younger years." The priest stared off into the darkness down the tunnel. "I am no one great and few men have ever known my name. But I have watched many things for many years, and have learned much."

"One may learn much and still be a fool!" Vincent snapped. Deep inside he wondered where this harshness came from.

"Truly so," responded the Priest without offense.

"I tell you now, it is an ill will that follows my life! I have been robbed of everything. If that were not enough, a fiery pain burns my gut and addiction continues to stab my tongue! Better to die."

"You speak of the Drink of Voluptas!" the old man came suddenly close and stared Vincent right in the eyes. Then, leaning back as if he had indeed seen a sickness in the specks of white, he proclaimed hopelessly, "Our people name it after an old pagan god of excessive festivity. It has plagued the whole land by this time with its foul pleasures, merciless addiction and late-coming pain. It is the *same* infestation from long ago before the King's death that we feared, but understood little of. I know now that abstainers lose the haunting cravings within a year, you seem to have been plagued worse than most! It is made from the vilest ingredients, mind you."

"It is wine imbibed with human flesh, cultist elixirs, and the curses of the damned!" returned Vincent as though he spoke out of a nightmare. But that place *was* a waking nightmare! Images came back to him like spear points to his skull! Steep slopes and jagged rocks, with a single road winding its way up amidst thick thorns and brush. The road that meant certain death and torture. Screams came from inside, like moans from the earth. Within the walls there was blood. Everywhere!

The Mountain of Darkness it was.

The Mountain of Octar's Voluptas.

If the old man could've better seen Vincent's eyes in the pitch black he might've jumped. They were furious and scared, bloodshot and dry.

Vincent continued, "In a foul and evil place, it was forced down my throat. If there was one thing worth living for, it would be to see those bastard cultists who murdered my Legionnaires tortured before me!"

The old man's voice suddenly became rude and powerful, "Even after all this, does your heart still ring with the tune of hate and empty vengeance!"

"Yes, and I tell you now that if I could line up all those who offended me, I would see them and their kin tortured a hundred days and then slaughtered before my eyes! Those who slaughtered my mother and sister and their whole race! Alongside them would be Bassus who stole the Legion from me. Next, the phony King Octar who no doubt now sits upon the throne, along with all his cronies!"

As if he had been hurt, the old man responded angrily "It is not wise to mention the name of this lord of slaves! And he is no *King!* Now, I suppose you would've gutted Arlen too, your old household headmaster, for his many times apologized cowardice!"

"Arlen? How do you know these things?" Vincent responded, half angered and half dumbfounded.

"It is of no concern to you! But that you locked him away for a crime you yourself committed in order to forget your cowardice, that is of concern! You who yourself ran in fear when your family was attacked! Likely he has rotted away in your dungeon by now." The old man suddenly sounded like a great leader of armies. "Would you also murder Kiathar, your brother in the Holy Order of Knighthood, because he is of the same race as the murderers?"

"Who are you! How do you know this!"

No answer.

Vincent suddenly curled up as an attack of Voluptas came upon him. The frothy wine was in truth sickness in disguise.

Cutting pain in his stomach grew and his hands began to shake.
He needed the spicy-sweet taste, the elixir meant relief.

"Would you also let your heart be consumed with revenge
to blot out the fact that you alone abandoned Iris and your estate
to be consumed by Hydrus and this Lord of Slaves while you were
gone? Torture and kill all tyrants but the knowledge of this will
remain!"

"Silence! No more!" Vincent pleaded, now twitching in
desperate agony from the sickness.

"Which is greater, the torments of the Drink, or of your
soul?!"

Vincent puked up blood onto the hard rock. "My soul, my
soul," he muttered to himself between coughs. Louder now, he
screamed to the old man, "Take it away, I want to die!"

The old man crawled towards Vincent and cradled his
spasming body in his arms. Vincent's cries echoed down the
blackened halls and the other workers wondered at the agony,
thinking that a guard had come to beat them while they slept. In
truth Vincent suffered from the tearing agonies much more than
any other in the kingdom with the same affliction, for concentrated
doses of its ingredients had been forced into him raw. Moreover,
a special curse from the Lord of Slaves himself was upon the
goblet he had drunk from, though he did not know it. His
throbbing hurt was in unison with the whole kingdom, yet
intensified beyond anything they could possibly comprehend.
Much time passed before the pain lessened. It never went
completely away.

"It was I who abandoned them," Vincent whispered when
he came to. "I left my family behind. God forgive me!" suddenly
he became hysterical. "It was I who left them behind! I ran like a
fool! How I have longed to behold their faces! In dreams I see
them only, in dreams of terror! How can they forgive me? Priest?
Arlen, he at least stayed, though frozen in his feet. And I blamed
him! The blame rested on me, but I was too horrified to admit it!
I blamed *him!* Hate filled my heart against Arlen so much that I
could not live there longer! But you were wrong Priest! You were
wrong about one thing! Arlen does not rot in my dungeon!
Without my aid did he escape. Escape and run into the jaws of
death! I found him dying at my doorstep! He died defending *my*
clan, *my* people!" Vincent broke into sobs and covered his face for

the shame of it. "A better man he was than I, who wasted my years philandering and seeking glory! Why did he die? Better that I should have died! Why him and not me?"

The Priest said nothing, but let the man sob. Out of sheer exhaustion, Vincent eventually slept.
"Rest at peace, you who grow to still greater stature," the Priest whispered to the sleeping figure, "For you will be forgiven."

The warmth of sunlight touched the miners nevermore. Eternally confined to the darkness they were, for the guards feared that they should rebel should they see the light. In the mines day and night was governed only by the guard's torches. Now the faint, glimmering rays of these could be seen filtering in from some far off tunnel. The old Priest knew the work would soon start. He could hear the clinking of hammers and picks as the miners prepared. The time had come.
"Vincent Kati, GET UP!" he commanded.
Awake now, Vincent slowly rose.
The old man continued, "The time of reckoning has come. I have been sent to you because the brotherhood, the Order of knighthood has all but died. It must be renewed should this reign of evil be ended. You are the last of the Equites, should you not find a way to do this, then no one shall. Will you do this?"
"Yes...But what hope is there while we are here?"
"There is always hope! Now kneel, and before God and his Church, renew your Equestrian vows."
Vincent did as bidden, for it seemed a light as of fire shot out from the old man's eyes. He kneeled and began, "I, Vincent Kati of the House of Cincinnatus, son of Gilroy, do swear before God, His Holy Church, and these here assembled..."

Though he thought himself to actually be alone with the old man, others soon crawled through the pits to the sound of their voices. They came because they heard voices resonant and alive; voices which defied the rock walls which tied them down; echoes which rung free from the monotonous blackness which bound them all in hopelessness. They sat listening as deprived creatures of the darkness, blind and dumb, smelly and sick, to catch a glimpse of this thing called hope. The words they heard went something like this:

In descent through the cold mazes of Numinous' crags,
I am steadfast and true.
Through fires of hell's wrath into mystic's halls,
Darts of lust I pay no due.

Against quaking fear and nature's bite,
I unleash fury and force.
Along winding roads and faded trails,
I keep true course.

When enemies surround me at every turn,
My sword is a deadly tide.
But when peace reigns in the land,
Justice is my guide.

Last of all I give homage to God,
Because of him, this I swear,
To the unarmed, parleys and cowards same,
All shall know me as Mercy by name.
For mercy I am shown, though I deserve none,
And I trust in the resurrection until Kingdom come.

"Very well," the Priest sighed as the ritual was completed.

"But where am I to go?" Vincent again began to doubt the old man. "Am I to lead Equites here under the earth?"

"Perhaps." Answered the old man seriously. Vincent wondered why he had ever bothered with the old fool.

"Follow the narrow path to the right and do not look back," The Priest commanded.

"But I have been down that path a thousand times, it only goes deeper, there is nothing but iron and rock!"

"The Lord said to Peter, lower your nets, but Peter replied, we have worked hard all day and caught nothing!"

"I don't understand, Priest."

"Who said anything about the path leading to freedom? I only tell you that you must go."

"Very well, If it is your command." Vincent stepped forward, but the Priest slid against the rock wall. Vincent heard it and turned, "Will you not follow?"

In broken, hard breaths he replied, "My time is nearly at an end, young one. Press onward now, and don't look back."

"As you will it, Priest. God be with you." With that, Vincent turned again to step off.

But the old man reached out with sudden fervor, "Yours is the seed which will renew the kingdom! Fail not!"

"I don't understand."

"God go with you!" the old man let out in a dying breath as Vincent walked away.

Like phantoms silenced by the long years, bodies followed behind Vincent. They were miners with a faint remembrance of talk, of people, of life and of light. The guards soon arrived to rouse them. They were ready for trouble after hearing talk, for speech was forbidden. Yet they found nothing but the corpse of the old man.

For what must've been hours, Vincent hobbled along that underground path. He soon became aware of the miners who followed at a distance behind, yet didn't think much of it. This had been a day of most unusual circumstances. Yet still his will faltered, and he came to a stop. All hope of escape had been killed for so long. To revive such thoughts was to raise the dead! He himself had murdered Hope long ago in fear that he might one day wake to find it strangle him. Wishful thinking was dangerous for the mind of such captives.

What did the old man mean? This path doesn't lead to freedom? Where am I going then? Wasting my breath and bringing the wrath of the guards on the others here? Foolishness! And there, slouching against the rock wall to catch his breath, for he was very weak now, he heard a great cry from below. Suddenly alert, he pushed on to discover what it might be.

Bound against a rock face was a man who must've once been great, for he surely towered above all other mortals. Yet he, like all others, was broken here in the dark. Defiant he no doubt had been in younger years. Perhaps he even had had a chance of escape on one of thousands of days in bondage! *But even the strongest fall, even the proudest break to pieces*, thought Vincent as he felt the damp metal of chains about the man's wrists.

The captive gave no gesture to Vincent, for he did not care if he lived or died. The yell of agony he had let out had been as one last cry before death. It was too late now. He had let go.

"Who has the key to your chains?" Vincent asked.

"What?" came a low grunt from the man.

"The key?" repeated Vincent with some urgency.

"All is lost. They have taken it away." Suddenly the man felt that he knew this faceless stranger in the dark. "Who are you?" he demanded.

"I am Vincent Cincinnatus Kati, a knight of this realm. I seek escape, or shall die trying." Vincent felt a sudden surge of determination flow over him, as if saying the words aloud had fortified him. "Who are *you?*" he added

The chained miner could not answer because he suddenly broke into sobbing.

***

"Luminares is alive still!" Evan told the frightened family.

"Alive? The Kingdom is dead! And I care not! Only for my son's life do I care!" The mother pulled two toddlers under her arms and hugged them tight. Tears rolled down a face marked by scars and lines of stress. "You people came here with your swords and horses bearing promises! Yet you have not brought peace, but division! I only ask for my son, my eldest! I do not want the protection of the Lady Regalis! May she order you all away from our town! You promised safety! You promised! But it was a lie! Curse you!" she squeezed the young boy and girl tight as though Evan would take them away if she did not hold them securely.

"We who serve the Lady break no promises, lady Monica. Even we cannot withhold those who go of their own accord during the black of night." Immediately after the words came out, Evan rebuked himself for trying to rise above her, to prove her wrong. Now was no the time for argument.

"My son is a good man! He would not have left unless he

was provoked or threatened! I should have listened to him!   We should have never stayed here and accepted your rule! You bring strife! We were better before!"

"Forgive me m'lady." Evan spoke defeatedly.

"No I will not! You have ruined everything! I have nothing now! How will I provide for the youngest when I am alone? Get out now! And do not back unless my boy follows at your side! Curse you for what you've done!"

If I don't have my word, what do I have? thought Evan as he walked his horse down the town's cobble road. It was not only a general promise to the people that had been made. He had seen her when they first took up rule and assured her personally. All their faces, the faces of a crushed people with desire for a better life, they had lined the streets to welcome them in those days. Hope had left now, like a thief in the night. *Like Monica's son,* thought Evan with some spite. Yet in truth it was not just this family that had lost trust, but most of the town. What had he and the Lady's men offered the people but struggle, hardship and division? *He* knew it would be so even in the beginning! Was it wrong to look beyond this? Was it deception? *Have we lied to them?* But such things were necessary to achieve the end! Division was inevitable if the Black Palaces were to be burned down! Hardship was unavoidable if slavery to the Voluptas was to be ended! They did bring war and division, not peace! But it was the only way! The only way to find true peace! Maybe it would be years down the path, maybe after their lifetime, but it would be!

With these thoughts pressed upon him, Evan mounted his horse and rode out of the town at a great speed. He would find this boy, if it meant the family would believe for a while longer, if it meant the town would stay together for a few more weeks. A promise was a promise. So he searched high and low along the countryside, but the outlaws were nowhere to be found. Rain poured and drenched Evan until his chain mail clung against his skin with bitter coldness. He held back his shivering and pressed on. Evening soon came and it was useless to continue the search in the dark, but it was then that what he sought at last came upon him.

Two shadows passed in front with blades drawn while another grasped the reins of his steed. Evan made no attempt at resistance. He heard the crunching of leaves as men emerged from behind him. He guessed that they had bows strung and ready. From that direction came a voice. In malignant tones it asked what he was seeking after the fall of the sun and beyond the town's wooden walls.

"I seek the son of Monica of the House of Steadfast," he answered without a tremor in his voice.

"I am he. Speak your message speedily now, dog of the Lady Regalis! For my patience runs short for your kind."

Evan turned to look at his assailer, "Augustus you are then, and I bring tidings from your mother. She is worried day and night at your absence and will soon be in dire straits should you not return. Think of your younger brother and sister, Augustus, and return she bids you! There will still be a warm hearth to welcome you away from these wild woods!"

"Hummph!" the young man growled in answer.

"Even amidst the Lady's followers could you find company should you will it." Evan wondered at his words, *an outlaw joining the sworn followers of the Lady?* But perhaps such an invitation would be the fatal blow in this battle, so he continued. "True, we are a meager brotherhood. But our aspirations aim high! Challenge you would find, but also no greater friends. Come now, and return with me, I beg of you."

"Out here, I don't respect anyone who can't stand for me!" he shot back. "This wasteland is not exile for us! Not in warm citadels and villas did I come to age! Along gloomy roads connecting town to town and in the dark corners of Luminares' shanty's we here were bred and formed! These places molded us! You come as one high and mighty, but you do not know us! I starved in the City of Burning Light while my father caroused in finery! I came to these roads and took what work the Black Palaces offered us. I saved my family with the silver I collected from their list of indebted strangers. This is where I grew up, fool! It's a dirty business, but you'll find I'm as sharp as steel! Perhaps we're hard of heart, but it only makes us stronger. You people who serve the Lady are like flowers, glamorous, soft and weak. You will not survive the storm! Now be gone with you!"

"Strength of will comes not from callousness, friend. But never have you seen the Trials, for the Equites are no more. Had you seen them, you would know."

"Would you care to feel the sting of my arrows in your spine? If not, depart at once, stranger."

"I beg you to reconsider, if not for me or the Lady, then for your Mother."

"My family is of no concern to you. Now you have spoken your last here, leave."

So Evan was left with no choice but to return to the town in failure. Alone he sat in a hovel and ate nothing, nor did he seek the solace of company, for the clouds of the future weighed heavily upon him.

***

Deep in the mines, the guards knew something unusual was transpiring. They heard voices near where they had chained the giant miner. Vincent heard feet rushing down the rocky slopes of the tunnels and saw blinding torches and men with clubs and whips ready in their hands. He expected the worst. Yet in their haste some of the guards slipped on the poorly carved tunnel. Vincent kicked the torches from their hands. Miners who had followed behind Vincent like wraiths emerged to aid him and the guards were overcome as flies by a swarm of ants. Their bodies were thrown into dark chasms.

Grasping one of the torches, Vincent shone light onto the face of the chained prisoner and the man turned away in agony from the spectacular brightness. Even Vincent was forced to squint until his eyes adjusted and he could perceive the form of the man. There, with a body horribly scarred from the lash, was the emaciated frame of Kiathar Strongblade! The face of the once detested knight was wet with tears and Vincent's so long angered heart was drowned with compassion. He knew in some deep cavern of his soul that it could not be chance that had brought about their meeting here.

"Fear not, Kiathar Strongblade, your deliverance is at

hand."

Vincent searched the body of a guard not thrown over the side for a key, but it was difficult to find anything with so little light.

After some time he returned to Kiathar. The weakened giant of a man fell forward after the click of the metal. "Call it providence that we didn't throw *that* guard into the chasm! Eh!" he slapped Kiathar on the shoulder. Vincent wondered at the sudden rise of his spirits. He was utterly overjoyed to see a face he knew.

Kiathar chuckled now with tears of joy in his eyes, and then they both laughed as though a great burden had already been lifted from their shoulders.

Kiathar exhaled in relief and then spoke, "It must be the work of God that you are here."

"Perhaps, but don't hope for too much," Vincent responded. "We are not free, not yet anyway."

"All these years I suffered," Kiathar's voice boomed even as a whisper. "I begged him to free me. I see now that it was simply not the right time. I was left here for a reason. I was left here so that he might put *you* along my path. I counted you, my lord, as an enemy. But he saw fit to rescue me with your hands! They say Christ was a carpenter, that his hands were gnarled from working with wood. If that is so, then *you* must be as his tool, for now he reigns from on high." Kiathar opened Vincent's hand and placed a medallion in his grasp.

Vincent brought the hand close to the torchlight and saw that it was a crucifix he had been given. "I don't know what designs the Creator may have for me. But I know that I wronged you horribly in past years. When you should have led the platoon of Equites, I placed you in the rear. When you could have fought by my side, I ostracized you. When I needed counsel most, I did not listen. Forgive me, brother."

Kiathar fell to his knees, "I will serve you faithfully master, from this day to death!"

"You will be the first to return to our Order, Sir Strongblade. Now reaffirm the oath."

Kiathar began, "In descent through the cold mazes of Numinous' crags, I am steadfast and true..."

When he was only just finished, a hissing voice came from the shadows, "Do you deceive us stranger?" It was one of the miners who had followed. "Are you truly concerned with such frivolities whilst trapped in this grave? Do you even have a plan of escape, or have you forced us into rebellion and a sure death?"

"Worms!" exploded Kiathar with a sudden vigor. He stood and walked toward them. "You who fear death even as you live a life worse than its sting! Better to die in attempt than to live a life of slavery cowering in fear!"

"Throw yourselves on pikes if you wish, but my life is worth more than that!" responded the miner. "I hear now from your accent stranger, that you are a Nordic, an outlander! Your kind drove the whole kingdom to war it is said by ravaging the Numantines and then fighting the Legion! You pillaged my farm before I was thrown down here! I for one will not follow-"

"Be silent stranger," Vincent broke in. "For this is no outlander, but a Knight of the Red Cloth! You may address him as Sire or m'lord." The miner backed off further into the shadows in fear of Vincent. "And what he says is true, for it is not life that you hold onto by skulking in these tunnels, nor is it death that we seek above though we may come to face it head on. Now come, tell me your name fellow prisoner of these wretched halls."

"Ignavus son of Fastosus is my name."

"Ignavus, I do not know how we may escape this prison. But I will wander and fight until my limbs may move no more. I will start by following the path of these guards. You are welcome to follow if you wish. The choice is yours."

So Ignavus followed, but he remained in the rear and could be heard grumbling the whole way. Up they climbed, poor undernourished souls, feeling their way with every footstep until another flickering light penetrated their eyes. This guard, realizing it was not his comrades who returned, fled the oncoming tide of miners. This was a godsend, for the mines were a great maze and no prisoner therein knew their paths, being restricted to the carved quarters of the lower regions. The frightened guard was followed until he climbed a great ladder and crawled into a tight passage beyond. No doubt this would've been overlooked had Vincent and the others been there wandering alone.

After they were through this passage, the going turned tough. Thirty or more slave drivers came upon them and they carried whips, spears and clubs while Vincent, Kiathar and the others wielded mere stones. It was then that Ignavus turned and fled with curses against his fellow miners upon his tongue. He descended back into the darkness and was there consumed. But for those who endured the hardship, and were led to acts of courage by the sight of their brothers' death and suffering, freedom was soon in sight. The prowess of Kiathar and Vincent, though greatly weakened, could not be matched when a mob of one hundred desperate slaves was at their backs.

Glorious sunlight that shone upon them and they ran west along the mountaintops until their legs begged for rest. Here, beside an enormous boulder, Vincent straightaway prostrated himself and whispered a prayer of thanks. From that day forth the place was called Humility's Rock, for there Lord Cincinnatus gave thanks to a God who forgets not even a sparrow that falls; a God who brings to light what is in darkness.

Vincent rose and stood beside Kiathar, who stared off into the horizon. The others were running about wildly, jumping and throwing dirt and grass in the air. Their joy was without bounds.

"So much suffering changes a man," Kiathar told him. "I am not so haughty now."

"Nor I," Vincent added. In full light now he looked at the crucifix Kiathar had given him. The gory wounds on the familiar image stood out like never before. He remembered the Priest's words, *Love is to lay down one's life for a friend.* He looked back up to the horizon. As far as the eye could see green plains and sloping valleys stretched out before them.

Kiathar sighed, "I have nothing left. No family. No possessions. I am the last of the Strongblades."

"You have your honor, your duty and hope, Knight," answered Vincent.

"How can we be Equites without lands to rule?"

"I suspect that in the battles that lie before us, power will not be found with any claims to territory. Instead, those who win the minds and will of the people will succeed. It is in this war that the Equites must now conquer."

"But Sire, we are only two. Do you know of others?"

Vincent laughed, "Not yet."

Chapter 14

The Master Returns

A BELL RANG FROM THE RUN DOWN CATHEDRAL where the
Equites used to swear oaths after the Trials. From its high tower,
beneath blocks of charred and rotting wood, came its deafening
tone of brass against brass. And it was the call to bring iron
against iron, to face the rain of a thousand arrow javelins, to
charge the field, to climb the hill, to scale the walls, to overcome
the enemy, and to die. The Companions answered the call without
question, without a word. Evan answered. Haste was made, for
all knew this time it was the Lady herself in danger. They would be
outnumbered, but it made no difference. None sworn to her
service would desire life should her body be taken by the
Legionnaires and their dream fail.

They rode over hill and field as though shot from a bow,
speeding their way to her stronghold, to the last domain of the Old
Kingdom. If that tyrant would raise a hand against her, so be it,
but also would he see two hundred hands fly to their sheaths! Two
Companions remained in the small town of Progenitoria to protect
it, as was promised. The lonely watchmen's eyes looked to the
east, wishing they too could answer the call.

Vincent led the sojourners away from the mountains and
they lived off the land as they could upon the way. With full
bellies, their strength slowly returned. But Vincent slept away
from the others and in the dead of night, Kiathar sometimes heard
his screams. He wondered greatly of Sir Cincinnatus' plight.

Most of the miners filtered into estates as the group

moved, but a few stayed with the two Equites. The deeds of these
lords in the mines had awed them. Besides, what else had they to
return to? A burning desire fired in Vincent to go home, to stretch
out roots, to plow earth, to start anew. But like his followers he
wondered, *where is home? And who is now my friend?* The world
had changed so much while they were away. Through villages
they passed as ghosts from another generation. People avoided
them like plague! From a few they learned of the crushing defeat
of the Keleres and Justinian Solis. The Savior Khan, as they called
him, ruled securely from his mountain in the Second Realm.
Wherever there were towns, Black Palaces stood atop trampled
crosses. The old Kingdom had truly passed away.

"Was there not a fierce outcry to answer these deeds?
Please tell me of this tale also!" Vincent pleaded to a stranger.

"Outcry? Hmmm. You mean a fierce battle?"

"Yes!"

"With people like me involved?"

"A tyrant has stamped his boot upon the common folk!
Did somebody, somewhere stand up against him!"

"You're out of your mind outlander! A person like *me?
Fight?"*

"What about when they murdered the village priest?
When they burned down the chapel and put that inn of black stone
atop it? Weren't you angered?"

"Well..." the man mumbled.

"You must have gone there to receive communion? What
now?"

"Yes, I attended mass. But the priest was telling folk that
the inns should not be attended. Well, that is against the decrees
of our land you know."

Vincent's mouth dropped in disbelief.

Kiathar stepped forward, "There comes a time when one
is so wronged that it is better to die attempting to right it than live
on in torture. You wouldn't know of this, for you are a worm and
a coward."

The villager's eyebrows twitched in anger, but Kiathar's
harsh and close-up stare cut short the villager's fury. Out of fear,
he hurried off.

"Try not to be so cordial next time," Vincent joked.

"I was only being honest," he appealed.

When they asked others for news that day they received only questioning stares and turned backs. "Such discourtesy should be punishable," Kiathar muttered under his breath.

"Look who is talking!" Vincent laughed. Yet in truth both their hearts were gravely troubled at what they had returned to.

"Perhaps we should go south instead of west? We might fare better with barbarian peoples and uncharted lands." Kiathar asked as the sun descended beyond the horizon.

"I cannot so easily leave a people that were once mine," Vincent answered.

In a busy market they were treated as beggars; pushed and shoved by authorities, thrown into crowded alleys. They found themselves amidst the sick and blind. People foaming at the mouth hugged and greeted them. Even ragged miners who had seen the worst of slavery pitied these townsfolk.

"Surely the lord of the land has had pity upon you and sent some form of aid?" Vincent questioned.

"There is no lord of the land any longer," answered some.

"Our townsfolk have a ruler," answered another with a crooked toothed smile, "It is the Committee. People meet in the old lord's halls every fortnight to write laws." He put his hand to a wrinkled chin. "But I don't recall ever hearing of a law being decreed."

"Voluptas alone rules here now!" remarked another angrily. Vincent wondered at his words.

"How did you get to be here?" Vincent questioned them, for never had he seen such hunger and homelessness. "Were you banished from your abodes?"

"Yes!" answered some. Thrown out for practicing old religion; ruined, for refusing to pay taxes subsidizing the black inns and shipment of their wares; fined and jailed for not warning a member of the Committee that a borrowed horse would kick hard; The stories of madness went on.

Still more bowed their heads in shame when Vincent

asked them how they had come to such a sorry state. One woman came forward with tears in her eyes, "I sold my possessions, my land, my sons, my daughters, piece by piece. I did it of my own will!"

"What made you do such a thing!" Vincent questioned in horror.

"This!" she screamed with frightening agony. In her hands was a golden cup filled with thick curdled red drink.

The smell wafted over Vincent and he immediately knew it as not just any drink, but Voluptas. Memory of the Mountain came back to him and of his torture and the stench of death. He turned away from the woman without a word, for an urge to drink of that cup filled him and he feared it. They slept in the chill evening air that night, beside the muck of a hundred hovels.

When day came, the woman left her golden goblet and followed them. There was something in the Equites, as they had called themselves. The clothes they wore were ragged, but they walked with pride. "A pride born of things beyond this world," she told the others.

Vincent, Kiathar and the few miners returned to the crowded streets again. Many of the poor folk followed and this earned them more scorn from the populace. Yet they did not give up on finding news. Had all the Keleres really been destroyed? Was there no man who defied the tyrant who sat upon the throne? Where did these Black Palaces come from?

"The elixir you drink is filled with the blood of dead Luminarian subjects and with the poison of slavery!" Vincent declared to one woman with a silver mask obscuring her face. She stirred the red porridge at a market stand near one of the black stone inns. All he could think of was the bodies of his faithful legionnaires being cut to pieces and poured out.

"From where do you hail stranger? For this is no news to me. But what do I care how the masters make the divine milk? It is our sustenance, our laughter, our life!"

Vincent wanted to reach out to the woman, to tell her something of the horrors he had seen. If only she realized the atrocity to which she was taking part! His thoughts were checked as he stared at the cold silver mask she wore with its lifeless smile.

"I will tell you my deepest dream, stranger. You see those women," she pointed to a tall parapet atop the nearby palace. Vincent looked up and saw a number of ladies dressed in mere silks that swayed with the breeze. Masked men surrounded them and more stared upward from a tower below. The faces of the women were a strange white. "One more year working in these markets and I shall be one of them. The painted ones they are called, goddesses of our time. Men adore and love them day and night."

"The love of which you speak has not beauty, reverence, compassion, nor hope, I deem. The love of which you speak is usury and power!"

"Speak what you will, poor fool. But I'd rather be up there than down here."

"I see only half naked women with ugly faces," remarked Kiathar with impatience. "Let us be done with this masked fool and be on our way m'lord."

Vincent too was impatient. He felt he had returned to a different world. "Become a goddess then lady. Perhaps you will find it most exciting when men dribble on you and crawl below you. Yet you will find yourself more alone than before."

"I know it now! You are the brothers who follow the Lady Regalis! HA! I should've known it when I smelled you coming my way!" she laughed in mockery.

"Tell me who this lady is, for I do not know her."

"You lie. I can see it now, you are her followers. You have merely hidden your brooches of white flowers! That poor dog, huddled up in the far corners of the Third Realm! The royal hag should know that her time is over. We live in a new kingdom now! One without titles, except that of our one Master! Here the painted and masked women have no need for men to swear to them! We stand on our own two feet! We have freedom to express ourselves! Tell her when you return that she should come to us! We will give her a night of joys she'll not forget!"

With that, a wooden shudder was slammed in their faces and the masked woman closed up shop.

"People of your kind should be wiped out with the sword,"

Kiathar spoke to the closed shudder only half joking.

"No," answered Vincent, his mind half lost in thought. "They are as unfortunate beasts that are led cooperatively to the slaughter; slaves who do not know of their bondage yet." He stared out into the market, deciding who to speak with next. "We have been asking for word of the wrong royal person, brother," he added with excitement. "It is not Justinian Solis but this Lady Regalis that we must find!"

All through the day and night Vincent roamed about asking for word of the Lady's whereabouts until his following grew tired of his wanderings. That her sign was a white flower was all that he discovered. Many fell behind or left his side. Kiathar and twelve others kept with him, but even the giant knight began to question Vincent's aims. They barely had food enough for one more day's travel and that was only for the two of them. *Where would I go now, if not in his footsteps?* thought Kiathar in resolution. Through another village and along many roads they traveled until yellow sunlight again peeked above the plains. Vincent began to wonder if he had indeed lost his sanity in this vain search.

It was then that horses stormed across their path, nearly trampling them. The lady who had sold off her whole family hid and prayed that these fast speeding riders would not cut them down. All but one sped on by. This one slowed until coming to a complete halt. A brown hooded face looked down upon Vincent. The rider was fair and strong with sinewy arms and a chin which jutted out like hard stone. Vincent wondered if this had been one of his Legionnaires from years past. His eyes fixed on the brooch below the rider's neck, white petals formed around a golden center. Vincent knew these were the people he was looking for.

He stepped ahead of the others and approached the rider. "Can you tell me, Sir, where the Lady Regalis resides? For though I am of lowly station, I am determined to place myself in her services."

"That I can, master." The rider pulled back his hood and tears of joy formed at Vincent's eyes because of the face he perceived. But the rider jumped from his mount and no sooner than his feet touched the earth was he kneeling before Vincent. "I thought you dead, m'lord! Forgive me! Forgive me for failing to find you! Long and hard did I follow your tracks from the capital to the Third Realm. I was robbed of hope when the tracks led to your ravaged estate. Not one was left alive! Battles raged everywhere! But for that whole year I traveled in search and heard nothing! Forgive me master, for failing! Great must have been your suffering!"

But Vincent bowed his head low to the level of the man. "Evan, it is I who owe the apology to you. My heart was haughty and full of hate and selfishness. I left *you* behind and it proved my downfall." He raised the man up but kept his own head bowed. Embarrassment filled his heart because of his ragged appearance in front of his old squire, yet he embraced this wound of his pride. "Forgive a fool who should have heeded your wisdom years ago."

"Everything I am, I owe to you, m'lord. If you have wronged me, it is but a grain of sand in a lifetime of blessing. Now command me, master!"

"Nay, from this day forth you will call me such no longer. But tell me why you hasten along this path?"

"Our Lady is in grave peril. The entire First Legion marches against her on grounds of insurrection. We who are sworn to her service hasten to her side to bring aid!"

"The years have weakened me, but there is a fire for battle yet in my veins, if this be a noble cause?"

"Never more noble a cause was there! One fit for a valiant death, I daresay. Yet my companions and I are mounted, while you walk. You may not reach the battle in time and I may miss my friends should I tarry with you any longer!"

"Kiathar and I could run many leagues before tiring, should our wills be hardened to it. Yet we must know the way or we will surely be lost in these valleys and forests!"

"Then thank our Maker, for this way you surely know well. It is the path to the Cincinnatus estate. Her abode is very close by to your family lands of old!"

Struck with amazement, Vincent questioned, "Tell me, Evan, who is this Lady Regalis?"

"The last of the royal line, some say. Others tell of her coming from across the Great Sea. One thing is certain, from wherever she hails, she has brought hope with her. Without her the Dominion will fall to disarray and all will be lost."

"The Dominion?" Kiathar questioned.

"There is no time to waste," Vincent interrupted. "Go ahead, Evan, and delay no longer. We will meet you on the field of battle, God willing."

"Until we meet again!" Evan declared as he mounted the steed. With a wild yell, he spurred on his horse and flew down the path and out of sight.

"I am with you my liege!" Proclaimed Kiathar in a booming voice.

"What of us?" asked one of those who had been enslaved with them in the mines. The vagabonds behind him echoed the plea. Among them were a few elderly.

"My brother and I must hurry ahead, but I promise you will not be forgotten if you follow behind. Master Evan will treat you well when you have arrived, you have my word. It is but a day's walk and I will tell you the way."

"What if you are dead when we arrive?" asked a homeless man.

Vincent felt foolish.

Kiathar stepped in, "Perhaps it is best you return to the villages from where you came. We walk a perilous road."

"You were right," Vincent said after they were away. "I just couldn't cast them away after their faithfulness."

"Do not deride yourself. Compassion should be prized, even in the fiercest warrior," Kiathar stated.

"Gird yourself against the onset of exhaustion," Vincent picked up a running pace.

Over hill and through valley without ceasing they carried on, lest they come to their objective too late. Yet behind them on the road, the miner whispered quietly to the vagabonds, "I saw that man find a way out of caverns so deep even the bats refused to live within. And I saw him charge twenty armed men like it was nothing, and *win*. He will not die. I was once a hunter and could track. I will follow." The miner stepped into the road and began to walk.

"I have water and food enough for the journey!" exclaimed the woman who had confessed her addiction. She held out a satchel and followed behind. The others followed suit. Along the whole path ahead she refused to drink water or eat until all the others had first partaken. Nor did she rest unless the others rested first. "I must give a good account to Lord Cincinnatus," is all she said when questioned.

***

       Evan gathered his Companions and came down the valley just as the advance guard of the First Legion marched onto the catacombs. Speeding on their horses, they fixed themselves between the enemy and the network of caves wherein the Lady resided. Their charge was sudden and the advance guard reeled from the force of the advancing lances. Yet the Companions, equipped with mere leather gauntlets and coverings, were no match for heavily armored legionnaires in a standstill of close combat. Once the charge of the horsemen had been stayed, the fight became evenly matched. Steel swords of the advance guard would cut down horse and rider until the Companions no longer outnumbered their foe. Moreover, the remaining nine centuries of the Legion advanced at a steady march from six leagues away. They would soon flank the horsemen and prevent any route of escape. The situation was hopeless.

       An hour later Vincent and Kiathar crested the hill above the caves. They paused and leaned on their knees to catch their breath. For three hours or more they had run and their legs and lungs ached like never before.

       "The fight has gone on for some time," Kiathar exclaimed between heaves of breath.

       "Look!" Vincent pointed down the hill. "The advance guard has cut through the horsemen's center!" he exclaimed in gasps. "They will soon have Evan's men split in two!"

       "Let us press on then. Perhaps we can yet break the advance guard before the Legion arrives. They will feel the sting of loss before they can win the day!" Kiathar began to run down the hill but then turned to Vincent who waited behind. His master stared at the nine centuries marching down the valley only half a league away from the caves below.

"We will fight against the remainder of the Legion."

Kiathar's face wrinkled in consternation. *Better to go down in a brawl than waste our lives without a fight!* Reluctantly, he raced after his master.

The tramp of their boots shook the earth and the clanging of the metal spears and shields was like oncoming tide from the Great Sea. Vincent ran before their lines and his intestines shook with fear. No man could face such might and not feel terror's sting! He steadied his feet and stood firm.

"I call upon you, Legatus Legionis! You who command this Legion come forth and make parley! Before your men are overrun like so many wooden playthings! Come forth!" So Vincent yelled against the mechanical wave of armor and blade. Ready to kill, trample and burn, there was no answer from the mass but a continuing advance. "Come forth!" Vincent declared again.

Kiathar at his side made ready to charge. He picked out two from the line he would take down.

The stamping boots of the Legionnaires stopped!

A legionnaire suddenly marched out from the left flank to meet them. The red crest of his helmet was horizontal, indicating that he was an officer and likely in command of the troops. A black cape flowed from his back and a scepter was in his hand. His men stood still as trees, yet from thirty feet away Kiathar could see nervousness in their eyes. *Why?* The knight was perplexed.

The walk of the officer was strangely stuttered, as one might be if delusional from thirst. *Is it Bassus?* thought Vincent with anticipation. He stifled a fleeting desire to take revenge. *A knight shows mercy to the worst of enemies in parley!* He reprimanded his thought.

"I am the Legatus Legionis, what reinforcements-" the Legionnaire paused and the eyes behind the iron helmet searched the faces of Vincent and Kiathar. "Impossible!" he suddenly declared with eyes fixed on Vincent. "I saw you go up into the mountain! None who enter that place come out alive! In the troughs they are filtered and destroyed! Has my disease killed my vision now also! Have I given way to insanity? Come, tell me your name?"

"I am Vincent Cincinnatus Kati, Knight of the Red Cloth."

"Truly so?" answered Exander. He removed his helmet to reveal a bloated face. Bloodshot eyes stared at Kiathar and Vincent in utter terror. Foam leaked from the edges of his mouth and dried fluids crusted against his eyelashes. In the face of the man before him Vincent perceived Exander Quickfoot. A surge of anger rose in him! Exander had betrayed Vincent and the Legion and caused thousands of innocents to die. Nothing less than death did he deserve!

"I am the Grand Dragon of the First Legion!" Exander now proclaimed raising his brow to the sky. "Ha!" he fell to his knees suddenly out of weakness and caught himself only with his left hand. "Master of the Lodges. Caretaker of our Sacred Vessels of Voluptas." He coughed up blood and began to break into shakes. Vincent suddenly feared the familiar signs he saw before him. "And I am breaking apart inside like pottery under the axe!" Exander bowed his head, "All my ways have brought ill and I revile myself, truly. The Communion of our Dark Religion is poison, I tell you!"

Vincent was surprised at the sympathy he felt for the betrayer.

"An unusual predicament we find ourselves in my lord. I don't know whether to smite him while he's down or beg our God for his soul," whispered Kiathar in Vincent's ear.

Vincent wasn't listening to the Nordic Knight, for there was a connection between him and Exander that none could detect. Only now did he see it and knew it came from the Mountain of Darkness. Their burdens were the same. "You were once a Knight, you were not always this way Exander."

"No, no lord! From the beginning I was corrupted! From the beginning it ate away my flesh! In the Second Trial! I took it willingly!"

Vincent's eyes opened wide in amazement. Now he realized after all this time that the cursed Drink had been under their noses for generations! It was an evil from the East! All along Luminarian Equites had been trained in immunity to the cultish ambitions. "But none who partake ever come out from that pagan temple!" Vincent questioned him.

"I did. Their acolytes let me loose. I was their seed." Exander looked up at Kiathar, "And you!"

Kiathar stared back in anger. He could've crushed Exander with his boot then and there.

"You lingered too long and prevented me from gaining the scepter of the Third Century earlier! The Legionnaires distrusted me because of you! You lingered for months even when all had abandoned you!" Exander pulled a steel spear from off his back and held it before Sir Strongblade. "Take it! Take it quick, before I regret my actions!" he laughed weakly at this.

Gold glinted from the spear, it was the platoon pilum! Kiathar took the weapon and his mouth gaped in astonishment.

"*Something* must be set right before I die!" The Legionnaire broke into furious shaking now and clung to his own body as though freezing from coldness. "I am all spent," he whimpered between chattering teeth. "Too far down those roads have I roamed."

Life oozed out of Exander slowly as does black puss from an incision, and then he died.

The troops of that Legion stared with great awe at Vincent. Whispers broke into loud questioning as rumor spread among them. "Who is this man who strikes down our captain without laying a hand upon him?" they asked each other.

Vincent bent over and closed Exander's eyelids. He grasped the helm of the Legatus Legionis, the same he had once worn, and held it aloft. "I am Vincent Cincinnatus Kati, Knight of the Red Cloth and rightful lord of this Legion!" he proclaimed with a loud voice to the whole Legion, as if in answer to their questioning. "I have come to reclaim what is mine and so do I now demand your allegiance. A return for the folly of betrayal has been visited upon your master. Let it not be so with you! Oaths were broken, redeem yourselves and fulfill them now."

A sudden loud crack ripped through the air! Vincent jumped from the sound.

Rain droplets began pelting the field now and a flash of lighting tore through the sky before them, followed by another crash of thunder.

"It is a sign," Kiathar whispered.

A few cheers arose from the ranks. The nine centurions

waved their scepters, treasures of the Black Cult, and ordered the march. Whips cracked from behind the formation, a tool the cultists originally planned for use only as extra motivation in the heat of battle. Yet as if wild dogs had been let loose in their midst, four of the centurions fell into the formation and were suddenly trampled on. Chaos ensued all throughout the nine-hundred! Who would have believed that many a man was still alive and forced to fight who had lost friends in that great treachery years ago? Moreover, veteran Legionnaires had missed promotion because of the sway of zealous cultists, yet these still commanded a faithful following in the ranks.

The legion was as oil that awaits a spark. Many fled now, preferring to run than face the confusion of a murdering mob. However, Vincent and Kiathar charged into the fray, cutting down all those who defended the scepter bearing cultist leaders. When all was done, Vincent stood in a pit muddied from skirmishing. Six centuries of loyal Legionnaires surrounded him.

An older veteran grasped Vincent's forearm and bowed his head, "Our master has returned!"

***

Octar, self proclaimed King of Ages, laughed a deep and horrid laugh. "You think you have beaten me, Lady Regalis, but I know you too well now! Your life is an open scroll before me and you are already my daughter!" So he spoke to the night winds. The bowing messengers quivered at his every word.

Before a great crowd of subjects his voice was like thunder, the reach of his arms like the sky, his thought as fast and piercing as lightning. "You are the Khan's flock which will connect all worlds. From the reaches of the far north across the Great Sea to the plains of Luminares far south and far into the east, we are one! True freedom I bring! Freedom from your old kingdom's tyrannical laws, freedom from your old kingdom's tyrannical God! Freedom to do as you please; to taste the sweetness of life; in spirit and body! To act from your desires and not regret! Like a blanket of black velvet I descend upon you!"

A great cheer erupted from the throng below Octar. They peered up at his silhouette in adoration and bowed before his massive black temple.

Octar plunged his daggers into the writhing body before him. The muffled victim's cries trapped behind the choking rag ended, the fists tightened against chain lost their tension, blood sprayed and spilled onto the altar and the people below greeted the splashing crimson with yells and jumping for it was the essence of Voluptas. "Luminares! Kingdom of the Night!" they screamed in altering tones and rhythms. Man pushed aside man and even climbed atop woman and child to reach the dripping dew, the honey from above.

"You are my children and you know me well. Now go forth and revel in the Night's loving arms!" The booming voice of Octar ended and the tall shrouded figure turned and walked away.

The people broke into revelry and tore a path into the city. Throwing horse, mule, market stand and beggar aside just the same, they pushed their way towards the numerous Black Palaces. Every one of them raced lest the darkness grow old and dawn come before their pleasure had peaked.

Octar's Mountain stood like a distant statue behind the temple. Its jagged slopes and angry thorns stabbed and scratched angrily against the stars and moonlight. Up that lonely slope Octar walked to his proud throne. From there he would look down upon his people in delight, with tortured cries from dungeons below to echo his every thought.

Chapter 15

The Lady Regalis

Two DOGS BARKED IN TERRIBLE FURY, wheezing from the bloodied sores on their sides. Jumping and clawing at each other, the pitiable beasts filled the crowded room with shrill shrieks and low growls. At last the smaller one let out one final whimper as foreign teeth sunk deep into its throat. The sound was pathetic and helpless.

Nicephorus Puter descended into the crowd, letting the loud ruckus of gamblers, traders, mercenaries, whores and travelers suck him in. It drowned out the screeching of his thoughts. He had seen it all, had satiated and drowned every dark desire in his heart until his belly was filled, his lust climaxed, his hands bloodied, his belt tied tight, again and again and again. But now emptiness cut him like the jaws of a desperate animal. With the hourglass's last grains of sand falling to their eternal tomb, he could not rise above the pangs any longer.

There, on the other side of the battle ring, were two women with painted faces flaunting their bodies. One breathed down the neck of a trader, the other laid upon a table. He knew the one standing to be Ishtar, for he had once possessed her. Yet in truth he had possessed nothing. A mistress of the Black Cult, she wielded hidden power. Many venerated her, but always from afar. A foul goddess she was who wooed men with promises. She tempted them into a web until at last they worshiped her with body and soul. Then, when her traps were set, with a cruel smile she would move onto a new victim, keeping the previous tied in knots, like a fly caught in a web. Gone beyond reach, a sharp eye she kept to watch him writhe in jealous agony. Nicephorus had cursed her. Yet not a hand could he have raised against her in revenge, for her power was without measure in the dark circles.

The other woman was a favorite among the men here. She didn't want love, she would tell them. The tantalizing stimulation was enough. "It's a simple bodily need," she had told him once from behind thick white paint covering her face. But Nicephorus' body was dying slowly now, for Voluptas kills a few everywhere. *Some people are doomed by God to be unable to abide the liquid long! Or perhaps I have drunk my life's share in but a few years?* Nicephorus would ask himself. Either way, the consequences were inevitable! *It is not fair that death should visit me so soon!* "I deserve better!" he would complain to the physicians whose potions did nothing. "I will sell all my possessions; sell my most valued servants into slavery, whatever it takes! Find a remedy!" He protested to no avail.

A tall standing man walked over to the whore on the table below. He leaned over beside the woman, affectionately took her hand and dared ask the painted one of her past.
"I have forgotten my name," she answered him with a haunted whisper, daring to look him in the eyes. A terrified look came upon her face as memory of the sharp pain of a lost life returned to her. Memories and meanings were pushed aside however, as she poured the Drink into their glasses and they filled their entrails with sweet numbness.

Nicephorus too drank the blessed cultish elixir in the balcony above. Sinking into a chair, he drowned himself in the liquids and watched two slaves brought into the theater below. They beat upon each other cruelly until life, the most precious of treasures, was snuffed out in a ring of blood. Nicephorus could taste the iron like malt in his mouth as the loser died. He knew what ingredients, what vicious bloodied recipe went into the Drink in some far off mountain. He knew he joined in the murder of so many thousands when he drank. Not everyone knew this! A privileged class he still was!

The dying man below peered into the world around him

one last time before he perished. As he looked out into the fading environment, his eyes chanced to meet Nicephorus'. Horrified, Nicephorus was unable to look away, for his own face he saw in the man before him! For that short moment, he wondered if he had indeed wasted his time on the green fields of this life; an inheritance spent away; friends who truly cared gone; a wife hurt and lost; a marriage failed; a life alone amidst a multitude; in the crowd, dying. Nicephorus lifted his goblet to his mouth in defiance and drained the ghoulish soup within. His eyes still stared below.

Walking away from the thoughts he bore in seeing the dying slave, he walked away from life itself. Nicephorus never left those halls.

***

"Sire, she is our hope and our life. Bow low before her. Never let your head be above hers," advised Evan.

"What does she look like?" Vincent questioned.

"Skin as soft and white as the lily, hair as black as midnight. She is soft spoken but commands a stare that burns like swords of fire!" Evan paced the tiled floor staring off into space. "Her words, when she uses them, pierce the heart like darts!"

"You speak as if you are given over to love!" Vincent slapped him on the back.

"Forgive me, Sire, I speak beyond my measure. I did not mean it in such a manner. You must understand, the Companions and I," He found himself at a loss for words. "She is our patron, our caretaker. Sire, if you had seen the starving children who fled to her side when the first villages came under our protection you would've," Evan stared at the roof again looking for words. "She is like a mother to us all," he finished the sentence. "And more, I suppose."

"She is generous *and* great then?"

"Magnanimous and powerful, sire."

"A rare combination. Well then, I shall not let it pass from my memory to lower myself in her presence!" Vincent made a show of pretending to bow. "Although, I may have a hard time if she is short."

"Our Lady is taller than you sire!"

"Then *you* must have truly had no problem when you went before her!" Vincent snickered as he looked down and patted Evan on the head jokingly.

"Oh no, I've never been given the honor to meet her before, Sire."

"You've never - what? But, tell me, you have seen her before?"

"Not in person Sire, no."

"How else would you have seen her," Vincent laughed. "But how then do you know these things?"

"She is our Lady Regalis, all who oppose the Dark Ruler know these things!"

"Is this so," Vincent stared down at his feet in deep thought.

A brown robed man entered the hall, "The Lady will see you now, Sire."

Vincent followed the man around the corridor and through bronze plated doors. Into a broken down courtyard overgrown with plants and flowers they walked. Vincent felt he had entered into another world! Green vines climbed the stone walls and purple tulips met them at their base like so many twirls of dark velvet, soft grass covered the ground and in patches there were deep rooted bushes, gatherings of pink Liatris standing tall, and scattered everywhere were pure white flowers dappled in morning due. The sound of running water tickled his ears and sweet vegetation filled his nostrils. On the far end, lit up by a ray of morning sun, was a mound of tall grass firmly set in place by the long winding roots of two trees of oak. Their greened veins of wood reached far above the roofless walls into the sky and provided a massive canopy. They approached the mound and at last Vincent saw what appeared to be an empty throne set between the two trees. A bare wine red cushion was placed at the base of the stonework and gold traced the winding sides up to its head.

"Pardon me, Sire, the Lady must have stepped out of the court. Wait here please," with that the worried little robed man was off in a hurry.

Vincent stood still with eyes wide and let the place absorb him. He stared at the swaying boughs of the oak where a ray of sunlight snuck through the foliage. When his gaze fell he saw a woman clothed in white and gold kneeling by a stream in the far corner. Approaching the woman from behind, he bowed low and spoke,

"My Lady, I, Sir Cincinnatus, am at your service."

"Awe yes, Sir Cincinnatus, you were expected." She rose and touched the green stems of the tree before her, but did not turn her face. "A great feat you have accomplished in turning the Legion on its heels."

Vincent scowled, "It was not my power that caused such a sudden overthrow. I am worthy of no such praise."

"The wood of the mighty oak still comes from the flesh of a small acorn. The word of your rising from the dungeons was as a call to arms for many older Legionnaires."

"My lady is full of wisdom, so I will not question. Yet my heart tells me that my part in these things was of no great stature."

"Perhaps it is only given to those of smallest stature to accomplish the feats of kings." The Lady Regalis turned toward Vincent now and he bowed his head in humility. Yet staring at her feet, a sudden inclination, a driving inducement, pulled the gaze of his eyes and lifted his head to see the Lady's face. The blazing radiance that he had momentarily perceived had struck a foreign memory, a past from beyond the grave he feared and yet hoped was before him.

Indeed, as his eyes met hers, he knew it to be true! A dreadful trembling came upon him as he got to his knees and crawled toward her with tears in his eyes. With a dark and sunburned hand he reached out and touched the leather of her sandal and his fingers, scarred from blades and gnarled from battle, felt the warmth of her unblemished skin.

"Do my eyes deceive me? Tell me this is not a nightmare sent from above to haunt me for my misdeeds! Are you real Iris? Is this your skin, is that your voice?"

"Yes Kati, it is I." She touched the folds of his bowed head. "Rise now and speak."

Two dark eyes stared at him from beneath falling locks of black hair. Her skin shone like moonlight and an air so foreign was about her that Vincent wondered if his senses had failed him. He saw in her the same light he had seen before, one he had cursed himself for extinguishing. Yet now it was radiant beyond imagination. *If the God of heavens still allows miracles upon the world, this surely is one crafted by His hand,* Vincent thought.

"What you said long ago was right," Vincent confessed. "Forgive me for not heeding your words!"

"Why did you not listen, but instead abandon us?"

"Hubris and hate for God and man clouded my sight and bent my will. I pushed you away because of your love for Arlen, a man I wrongly persecuted. But he was willing to right his wrongs, even to the cost of his life! Alas, I hid the evils that I once committed! For I ran away on the day of my family's demise and thereafter swore to never tell a soul! I kept this secret from you all these years. For it was easier to flee than to face down my faults, easier to blame Arlen than to see the monster in my heart. This is the truth Iris, as you have never known it. Tell me now how horrid my face is to behold. I perpetuated the evils I started that day with endless wrath and little pity. I abandoned you, I left behind my family's people, the clan, to pursue what I thought was justice. To pursue worthless revenge and hate and glory! All the time trying to forget what was imprinted permanently on my memory! But I have lost title and wealth and all that I possessed, I have come to ruin and now do I see my folly. Just as you said would happen."

"Vincent Kati, were there earthly medicine to heal the wounds you have suffered, I would've spared no expense in procuring them long ago."

His thoughts lightened at her speaking his name. *Kati.* Only those closest to him had ever used it. It was refreshing, like the smell of the growing grass around them.

She squeezed his shoulder with her delicate fingers, "Your wrongs are lessened by the fierceness with which your heart has tried to rectify them. I forgive you!" Vincent let out his breath. "Here you will find comfort and rest," she continued. "Here you will win true glory from the praise of your people."

Vincent glanced up when she spoke of the people as his.

"Valor with humility," she continued, "Strength with gentleness. Power with love for the disempowered. The code is already written upon you. It was in you when you returned from the Trials so long ago. Knight, you have but to renew it and spread it to my people." She knelt and clasped his hands and looked hard into his eyes. "My Dominion is wide, not yet has the Slavemaster crushed us in his merciless fist. My pardon is upon you, Kati. Rise now." Vincent finally stood and they began to walk together through the garden.

"But, m'lady, how did you come to take such power?"

"I *took* nothing. Where there were sick, I healed. Where there were hurting, I comforted. Where there was disarray, I spoke of unity. I never demanded homage, nor did I ask for this garden, this fortress of hope. I only gave. And some gave in return. But the Lord of all lords has seen fit to exalt me above all women we have known, save one. And ever do I ask her who is enthroned above for the grace to serve her children."

"Truly, the handmaid of the Lord must have a place for you close to her heart. But tell me, two hundred Companions would die for you and you have not demanded homage of one?"

"I did not write the book of oaths to which the Companions swear. That was the working of one whom I am told bears no name from his kin. But he is called Evan, which means Young Warrior in his native tongue. I have yet to meet him in person, for he is ever busy, as am I."

Vincent laughed.

"What amuses you?"

"The Companion of whom you speak is my squire of old. You have known him in days past. But I see clearly now that he has since grown to great renown and gallantry."

"Is this so?"

"It is, dearest one."

Iris' heart stopped at these words and she turned her face away. "The ways of Providence are beyond reckoning. And life sometimes takes turns unforeseen." She bowed her head, *So shall my life be lived forever in solitude and my womb ever barren.*

"So it does!" responded Vincent joyfully, unable to detect her thoughts.

Vincent Kati spoke with the Lady Regalis of times long lost and of the matters of the Dominion. She ordered a feast prepared in two days time to celebrate the victory achieved. Vincent also learned from her that there was at least one other Legion fielded under the Dark Lord's banners and another in the making. His heart was greatly troubled at this, for he could see no way of defeating such armies or winning over a populace that served this Dark Lord willingly.

***

The surviving Companions of the Dominion were seated at a great oaken table in a corner of the great hall. Vincent made his way to its head, all the way receiving acclamations from common folk for his victory on the battlefield.

"The Legionnaires melted as wax before you! God is at your back, lord!" exclaimed one as he bowed.

"Is it true lord, that your words send men into turmoil?" asked another.

"What spell did you cast upon so fierce an enemy?" a rich looking man grasped Vincent's arm.

Vincent looked him square in the eyes, "Do you think me to be a Knight of the Black Palaces? Whatever power it was, it was not mine and it certainly was no spell!"

"Our Knight, Savior of the Dominion!" cried an old woman as he passed.

Vincent was troubled at their words. *They deceive themselves. It was but one favorable battle. What can one man really do in such a hopeless war?* He thought. But he paid the commoners little heed, for his eyes were on the Lady at the opposite end of the hall. She passed amidst the guests in a flowing white gown bequeathing her infectious smile on everyone.

Coming to the table finally, Vincent greeted the Companions and they took seat. Kiathar Strongblade was to his right with the platoon pilum in his hand and Evan was to his left.

"You treat me as a Count by placing me at the head, Evan. You forget that that kingdom has passed away."

"Honors are not given for the sake of the land, lord. But for the person."

"Evan the Loyal I will call you, for never have I known one so true to master and cause!"

Evan bowed his head in response.

"I never had to sit beside a barbarian when I reigned over my estates in the first realm! Must I now be humiliated in this manner m'lord?" a stranger beside Kiathar asked Vincent.

"You will sit!" Vincent commanded with sudden anger. "I have seen the darkness of slavery with this man and walked many a battlefield at his side! If you are not *honored* to be in his presence, then you best leave."

The man took his place in embarrassment and spoke no more that night.

The most delicious meats, vegetables and fruits were now brought before them along with mulled wines. Mead also was served, having been brewed under the special direction of Sir Strongblade. A broad smile came across his face as a keg of the stuff was placed before them.

"It has been many years since I have tasted the mead of my forefathers!" he exclaimed.

"It is long since any of us have tasted the fruit of a customary life!" A Companion near the end of the table spoke out in a loud voice. "Yet we now rejoice while the enemy still poisons our wives and daughters and lands with the lies of the Black Palaces! And his Legions march closer by the day! When will we attack?"

"Would you ruin the people's happiness with your drawling tongue!" Kiathar answered. "You will spoil the feast with worries of tomorrow! Come man!"

"I cannot enjoy anything whilst there is such suffering, such trickery..." his voice trailed off, but there was a genuine glare in his eyes that Vincent saw.

"What is your name, brother?" Vincent asked.

"Golro my lord."

"By your mannerisms I judge you have seen the grave sin of these palaces and your passion to wipe them out is just. But lord Strongblade speaks truly, there is a time and place for all things. Do not let your mind be divided on this occasion of jubilation." Satisfied with his judgment Vincent sipped his wine.

"I stand on the threshold of the dark lord's abyss and my eyes are ever upon those suffering within. You speak of jubilation my lord! Jubilation is as sickness to me now and fine meat as gravel and sand! My spirit is unable to sit idly any longer!" Golro burst out as he threw his meat knife clattering across the table.

"Forgive him Sire," interrupted Evan. "He was raised to the Companions from the lowly ranks only recently, and is a foreigner himself. He is unpracticed in the courtesies the Knighthood held so dear."

Yet Vincent did not despise Golro's brashness, for he knew himself to have been of like mind in younger years. Lingering fresh in memory were days when to sit still meant agony and dissatisfaction. But now he felt peace flowing over him like the slow assault of the endless tide. He eyed Iris across the hall, still flowing about the common folk like Life itself.

"Truly I am of common blood, raised up only by the Trials. But God granted sense to all men, and I see not the sense of you lords of old."

Kiathar slapped his mug on the table in anger. "Let me take him outside and rebuke him, master."

Vincent looked at Kiathar, then Golro, and then down at his plate. He frowned, *the peace I retain for today is surrounded by raging storms.*

"This one is strange, my lord," Evan whispered to Vincent. "We found him roaming the highways in the red armor of a knight, but he claimed no title. Under my command he has always been courageous to the point of rashness."

Vincent wondered at the meaning of this.

"What would you have us do, Golro?" Vincent asked the man. "Ride out to demolish the Black Palaces and meet the black Legions head on? To what end? Mounted riders of the finest armor cannot stand against such a wall of spears covered by a deathly hail of javelins. Do not forget that I commanded the First Legion before its corruption! You and your brothers would be annihilated and our Lady's dominion conquered soon thereafter! Is this what you want?"

"If that is my fate, so be it!" Golro answered. "I am ready to die!"

"So you are!" broke in Evan. "But what of the women and children of the Dominion, what of our Lady! You would kill them also with your recklessness!"

"The same fate awaits us here, deep in the Third Realm!" Golro came back. "The False King Octar knows where the Lady's palace now lies! It is only a matter of time before the Legions meet us here and the Dominion falls! Better to ride out and meet them on our terms!"

"You shall NOT mention that name at this table!" Vincent
pointed a vindictive finger at the brother. "Nor in this household,
ever again!" The name conjured up horrors of the mind that none
there, save Evan, who also had been in the Mountain, could
imagine.

But Vincent knew he was right, and a deep hurt panged
him, so that he no longer desired food either. His gaze chance met
with that of Iris from across the hall. Past server and guest, table
and torch, their wills were glued to each other from a great
distance. Vincent wondered, for though the Lady had looked as
exultant as the stars themselves, the sorrow in her eyes suddenly
seemed twice that of his own. She looked away from him in pain.

The time for dance soon came and the hall was filled with
laughter and the tunes of the lyre, harp and flute. The ladies made
a line on one end and the men on the other. Purple gowns the
color of grapes or as orange as the setting sun, flew and waved in
glee. Colors of the royal houses of old mixed with those of the
common folk on this occasion of occasions. Great and generous
was the Lady Regalis, so did all whisper or proclaim at that feast.
The colors of the house of Cincinnatus were also seen on that
wooden floor. A great cape of red with golden trestles and the
emblem of sword pierced star flapped as he passed into the hands
of many fair maidens. The time came when the partners switched
and his cape mingled with the pure white gown of the Lady Regalis
herself. A daisy was in her hair and her lips were as roses. She
smiled as Vincent took her hands.

"My lady, I fear my coming to your wondrous side will only
rebuke my humble skill," Vincent said with a smile as the line of
partners turned to the left to promenade.

"And should your skill be found wanting?" she pretended
in a most stately fashion.

"Then I should spend a thousand years begging your
forgiveness!" Vincent joked, but there was more truth in his
pleading eyes than jest.

"At what do you stare, Lord Cincinnatus," she asked.

"At you m'lady," Vincent answered taking her by the waste
and turning to the right.

"Do a thousand bended knees cause you to look at one so differently, who was betrothed to you so long ago?" she whispered, all jesting aside.

At that moment the line switched partners and Vincent was left with another maiden looking starry eyed at him. He pulled the poor girl along and danced over to the side of Iris once more. Then, in a very brutish manner, pulled Iris' new partner aside and took her hands once more.

"Your manners are lacking, Knight. Forget not your station," she reprimanded him, but did not let go of his hands.

"Forgive me my lady, I come from years in the mines and have forgotten much in the ways of custom and courtesy," he smiled hard at her and she rolled her eyes in pretend annoyance. "Things have changed." Vincent tried to make an answer to her previous questioning.

"So they have," she responded blankly.

"I have changed," Vincent continued, feeling frustrated. "I am not the man I once was. A thousand bended knees makes no difference to me, but does one bended knee mean anything to you?"

She turned her face away. "Ask me not."

The song ended now and Iris slipped through the crowd as a raindrop through fabric. Vincent was left alone with a heart thumping louder than the music which now began again. He cleared a path and searched her out. Not seeing her familiar form amidst her retainers, he headed outside to the portico. She was there beneath an undergrowth of vine staring into the skies.

"We can escape from here," Vincent whispered at a distance. "Away from the violence, away from sorrow, to make a new beginning across the sea! Come away with me Iris! Before it's too late."

"And leave my people behind to face war alone?" she looked at him now, and anger was on her face.

He rushed to her side, "Be realistic, Iris. Your Dominion is but a fraction of the Third Realm of old! Our enemy commands the populations of the entire Kingdom! And they willingly follow! I do not like leaving any more than you, but is there any other way? If so tell me for I don't see it!"

"What you say shall not come to pass," she responded firmly.

Silence.

"You wish to take my hand, but this cannot be. I am wed to a man living in a distant land."

Vincent was shocked.

"Who? When?" The words finally came out.

"Nicephorus Puter. A year after you left in pursuit of the Keleres. He was previously a rich landowner and vineyard grower and I needed to marry to save the estate. That is of no consequence now."

"Do you know of his whereabouts?"

"I have not heard from him in two years."

"Then he is likely dead, along with the rest of the old ruling order."

"You don't know that! Nor do I. I will not interfere with the plans of God."

"This cannot be the plan of God!" Vincent hit the portico wall angrily; woodchips flew from the force of his hand.

"If you loved me, then you would love my people. They are my children since I can have none of my own." She looked hard at him but there was care in her worn eyes. "And they would be your subjects, should you lead them."

Vincent shook his head, "A title born of lies and treachery, I care not to claim it any longer."

"And yet they hail you as such. All men falter. It is what they do afterwards that makes them."

Vincent waved his hand as if brushing aside what she now said. "You call these people your own, my lady, but they are immigrants and exiles; Homeless peasants fleeing from the west. Do you really owe them this?"

"I will forgive you that slight this once Kati. You forget that your own kin came from afar. My dominion rejects no sojourner who comes in good faith."

Vincent stared off into the night angrily.

"Your estate lies not far from here, I trust you have not forgotten."

He looked back at her longingly, "What good is dead land without the people you love?"

"No good. Then my feelings are the same as yours. I cannot leave the Dominion behind to go to a far off place." She placed her hand on his shoulder, "We have not lost all hope! The Tyrant will not risk losing another Legion in battle. He will muster all his servants before he strikes again. There is still time to prepare!"

Vincent took a deep breath. He shook his head, "I am sorry. Even after all these years I am tempted to run from my struggles, to take the easy path! But you are right, there is no way I could leave my brother Kiathar, or Evan. Not even the strangers who look to me for hope could I so easily abandon." He paused in thought and then continued, "I am coupled even with the wretches beyond the Dominion; those enslaved to the foul Drink which plagues our land."

Iris gave him a questioning glance at this, but because of the shame she bore she asked nothing more of it. *He must not discover Voluptas in me!*

Vincent gazed up at the stars, "There was a priest in the mines who sent me down what turned out to be the path to freedom. He told me before I left, 'Who said anything about the path leading to freedom? I only tell you that you must go.' I will never forget those words." He looked back at Iris, "I cannot see the end of the road in life any longer. The ground falls from beneath my feet every time I think I catch a glimpse. But I know which path is the right path, and I will take it, come what may."

"What direction will it lead you?" Iris asked.

"I will raise up the Order of the Red Cloth once more. The Equites shall contend against this Lord of Slaves!" Vincent turned to go but then paused, "It is best that I see you no longer without the company of others. For the sake of our friendship I wish it were not so, but my heart cannot abide it any other way."

"I understand," she replied softly.

She walked to the edge of the portico doorway after he had left. Her eyes followed him as he weaved through the bowing crowds within the hall. He pulled a saluting Legionnaire aside and they clasped hands. Raggedly dressed travelers she did not recognize were entering now on the far side through the main entryway. Vincent headed directly to them and embraced them as though they were family! Within minutes he had placed silk cloaks on their backs and set them down on a table littered with bread, meat and soups.

In that moment, Iris loved him with all her heart. She turned away in misery.

***

Vincent lifted the sword from Evan's right shoulder and placed it on his left while the priest beside them made the sign of the cross.

"I Knight you Sir Evan the Loyal, may your hand ever be true to justice and truth, no matter the cost. Stand, Evan and take your place." Evan walked to the front of the altar. He was proud and fierce to behold, first of the new Equites of the Dominion. His platoon's pilum was in his hand and fiery light shone through the broken windows of the cathedral onto his face, as if angels stood by him. They were all strangers in a decayed land, a spark of flame in an ice cold winter. They had no bishop to perform the rites, nor a building without rotting timbers to celebrate in. Yet their aged traditions were as strong as iron.

Blacksmiths were called upon from far and wide and many a smithy set up shop in the inner sanctum of the Lady's dominion. Once again the red armor was donned! In those months the Equites grew until they numbered in the hundreds. Out into the far reaches of the Dominion Vincent planted the most worthy of them as lords, anchors of peace in a storm of unrest. Evan the Loyal was the greatest among these.

Still others served as officers in the Thundering Legion. So the Legionnaires had named their organization after Sir Cincinnatus' demand for allegiance had been echoed by the heavens. Its composition grew to twenty-four centuries and when the time was right, Vincent delegated command of the Legion out to others. Every three centuries was led by an Equestrian commander and Sir Strongblade was empowered over the entire force as the new Legatus Legionis. Kiathar held the Legionnaires to a grueling standard of physical prowess and moral strength. Wherever the Equites called for aid against raiders or enemy incursions, the Legion struck like a fierce storm and won the people's praise.

Meanwhile, Vincent presided over a new elected council as sole tribune. With his power to veto, he guided the infant assembly in passing laws both shrewd and just. The whole Dominion looked to Sir Cincinnatus and the Lady Regalis with absolute trust and confidence. Extensive fortifications were built and defenses prepared against the coming enemy. For a whole year this continued until the people forgot the dread of war and doubted an attack would ever come. The humdrum of normal life returned.

Even Vincent became assured of the Dominion's security. Any invader would be delayed by extensive fortifications and the advances of Equites, giving the Legion time to position itself and hammer the enemy to pieces. Still, he was not content, for expanding the Dominion remained next to impossible. He stared out into the lands of the Second and Third Realms, where he had once ruled, and saw a tortured people whose stubbornness prevented liberation.

As the Dominion grew in power, Iris too fell into the snares of worry. Her spies were many in the lands and the word they returned with was of doom. The fingertips of Luminares, blackened by ingestion of the palaces' drink, stretched out again with foul intent. A reclusive shadow darkened her routine at day and in the night she walked the watches without sleep. Vincent heard of this and knew it did not bode well. Yet she told no one of her fears or activities. The common people trusted in the Equites and no dread could grip them.

Chapter 16

A People Lost

"YOU CAN SPARE ME YOUR ENTICEMENTS! I have not come for the pleasure of a night or to lose myself in Voluptas. Tell me what I need to hear."

"But my Lady, you know how delighted we of the Black Palaces would be at your return." The pale moonlight showed the smirk of the black robed man. "Yes I say *return.* I have discovered a little secret! It seems the Queen of the Dominion, the Lady Regalis has been plucked from the field many a time! The Palaces forget no one, lady. Why not return to your home for a night's stay?"

"Silence vagabond of the night! Those days of slavery are gone. Nor was I ever a willing guest."

"You know that you thirst for it! The desire never dies. Voluptas is in your veins, admit it!"

"There are many burdens to be borne in life. But never again will I imbibe the organs and blood of those who are crushed in the dark cellars of your capital."

"You speak as if you are better than us; you who drink the blood of your Christ!"

"Your practices are a mockery of religion! You kill and curse and then pour it upon the people until they are enchained to your golden vessels. The blood of Christ is a living sign that God laid down his life for the impure. He washes, you stain."

"Your God is dead. Just as your people soon shall be."

"Enough. Give me the news."

"Give me the gold!"

"There will come a day, even for you, when gold will cease to sparkle." Iris handed over five shining coins. "Remember that

I promise you no protection from the law of my lands."

The man frowned at her and stuffed the coins greedily under his robe.

"Your lands will soon be a burning heap! Yes, the Khan's forces march within the month. And yes, Nicephorus Puter is alive. He promises an answer will be given within a fortnight."

Iris felt dirtied by the transaction. She returned to her retainers waiting in the tree line. They had no idea with whom she spoke, but the guilt still gnawed at her. *I have done this for the Dominion, not myself!* her mind protested.

***

"From the poorest villages they scour for them. Little ones, innocent and clean. Marched to the black palaces to serve foul whims of polluted minds! Forced to consume Voluptas, to perform on stage, to do things no children should do! To be the laughingstock of wicked men who feed their twisted imaginations upon them!" Vincent remembered the villager's words and anger spewed out from him like volcanic ash!

Boots dug into horse's flesh and the steed flew forward. Vincent drew his sword. Galloping hooves pounded the dirt and hard breaths came from the chain mail covered beast. The black cloaked men looked up the road and their faces were filled with sudden terror. Frozen in fear, they would soon be trampled by the obedient warhorse. They closed their eyes, anticipating the crushing blow. Children fled from the path! Screams pierced the damp morning air! Vincent's taut muscles pulled the reins just before them and his massive brown mare went up on its hind legs. A woman escaped from the grasp of the men and backed away from the raised hooves. Immediately, Vincent leaned forward and the horse's fury came back down, pounding one of the cultists into the earth. Urging the beast forward, he swung hard to the right and cut another down. A spear scraped against his metal shield as he parried what would've been a deadly blow on his left. Speeding forward, Vincent maneuvered away from another spear point and pounded a bow equipped cultist with his blade.

Vincent turned his mare to face the two remaining enemies. Having struck their hearts with fear, Vincent lowered his sword point away, but his voice remained firm, "Your night's work cannot evade the eyes of dawn!" The children were quieted now and stared up at the red armored man in awe.

"These are not children of the Dominion! To the Black Palaces they go. They are mine!"

"Perhaps you would like to finish this fight?" Vincent's horse began to trot forwards.

"No!" replied the shorter of the two. "We will leave our baggage for you and return to the Black Palace yonder." He pointed to the dark tower a stone's throw behind Vincent.

"You will not return there, but walk instead to your master's domain deep in the Second Realm. This land now belongs to the Dominion!"

"Well if it isn't our lord Cincinnatus!" mocked the first as Vincent came closer. "You must know that the people here won't abide your rule! They will relocate to the next estate before living under your draconian laws!"

"Perhaps. But they will make that decision themselves," Vincent replied coolly.

"You just don't understand, Sire. Not everyone is like you. Did you know there is a rumor the Lady Regalis herself makes visits to the Black Palaces on occasional lonely nights?"

"It is a lie. She would never do such a thing," he responded unperturbed.

"Come now, why can't we be friendly with each other? We all-"

"Leave this instant or you shall meet the fate of your fellows." Vincent commanded with composure.

When they were gone, Vincent saw that the children were unchained and set on their way under the watch of the lady who had also been in bondage. He rapped hard on the Black Palace's doors and arrested its porter. Those who inhabited the inn watched as its tower crumbled under the flame and crashed down to the dirt. None dared oppose the armored knight. Vincent then told them of the horrors they perpetuated by their actions. "You are free," he said. "Return to your homes and commit these crimes no more."

One by one they spat at his feet and traveled down the road the cultists had already gone.

"Why should we care about the lives of those we've never met!" many complained.

"It is probably thieves and foreigners whose blood is poured into the elixir!" added one.

"I will probably die from this. But it's too late to stop now," another sighed.

"You are right, m'lord. But I cannot live my difficult life without Voluptas. It eases my burdens!" confessed another.

"Only for a short time," Vincent responded to him with defeat in his voice. "Only for a short time."

There was but one of the fifty who thanked him and returned to his family and estate.

***

"You must forget them, Tribune," a councilor told him later that night. "They are all lost. Think instead of your people within the Dominion!"

Vincent stared into the bonfire drearily. He shook his head, "That cannot be the right path!"

"No perhaps not," Lord Evan chimed in. "But the councilor has a point. We have plenty to contend with inside the Dominion as it is. I hardly found time to return to the inner sanctum myself! All of the lords are hard pressed in preparing for winter. The harvest was far from impressive! The people of the outer rim are not lost, but left to their own devices until the Dominion can afford a more aggressive posture."

Vincent made no answer but continued to stare into the flames.

"What is your opinion Legatus Legionis?" the councilor asked Kiathar.

Kiathar was eyeballing Vincent questioningly from the corner of the room. He shook his head and kept silent.

The lady is not here, but on errand, they had told Vincent when he had gone to seek her council. Vincent watched the crackling flames leap onto a fresh log. *Every night she wanders*

out alone. She tells no one of her travels. He remembered the accusing words of the acolyte he had heard that day.
No! I refuse to believe such lies!

That night the Legatus Legionis donned his broad rimmed helmet and prepared to return to his men. The red plumes standing high off his head commanded discipline, the Equestrian red breastplate covering his chest resounded of the dignitas he had earned, his short Legionnaire's sword spoke of swift force and the giant axe strung to his back was as fearful as death itself. Kiathar knocked hard on the Tribune's door, wishing to bid his brother farewell.

No answer.

Kiathar pushed open the door. On the floor Vincent writhed in silent agony, shaking and shivering, beating the stone ground with his palms and clutching at his stomach. Kiathar knew it was the plagues of Voluptas, but worse than he had ever seen.

He shut the door quietly and headed out to his waiting horse. He mounted the beast and started off at a trot, but then slowed and looked back. A sigh escaped from his mouth and he jumped back off the steed.

***

Iris sat alone in her court. Sleep no longer came to her wandering mind. At times she would walk in the garden, her long white flowing gown trailing behind her in the cool stone hall. The fabric rustled over vines growing across the floor and between the wedges of the brown bricks. Long she pondered how her people might be saved.

I was wrong to speak with those cultists! she reprimanded herself in thought. *I should have given them nothing!* Her heart lay in fervent prayer when her steward broke the trance into which she had slipped.

"My lady," he bowed low. "A messenger comes from Luminares. He claims to bring word from the Council."

Could this be the answer? "Show him in."

Through the entryway walked a man of stately garb, but very young. He bowed low and began to speak, but the Lady interrupted him, "Do I know you, messenger?" she asked.

The boy looked up uncomfortably, "No, my lady."

"Yes!" she stood from her seat beaming. "Augustus of the house of Steadfast! From the town of Progenitoria. Monica is your mother and I broke bread in your house when I made my second tour of the Dominion."

Impossible that she could remember such a thing! It was but a few minutes of her time! The messenger thought.

"I never forget a face," she said as if reading his mind. Augustus wondered if his intentions would come to ruin.

"I have lived in the City of Burning Light, as it was called in days past, for two moons now. I have come into the service of a certain Nicephorus Puter, whose message I bear upon me."

Iris' heart stopped.

"Shall I read it?" the messenger asked.

She motioned with her hand, suddenly at a loss for words.

"To My lost wife, the Lady in Hiding. I know now that the esteemed Lady Regalis, mistress of the rebel Dominion, and you, Iris, are one and the same. It is beyond belief that you found me! I send you this most important counsel. Listen not for my sake, for I am but a poor fool who rebukes himself for his shortcomings. Listen for your people. Grave are the times, even now the dark Legions march to you and they know no defeat. Yet there is hope even here within Luminares! Not all respect their allegiance to our present Master. There are some in the council who would listen should they see your face and know that the Dominion and its people are real. Should they hear that you intend to defy the Master to the last, perhaps their hearts too will turn to open defiance. Much power is wielded by some, the second Legion may even turn its course. One thing is certain, there is no hope for your Dominion in waiting! Come now, or I fear I will not see you again. Yours always, Nicephorus." Augustus rolled up the scroll and handed it to Iris.

It would be just like him to send a servant rather than come himself, she thought in morbid mockery.

"Well spoken, Augustus of the house of Steadfast. You will need no return message. For I shall answer myself and most speedily." She waved her hand and the young man bowed low and left.

The steward walked forward. "What are your orders my

lady?"

"I am left with little choice, it seems. If I stay, I fail. Prepare my horse and wake six of my retainers. We will set out on our long journey immediately."

"Should I not rather wake one of the Equites? Their horsemanship is far superior, as is their talent with the sword my lady."

"No," she replied softly. "The Equites do not believe the Black Legions to be a threat. But I cannot bring myself to trust in this."

"They would still follow and protect you m'lady."

"I know they would. But I intend to deal with a personal matter on this journey, one better suited for the company of private retainers. Besides, this matter must be kept quiet, lest I be endangered more."

"You will find your husband my lady?"

She stared back in silent assent. "Wake my retainers."

***

Vincent did not sleep that night, nor had he truly rested in days. His weary brown mare followed behind its master and traced his endless march on. No warm stable or fresh hay awaited. They were far from the Dominion now, far from neighbor and friend. The Count of the lost realms marched to doom.

For three days Kiathar followed Vincent's tracks in stealth. The dreadful course he feared his brother would take proved correct as Vincent led far off to the old borders of the Third Realm. Just beyond sight Kiathar remained each day, but when evening came the third day, he spotted brigands lurking in the shadows of a nearby forest. Fearing an attack, he drew closer.

"Hail, brother. Come down from your hideout!" His old master's senses were too keen, Kiathar was discovered.

Strongblade emerged from behind the shadow of a tree. He noted the figures of black disappear into the forest beyond Vincent. "There are bandits in the trees beyond you, Sir Cincinnatus!"

"Yes, we both have seen them then, but they are mostly youngsters. No doubt they have been hesitating to assault an armored horseman. With two of us, they surely have turned back in fright."

"I feared they would give battle as you crossed the forest, else I should not have ventured so close and I would not have been discovered," Kiathar walked closer. Vincent's face was pale as death in the waxing moonlight.

Vincent clasped him on the shoulder, "I still would have found you, friend." He smiled, "I discerned your figure on my trail a night ago, though I thought you to be a spy then."

Kiathar shrugged, "I was never a hunter who tarried long in tracking his prey."

"The only prey a knight of your breadth can fairly hunt is the Extraho Prodigus!"

Kiathar, staring at the last rays of waning sunlight, tucked fingers beneath his breastplate and touched the jagged teeth twined around his neck. *So long ago. That world is lost now.*

"I battled the striped monster in the Third Trial also," Vincent whispered reminiscently.

"Truly?" Kiathar questioned.

"But I didn't kill the beast in thirty seconds!" Vincent smirked, but cold reality thinned his joy before he could laugh. "You know my destination then?"

"I know that you head alone into the very hive of wickedness!" Kiathar answered.

"You cannot understand, no one can. But the people of this land are my brothers and sisters. I must take their burdens!"

Kiathar squinted hard at Vincent. It was not out of mockery or distrust that he stared, but as if he might peer into the guarded heart of his brother. "Your wisdom is beyond mine, brother," Kiathar's raspy voice explained in forfeit.

"Humility is the beginning of all wisdom," Vincent came back.

"It would be wise for us to journey together. Two are stronger than one!"

Vincent sighed, "Where I am going you cannot come. Return to the Dominion, return to the Thundering Legion and take pride in your duties. A bright future awaits those who dwell in the Lady's lands. I must go alone."

This was not the end of their conversation, for Kiathar possessed a will of iron sharpened by their brotherhood. Not even Evan understood the unique connection of the two born of their experiences in the mines. Kiathar relented at last but afterward decided on tracking Vincent again from afar. This time Sir Cincinnatus rebuked the knight harshly and forced him to turn back.

Finally, after another two days travel, exhaustion overtook Vincent and he set up camp.

***

Evan was visiting the blacksmith when a boy came running in fields afar yelling out his name. He took his breastplate, a large dent in its center from the hammer strike, and placed it on the blacksmith's table. A smuggler found on the highways carrying Voluptas and other forbidden wares from the Black Palaces had not taken well to arrest! The untimely run in had delayed his trip home. Evan dropped silver pieces into the sooty hand of the blacksmith and walked speedily to the boy who called his name.

Out of breath, the boy slid to his knees before Evan, "Master, forgive me I pray and come quickly. I was wrong! I listened to them but now they are taking her away! I am unfit to battle them alone and all my friends have left me! Curse them! Please!"

Evan saw that it was Augustus, whom he had sought out and found in the wastelands for naught. "Slow down man for I'll not help you any sooner than I discover your ill."

He took a deep breath. "Three days past was I here, sent by the acolytes of the palace with whom I make my dealings. I saw your Lady."

Evan's face turned white at his words and he feared the worst.

"I bore a false message intended for her. It was to be a trap to draw her out of the Dominion. Damn me! The silver from the acolytes is worth nothing to me now. Curse it!" the boy emptied a sack of coins into the mud. "They have taken my sister to the black palace with them! It is no place for young girls! I fear what the bastards will do to her! And now my mother is near death from the beatings she received! Come quickly my lord or there will be no hope. Think not of my ill deeds, I beg! I care only for my sister!"

"Aid you have pleaded for and aid the Equites of the Red Cloth will give unto you. But you must come first with me." Evan threw the young man atop his steed and then mounted to the front of him.

Evan searched frantically for Vincent in the council halls of the inner sanctum, but he was nowhere to be found. The Tribune's horse too was gone, which left Evan greatly troubled. He headed for the court. When Augustus had again explained what he had done to Evan's fellow Equites, Golro raised his fist to strike him. Just before the blow was loosed, Evan commanded, "Stay your hand Golro!" Though his own first impulse had been to do the same. "Your anger is just, but this boy's wicked deeds have already punished him enough."

Then with a word from Evan, three Equites were dispatched to destroy the abusive acolytes. Augustus fled the court in shame. Golro was eager to go too, but Evan held him back. "Patience, Golro," he told him. "I fear a task of most severe challenges now awaits us. I will have need of your valor before long."

"Lady Regalis has already departed?" Golro questioned as the realization set in.

"The Lady Regalis is captured!"

Evan wasted no more time. Gathering up the most able of the brothers, he departed immediately with what little stores he had time to gather. Every hour that passed her tracks would be more difficult to find. There was no time to gather a century of Legionnaires, nor could they be spared from the Dominion's defenses.

Sir Cincinnatus will discover this ill when he returns to the inner sanctum tonight and then he will follow after us in haste. He is the best hunter I have ever known! We will find her within two days! Evan thought reassuringly. The predicament did not seem so optimistic when night fell and still they wandered alone. Word of the Lady's passage was hard to find and it was many more days before the Equites were even onto her tracks.

***

A young woman lay on a wooden table. Her white gown draped over the knotty table's sides and weighed flush against her small frame. She stared at Vincent with deep anger and it troubled him so much that he stepped forward to ask her what was wrong. To his shock her gown was transformed to black and she began to smile. Vincent tried to ask his tiny sister why she would wear the clothing of the acolytes, but to his frustration no words would come out. He realized then that he could not speak because he was drinking, gulping down thick liquid from a cup of gold. But as he did so she bled. And the blood was horrid.

Vincent sat up in a sweat. He wiped his brow with a shaking hand and held tight to his legs. *An attack of the addiction.* Vincent had hidden them well from the others. The pain began to swell up. Suddenly shaking uncontrollably, memories flashed before him of dark places and whips and his mouth being forced open, all before a silent mountain. It passed.

Blood of Christ, wash me clean, he prayed. He clutched tight the crucifix Kiathar had given him a year ago atop a different mountain.

It was a dark day. The smell of wet grass filled his nostrils and rain fell onto cold ground. *I abandoned my family. I forsook my clan.* Vincent hung his head in despair. *I was blessed with title and the stewardship of an entire realm of people, but exchanged them for revenge and hate.* He cried out internally, the hurt and anger radiating from him even in silence. *But not again! Now at last do I see!* Vincent sat alone in the red draped tent, his sword in his hands before his bowed knees. *At last I see my family clearly before me; the faces of a thousand boys and girls! A thousand mothers and fathers!*

The tent door flapped angrily with the wind outside. *It is not too late yet.* The stings of cold air's touch reached through the drapery and between the links of Vincent's steel armor. He breathed it in. *God grant me strength!* he prayed, anticipating the tortures soon to come. He stood and walked out into the cold morning where the sun was still far below the horizon. The dark silhouette of a distant mountain pierced the night sky far away. *Where I am going you cannot come,* he remembered his words to Kiathar. The flickering light from inside the tent went out with a gust of wind and Vincent felt chilling solitude sink into his bones. Against the wind and rain he stood as flint against stone, but the sight of the mountain cut right through his veins and pierced his heart. He shook uncontrollably. *I go to the place I fear most!*

Chapter 17

The Last Trial

THE CITY WAS CRAWLING WITH HOODED PEOPLE who spoke no words. Seven days Vincent had traveled to come to the repulsive city. Helles. This wretched hive of nightmares, the one land he would never have desired to return to! Even here, at the base of the Slavemaster's mountain, there was life, but so long had corruption eaten it away, that they were hardly men and women who walked the streets. The figures moved away from Vincent with uncanny ease, suffering displeasure in his presence even from a distance. A hundred eyes stared at him hatefully, but their faces were hidden by horrifying white paint. It stole the life from their expressions. *There must be humanity left in them?!* These frightful sculptures of human form bore into him with their angry glares but looked away when Vincent's prying gaze searched for their eyes. Just as quickly they stared again when he moved on, the loathing resentment seeping through gobs of thick paste.

A miserable drizzle was coming down. Vincent tucked his tunic under his gauntlets to keep out the cold water. He weaved around piles of refuse obstructing the cobblestone road, pulling his steed behind. A pile of wood came up before him in the center of the road. From the rank smell and the buzzing of flies, he knew there were dead bodies inside the burnt carriage. Cruel eyes stared up at him from someone hidden behind the mess. They shone like those of a cat, but they were human.

"Humph," came a low growling voice. "A knight come to the lord's mountain?" the eyes spoke tellingly.

Vincent froze in a questioning stare.

"You will be crushed 'neath its roots!" scoffed the urchin of a man. Pale hands pulled a black hood over the face and Vincent saw a cloaked figure emerge from the wreckage and scamper hurriedly away.

The gates to the sole road up the mountain were guarded by one hundred Legionnaires. They were formed up as if ready for an inspection. These were not soldiers like those of Vincent's old command, but a new breed sinister and mean. Their armor was draped with black cloaks fastened by a single golden brooch and their helmets were molded to the form of ogres, giants and wyrms. Gargoyle like forms of terror covered their heads frightfully. This was the elite guard of the Lord of Slave's Legions! The steel bulwark they wore rendered them as inhuman as they had already proved by their actions throughout the kingdom.

But this is not what troubled Vincent most. Climbing up the mountain's lonely road he saw three thousand or more mounted figures! Vincent dodged behind a stone building and moved closer down a back alleyway. He peaked out from behind a low thatched roof.

Impossible!

Vincent recognized the eastern like armor and curled bows of the men in the rear of the train.

Nothus! An entire army!

The horde rode slowly up the winding trail and disappeared into the mountain's peak.

Vincent pulled his head back behind the stone building and clenched his forehead in desperate thought.

The Dominion is doomed!

On sudden doubt rushed upon him. *The kingdom is surely lost now! Must I pay the price when there is so little hope?* He forced his eyes open and this time stepped into full view beyond the roof. There stood the giant mountain before him like the silhouette of the Extraho Prodigus waiting to pounce. It was a giant shadow stabbing into the sky and impregnable to attack. Vincent's eyes focused hard now on the peak and his mind stretched out. Just as if the Lord of Slaves stood before him in challenge, Kati's blood began to boil. His arms became like iron as he stretched out his fist, "By God you will not make me turn back now! My people will be free!"

As the words issued from his mouth, the elite guards turned the horrible faces of their masks his way, ten gave chase. Vincent was an outlander, a tarnished one. He whose face was unpainted or who wore no mask was unfit to be in the Lord's domain! Mounting his steed, Vincent overran two of these guards and flew to the east. He recalled the hidden narrow path upwards and set out for it. Yet the elite guard was not without horses of their own. Born and bred in the desolation of Helles, the animals were at an advantage. Two score men were closing upon Vincent within the hour.

But at last he came to the foot of the mountain and for the moment, still held the lead. His brown mare sprinted away in fright as he loosed her. Once before, Vincent had walked this way in flight from terrible captivity. Faint rays of morning light crept through gray clouds. It seemed as if even the hard rock itself had drunk the Slavemaster's venom and sprouted into distortion! Thorns grew everywhere. The jagged saws reached from the foul earth and scratched the sky. A way fraught with ills this was, with steep slopes and jagged rock enmeshed in the prying fingers of the razor like vegetation. The foul branches were not planted by any gust of wind or natural growth, but by the devices of the Lord of Slaves himself. And they were great plants standing to the size of a man with briers as of blades reaching out.

It had not stopped raining for days now and beneath shining red armor, Vincent's clothes were drenched. *God forgive the doubt I gave quarter to for a moment! I know my task. The engines of Voluptas must be destroyed! I will find a way or die trying!* Vincent breathed in deep the moist early morning air, lifted his bowed head. He saw before him the faces of all the tortured people he had met; young, searching girls; hopeless fathers. They looked to him! This mountain was the vile heart of the black palaces which poisoned them all. Voluptas and a thousand curses were pumped into the kingdom from here!

There is only one way forward! Vincent stymied his shivering muscles and began the ascent. Thorns sticking and stabbing between chinks of armor every inch of the way, he pressed on; over rock and through bramble, up sheer cliff holding on by bare hand; no fortress of rock or steel could withhold him. The elite guards in pursuit were hard pressed to keep this foreigner's pace. But the wiles of the Lord of Slaves are a slow toxin and there were yet many ordeals that Vincent could not foresee.

From base to summit he climbed, clambering and falling, slipping and rising, pushing onward though blood poured from cut brow and from bruised elbows. The thorns stabbed as angry talons against him until every inch of exposed flesh was hewn. Yet with his sword he carved a way where he could.

Exhausted from the struggle he at last stood before the gates that entered into the foul chambers beneath the mountain. They were rusted iron gates ritually stained with the blood of those prisoners who had entered. Vincent watched intently from behind a boulder as countless fearsome Nothus warriors crossed the threshold on horseback. They wore plated metal armor covered in animal skins and carried long spears. Bows were strapped to their backs and many wore frightful red masks looking like terrible dragons and helms with long bull horns protruding upward. Plumes blew from their iron helmets in the winds of the rain storm.

Rigid jawed with high foreheads; those faces he could see

were toughened by years of battle. They were fierce. Skulls hung from the horses of many. The Nothus knew no defeat in the attack. Years ago they had been beaten only because the Equites had taken them by surprise in their homeland. Even then, the Luminarians had barely claimed victory.

In the First Nothus War, six Luminarian villages had been wiped out to a man. The Nothus were butchers! They were barbarians descended of witches and had no care for humanity! Their tribes as a whole had slaughtered entire civilizations without compunction. These Nothus had come to extinguish his people from existence!

The sun had been down for hours when the last of the long train of foreigners disappeared behind the gates. Vincent emerged from the shadows. As a hunter sneaks upon prey, he took the hooded acolytes guarding the gate at unawares. He cut down the white faced sentries with precision and stealth. Into deep caverns he now clambered, suddenly dreading the screaming memories of pain and dismemberment that came back to him. The smell of the halls was rank with the Drink and he could taste flavors of iron rich blood, wine and wet dirt.

Deeper and deeper he went until he came to the glorious golden hall. Pillars of ornately painted wood reached to carved rock above and mud gave way to a marble floor below. Flames leaped high from a raging bonfire at the center of a crowd of seated Nothus.
There must be five thousand of them! Vincent was shocked.
They were at tables as if prepared for a feast, but they kept their weapons with them. High up, on a floor above them, a dark figure called out in a loud voice continually. He screamed out incantations of a foreign tongue, shrill words Vincent could not understand. Just the same, their evil resonance caused him to look away.

Vincent pressed on through the side tunnel. He again walked through darkness, but could hear the incantations of the shaman becoming louder as he slowly ascended. With but one more step Vincent should have been free of the darkness and on his way up stone stairs, but alas, as though it were the hand of the angered Lord of Slaves, a great chasm seemed to open up under Vincent. Down he fell into a cistern wide and long; not so easily does a stranger of pure heart lurk in the Khan's stronghold, the King of Ages' dungeon. The Slavemaster was learned in the secrets of guile and there was more to his terror than mere darkness and elite guards. Octar laughed from his throne high in the Mountain and the halls shook with his malice, for he had seen Vincent.

The cries of children could be heard from somewhere, somewhere he could not get to. Here there was no order, no justice. He breathed terror in from the humid air. Frantically Vincent ran amidst splashing waters. Before he knew what was happening, he was up to his chest in the cold liquids. Crying out brought him no help and though he raved and ran, he could find no escape, nor a path back to shallow waters. *I'm alone in the darkness,* he thought in despair. The iron like smell of Voluptas filled him, soaked through his skin and sponged away his strength. *This is my end, I shall become a victim, digested slowly here and consumed in goblets of Voluptas in years to come.* As he sank down into the rising swamp he searched for and grasped hard to the crucifix he kept.

***

Dim candles floated up the aisle and Iris watched their fluttering flames dance about freely. Lifeless forms, human figures bereft of will or desire, soulless bodies, carried them to the altar of death. From somewhere far above, somewhere hidden in darkness atop the great staircase behind the altar, wicked eyes stared down. She could feel his presence, the Enemy.

The Grand Dragon, highest shaman of the Black Order, was to make sacrifice in charm of the Nothus hordes and Black Legions. Flames leaped from the bonfire just in front of the altar, allowing all in the golden hall to see the spectacle. Even now the Nothus stared up at the Grand Dragon from the wide hall below, ready to greet the spray of blood and outpouring of drink. Tomorrow they marched. It would be the last assault upon the Dominion and all the dissenters who remained. Her spies had been right! The annihilation of her people was at hand.

The victim was brought forward with her white mask upon her face and her wits in a haze, as was the customary preparation. Ropes tied to flesh and daggers made ready, the attendants of the ritual removed their hoods to reveal their own masks, which glowed eerily in the dark. *God help us!* she prayed. As one body, the attendants lifted their goblets, ready to drink to the victim's death, but Iris' hands were empty. A tall figure carrying chalice and mask then appeared before her. Iris' heart stopped. Hard hands took her fingers and squeezed them against the cup until she thought her bones would be crushed. Now he grasped her face and holding it against the hard stone wall shoved the chalice against her mouth. She spat the Voluptas back at the menacing figure stubbornly. Thick, red, curdling juice spilled all over. But it was no use, there was no escape. This time he plugged her nose with one hand and again forced the cup against her. Gagging and choking, she gave in and swallowed. Swooning from the elixir, a tear fell from her eyes and a white mask was now pressed against her face.

She looked upon the world now from two carven slits. *Lady Regalis no more! A farce it ever was. The glorified garb of a wretched widow! Motherless! Killer at birth! Unloved by father and betrothed! Childless. Abandoned. Abused. Cold in marriage. Addict! Prostitute!*

"Embrace now your true self." The rough man spoke.

Iris stared out into a pale world.

***

Thick red fluid dripped from his armor to the floor. He shivered with coldness and rage at having come so close to death. Sinking deep into the cistern, a path had become apparent from whence the dark fluids flowed. Even through the thick vomit of blood and wine a flicker of fire can shine through! Up the tunnel he had climbed, gagging on the fluids as he ran out of breath, until at last he took in free air and the warmth of a torch breathed upon him. *Call it providence,* Vincent had thought.

He stood in a small carpeted hall lit by more blazing torches. Twenty bare cushioned seats sat along the wall, but there were pitchers fresh with Voluptas that stood upon the large wooden tables. An uncanny feeling that he was expected singed a deep nerve in Vincent. He could taste the piercing drink as though he had already partaken. At once he hated the liquid and desired it! He cursed his ambitions.

How can something be so repulsive to my wits and desirous to my flesh at once!

Vincent made war upon the leanings of his thoughts so that he should not falter and stray down the wayward path in this time of need. He stepped forward and scattered the pitchers to the floor. As he did so, the hall suddenly filled with bodies. Women with painted faces came from hidden rooms and crowded him with alluring embraces. Vincent refused to draw his sword against them, but as one they obstructed his path in a phalanx of skin and silk; of bare leg and hip and warm touch and breast. They were before him and they were upon him at once. So close that their paralyzing breath whistled in his ear. A cup of gold they pressed against his lips, and Vincent could nearly taste the bitter fruit within. Yet he pressed on as one warily pushes sleep aside in the morn. Then, as if waking from a dream, they were gone and Vincent was alone on a dark ledge.

Your friends have embraced the night, you alone push me away, a voice seemed to tell him.

He stared down lengthy stairs to a candlelit hall below. This room overhung the enormous Nothus horde seated further down. The number of their spears was like a boulder crushing Vincent's discouraged heart. Thousands of invaders stared up at the robed individual still chanting at the hall's edge. A black altar was beside him and two acolytes brought a robed woman toward him.

Vincent was obscured by darkness, but could see clearly faces lighted by fire directly below. Now his faith turned to pain as he focused on the figures in the chamber.

Iris is there!

Her features were undeniable; long black locks of hair on a high brow. A horrid mask of white was being placed on her face! She did not fight it, but remained motionless.

How could you!

She stood with *them*, with turncoats and men of foul heart, with prostitutes! Odd chanting with moans and the clashing of cymbals floated up to him like soiled incense from below. The ceremony had begun. *She has betrayed me! I have come over mountain and through trial for naught!* Vincent sunk to his knees in dismay, but kept his eyes fixed on her figure within the chamber. In his agony Vincent could not wipe away what his eyes had seen. *What magic does this lord possess that he may so easily turn my friends?* A tear fell from his eyes in his moment of weakness. He watched the acolytes march to the altar where soon the blood of a live human would be spilt. Vincent scrambled away from the ledge in shock and disgust at the sight. *What now?*

As this thought passed through his mind, Vincent abruptly became aware of a great shadow before him. Though already shrouded amidst darkness, the form hauled in the blackness of night as though it were a garment.

"You recognize the woman below?" spoke the blackness.

A spear pierced his heart with fear and Vincent was unable to move.

"I know you well. You who were once betrothed to that simpleton they call the Lady Regalis. That hoar!" came the voice, like thorns scraping against soft tissue. "She, like so many of your so called people, is secretly an acolyte in my following."

"You lie," Vincent whispered.

"Do I? Look down upon her and tell me again."

Vincent stared down to the chamber below where the women danced about the altar with swaying sashes. Iris was there. He remembered the accusing words of the acolyte on the border of the Dominion. *I have been so naïve!*

"She belongs to me, as do the people of the Third Realm," came the voice now as terrible as thunder. "Face it, they have betrayed you! Your efforts are useless."

Vincent started at the accusation, but found himself sinking back down against the wall.

"Yes you knew it already," continued the voice in soft tones. "In the hour of need, Iris hid beneath my cloak. You cannot blame her. You cannot blame any of them! My armies will soon cover the entire kingdom! What they did is only rational. But this is not Iris' first time in my presence. She never spoke a word to you of it, but she has long been a caller of the Black Palaces. In the suburbs of New Antioch my shamans know her by name! Even in her reign over the rebel Dominion she crept out in the dead of night to my palaces. So do not pretend to be the savior of the Third Realm. They, like Iris, serve me! I am Khan, their caretaker and lord. And you are very arrogant if you think that so many people might change because of *your* actions here! Don't be a fool! What can *you* do here? Don't throw your life away! Behold my might!" A long finger pointed to the Nothus horde beyond.

Vincent searched his heart in great fear. *Does he speak the truth?*

The figure sat down now on what appeared to be a throne. Iron spikes shot out from its sides and skulls were piled at its base. Vincent had not seen it in the darkness. The dark lord had been there all along.

"Go now, I release you!" With a flip of his hand a passageway opened up beside them and dim moonlight leaked in as from watching eyes. "You come to save a people who do not desire saving. They are my servants."

Vincent, in utter loneliness and consternation, took a step.

But the glimmer of light which then shone upon him from outside burned as prongs of hot iron upon his flesh. He recalled with pride the branding of Knighthood upon his arm; *We are never alone,* his own Equestrian master had told him after the Trials. *He, is always watching.*

Vincent looked out at the stars and confidence again began to wash over him like heat from a warm hearth. He remembered the Count's crest of sword pierced star. *I cannot betray my word. What I say I will do, I will do; though it leads to death.* Vincent turned. *I don't do this for myself.*

The horde of Nothus was before him and the prowess of the Dark Lord at his side.

Love is to lay down one's life for a friend, the priest had said to him in the mines. *I will not abandon my people, nor her.*

"I will no longer run," he spoke pointedly to the shadow

on the throne. "Here I make my stand, come what may. Die with traitors or with the true, I abide by my people. Neither those who were once my subjects here, nor in the Dominion far away shall bow before you while I, or any Knight, lives. Mark my words!" Light from the moon and stars outside illuminated Vincent. His battle glare was not despondent, not death seeking, but unafraid and proudest of all mortals yet alive.

"Reckless fool," the self proclaimed king growled back. He snapped his fingers and the opening to the world shut again, leaving them in utter darkness. Then with one fell swoop of his forearm, he knocked Vincent to the ground. Armor clanged against stone and bone hard against armor. The shadow towered above the knight.

But the blood of a Knight of the Red Cloth, simmering with mercy by nature, boils red hot when called to challenge. Moreover, Vincent was of a long line of strong willed lords of the Skilurus clan. Therefore the speed with which Vincent Cincinnatus rose and drew sword caused the Lord of Slaves to step back in fear.

"Octar, sorcerer and deceiver! You are naught but a slave-driver!" Vincent bellowed. "Lies cannot enchain me, nor am I yoked by your condemnations. Your fearful proclamations and curses are but a filthy garb in my sight!"

These words of Vincent, like a meteor ripping through the night sky, burned the heart of the Dark Lord ere the sword fell upon him, so that he bounded down the stairs in dread.

Then from the mouth of Vincent there issued forth a war cry so fell and glorious that the blackened halls shook and the entire Nothus horde below stood at the force of his breath. He charged after the Slavemaster with sword raised. Because of his trembling limbs, the Khan fell upon the stairs and the stolen Luminarian crown flew from his head. Shaking in mortification, Octar then fled down hidden passages and was not seen again, for even a sorcerer and Nothus khan feels fear. Even one so great can turn coward! For true greatness is not found in darkness any more than courage is found in hiding. And true courage comes only from love, which the darkness cannot possess. Vincent sealed away the royal diadem in a satchel and hurried down the stairs.

In answer to Vincent's war cry there came a low and ferocious bellow from below. Then, throwing away cloak and gargoyle helmet, Kiathar Strongblade revealed himself in his prowess. Forgetting all care for disguise he wielded his axe with untold ferocity and single-handedly slew every acolyte or guard that was unfortunate enough to block his path. Vincent smiled at the sight of his friend.

"How came *you* to this stinking place?" Vincent asked Kiathar between sword thrusts.

"By the front gate, how else?" answered Kiathar, pulling his axe from a fallen elite guard.

"Ha!" Vincent laughed.

"You came not by this-" he knocked one of the guards back with a jab to the helmet. "Road, Sire?" he finished.

"No! There is a secret path which winds around the sides."

The last few acolytes were forming up now before them.

"Indeed Sire. Hmpph. I wish I had known it."

"I am sorry I never told you, Sir Strongblade."

"No worries brother, they thought I was one of them. Well, I had to kill one of 'em and take their armor first of course."

"I thought you were one of them!" Vincent exclaimed.

"HA!" Kiathar beamed. "What do you think now?"

"I think I would run thirty leagues before facing that axe, were I them!"

"Indeed!" exclaimed Kiathar.

The last few fighters perished, including the Grand Dragon, who fell from the ledge to his death. A great roar erupted from the Nothus hordes below and thousands of the foreigners were now running and yelling beneath them.

"Kati!" Iris cried as she fell into Vincent's arms. "How did you get to this place?"

He unclasped her mask gently and threw it to the floor. "You will no longer be a slave, but free."

"I had lost all hope, forgive me!" Her face was wet with tears.

"I cannot reject my own people. Nor you, above all, who are of my own clan." Still Vincent's expression could not hide the hurt and confusion he still felt.

"Kati, what dark power engineered this chain of events? I did not come here of my own will. You must believe me. You must!"

Vincent pulled her close and squeezed her small frame, "I believe you, I believe you," a tear fell from his face in relief.

"I set out for Luminares in secret," she explained between sobs. "To meet my husband and a few loyal councilors. But my husband is dead and the council is no more! It was a trap!"

"I believe you," he answered again. His wits returned, Vincent looked hard at his surroundings. He clasped her hand and walked towards the altar.

Near the bonfire beside the ledge were ten large jars. The revelry was meant to be fueled far into the night. Vincent reached down and with the strength of his whole body, heaved a jar onto his shoulder. He turned to Kiathar and Iris, "Follow me," he said.

The three went up a dark staircase which led to a room above the golden hall. Moans and cries came from prisoners ensnared in every corner.

"I was trapped here once," Vincent remarked solemnly as he stooped near a ledge. His back and arms flexed taut as he poured the giant jar of oil into what seemed to be a trough. When at last it was emptied, he threw it to the ground and took a torch from Kiathar. "Voluptas will be their death." He threw the torch onto the trough. Iris and Kiathar watched over the ledge in amazement as an entire aqueduct crossing the roof and spiraling down the golden hall's pillars sprouted flames. "What once fed them drink, will feed them fire." As he said this sparks of yellow flame exploded out of a duct far below and onto a prepared table.

The three busied themselves unlocking the long chain tying all the prisoners now. Within minutes a hundred refugees followed Vincent's lead in pouring destruction down the aqueducts. For many years Octar had been storing up men and women like cattle. Readily they aided in wiping out the nightmare in which they had lived for so long. Soon innumerable flames were licking the roof and wooden pillars of the golden hall. The Nothus below panicked and began to clash with each other as the feasting room filled up with smoke. Five thousand armored bodies clambered to escape from two single doorways in the rear of the rock enclosed hall.

Vincent led a great host out of the mountain now.   When they had nearly reached the Mountain's gate at the peak, Vincent and Kiathar watched through a crevice as the golden hall collapsed atop thousands of the Nothus invaders. Its high roof, built by haughty hands, could not withstand the heat of the inferno now blazing within. Crags and rock crashed down upon the fleeing horde. Their tables and drink were smashed to oblivion beside them.

***

Vincent saw a thousand torches below the mountain as he came out from the gate at the peak. Many Nothus had still escaped. They set up rigid formations at the base of the trail.

"What now?" Kiathar questioned.

"We must make haste and climb down the secret path before dawn. When the sun rises we will be discovered." Vincent looked back to the hundreds of captives who still piled out from the iron gate onto the mountain's path. Smoke billowed into the sky behind them.

In that moment, three suits of red armor pushed through the crowd towards the three. The tallest of them stepped forward and removed his helm.

"My lady and Tribune, we meet in a fell hour."

"Sir Evan the Loyal! And how came *you* to this place this hour?" Vincent asked.

"My brothers and I," Evan gestured to forty other Equites standing behind. "Came in search of the Lady Regalis." He bowed his head towards Iris. "I see that we are late in coming, but we wasted no time in beginning our pursuit after we learned of her capture. Tell me now how you learned this news of her, for I searched but could not find you before our departure."

"I knew nothing of her capture until Providence had us meet here in the jaws of death. I left well before the incident."

At these words Evan bowed low, "Sir Cincinnatus, don't you know that I would have followed you through hell itself, had I known of your journey?"

"Evan, truest of Equites," Vincent placed a hand on his shoulder. "Rise, the battle is not over yet. By what path did you ascend?"

"You forget, Sir Cincinnatus, that I too have walked the secret path to the summit. For I was with you when we first left this wretched hive of evil."

"You speak the truth."

"And you two shall be leaving by this path again, and soon!" Kiathar chimed in.

As the sun peaked above the horizon, the Equites still lingered at the base of the mountain. A dark plume of smoke rose up from the peaks above them. The hall of nightmares, the heart of Voluptas was destroyed. Obligated by the Code, Vincent and the nobles waited until the last of the captives had escaped from the thorny slopes and gone into hiding within the city before they departed. When at last this was done, they mounted their horses and looked to the east. Here, a foul army of Nothus and Black Legionnaires blocked their path.

"We are with you my lord!" Evan, Kiathar, Golro and the others exclaimed, though Vincent had claimed no lordship over them since his return from the mines.

Vincent bowed his head in humble acknowledgement of their loyalty and started off at a trot ahead of them. Iris rode close behind the formation.

The enemy lines were thin and disorganized, for many chiefs and leaders now lay buried in the mountain. Close to the altar and to the Voluptas, the golden hall's places of honor proved a bane when the hall lit with fire. They were trapped far from any route of escape. Lust proved their downfall.

Moreover, the enemy was disheartened at the complete disappearance of their Khan. Was he also dead? Or had the King of Ages fled with the cowards?

In contrast, Vincent's men were unified in passion and purpose. For each other, for their honor and good name, and for the heritage of their forebears, they would happily accept death.

They were the right hand of Lord Cincinnatus and the aid of the afflicted. They were the Equites. As one they charged the mass of enemies. Like a thin axe head cutting through a log, Vincent and his men chopped a way through the enemy. Before the Nothus could regroup, the Equites had dashed out the city walls to relative safety. Many deeds of valor transpired in that fight. Whole ballads would thereafter be written of the heroics of Golro, Evan, Kiathar, Angelus, and others. Far above all, however, was the prowess of Sir Cincinnatus, who was at the head of the charge when the battle began, and guarded the rear when they had pushed through.

Chapter 18

Dignitas

WHEN THEY AT LAST RETURNED to the Dominion, the people acclaimed Vincent King, but he would not accept the title. Instead, he placed the crown he bore in the safekeeping of watchful guards within the Cathedral. There, where the Equites took oath, it would serve as a constant reminder of the weight of the Order's vigilance.

Countless people swore allegiance to the Dominion. Her borders grew until the entire Third Realm was reclaimed, but many turned an angry brow away from Vincent and his Equites. They returned to vile ways and hid their faces from the East.

"Voluptas will disappear slowly, and with it, addiction and decadence," Vincent told his Equites. "But the path these people choose springs from no mountain or palace, nor from allegiance to the Khan who has fled. Their devotion is to the heart of evil itself, which throne I am unable to conquer. But we will do what little we can, day by day, to contest this throne wherever we go. Our victory will never be complete, but let the world know that wherever we go, the chains of vice are broken. Our people will be free to choose a path of hope."

Vincent, for his part, rejoiced not so much in acclamations, but was content with a small estate and loving family. When his term was finished, the Tribuneship was relinquished to another and Vincent set himself to hard work on his father's fields. Countless friends never ceased singing his praises, even as he retreated to a quiet life. The unusual pains of Voluptas which he had suffered never disappeared completely; but Vincent told those closest to him that the sting from those dark times had lessened greatly when the engines of the Mountain were burned away. Moreover, at peace for having saved his people, Vincent's dreams troubled him no longer. Iris Cincinnatus rested easy in her Kati's embrace, being at last wed to a man of *dignitas*. Together they looked onto fields of fruitful harvest, where fathers and mothers of the Skilurus clan were buried, and the two were at peace.

***

Years later in a small town bordering New Corinth, villagers gathered around a warm fire. Falling raindrops pattered against pots and pans left outside the hut as a gnarly nosed, tall beggar questioned the cottage dwellers within.

"Surely there are others who have matched him?!" the old beggar exclaimed.

"Never has there been a knight so pure of heart, so skilled in battle, so faithful, so fiercely loyal and brave, or as pious as Vincent Cincinnatus Kati!" a villager reassured the old blind man. "No one knows the Equestrian Code better, or holds the Trials more dear!"

"You truly believe this?"

"Have you not heard of Sir Cincinnatus? Disputes which

cannot be remedied, he judges fairly. Enemies no one dares touch, he lays low. The widow and orphan have no better friend!"

"I have heard enough of these stories," the blind man cut the villager off. "I must be on my way. The path to the Great Cathedral is long." In a sudden hurry, the blind man hobbled down the muddy road and disappeared in the rain.

A month passed before the strange, blind beggar was seen again. Kati and Iris stood in each other's arms on one of these brisk Spring morns and watched the first fiery rays of daylight peak above the countryside. It was then that the old man reappeared, hobbling down the dirt road to the Cincinnatus estate. Greeted kindly and fed a hearty meal, the raggedly dressed stranger beamed as he reclined with a full stomach.

"You have treated me graciously," he thanked them. "Though I am a dirty and smelling sojourner."

As if he might look into the stranger's soul, Vincent peered hard into the scarred holes where the beggar's eyes had been burned out.

"God has smiled upon you both," the beggar added. He then pulled them very close and whispered, "Shadows darken again in the East and the Dominion stands alone! The Nothus hordes ride again! For a decade the people have lived without King or Queen. Shepherdless!"

At that moment, Vincent's eyes were suddenly opened and he fell to both his knees.

The blind man pulled a golden crown from a satchel at his side and held the diadem aloft.

"My liege!" Vincent cried out. "Justinian of the House Solis, last of the kingly line! Forgive our impudence, lord!"

"There is nothing to forgive any longer. You alone, Sir Cincinnatus, have been found worthy of bearing this burden. I chose to forge my own crown when Keleres swords were at my side, and so was not chosen. I am the last of the Kingly line, a line that must perish. But all things have a beginning, and God has deemed fit to begin our people again in you. I have followed many dreams, witnesses and stories to this home. Therefore, I will delay no longer. By the power vested in me through my fathers, I name you Vincent Cincinnatus Kati, King of Luminares Novus! The Lord makes poor and makes rich, he humbles, he also exalts! He raises the needy from the dust; from the ash heap he lifts up the poor, to seat them with nobles and make a glorious throne their heritage. He gives to the vower his vow and blesses the sleep of the just. For the pillars of the earth are the Lord's, and he has set the world upon them."

THE END